The Last

Kincaid

Also by

Ted Miller Brogden

Jigsaw

Copyright © 2012 Ted Miller Brogden

All Rights Reserved

ISBN

978-0-615-56319-0

M E Publishing

Beaufort, SC

Very Special Thanks to Photographer:

Catherine Ford

For contribution photographs used on the cover.

———————————————————

Cover Designed by:

Pamela Diffee

———————————

Acknowledgments:

Many thanks, to Betty and Steve Smith and Betty's parents Bill and Magdalene Herring for inviting me down to Chub Cay, the "birthplace" of The Last Kincaid.

For sloughing through the rough drafts: Tracy Draughon, Ray McDonald, Rhonda and Bob Quinn, Cassi Broach, Linda Ammons, Mo Everidge, Kymbra Bryan, and, Lisa "Bodacious" Thompson. I can't thank you guys enough.

A most special thanks to Ms. Penni Bland, a truer Cardinals' Fan never will be known, nor a more beautiful person ever found!

To my son Gabe, thanks for making fatherhood the greatest joy I've ever known.

Pamela Diffee, the most multi-talented editor in the world, English, French, and Russian…amazing! Of course your hardest challenge was making English look like my first language. Thanks for the Herculean effort, Pam.

Ted

Miller

Brogden

THE LAST KINCAID

Prologue

Golden rays from the late afternoon sun reflected off the cirrus clouds floating on the horizon and five-year-old Caleb approved the colorful display with childish joy. Yards across the furrowed ground his parents, Iris and Grover Ferguson, marveled at the wonderment provided by God and nature. Any event that softened the harshness of these depressing times was welcomed. And in their minds, this priceless spectacle was a sign from the Almighty that the long battle with the deep-rooted pine stump was finally over.

Inspired by that thought, the sharecropper couple braced hard against the fat-lighter monstrosity and inched out a space just wide enough to hold another stick of dynamite. For years the stump and surrounding root mat had withstood the efforts of Demon the mule and the backbreaking labor of the entire Ferguson clan. Today, thanks to an anonymous donation of a half-case of dynamite and box of blasting caps, victory would be theirs. Stirred by the pending achievement, Iris Ferguson performed a little soft-shoe-shuffle to the delight of husband and young son.

Smiles faded as Demon brayed the arrival of an unexpected visitor. Usually there was nothing that intimidated Grover Ferguson, a powerful man whose strength made the tenant legendary in these parts. But even the man possessed with the brawn of two men could not quell the fear rising in his gut. Brute strength has its place but is never a match for pure evil.

Though small for his age, the boy staring at them cast a domineering spell over the scene. Vast wealth and privilege magnified the boy's difference to the ignorant and impoverished sharecroppers.

As the intruder approached, Demon, sensing the slack in his plow line, edged beside Caleb like an overgrown watchdog. To ease the tension, Grover nodded to the visitor. As expected, his greeting went unacknowledged. The slight figure moved past Caleb and stopped when his shadow darkened the plunger box hard-wired to the dynamite surrounding the stump. The boy removed a lollipop from his pocket and, dangled it just beyond Caleb's reach. He grinned as the child honed in on the treat, then tossed it as far as he could toward the pine stump.

Cold sweat dampened the threadbare garments of the aging couple as they raced a beeline course toward their youngest child. Together, inches away from the dynamite, Iris and Grover realized their mistake; the explosive materials had not been a gift, but a set up. Nothing about the boy hovering over the plunger suggested mercy. Today they would die but they would die as they had lived, hand-in-hand.

Flames from the explosion burned white-hot into the resin canals of the stump and ignited a fireball across the sun-set sky. Ten miles away the force of the blast rattled windows of mansions cushioned by the Cape Fear River. Closer to the devastation, veterans of wars past ducked for cover, and animals, domestic and feral, cowered against the shaking ground.

Ganna Mae Ferguson ignored the dirty water sloshing from the dishpan that soaked what her mother would call her, "city clothes." She barely noticed the shards of glass from the shattering kitchen window peppering her face like porcupine quills.

The ringing in her ears stilled as the fury of the explosion swirled past the shotgun hovel her parents called home. Dust from the blast sifted through the torn window screens, coating her new suede pumps, bought especially for this surprise visit home. Ganna Mae scanned the field for a glimpse of her parents who had been visible only seconds before. Nothing. With a quick flick of each foot, the stylish shoes clattered across the worn pine floors.

The loamy grit of the sandy path tore away the expensive silk stockings covering her feet. A thin voice guided Ganna Mae like a beacon through the angry black smoke and afternoon haze. There, next to a huge hole in the ground sat Caleb Ferguson muttering the only words he ever would speak again; *"Mule did it. Mule did it. Mule did it."* Cradled in his tiny arms were the entwined hands of Iris and Grover Ferguson.

Chapter 1

Ganna Mae Ferguson had been hard to find, and even harder to convince, but Wyatt had finally gotten the old woman to sell. As soon as the deed was recorded, he would officially own the best piece of commercial dirt left in North Carolina. Not that his board of directors would feel that way once they found out what he paid for the place, but what did they know? Soon he would be zipping along at 500 knots headed back to his corporate offices in Wilmington. Wyatt Kincaid, CEO of the Crown Kincaid Development Company, comforted by that thought, released his grip on the alligator briefcase glued to his chest. Though the deal was done and Ganna Mae's signature, the last signature, was on the deed, something was missing. Instead of rejoicing over buying *"the tract of land that couldn't be bought"*, and leaving other land-starved developers across the state crying like hungry babies without milk, Wyatt's thoughts turned introspective.

Getting the signatures of thirty-eight heirs scattered across sixteen states and two countries would have persuaded most men, including his board, to aim their sights elsewhere. But he was not like most men.

Six foot six and two hundred forty-five pounds of sinewy brawn ensured that he never would be a member of the genus *homo vulgaris*. "Never," Wyatt grunted, tossing his briefcase onto the adjoining seat. He tugged at the lapels of the expensive suit tailored to accentuate his broad shoulders and narrow waist, two features that certainly set him apart from his roly-poly board members.

Aping the expression of a criminal posing for mug shots, Wyatt studied his reflection in the etched glass mounted on the bulkhead of the Challenger jet. Time had softened his chiseled features, but only slightly.

Nips and tucks were the latest craze for aging CEO's, but ever averse to vanity and herd mentality, Wyatt had bucked the trend. One more peek at the glass, and his mind was made up. No surgery. All things considered, fifty years of the good life had done little to diminish his imposing presence. In fact, his silver gray hair and fine character lines merely enhanced the ripened perfection of his manly countenance.

Satisfied with his exceptional visage, Wyatt located the iPhone inside the gentleman's pocket of his jacket. The hidden compartment, originally designed for a nipping flask, now served a more mundane communication function. With the flair of a gifted swordsman, he pierced the current date dead center. Board of Directors meeting was the single entry. "Sons of bitches," Wyatt muttered, and then aloud, "A necessary evil."

The Crown Kincaid Development Company had been family owned for over seventy years with no board of directors. That had now changed. He had certainly profited when he gave up complete ownership, but he despised having to kowtow to the knuckleheads who sat on his board.

The Board was comprised of third-generation overseers of vast family fortunes. Unlike the first generations who had built the fortunes, or the second generations who had expanded them, (strong, cunning men like himself), members of his board roosted on the third branch of their family trees, the squanderer's branch. This high up on spindly third limbs, decisions were made by whichever popular wind prevailed at the moment. Wyatt shook his head at the analogy. Maybe he was being too hard on them. They did, after all, stand while pissing, a trait generally associated with the male gender. One thing was certain; none of them possessed one calcified shard that could be mistaken for backbone. In fact, even Ganna Mae, seventy years old, half-blind, one-hundred percent crazy, and *Magna Cum Laude* School of Hard Knocks could have whipped them all. Yet, Wyatt knew that the board would find fault with him for doing what they never would have even attempted, beating the old woman into submission.

The scandalous price he had paid for the property would have been less had Ganna Mae passed on to her reward like her other siblings. The third-generation Ferguson heirs, true to form, had been eager to sign, and why not? They had no connection to the land. Hell, for that matter, few of them even knew where the land was located, much less the real value of the old home place. Not so with Ganna Mae, the youngest daughter of Grover and Iris Ferguson, two hardscrabble old coots who had eked out a living on the forty-acre spread during the Great Depression. Second generation, Ganna Mae had been different, as expected. So today, the old woman had merited his best negotiation skills. Truth be told, he would have charmed her pants off, if that's what it would have taken, but thankfully...(*Whew baby!*) it hadn't come to that.

Ganna Mae had worn the poverty of the Ferguson family as proudly as decorated veterans wore medals for bravery in combat, and she, like some veterans, had viewed the past through tear-filled eyes. But he had heard war stories before and hers, much like those of the vets', had probably gotten better with time and the telling.

A skeptical smile spread across his face as he remembered the old woman's recollection of slingshot gravy in times when meat was scarce, poured over cat-head-biscuits made with lard and washed down with Mason jars of tea sweetened with King Syrup. "And that's just about all we had to eat, boy!" Ganna Mae had snapped, the depths of deprivation still dark and glinting in her stricken eyes.

Apparently the Ferguson's had suffered meatless months; hell, meatless years, except for the occasional slab of streak-o-lean donated in the dead of night and left on the porch by an anonymous neighbor. And what self-respecting pauper lacked a story of walking shoeless to school in the winter? Certainly not Ganna Mae, and, not surprisingly, her trips to and from school were uphill, both ways, in a blizzard. Blizzard in a town that Wyatt knew averaged less than an inch of snow per year.

For hours he listened to the hard-time stories of sly-ass Ganna Mae, and with each story she had gotten more dollars per acre to sweeten the deal. Ganna Mae, however, like any good negotiator, had saved her best for last.

Her blizzard of 1937 was hard enough to buy, but then the old woman had thrown in the heat wave of 1942. Eight days of one-hundred-degree heat had killed the family's two mules, so the story went. Ganna Mae and her five older brothers had taken the mule's places in the harnesses during the planting season of 1943 just to survive. Oh yeah. The tearjerker Wyatt remembered. The youngest son, clubfooted Caleb, had ridden on his father's shoulders and shouted the gees and haws to the improbable team. When the crops had been harvested, Grover had replaced the two mules with a stalwart hybrid named Demon. The mule had been a bargain. For half the price of one mule, Demon had done the work of two. Unfortunately for the Fergusons, the mule, as his name implied, had an evil spirit. In a deliberate attack too horrible for Ganna Mae to relate, the fiery black mule had ended the humble lives of Grover and Iris Ferguson.

Wyatt had wanted to know more about the mule, but not as badly as he wanted to get back to the soundproof cabin of his jet, so he passed on his chance to learn more of the murderous Demon. Instead, as the tears streamed down her face at the story's end, Wyatt had done what man does best, gone for the kill.

"Ms. Ganna Mae, you should sell that land and free yourself from the burden of this terrible memory. I've offered you more than a fair price, don't you think?"

Ganna Mae composed herself and nodded agreement. Wyatt wasn't sure, but there seemed to be a shadowy smirk on her face. He convinced himself that it was actually a smile.

Hiding her hatred of Kincaids was an art Ganna Mae had practiced for decades, but Wyatt's insensitivity, the big lummox, had almost caused it to erupt. Blessed with the best theatrical training available in Europe, she recovered. She was sure the idiot hadn't noticed her slip. After the "land-sale" game was over, everyone would see the signed deed for what it really was; a death warrant for Wyatt, the *Last Kincaid*. Something she had planned before he was even born. At least now she could take solace in knowing that she had served subtle notice of the beginning of the end of the Kincaid Dynasty. Maybe too subtle she feared.

Reverting to character, that of a dried-up sharecropper's daughter finally accepting the inevitable, Ganna Mae told Wyatt her reason for vengeance.

Vengeance this idiot would undoubtedly perceive as stipulations to his precious contract.

"Mr. Kincaid, I won't need this in writing, so you don't have to draw up a new contract, but I want your promise of two things: one, I don't want my parents' remains disturbed, and two, there is an old chiffonier in the home place. I want it."

Agreeing to any condition not in writing was easy enough, but agreeing to Ganna Mae's last requests would be even easier. The laws of North Carolina already protected Iris and Grover's graves located on the property and retrieving the chest of drawers would take little effort. It was time to seal the deal.

"Ms. Ganna Mae, that won't be a problem, we've got ourselves a contract." Wyatt laid the contract on the table for her to sign. "I can understand your concern for your parents, but the furniture...That old house has been wasting away for fifty years, and with the humidity and all, I doubt the furniture is worth anything."

"Maybe it has no value to you, Mr. Kincaid, but the chiffonier is the only reason I'm doing this at all."

Good, just a one-sentence explanation. Before Ganna Mae could launch into another story, Wyatt cut her off. "Well, in that case I'd be glad to get it for you. Now, I know a lady your age doesn't drink the hard stuff, but when I do a deal, I think it should be sealed with a drink. I keep a bottle in my briefcase just for these occasions. Maybe you could join me in a toast with some of that buttermilk I spied in the icebox over there."

Ganna Mae parted the calico curtains covering the pie safe and retrieved two tin mugs. As she sat the mugs on the washboard basin, murderous acts, as murderous as any Demon had ever plotted, ran through her mind.

In the quiet interior of his jet, away from the board, and more importantly, away from Ganna Mae, Wyatt tried to savor his victory. Two obstacles stood in his way: the board's negative take on his victory, and the conniving Ganna Mae. Convinced he could deal with the board later, Wyatt opened the briefcase and studied the deed.

Everything about the document was standard, except for the seller's elegant signature. Nothing about her penmanship suggested any septuagenarian scrawl he had seen before. Old people scribbled, but Ganna Mae had signed with flair, form and a steady hand. In fact, her name looked more like an autograph than an endorsement of a legal document.

Then there was her reference to the furniture. *Chiffonier* the old woman had called it. Preposterous! A woman one generation removed from sharecroppers should have referred to it as a *chest of drawers*. Wyatt's contempt for any woman who referred to furniture by its French name was well-founded. After all, three of his four ex-wives had favored French *chiffoniers, étagères,* and *armoires,* items with much more appropriate domestic appellations, chest of drawers being one of them, damn it!

Little matter. Once the furniture, French or English version, found its way into his divorce settlement--the pieces soon found a domicile far from the original purchaser. Since then, Wyatt had embarked on a campaign against anything French. With that thought, as Ganna Mae had predicted, Wyatt had failed to see the chiffonier for what it was; the clincher in the plan she called *The Last Kincaid.*

"Back home, Bossman?"

Trent Rayle looked like a pilot, seasoned with just enough gray to temper his bravado, but still gutsy. He was an ex-fighter pilot, a combat veteran from the Gulf War, and a former captain with FedEx. Wyatt had been insistent that his pilot not come from the airlines. Too regimented. He wanted a guy with balls. Someone who knew the rules but didn't mind pushing them.

Having a private jet and a pilot to fly it had not been high on Wyatt's list until 9-11. Flying first class in commercial had been good enough and, besides basking in the green-eyed envy of the coach passengers filing past him on their way to steerage, he had enjoyed flirting with the flight attendants. Thanks to the bullshit rules of the FAA, and the airlines' general disorder, that had changed.

Airports remained in a constant state of delay. If it wasn't the weather, it was the security directed by politically correct, dumbass-policy makers. Security searches on ninety-year old women, five-year-old kids, and captains of commerce such as he?

What idiocy! Hijackers were Arab men, Islamic radicals. To hell with politically correct! Search the obvious—the terrorist in our midst for Christ's sake! In fact, Wyatt had made just that statement and paid the price at a gate at O'Hare. Who knew Sikhs weren't Muslims?

Chicago officials had pulled him aside and caused him to miss his flight. Best thing that ever happened to him. He ordered his own jet right from O'Hare and Bombardier deliver the Challenger jet to Wilmington the next day. To hell with security. Let someone else bitch about the camel jockeys and be detained. Wyatt's days of x-rays, shoe-sniffing-dogs, and probe--wielding perverts were over.

"Yeah, Trent, but go ahead and file for Chub, too. I want to have dinner on the boat tonight. Have someone from legal meet us at the airport. I need this deed recorded today."

"How long are we going to be on the ground in Wilmington?" Trent paused before inserting his last urgent text message from the corporate office into the conversation. "You still have a board meeting, right?"

"Naw, that's been cancelled." Wyatt's statement wasn't a lie. The meeting had been cancelled, but not by consensus. "I just need to get the deed picked up. Shouldn't take but a minute."

Cancelled? "OK, Bossman, anything else?"

Wyatt savored the moniker Trent used for him, *Bossman*. Even though he had insisted on Trent continuing to use it, for the first few weeks the pilot had stuck with Mr. Kincaid, just to be on the safe side. Trent, like some of the office staff, didn't understand the importance of a good nickname. A company needed a leader with a name people remembered, and *Bossman* filled the bill.

"Naw, I can take care of everything else from back here. You want to have dinner on the boat?"

"No thanks, Bossman. I need to get back home. My wife's still in the hospital."

"Yeah, I forgot. How is Sherry?"

"Cheryl," Trent said. "Not much better, but thanks for asking."

Nothing embarrassed Wyatt more than using the wrong name, and nothing irked him more than being reminded of his miscue. Golden Rules of any Crown-Kincaid business deal: Learn the names and use them often. Shake hands, pat them on the back and watch how they handled the physical part. If they touched back; Good-old-boy'em to death…If they stiffened or recoiled, just screw'em real quick. No need to waste foreplay on a bad date.

The Kincaid Golden Rules of Business didn't apply to hired help. No one had told Trent all the rules of Crown Kincaid, but he would learn. Rule number one: first and foremost, never correct the Bossman. Cheryl became Sherry and Tim became Tom…and anyone who couldn't remember that became unemployed.

Chapter 2

Timothious Ridell, "Tim" to his friends and "Tom" to the Bossman, had been chosen, no, ordered, to pick up the deed at the airport. Phillip Moole, head of the legal department at the Crown, never requested the services of any of his staff, and today was no different. Dispatching an attorney to perform a menial task obviously more suited to a paralegal, was a subtle act of vengeance designed to remind the chosen pettifogger of his diminishing status in the legal department.

Tim Ridell needed no such reminder. Moole, a Harvard grad, had made no attempts to hide his disdain for any attorney not educated by an Ivy League school, Duke being the only exception. Before Moole arrived, Tim Ridell had proudly displayed his Campbell University Law School degree on his office wall. Now, the unframed certificate resided in the lowest drawer of his desk.

The ink had barely dried on the sole graduate degree in the Ridell clan, when Tim landed his job with Crown Kincaid. A hiring decision new comer Phillip Moole questioned at his first introduction to office staff. But Moole, like everyone else in the office, quickly learned that Tim Ridell hadn't actually landed the job. That distinction belonged to Sally's father, Jim Boykin, a distant cousin of Wyatt Kincaid II. Sally's decision to marry a man with no pedigree was bad enough, but damned if Jim was going to let "Baby Girl" marry a man without a future. Big Jim Boykin's suggestion, to the Crown, as expected, had carried enough weight to crush Tim's hopes of becoming a public defender. To no one's surprise, Sally had sided with Big Jim. Rather than see the intrusion for what it was, Sally referred to it as a simple correction of Tim's ambitions.

"Honestly, Tim, I don't understand why you get so upset when Daddy takes an interest in your career. It you weren't married to me, can you imagine how much his advice would cost? Why don't you write him a thank you note? It's the least you could do. Daddy would like that."

Aware of the futility of disagreeing with Boykin and Boykin, Tim did not write the note, but he did sign the gushing accolades prepared by Sally. And, as promised, the bonds of nepotism delivered a better mousetrap--

Unfortunately for Tim, neither those bonds, nor his good old boy antics had been strong enough to maintain his third-chair status in the legal department. His divorce from Sally had severed the family connection and the recent changes in the Crown's legal hierarchy had made Moole "Good Old Boy Emeritus".

While the two events were not connected, both had proved detrimental to Tim Ridell. Moole's promotion to head of legal had come without warning. Sally & Company, on the other hand, had advertised his imminent demotion after the divorce like a weekly special for ham hocks in the *Wilmington Star*.

His union with Sally was fraught with omens, only he had been too greedy to heed them. The first warning had come on his wedding day in the vestibule of the Jacob Street Presbyterian Church. Watching two women making love was a suppressed fantasy he had harbored for years. Seeing his bride-to-be and her Maid of Honor, Celestine Bryce, performing the act like two accomplished porn stars, squashed the erotica. "Sorry, honey, I thought the door was locked," was the only apology he had received for her infidelity.

Bolting from the ceremony had crossed his mind but Sally Boykin, by popular consensus, had been a catch too good to release. His ship, the unsinkable S.S. Boykin, had come in, and stowaway Tim Ridell was on board for the ride. But this ride, like most, had come at a very steep price. Giving up the public defender job was the first withdrawal from the Tim Ridell Manhood Account; the divorce from Sally and later rejection by Jasmine Dubois had depleted it.

Sally had sent the terms of the divorce by fax in a two-sentence explanation and postscript. "Tim, I needed your sperm. Too bad I had to suffer your inept pawing to accomplish that goal." P.S. "Your genes over achieved as soon as they reached my womb. You have undoubtedly fulfilled your purpose here on earth, now please die." Judging by the two initials in small caps following Sally's name, the note had been signed by her legal secretary.

The monetary terms of the divorce were as cut and dried as the note. $3500 per month child support and $3500 per month alimony payments until Sally remarried. And how likely was that to happen? Never in a million years would Sally remarry. How could she? States that were considering legalizing same sex unions didn't include North Carolina, and probably never would. She had reminded him of that at least twice a month for the last three years. Sally, the consummate know-it-all, was always on top of things, (and probably the reason the Dominatrix had to suffered his inept pawing) even the laws of North Carolina, though she steadfastly refused to reside there.

Had Sally and Celestine Bryce quietly faded away to Charleston with the child, things might have been different. But doing things quietly never had been Sally's style. When the *Wilmington Star* had refused to print the announcement of her union with Celestine, Sally found another way to embarrass him.

He, like everyone else in his office, had learned of the cohabitation via interoffice email. The divorce papers arrived the next day by registered mail in an envelope marked with the return address of Celestine & Sally Bryce.

No hyphenated last name like the one Sally Boykin-Ridell had insisted on when she was married to him. Just plain Sally Bryce.

Visitation rights, every other weekend and alternate holidays, had seemed fair and out of character for Sally. Not until he had tried to exercise his parental rights had he understood the reason for Sally's fairness. Court-ordered visitation was a joke. Four years had passed since the divorce, and his son no longer called him *Da-Da*. Now, he was known as "the man in the smoking car". Court battle after court battle and the results were always the same visitation rights confirmed, but not enforced. The Dream Team, as Tim referred to the brain trust of Sally, Celestine Bryce, and Jim Boykin, had no problems prevailing in court over whatever shyster he could afford to hire. Jurisprudence proclaimed truth as the only ballast that could tip the scales of justice, but in the harsh reality of the courtroom he had learned the absolute truth: money was the real procurer of justice.

Paychecks from the Crown supplemented by a generous helping of credit-card debt were the resources Tim Ridell had relied on to finance his quest for parental equality. Using one card to pay another had worked as long as the pre-approved cards rolled in, but when the supply dried up, so had the outgoing monthly payments. Skipping his trailer payment one month and lot rent the next had been an effective strategy for a while, but the thickening trail of blue smoke emitted by his aging BMW would soon change that.

Engine replacement for the fancy sports car would be $12,000 and with his Beacon score, trading the car wasn't an option. Not a problem he would have to worry about if Sally hadn't insisted on buying a European car. Engine replacement for the Chevy Lumina he had picked out would be half of the BMW repair bill, but "Daddy's Baby Girl" wasn't about to be caught dead in a domestic car. European sports car: $60,000--custom sound system, $2000---and an "atta boy" from Big Jim Boykin--priceless. And worth at least another thank you note, Tim thought, as he slammed his fist into the padded dash of the aging car.

Child support, alimony, and car repairs, as bad as they were, paled in comparison to his latest problem. His last routine check of the Ferguson chain of title, which should have been a formality, was anything but. There, in the Grantor book, where the entry should have read: Ganna Mae Ferguson et al to the Crown Kincaid Development Company, was an entry that would ensure his unemployment: Ganna Mae Ferguson et al to Yasnaya Polyana, forty acres Brunswick County. The letters ran together on the page like a black cloud. Bossman had just paid $100,000,000 for a piece of property to someone who didn't own it. And Wyatt Kincaid wasn't likely to understand the reason he hadn't recorded the Memorandum of Option immediately after he had received the phone call to record.

A reprimand from the Clerk of Court, Art Boykin, brother of Jim, uncle of Sally, for being late on his child support payments had taken no longer than ten minutes. But the delay had been long enough for someone to record ahead of him.

The big jet taxied on to the ramp at Air Wilmington. Tim Ridell ran to the plane and stood by the air stairs like a lap dog waiting for his biscuit. A treat the Bossman would be glad to give if he could just answer his next question with a *yes*.

"Did you get that option recorded?"

Every bone in his body told him to say no, fess up to his mistake, and throw himself on the Bossman's mercy. Instead, out came. "Yes, sir!"

"Good man. Record this deed and tell the boys to have a road pushed into that tract. I'll be back Wednesday, and I expect to be able to drive that road in my car. One more thing, there's an old chest of drawers in the house, get it out. Then have 'em bulldoze the thing down…but make sure they protect those old grave sites out there. Got it?" Wyatt Kincaid moved back into the plane's interior. Tim's response was directed to Trent Rayle's backside. "Yes sir, Mr. Kincaid. Have a good trip."

By all accounts the trips to Chub Cay were always good trips. Not that Tim Ridell would ever know anything about the luxuries aboard the 92-foot Hatteras Motor Yacht berthed on the little island of Chub Cay north of Nassau. He'd never been invited. The only lawyer in the legal department who hadn't been. Janis Farrior, the department's senior legal secretary, had been many times. And so had Jasmine Dubois, the leggy blonde paralegal, AKA "One-trick-Pony" Jasmine was the eye candy of the legal department and the Bossman's little trixie. Sure, when she had first arrived the initials after his name had piqued her interest. Not that his physical attributes had turned her off either. Six-foot-two, skinny, but still good-looking and single/divorced. One date and a glass of wine at his trailer had ended the attraction and given rise to his equine nickname for Jasmine.

In fairness to Jasmine, the office gossip was chockfull of stories about Tim and Sally's divorce. Jasmine came after the divorce, but even she was privy to the outrageous screen saver Sally had installed on the office computers. The Crown, like most corporations, gave bonus checks at the end of the year. Paralegals had gotten hundreds, and Janis Farrior had snared a couple of thousand. Junior lawyers had gotten new cars and trips and Tim Ridell, third in seniority of legal, had gotten $25. Rather than base the bonus on job performance, Big Jim and Moole had set Tim's bonus. Wyatt Kincaid had questioned the small bonus, but Big Jim and Moole had passed it off as a practical joke. Like the hundreds of other practical jokes the two had pulled off at Harvard, the pain caused by the prank was lost in the euphoria of their brilliance.

Inspired by the jokesters, Sally had provided the screensaver for the office network. The split screen pictured a naked Tim Ridell sporting a shriveled gherkin for his manhood and a copy of the bonus check taped to the pickle. On the opposite side was a picture of Sally's buttocks covered with the joint financial statement of the law firm of Boykin & Boykin. Over the statement was a sign that read, "Look what my ass made!"

Copies of the screensaver had been removed, but saved. New hires like Jasmine were treated to the spectacle as a right of passage and a reminder of what happened to people who crossed the Boykins.

Sally's sexual proclivity wasn't brought up during the divorce settlement, nor was his twenty-five dollar bonus check, but the balance of the marriage's dirty laundry was thoroughly washed in public. Like everyone else in the courtroom, Judge Axle Rand, divorced by his wife for looking better in her clothes than she did, was fixated on Sally's low-cut blouse and tight skirt. Sexual attraction flowed from the plaintiff to the cross-dressing judge, and no one noticed the sparks more than a smoldering Celestine Bryce. Any doubts Tim Ridell had about the outcome of the divorce proceedings were dispelled when he overheard Judge Rand during a lunch break. "Sally, you have to tell me. Where in the world did you find that outfit?"

In the courtroom, Sally had portrayed him as a successful high-powered attorney with vast earnings potential. Even the cross-dressing judge had known her characterization of him was a stretch, but intent on obtaining the address of Sally's clothes source, the judge was more than generous in his ruling. If the judge could have seen the high-powered, potential money-making machine, Tim Ridell filling in for Jasmine, the paralegal trixie, while she was off in the Bahamas bopping the Bossman, the alimony payments would have been cut in half.

Tim swung back by the courthouse to check the title. There had to be a mistake. No one sold the same property twice in one day. A search of the records verified his assumption. The property had not been sold twice in the same day. Dates, on what he hoped was a bogus deed recorded only minutes after the Bossman had called to say the deal was completed, predated his deed by exactly one year. The unscrupulous maneuver effectively established a chain and color of title on the property claims of the Crown Kincaid Development Company. The forty-acre centerpiece of a billion project was useless until the courts could determine otherwise. Wyatt Kincaid would fire him long before the court ruled, though; that outcome wasn't in doubt.

The Dream Team would hound him for the alimony and child-support payments even after he lost his job. He could already picture the lawsuit demanding he make payments even if it meant selling his vital organs. Then there was the Crown. The only body part they would be interested in was his head.

The answer was simple. Find Ganna Mae Ferguson and Yasnaya Polyana, whoever in the hell she, or she was. Explain the mistake and straighten everything out by the time the Bossman returned. His brainstorm was interrupted by a call from the Challenger,

"Tom, send the old woman, Granny Mae...Ganna Mae, some flowers. She was a hard case, but I liked her. Wouldn't want her to think the Crown doesn't have class...and put a wreath on her parent's graves. That'd be a nice touch."

"Tim."

"What?"

"Tim. My name is Tim, Mr. Kincaid."

"I don't care! Just get the flowers and the furniture."

"But, I don't have a pickup truck. You want me to get one of the construction guys to pick it up?"

"No, and I don't give a damn if you have to walk it home, but get it today, Tom."

The cloud of blue exhaust smoke and dust from the dirt path billowing behind Tim Ridell's BMW resembled the smoky chemical fog sprayed by the city of Wilmington to fight mosquitoes. Enough so that irate citizens bedeviled by the pesky varmints placed calls to city hall to complain of the attention being lavished on the countryside south of the city limits. Oblivious to the sound of pistons slapping against dry cylinder walls, Tim Ridell, for the moment, was thankful for the car's feeble performance. No doubt, that was about to change, Tim thought as he eyed the blinking check engine light. True to form, the Sally-cursed-car sputtered, coughed, and finally rolled to a stop fifty yards short of his destination.

Through rising puffs of burnt engine oil, Tim surveyed the Bossman's latest acquisition. The shotgun house, bound by a cocoon of lush green vines and thistles, looked more like a vegan Happy Meal than a homestead. Rough-hewn slats of fresh pine lumber covered the windows and doors of the structure. "Great," Tim muttered. "How am I supposed to get in?" From the far side of the house, glints of reflected sunlight posed a possible solution. Tim followed its faceted path and observed a new Chevy pickup backed up to an afterthought side porch clinging to the house. Through a knothole in one of the pine slats, Tim Ridell peeked inside. Nothing in his thirty-seven years, not the two summers he had spent as a lifeguard at Myrtle Beach, nor even the week on the French Riviera on a Euro Pass, had prepared him for what he saw. Both locations were renowned for the resplendence of beautiful people per capita, but neither could boast of the beauty he ogled through the fortuitous knothole.

Braced against a chiffonier was the most exquisite female Tim Ridell ever had seen or even dreamed about. Strands of honey blonde hair neatly coiffed into a French braid crowned a face more perfect than that of Venus de Milo in the Louvre. Soft, delicate tendrils, sun-ripened and liberated, floated around her face like silky webs riding thermals.

As he watched, the goddess strained against the furniture and moved it a few inches across the torn linoleum floor. The muscles in her flat stomach compressed into six distinct quadrates almost equal in size. Under the cotton halter-top dampened by perspiration, firm breasts adorned with pebble-hard nipples brushed against the veneer sides of the chiffonier. His hands trembled as he watched the woman's sculptured buttocks swell against her pressed silk shorts. Weakened by her efforts, but determined to move the object, the beauty once again shoved against the furniture until the muscles in her legs quivered.

Covetous, lustful thoughts ran from his mind deep down into his groin. The feeling invigorated him, and deposited one installment of masculinity back into the depleted Tim Ridell Manhood Account, subsequently reminding Tim of the painful withdrawals. Sally and Celestine's affair had drawn little attention. Even in some circles of the conservative South, The Gay Way was becoming chic. The manhood gherkin on Sally's screensaver was seen as the reason that he had lost his woman to a woman. Jasmine's infatuation with the Bossman, a man nearly twice her age, only added to the rumor. Images of the long-legged blonde and the old man steaming up the mirrors in some hotel room chafed against his strict Baptist background. True, nothing the Bossman and Jasmine were doing was illegal, but it had to be immoral...twice her age, disgraceful!

He had not been out with a woman since his fiasco date with Jasmine. Instead, to satisfy his needs, he had driven once a week across the state line to visit the girls of Santee Cooper in South Carolina. Fifty dollars a trip was an extravagance on his limited budget, but there Tim found no rejection, no mission to destroy his manhood. The transactions were straightforward; sex for money. Tim Ridell understood the concept of more sex = more money. But sex was not the reason he made his weekly trips across the border into the degradation of South Carolina. Each week for one hour with a girl named Rosalyn, he enjoyed the only pleasure his limited resources could provide, friendship.

Thirty minutes into his first visit, a knock at the door reminded Rosalyn of the customers waiting to be serviced in the larger adjoining room, aptly called the paddock. Tim had wasted three earlier visits on girls named Joy, Candy, and, the crudest of all, Hot Body. The motto at the Rocking Bronco was "Be rocking while the door is locking," a canon each of the previous three girls had repeated as soon as the door to the stall had closed.

Rosalyn was different…a hooker with a heart, and for that reason, Tim Ridell had become her regular. To satisfy the madam's demand to "Hurry the hell up!" Rosalyn, fully clothed, had bounced on the bed and then given the performance of her life. "Stars…stars…oh, baby. Fireworks, fireworks--aaah, yes, yes--oooh, somebody get Smoky the Bear on the line…I'm on fire, honey!"

Back in the paddock, men salivating with anticipation ignored the other girls and demanded an appointment with Rosalyn. Applause and catcalls of "You Da Man!" greeted Tim as he rejoined the studs in waiting. "Go Mac--Daddy!.. Hell, you da *Sixty Minute Man*!" Tim Ridell soaked in the standing ovation, and why not? No one else had withstood sixty minutes of the steamy pleasures offered at the Rocking Bronco. He was *the man* for that brief moment. But each night on the drive back to Wilmington, Tim Ridell prayed that no one in the Rocking Bronco would discover that the Sixty-Minute Man had sampled only conversation and humanity from a wayward courtesan.

Again Tim Ridell peeped through the knothole, and again the sexual desire Rosalyn was unable to arouse shot through him. Short hot breaths warmed his face pressed against the clapboard siding and beads of sweat moistened his cracked lips. Weakened from the sight of the goddess, he turned to face the overgrown fields of the farm, and sucked in deep gulps of air. He made it back to the BMW before his normal breathing returned. From the seat of the car he grabbed a golf towel and wiped his face with trembling hands.

Lawyer logic told him that women that perfect didn't exist…well maybe in a bar just before last call. In two more breaths he came up with as many reasons why such a perfect package couldn't be inside the house. Beautiful women didn't drive pickup trucks, and the dimly lit house was hiding imperfections daylight would expose.

"Hi."

Tim Ridell did not answer; instead he studied the figure standing in front of him. In the light of day his false assumptions died. Pygmalion's creation, Galatea, would have been relegated to Miss Congeniality in a beauty contest with this woman. Warm eyes, as soft as blue flame and flecked with violet, stared back at him. Through full-pursed lips, she made a request, "Could you give me a hand?"

With the golf towel still in his hands, Tim Ridell began to applaud.

"Funny, really funny, hotshot, but I need a real hand. I thought I could load it myself but it's too heavy."

"I wasn't being funny, and I don't know why I did that….and why are you taking things out of this house?"

"Why shouldn't I?"

"Because, my company, the company I work for, owns this house."

The woman leaned into the car until her face was inches from his. "Says who?"

"Me…I'm Tom, er Tim Ridell."

"Well, which is it, big boy, Tom or Tim?"

"Tim, Tim Ridell, I'm an attorney for the Crown Kincaid Development Company."

"I see, and you're full of crap. I know the owner, and it's not Crown Kincaid, or the Crown as you flunkies refer to it."

"No, really, we bought it today. I just recorded the deed."

"You might have recorded a deed, but you don't own it, hotshot."

"Why would you say that, and who are you, anyway?"

"I'm Yasnaya Polyana."

Chapter 3

Ganna Mae pulled the Timex watch from her apron pocket and noticed the hour, 5:05 p.m. The Registrar of Deeds would be closed by now, and someone at the Crown would be crying foul. A smile cracked the heavy stage makeup covering her face. They had done it, beaten the Crown at its own game. The vendetta had been fifty years in the making, and the long years had done nothing but sweeten her revenge.

Wyatt Kincaid, as she had figured, was oblivious to everything but the signature line on the deed. What a pleasure watching him squirm for hours as she belabored her horrid childhood. Oh and how he had commiserated with her...Ms. Ganna this and Ms. Ganna that. When that hadn't worked he had poured on the charm, and when that hadn't worked he had piled on the money, raising his already outrageous offer. She broke into uproarious laughter thinking about how quickly Kincaid would have screwed her if that was the only option to seal the deal. Swine!

From the kitchen window in the cabin, Ganna Mae watched the last rays of the dog days sun bed down for the long night ahead. A night that she wouldn't be spending in the shack she and Yasnaya called *the scene*. The cabin was clean. She had left no clues of her presence except for the two tin mugs she and Wyatt had used to toast the deal.   Clumps of butterfat, bourbon, and whole milk spattered in an abstract pattern against the blue speckled tin basin that doubled as a makeshift sink. What had been called slops in her youth could easily pass for a masterpiece in any of the galleries on West Street in Manhattan, the place she would be spending the night.

None of the roles she had played on the stages of London, New York, and Paris had provided the satisfaction she felt at this moment. Wyatt upstaged her by suggesting the toast, and his insistence that she was too old to handle liquor had pissed her off. None of that mattered now. What did matter was getting the taste of clabbered milk from her mouth. Using the boiling water on the kerosene stove, Ganna Mae rinsed out the remnants of her buttermilk and poured in four fingers of the Early Times she had bought to toast the deal. Great thespians were insistent on stage design and props. The cheap bourbon and cabin symbolized her sharecropper's background... and the ogre hadn't noticed. "Crass bastard," Ganna Mae muttered, and then curved her lips into a wicked smile.

"Oh, but you will notice my next scene, Mr. Kincaid. Yes...even you will notice next time, Jackass."

One more drink and a couple of cigarettes, then it would be time to leave for the airport at Raleigh-Durham. Between sips of bourbons and cigarettes she washed off makeup and moisturized her face before applying her Borghese base. In one quick-stitch motion the flour sack dress fell to the floor. And almost as quickly a Chanel wool bouclé suit with a fox wrap covered her svelte frame. Agility and septuagenarian were generally worlds apart, but a lifetime of professional dancing had closed that gap for Ganna Mae, or Gan Mana, as she was known on stage. With the same deftness she had used to change, Gan dialed the number of her accomplice.

"Hello."

"Hi, sweetie. Did you get the chiffonier?"

"Gan, can I call you back. I have a little situation here."

"The Crown?"

"Well, not exactly. More like a pawn of."

"Can you handle it, or do I need to drive to Wilmington?"

Tim Ridell processed Yasnaya's remarks. The pawn would be him, and Gan had to be Ganna Mae Ferguson. Like a punch-drunk fighter he shook the vision of Yasnaya Polyana from his head and stood to rejoin the fray. "I know who that is and I need to speak with her."

Ganna Mae heard his voice. True enough she would have to talk to the Crown, but not now, too early. "Yas, tell him the call was from Fran. I'll call you when I get in. Leave the item if you must."

Yasnaya Polyana folded her phone and stared at Tim Ridell, then spoke. "You really have trouble with names, don't you? First you can't remember your own, and then you change the names of my friends. And just in case you've forgotten it's considered bad manners to eavesdrop, Tim, or is it Tom now?"

"It's Tim, and you said Gan. I need to talk to her about a little matter of fraud and--"

"I said *Fran*, and since you mentioned a point of law, let me remind you, Mr. Ridell, you're the only one who is breaking the law."

"Breaking the law?"

"That's right, you're trespassing. Leave now, or I'll call the police."

Yasnaya opened the phone and began to dial.

"No, wait, let me explain."

Yasnaya finished dialing and put the phone to her ear, Tim Ridell moved in front of her. "Please, let me explain."

"911 What is your emergency?" The operator asked as.

Yasnaya held the phone away from her ear and watched the expression on Tim Ridell's face. Whoever this man was in front of her, he wasn't a threat, and hardly a worthy adversary. The fear induced by a call to authority had completely undone the man. No longer bolstered by his employment with the Crown, Tim Ridell folded like a bad hand at the poker table. His disputes with Sally had resulted in the same hangdog demeanor he now displayed.

"911, what is your emergency, please?"

Something, maybe the hurt in his eyes, or the puppy-dog meekness of Tim Ridell, softened Yasnaya. Beating up on people wasn't her way. Never had been. Besides, vulnerability was sexy.

"911? I'm so sorry. I must have dialed the wrong number." Yasnaya folded the phone and smiled at the dejected puppy in front of her. Relief washed over Tim as he rushed his words out in a hoarse rasp. "Thank you. I'm leaving now." With his tail tucked safely between his legs, he retreated to his BMW.

Lights from the instrument panel glowed, but no sound came from the engine. Tim banged the gear shifter like a drummer in a punk rock band until the park position lit. "Come on baby, one more trip to the bus station that's all I ask." Tim urged as he frantically pumped the gas pedal. "One more trip, baby--please!" The car, flooded by the needless priming, ignored Tim's pleas and refused to start. But why should it? Why should anything work for him, especially anything connected to this damn albatross of Sally's?

"Do you need a jump?"

The words were spoken in a soft tone, almost caring, almost uplifting enough to raise his head from the steering wheel, but not quite.

"No, I need a gun."

Yasnaya reached in the window and patted Tim on the head. "Come on, you'd kill yourself because your car won't start?"

"Oh no. The gun's for the car. I have enough compassion to put it out of its misery, but I don't like myself that much. Besides, why should I do the company's job for them? As soon as they find out we don't own this farm. I'm a dead man."

Having his head patted by this beautiful woman was more than he expected. What she said next was a troubling bonus. "It isn't your fault. Phillip Moole was in charge of gift wrapping this little project."

"What? Who are you, and how do you know so much about the Crown?"

"Tell you what, Tim, you help me load the furniture and I'll give you a lift back to town. Maybe I'll even answer your question as to who I am, deal?"

The chiffonier slid into the bed of the truck and Yasnaya passed him a rope to secure it. Perspiration had soaked her cotton halter-top once again, exposing the absolute magnificence of Yasnaya Polyana. Tying a slipknot should have been an easy task for a former Eagle Scout, but it wasn't. Unlike Sally or Jasmine Dubois, this woman was being nice, even if she had compared him to a chess piece of the smallest size and value.

Technically he was doing nothing more than helping the rightful owner move her furniture...even the Bossman would understand that. No, he wouldn't understand. But nothing that Wyatt Kincaid or anyone else understood mattered now. Hell, life was over, or, life as he knew it was over; a blessing in a way.

Sally would hound him until the last drop of his blood was safely tucked away into her bank account. Phillip Moole would have him disbarred even if he wasn't responsible for the land debacle. Yasnaya would forget him as soon as she dropped him off at his metal mansion.

For the first time in four years, Tim Ridell faced what he had tried so hard to avoid...rock bottom, and it wasn't so bad. True enough, he was screwed. But so were the Crown, Sally, and some unknown mechanic waiting to sell him the $12,000 replacement engine for the BMW. The prospect of winning by losing less than his opponents suddenly hit home. Tim Ridell lifted both arms toward the sky and shouted in rapture. "Hot damn! Free at last, free at last! God Almighty, I'm free at last!"

Yasnaya watched as the man she had deemed harmless danced a jig in the dust around the truck bed, and then second-guessed her hasty observation.

"Hey, are you okay?" Yasnaya asked.

"Fit as fiddle, and free as the breeze."

"And that would mean?"

"That would mean, Miss Yasnaya Polyana, I couldn't care less how you beat the Crown out of this tract of land. Nor does it bother me that you are taking the furniture I was directed to pick up. As a matter of fact, if there's anything else in the house you want to load, I'm game."

Yasnaya looked at the head of Tim Ridell, the same one she had patted minutes earlier as he sat in his broken-down car and spied no new bruises or abrasions since her last contact. Which meant the reason for his transformation was internal, more than likely a mental breakdown. Great, in the middle of nowhere and she was alone with an insane person. Just to be on the safe side, she moved to the driver's side door of her truck and retrieved the 25-caliber Raven automatic and stuffed it into the waistband of her shorts. "I think it's only fair to warn you I have a gun, and I know how to use it."

"What? I wouldn't--look, you've got me all wrong. I know I sound a little crazy, but all I'm trying to say is, game over, and you win."

Yasnaya put her hand on the walnut handle of the pistol, "Well, that's a pretty big mood swing you're having there."

"I'm not having a mood swing; I'm having a life-changing experience, that's all. I've seen the light--."

"Yeah, I got it. Free at last, and all that, but still, you're acting just a little weird to me."

"Yasnaya. May I call you Yas?"

"I guess...as long as you don't start singing and dancing again." Yasnaya pulled the gun from her shorts, "And keep your distance."

"Yas, I wouldn't hurt you--."

"Oh, OK -I'm supposed to believe that, and only fifteen minutes ago you were going to shoot your car!"

"I'm an attorney, for Christ's sake."

"And that's supposed to make me feel better?"

"What's that supposed to mean?"

"Attorney, shyster, scum of the earth... any of that ringing any bells, Tim?"

"I'm not that kind of attorney. I'm just a mouthpiece. The worst I could do is talk you to death."

Yasnaya put the gun back into her shorts. Tim Ridell was right. He wasn't dangerous. Unbalanced maybe...possibly crazy, but not dangerous. "So--is that what happened to your car?"

"I don't understand."

"Your car. Did you talk it to death?"

Damn, the girl was gorgeous and funny. "You know, that was pretty funny. I'd laugh but I'm scared you might shoot me."

"Laughing is OK, but if you start dancing again, you will be a dead man."

The ride back to Wilmington was quiet, and Tim's mind was clouded with thoughts of his next move. He had no idea where he was going, but his mind was made up. He was going somewhere far away from the Dream Team, the Crown, and the greedy mechanic. The best part of his plan was that no one would miss him, with the possible exception of the mechanic and the credit card companies.

"Do I cross the bridge?" Yasnaya slowed the truck as she waited for instructions from her unstable passenger.

"No, turn left onto River Street. You can drop me at the Harbor Bistro."

"I thought you said you lived in Columbus County?"

"I do, but I'm not ready to go home yet. I feel like celebrating. Why don't you join me?"

"I don't think so." Yasnaya took her eyes off Tim and made the left turn onto River Street. "You're acting weird again."

"Come on, it's a crowded place. You'll be safe there. Besides, you promised to explain who you are."

"I said I *might* tell you who I am."

Lights from Harbor Bistro glimmered from the elevated dining patio and mixed with the convection fog hugging the warm waters of the Cape Fear River. Yasnaya swung her door open as soon as the pickup jerked to a stop. Her actions provoked a question from the still giddy Tim Ridell. "Change your mind?"

"No, my stomach. It growled. Besides, you were right. It's crowded."

The restaurant patrons were divided into two camps Camp One: the gaggle of women who disapproved of Yasnaya's attire. Camp Two: the smiling men who did approve and were amused at Camp One's ire. Tim Ridell was firmly entrenched in Camp Two.

"Table for two, by a window."

"Do you have a reservation, sir?"

"No, but I do have this." Tim opened his wallet and pulled out two twenties and a ten. Fifty dollars enough for another hour with Rosalyn and another chance to be admired for his pseudo-virility--Sixty-minute Man.

The hostess looked them over.... Not exactly appropriate attire for the Harbor Bistro, but for fifty bucks, who needed a dress code? "I think we do have a cancellation. Will a patio table be okay, sir?"

"Perfect. Thank you." How long had it been since people had treated him like someone? Oh yeah, since he had been Mr. Sally Boykin. "Oh, and miss, could you bring us a bottle of Cristal?"

"I'm not your server, sir, but I'll pass your request along. Have a nice evening."

"Cristal? Ooh."

Good, Yasnaya knew the champagne. If she knew the wine, she knew the three-hundred-dollar price tag that came with it. Under the table Tim checked the credit cards in his wallet. One had a five-hundred-dollar limit, and the other had a thousand, the remaining eight cards were maxed out.

Chapter 4

Trent Rayle lowered the nose of the Challenger until the ninety-two-foot Hatteras yacht was dead center of the windscreen. Level at 200 feet and one half mile from Chub Cay, Bahamas, Rayle bore down on the hapless *Crown Jewel* berthed in the harbor.

Buzzing the boat, while fun as hell, also gave the crew time to make the *Crown Jewel* ship-shape, just in case it wasn't. Corporate flying would never replace the adrenaline-pumping F-15 fighter jets Rayle had piloted. But neither was it as boring and monotonous as flying for hire or hauling freight. Plus, corporate had another bonus, other than the occasional European or Asian trips he was home every night.

For fifteen years Trent had fought Cheryl to stay in the job he loved. But then the cancer came, and leaving the Air Force wasn't as important as granting the dying wish of his high-school sweetheart. Six months when you were fifteen going on sixteen was a lifetime, but six months for a terminal cancer patient was barely a day. Soon it would be over. Cheryl had already picked out her burial dress, the flowers, and even the music for her funeral. But Trent refused to talk about her approaching death, or believe it. Miracles happened and they happened to good people. No one deserved a miracle more than Cheryl, and no one believed more than Trent Rayle that she would have one.

From the cabin came the booming voice of the Bossman, "I bet that woke their asses up."

"Bossman, that buzz job woke the dead."

Dead. Damn, he'd said it. Death was a word he banished from his memory as well as vocabulary. Perhaps by ignoring the unwelcome visitor, he had reasoned, it would bypass his home, his family, and most of all, his beautiful wife. Superstition and sports go hand in hand, the same is true in aviation, and for good reason in his case. Once, in the Gulf War, Trent had worn the same socks for thirty sorties. Sure, his feet smelled like spoiled bologna, but the lucky socks had worked, and he had come back home to Cheryl.

"Want me to buzz her again?"

"Naw, you better not. That old bastard on the Broward hates it when you do that. If I didn't think I'd do some business with him...."

Wyatt's voice trailed off as he thought about Jarek Denton, who owned the 126' Broward Motor Yacht, *Slice of Life*, berthed next to his Hatteras. Denton owed all of the Cheesy Pleasy pizza chain franchises on the East Coast. The pizza tasted like crap, but the games and kid-oriented theme drew starry-eyed tykes and their cash-laden parents to the Cheesy Pleasy locations like barnacles to boats. Denton's pizza parlors were a perfect anchor for the strip development the Crown owned at the Down East interchanges of I-40, but Wyatt had unwittingly blown his chance to land Jarek Denton as a tenant.

Never one to stand on ceremony, Wyatt paid little attention to crew apparel and thought the crew uniforms favored by some of his fellow yachtsmen stupid. Denton, a traditionalist boater, visited Wyatt on board and suggested that he correct his oversight, demanded actually. The man was even brazen enough to give him a catalogue of uniforms acceptable as crew attire. Rather than bother to find out how Denton made his money, he gave a very public apology to Denton in the club dining room and abruptly whisked the crew off for a day of shopping at the marina haberdashery. Instead of pullover polo shirts and shorts, acceptable attire, he had outfitted his crew with wife-beater T-shirts and cutoff jeans. His gang had applauded Wyatt's moxie, and with the exception of Yvette, the chef, all had donned the outrageous getups and joined him for lunch at the dining club on Chub Cay. Denton, smoldering like a pig over a pit, observed the show from two tables away. Angered by the insult, Denton had retaliated by lining the dock between the *Slice of Life* and the *Crown Jewel* with twenty-foot high potted evergreens to hide the unsightly view of redneck chic. Yvette, in her traditional chef's whites, was the only crew member of the *Crown Jewel* with whom Denton was on speaking terms, including Wyatt.

Jim Williams, second mate, loaded Wyatt's bag onto the four-wheel drive mule, then dusted off a spot on the bench seat for Wyatt. "Just the one bag, Bossman?"

Wyatt winced as he observed Jim's T-shirt and cutoffs. Changing his directive for crew apparel would mean another shot at doing business with Jarek Denton, but that would lose him the respect and affection he had gained from the crew. Besides, when his new development opened, the high and mighty Jarek Denton would beg him for a tenant slot. Hell, old Denton might even have his *Slice of Life* crew dress like Wyatt's just to bury the hatchet.

"Yeah, won't be here but a few days. Business."

"Going to have time to get in some fishing, Bossman? The yellowtails are eating it up."

"Nah, just want to relax a little...wouldn't mind eating some, though."

"Already cleaned some for you and the crew bought you a little present." Jim said as he pulled a wife beater from a plastic bag. "Check out the writing."

In bold black letters on the front and back of the shirt were the words: **To hell with a Slice of Life, I've got the whole pie!** Jesus, Jarek Denton never would do business with him if he wore this. Maybe he wouldn't have to. "Thanks, Jim. That was mighty nice of y'all. You shouldn't have."

"We knew you'd like it. Want me to wait while you put it on?"

Wyatt hesitated. Key tenants were more important than an admiring crew. Hell, somebody had to help pay for his new project. Cheesy Pleasy would go a long way…. Damn, it was hard being a hero. "Thanks. Maybe I'll put it on later."

"Come on, Bossman, Yvette bet $100 you wouldn't wear it. Said you didn't have the nerve."

Wyatt peeled his suit coat and shirt off. "Well, damn if she won't see."

"All right! I knew you would. Hundred bucks…K-ching!"

Great, twenty-year-old kid wins a $100 and I lose every damn Cheesy Pleasy from New York to Miami. Wyatt slumped down on the seat of the mule. Denton was a reader and there was good chance he wouldn't even look up, and, with the evergreens, he couldn't see over the next berth once he was on the boat. Good plan, good plan.

Wyatt tucked further down in the seat as the mule rounded the dirt path that ran parallel to the harbor and docks. The bald head of Jarek Denton glowed in the sun. Good, he was reading. Ease on by, no harm…no foul. Jim Williams blew the horn on the mule and waved to Jarek Denton. "Show him, Bossman!"

Wyatt looked at Jarek Denton and sank further in the seat, at the same time Yvette yelled out, "Told you he'd hide."

Hide? Damn if Wyatt Kincaid would hide, not for any amount of money. "Afternoon, Mr. Denton." Jarek Denton got the Full Monty from Wyatt, closed his book, snapped off a one-finger salute, and disappeared into the *Slice of Life*.

As he walked up the gangplank of the Hatteras, Wyatt did damage control. At least he had said, "Mister." Denton had to give him points for that, right? Millions, hundreds of millions, and Denton wouldn't be giving but taking, and taking….Damn it!

Wyatt kicked his shoes off at the top of the gangplank, grabbed his waiting Scotch and water from the pilothouse, and then made his way to the upper deck of the boat. Thirty feet above the dock, he had a clear view of the *Slice of Life*, but that made him reconsider his excellent perch. No need to give Denton another look at the stupid shirt. Back below on the aft deck Wyatt silently appreciated the landscaping provided by Denton. Snuggled safely behind the firs, and determined to forget about Denton, Wyatt rehashed the Ganna Mae deal again.

Nothing about the deal had gone badly. In fact, as deals went, this one had been perfect. Two items in Ganna Mae's cabin in Asheboro had troubled him, though. Louis Vuitton luggage wasn't rare, but it was rare for such a fine bag to be owned by a poor old woman. At first glance he had thought the bag was a knockoff, but the smell and feel of soft leather had convinced him the bag was authentic. Then there was the tin of face cream from Clé de Peau Beauté, $450 per ounce and sold by only exclusive retailers like Bergdorf Goodman, Saks and Nieman Marcus, a fact he knew thanks to his last wife's taste in cosmetics. Had it not been for choosing the wrong door for the bathroom and winding up in Ganna Mae's bedroom, he would not have these troubling thoughts.

Explaining them away had not worked either. Sure, she could have been spending the money from the land sale before she had gotten it. But why spend money on luxuries rather than necessities? Even the newest of the nouveau riche would take care of needs before wants, unless they were as dumb as the Brinks robbers had been in Charlotte a few years back. *Velvet Elvis paintings*! The FBI should have shot them on the spot. No wonder prison reform was hopeless. *Bad taste* lived on after criminals were convicted. Wyatt thought about the earlier stunt with Denton; he should be shot too. Dumb! No, stupid! Tasteless--jeez…he would fit right in with the Brinks Gang.

"Would you like another drink, Mr. Kincaid, or perhaps an hors d'oeuvre? I'm sure it would be more satisfying that the ice, oui?" Yvette had the same snooty European accent of his last wife. She had been French and Wyatt's habit of crushing the rocks in his glass of Scotch had bothered her, too. Bothering a wife was one thing, but he couldn't care less how agitated his galley cook became at his bad manners. With malice aforethought, Wyatt filled his mouth with the last cubes of ice in the glass and crunched loudly. "Yeah, another Scotch and water please. Oh, and Yvette, put a lot of ice in it…matter of fact, bring me a separate glass of ice."

"A separate glass of ice, sir?"

"Yes, if you don't mind. You know, a little something to nibble on before dinner."

"Sir, may I remind you, ice is not considered one of the food groups. How about a nice sorbet?"

"Tell me, Yvette, what damn food group does sorbet fall into? I want ice, preferably crushed, but cubed will do. And tonight, for dinner I want a side dish of ice, plain ice. No sprigs of mint to dress it up and no slushy fruit-flavored crap--sorbet--just ice."

"A side dish of ice, very well, sir. And what entrée would you like with this ice?"

"Oh, I don't know, whatever you think might go well with ice. I'm open to your suggestions, Yvette." The Le Manoir Culinary Art School-trained chef did have a suggestion: Braised Redneck, simmered in diesel fuel and smothered in a nice toxic-waste sauce came to mind. In her native tongue, Yvette suggested her choice.

"Rouge?..whatever in the hell you said. What kind of meat is that?"

"It's a *foul* dish, sir."

"Not that pigeon dish, is it?"

"Squab? No, it's not squab."

"Not tough like duck, right?"

"Well, is does start out tough, as you say, but first I will marinate it in *ciguë*, then it will not matter how tough it is."

"What kind of wine goes with that?"

"I think perhaps a nice bottle of *pisse rouge de taureau* would be appropriate, sir."

Captain Clark Guilford, fluent in French from his stints on the French Riviera, silently translated Yvette's two suggestions.(Ciguë: hemlock. *:* Pisse rouge de taureau : Red bull piss), and wondered if Wyatt Kincaid had done the same.

"Okay, that sounds good. I'm tired of seafood anyway. Thank you, Yvette."

"Nope," Clark mumbled.

"The pleasure is all mine, sir." Yvette gave him a slight bow and headed for the galley.

Controlling staff on a yacht had proved no different than controlling office staff, contrary to the warnings of his more seasoned yachtsmen friends. Captains were professionals, and mates were mates, but cooks…that's where the trouble was. Temperamental, obstinate, and downright ornery, cooks couldn't even be happy being called cooks. Being a cook was good enough for his cook in Wilmington, but Yvette insisted on being addressed as *Chef*, a demand Wyatt steadfastly refused to honor.

His introduction of guests and crew had become a competition between himself and Yvette. Rather than wait to be introduced, Yvette had taken to introducing herself as the boat's chef. Wyatt undermined her gambit by insisting that the guests call her *Cookie*, which inevitably led her to offer another lesson on foods. "A cookie, monsieur, is something that sometimes appears at the end of a meal. If you insist on insulting me, your chef, I shall do the same."

The guest got the message though Wyatt did not. No matter how many times his guest sent compliments to the chef, Wyatt's compliment was always the same. "Yeah, that Yvette is a hell of a cook, all right." Guest and crew alike pretended not to hear the sounds of crashing pots and pans in the galley after the Bossman's remark. While Wyatt basked in his one-upmanship, Yvette plotted a French revolution of her own. The guests were served sweet postprandial drinks, while Wyatt consumed a slightly more saline version of the same vintage. On the days Yvette had eaten fresh asparagus, Wyatt's drink was always darker and more aromatic. Rather than complain, Wyatt considered the signature drink an owner's perk.

"Bossman, you have a visitor," Captain Clark Guilford announced from the pilothouse.

"Who is it, Clark?"

"Your attorney, sir. Mr. Moole."

Why would Phillip Moole come to Chub uninvited? If it was business it could wait until Monday. The last thing Wyatt wanted to do was explain to Phillip Moole why he and Jasmine Dubois were spending the weekend on the boat together. The meeting would just have to be short. Besides it wouldn't be a meeting. Moole's trip was of the congratulatory nature as surely, he would be responding to the land deal's closure.

Wyatt filled his mouth with ice and bellowed his reply to Clark Guilford. "Tell him to come aboard!" He then whispered to Jim Williams, the second mate, "Come back here in ten minutes and tell me we're ready to shove off, got it?"

"Sure, Boss. Ten minutes. You want me to hide Ms. Dubois until he's gone?"

Wyatt Kincaid grinned at the young mate. No wonder he was going to medical school. The kid was bright. "Yeah, tell her what's going on, but don't bring her to the boat until he's gone."

Phillip Moole committed the cardinal sin of the sea: wearing black wingtips on board. Before Wyatt could chastise him, Phillip Moole opened a dialogue that would change the glamorous life of Wyatt Kincaid II forever.

"Wyatt, if you're waiting for Jasmine she won't be coming. I saw her in Nassau, and informed her that her weekend plans had changed. She's on a plane back to Wilmington."

"The hell they have, but your plans have changed. You're fired, Moole."

"I'm afraid you can't fire me, Wyatt. Not anymore."

"Hell if I can't! And I can also throw your ass off this boat."

Like a bouncer in a honky-tonk, Wyatt grabbed Phillip Moole by the collar and crotch.

"Wait a minute, Wyatt, before you do that you need to look at this." Moole reached into his jacket pocket and pulled out a document. "This is a directive from the Board of Directors of the Crown Kincaid Development Company which authorizes me to seize this boat. The boat will be taken back to Miami and put in possession of the rightful owner."

"What the hell are you talking about? I am the rightful owner!"

"No, Wyatt, The Crown owns this boat, or used to own this boat. It has been sold."

"They can't do that. Not without my permission, and that's something I haven't given."

"Wyatt, take your hands off me and I'll explain, step by step."

Wyatt looked down at the water beside the *Crown Jewel* then back at Phillip Moole. "Better step-by-step fast, Moole, the sharks are getting hungry."

Phillip Moole pulled his pants out of his crotch and flopped onto the aft deck divan. "Wyatt, you no longer have control of the company. The Directors now have controlling interest."

"Well, Moole, I guess the Harvard School of Law wasn't big on math, so let me help you out. I own forty percent, and the board, collectively, owns forty percent. A party that will remain unnamed owns the other twenty percent. That, my friend, makes you all wet." Wyatt said, grabbing the lawyer again and steering him to the rail.

"Yasnaya Polyana!"

These were the last words of Phillip Moole before he hit the deep waters of Chub Cay harbor. Surveying his handiwork, Wyatt leaned over the rail of the aft deck. "Who did you say?"

"Wyatt, you bastard!" Moole, never a strong swimmer, floundered in the water as he raised one arm and pointed toward the dock. "I was going to do this the easy way, but that's changed. Meet Mr. Jacobs. He's an inspector with the Bahamian Police Force." A tall black man on the dock looked up at Wyatt. "Mr. Kincaid, I need to see the paper work of the *Crown Jewel*. I think we have a problem."

"Well, come aboard, Mr. Jacobs. I can get this straightened out in a hurry. Clark, get the papers for the boat." Rene Jacobs removed his shoes and boarded the boat. Although a powerful man himself, Jacobs had no desire to tangle with the lumbering giant hulking over the aft rail of the boat. "Mr. Kincaid, I have a copy of a bill of sale for this vessel. The owners have asked that we take possession of the vessel until they arrive here tomorrow." Wyatt dumped the ice from his glass, filled it with Scotch, then took a long drink. "Well, looks like there has been a mistake, Jacobs. You see, I own this boat and if I had sold it, why don't I have a check?"

"I have a copy of the certified check if you would like to see it, Mr. Kincaid."

"I would. I'd like to see that."

Rene Jacobs opened the folder and produced the copy.

"Hell, this check is for only $5,000,000 dollars and this boat is worth at least $8,000,000. Ain't that right, Clark?"

"Closer to ten million, Bossman."

"See, I told you. But that don't matter, Jacobs, because I also own the company this check is made out to, the Crown Kincaid Development Company. You might have noticed--I'm Kincaid. I also own this slip where the boat is berthed. Now, what I suggest is that you fish that wet dog Moole out of the drink, and the both of you get the hell off my property."

Rene Jacobs looked the big man over. Typical rich American, too good to be bothered with small things like the laws or officials of small, insignificant countries like the Bahamas. The British could be forgiven for their colonial attitude but the Americans, who had been colonized themselves, could not.

"Mr. Kincaid, this bill of sale originated in Miami. And, sir, according to that city located in the USA, your country, this bill of sale is valid. Vacate the vessel, or I'll have you arrested." Having said that, Rene Jacobs waved his hand to the Bahamian police squad on shore. "I can also assure you, Mr. Kincaid, that if you lift a hand to me, you will spend a lot more time in the Bahamas than you planned."

Wyatt looked down on the dock at the drip-drying Phillip Moole. "Moole, get your ass up here and tell this man who owns the Crown…and take your damn shoes off!"

"Go to hell, Wyatt, I'm not telling him anything. I'm telling you to get off the boat. Now." Wyatt looked at the police squad's drawn weapons, then back at Jacobs. "I'll tell you what I'll do, Mr. Jacobs. I'll leave for now, but once we get this straightened out, I'll be back with the Prime Minister, and then you won't be staying in the Bahamas as long as *you* planned."

"You may do as you please, Mr. Kincaid, but you will not be doing it on this vessel. You have five minutes to leave."

Yvette, who had overheard the conversation, had already taken matters into her own hands, literally. The small suitcase of Wyatt's had not been unpacked, nor would it be. Finally freed of her bullish employer, Yvette performed what would be her last official duty aboard Wyatt's *Crown Jewel*.

"Yvette, where are you going with my suitcase?"

Without answering Yvette moved to the aft deck and tossed the suitcase overboard.

"Yvette, you're fired, damn it!"

"Monsieur, I quit."

"My damn passport is in that suitcase, Jacobs."

"That's too bad, Mr. Kincaid. I suggest you retrieve it. Without your passport you cannot leave this country. You now have four minutes. I advise you to hurry."

"I'll get it for you, Bossman," Clark Guilford said as he descended the stairs to the aft swim platform.

"Captain, the new owner has agreed to retain the crew, but if you get that suitcase you will be unemployed," Phillip Moole said as he moved over behind the armed Bahamian police squad on the dock.

"Three minutes, Mr. Kincaid, then I will have no choice but to arrest you."

"Jacobs, for crying out loud, at least let me get a gaff from the tender boat."

"You now have less than three minutes, Mr. Kincaid, and the order to vacate covers the dock."

"Sons of bitches." Wyatt concluded, then downed the remaining contents of the bottle of Scotch. "Let's see you confiscate that!"

Chapter 5

Tim Ridell waited until Yasnaya finished her sip of champagne before he asked his question. "I don't understand this game you're playing, but I would like to know more about my competitor. Are you going to oblige me?"

"I bought a piece of property, fair and square. How does that translate into a competitive game?"

"Fair and square?" Tim swirled the champagne in his glass and marveled at the honey colored liquid. "You know, just by the color of this wine you can tell its special, different, not an ordinary bottle of champagne. It sort of reminds me of this 'fair and square' land purchase of yours. Maybe if you had recorded the deed a year ago when you first purchased the property instead of waiting to the last minute so the purchase wouldn't show up on my title examination, it would have been a straightforward deal. But we both know you changed the rules at the last minute, and that's unsportsmanlike conduct, which makes this a game."

Tim Ridell watched Yasnaya spear a chestnut wrapped in bacon with her left hand and guide it to her mouth without changing hands. Europeans ate like that. In an attempt not to be identified as an "Ugly American" he, too, had eaten his meals like a southpaw while abroad.

"Well, am I right?"

"Why do men have to equate everything to sports?"

"I wasn't aware we did."

"Oh come on, Tim. *First base*: hand on her breast. *Hit the old home run*: made her see stars in the sack. Even the rating system you guys have for women is straight out of Olympic scoring for gymnastics. What was I by the way...7-8?" Yasnaya held her hand up. "Don't tell me, let--"

"Yasnaya, I concede your point. We do think in terms of sports, but only because it makes things clearer. In sports you win or lose, and on rare occasions play to a draw. It's a simple concept. I don't have a problem admitting defeat in a game you won't even acknowledge."

"How about this? For the sake of argument we call it a game and you a loser. Quite a gracious loser, by the way." Yasnaya toasted Tim with her glass of Cristal. "But a loser nonetheless."

"I appreciate your concession, but, since you put it that way, your admission rings a little hollow."

Yasnaya smiled as Tim Ridell corralled an angel on horseback with his left hand, then mimicked her eating style. American men, for the most part, had atrocious table manners. Although this man's attempt to emulate her savoir faire was awkward, she appreciated the effort.

"Just curious, Tim. Will Wyatt Kincaid lose as graciously as you?"

"Unfortunately for you, I'm the only one at the Crown who is well-versed in losing." Tim stared into Yasnaya's eyes. "Make no mistake, the Crown will fight back. Their first strike will be to color your title with a notice of pending legal action and then there's the little matter of fraud charges against Ganna Mae Ferguson. I suspect they will have the D.A. file those charges. Fraud is a felony, after all."

"The Crown won't file. Wyatt Kincaid will, but he won't have a leg to stand on."

"If you've based your strategy on that assumption, Miss Yasnaya Polyana, may I remind you Wyatt Kincaid *is* the Crown."

"Wyatt Kincaid made a tactical error. Are you aware he bought all of the properties for the project with his own monies, but titled them to the Crown?"

"Yeah, he does that all the time, then sells them back to the company for a nice little profit. He doesn't title the properties to himself so he can avoid the tax liabilities on the gain. The practice is questionable, but profitable."

"The practice is illegal, and this deal won't be profitable. The Crown won't be bailing him out this time," Yasnaya said.

"You sound so sure, but I'm telling you the company will do what Wyatt tells them to do. The board of directors is a rubber stamp. I've met them all, and not one of them has the nerve to cross Wyatt Kincaid."

"That was before the board gained controlling interest of the company. I think you will find things have changed quite a bit now."

"The board can't gain controlling interest. I helped draw up the stock purchase. It's a fifty-fifty split."

"Fifty-fifty or even split of available stock. It makes a difference you know."

"I was told by Mr. Kincaid it was fifty-fifty. Do you know something I don't?"

"Did you research your work? Have you ever gone though the company archives?"

"No."

"Maybe you should have. You might have saved your job. You might have even gotten Moole's job."

"Moole drew up the papers, and he did the research. I just verified his work to Mr. Kincaid."

"I guess you've never looked at the document. According to the recorded copy, you prepared the papers."

It wasn't a surprise that Moole would frame him with shoddy paperwork. Moole would do anything to get him out of the legal department that was no secret. Still, it bothered him that Yas thought him incompetent.

The server kept a respective distance then held the bottle of wine for Tim to view.

"Your wine, sir. May I?"

Tim Ridell swirled the half-filled glass of Oregon Pinot Noir and watched as the long legs formed on the side of his glass. Sally had taught him well. Only a connoisseur of fine wines could appreciate the implicit phenomenon of the long trails clinging to his glass. The wine was exquisite, long legs, a little light in body, yet complex and structured. A perfect choice for the hors d'oeuvres. The delicate body of the wine complemented the tannin of the chestnuts. Yes, indeed, a very fine wine.

"Good choice," Yasnaya said as she raised her glass in a toast.

Nice, the topic of the evening had changed and that suited Tim Ridell just fine. Maybe he wasn't the greatest legal mind of the century, but he did have other talents, which Yasnaya had noticed, and even complimented.

Apart from her lack of a Southern accent, something else was different about the woman across from him, very different...definitely not from these parts. But which parts was she from? So far she had used no colloquialisms that he could use to identify her origin. Though her mannerisms and dining habits suggested European, he was certain she was an American. Perhaps a Midwesterner. That would explain her lack of an accent, but where had she picked up her continental flair. "Chicago?"

"Excuse me?" Yasnaya asked.

"I'm sorry. I was thinking out loud. Are you from Chicago?"

"No, and please don't ask me my sign. I'll puke if you do."

"Any other question I shouldn't ask? I wouldn't want you up-chucking before we get to the entrée."

"Rather than go through the boring ritual of asking questions to find out about one another, let's try something different." Yasnaya's eyes sparkled. "You like games; let's play the powers of observation game, OK?"

"Never heard of it."

"I think it's self-explanatory."

"Maybe, but then you have this penchant for playing by a different set of rules." As soon as Tim spoke, he worried he had steered the conversation back to the unpleasant subject of the Crown. "OK, but you first."

"Just for the record, there are no rules. But are you sure you wouldn't like to toss a coin to see who goes first?"

"Naw, you probably have a two-headed coin."

Yasnaya rolled her eyes. "Very well, do you like Christmas?"

"Christmas?"

"Yes, how does Tim Ridell feel about Christmas?"

"Over-rated, at least now. I grew up and realized the holiday was based on a hoax, and it hasn't been the same since I was eight. "

"Your answer says a lot about you," Yasnaya said. "For one thing, you are either a slow learner or a hopeless romantic."

"Why do you say that?"

"Come on, Tim, eight? Most people figure it out long before then."

"Figure what out, Santa Claus?"

"Exactly."

"OK, I'm a slow learner, but you could have found that out without the Christmas question." Heck, just ask anyone in Legal at the Crown, Tim thought.

"That's true, but I couldn't have found out you were an only child."

"So how did you know that?"

"You were eight when the great hoax was exposed, which means you were the eldest or an only child. I went with 'only'. Why? Simple. Had you, had siblings, chances are you would have said '*we* grew up.' I played the odds."

"Lucky guess."

"Maybe, but how's this? You went to college locally...even law school. Here's a bonus...nothing to do with my earlier question, just my observation. You have a taste for the finer things in life, but not because you are used to them. Someone else introduced you to them. On the face of it you appear worldly, well-traveled, but you are not. You have been to Europe, but at an early age, and, forgive me, probably on a Euro Pass. Still think I'm lucky, Tim?"

A redness crept up Tim Ridell's neck and spread across his face, finally settling in full bloom atop both ears. "Heck no, not lucky. You've had me checked out."

"Checked out? Hardly. I do find you attractive and, to some degree, even interesting. But let's face it, Tim, you don't have the clout to justify an investigation."

Scaled, gutted and filleted by a woman, the gentlemanly thing to do was wait until the grease was hot enough to fry him. Not tonight, not ever again would that happen. Sally had reveled in, and been a master of the belittling game as well. And for all his hope, Yasnaya was nothing more than a blue-blooded debutante bitch, just like Sally. The only way to win this game was not to play.

"Waitress...oh, Miss."

"May I help you, sir?"

"Yes, you may. I need my check, please."

"Right away, sir. Is everything okay?"

"Everything is fine. I need to leave. I'm in a hurry."

Yasnaya spoke softly, "I didn't mean to hurt your feelings. I was simply trying to show you the power of observation."

"Powers duly noted. Thank you for the lesson."

"Come on, don't be so thin-skinned. I was just relaying what I see."

"Let's see, that would make me an unimportant lowlife imposter with a spent Euro Pass tucked away in a picture album as a memento," Tim said. "So why would you want to have dinner with such a person?"

"That's not what I said."

"Oh, sure. You were more eloquent but that's what you said, lady."

"Sir, excuse me, your check." Tim fumbled in his wallet, found the new credit card and put it in the folder and gave it to the waitress. "I'll be right back, sir."

Yasnaya sipped her wine and waited until he faced her. "You're behaving badly."

"I'm behaving badly? Lady, you were downright rude. I can't see where a little breach in manners should bother you."

"Tim, I was guessing. I didn't mean to offend you. Please--"

"I'm not offended. Is that what you thought? 'Cause if you did, your powers of observation have failed you. I'm pissed, Ms. Polyana." Instead of standing and waiting for the conversation to finish, the server blocked Tim from Yasnaya's view and whispered, "Sir, I'm sorry, but your card isn't valid."

"It has to be," Tim hissed. "It's new."

The waitress pointed to the date on the card. "I'm afraid it won't be valid until next month, look at the date." Tim pulled the other card from his wallet, same deal. Eight cards left...one of them had to have some credit left. Yeah, the American Express. "Here you go, try this one." Tim smiled a big smile in appreciation for the compassion displayed by the server. As she left with the card he remembered the memo on his desk: *Return call to American Express*. He hadn't.

"Tim, let's start over again. I'm sorry."

"Look, I just wanted a nice meal and a little company, but instead you decided to make me the meal. Thanks, but no thanks."

From the look on the face of the cashier, things weren't going well with the American Express card, either. Ignoring Yasnaya, Tim opened the bill section of his wallet, three twenties and four ones. The bottle of wine had cost way more than that.

"Sir, the card service asked us to keep your card." This time the waitress used no polite ploy to save the customer. This guy was a deadbeat. No sense trying to savage a tip from this peckerwood.

Tim looked at the waitress then back at Yasnaya. She had called it right; he was lowlife. Maybe the restaurant would take an IOU.? Probably not, and nobody in Wilmington was stupid enough to take a check from him. Like a dealer in Vegas, he ran his fingers over the remaining cards. Maybe the Visa...no, it was full. He had tried it at the self-serve pump.

Yasnaya excused herself and headed toward the ladies room, leaving Tim and the waitress alone. "I have to pick up another order, sir, and I really hope I don't have to bring my manager back...I'm not getting stuck for your tab."

Tim nodded and smiled at the waitress. Too late to use the old left-my-cash-in-my-other-wallet ploy. Maybe charm would work?

"And don't tell me you have cash in your car. You're not leaving until the bill is paid."

Nope, that wasn't going to fly either.

Being seated at the rear of the patio had felt good when they first arrived, but now the door and freedom were too far away. He'd never make it out before they caught him. The cashier gave him a look to let him know she was watching. Slowly he turned his eyes from the door and looked over the patio. Hop over the railing, hit the river, and swim like heck. His only out, but before he could make his move, the waitress was standing next to him.

"Everything has been taken care of. Have a good evening," the waitress beamed as she realized the large tip. "And I'm sorry I was rude to you."

There was a God. He smiled, and then it hit him. "Hey, where's my receipt?"

"Your friend has the customer copy."

Great! Now he was obligated to suffer more embarrassment. Before he could make a mad dash for the door, or dive in the river, Yasnaya was back at the table.

"It was just a misunderstanding, I'll pay you back."

Yasnaya batted her baby blues and smiled warmly enough to give scientists new concerns about the source global warming. "Oh, don't let that wounded-male pride get in your way. It's quite acceptable for women to pay."

"Well, we're a little behind the times down here, ma'am, I insist--"

"Tim, I made you angry. It's my way of apologizing, OK?"

"I wasn't angry."

"Oh, really?'

"I was pissed."

Yasnaya patted him on the head like she had done earlier when he was in his car.

"And how are we now?"

"Better, but how the heck did you guess all those things? You were right, by the way."

"Let's not go there again."

"Come on, I want to know how you did that."

"Tim, I don't want to hurt your feelings again."

"You won't, I promise."

"OK, I'll tell you, but first you have to tell me what you observed about me."

Yasnaya wasn't going to let the game end until it had been played out, and for good reason, her victory was assured. In his mind, Tim Ridell filled in the blanks about himself that Yasnaya did not know, and hopefully, never would know.

His mother was a bank teller and his father had been in charge of maintenance at a textile factory in Mount Olive. Not one ounce of Ridell blood was blue. The staple of their lineage was salt of the earth, common folks, decent. His parents had taught him manners and respect, and punishment for a breach of either was swift and severe. Sally had known his background, and had used it against him in their little battles of one-upmanship. Her first volley had been fired on their wedding day. The insult had been directed at his mother, or more accurately at the dress she had worn for the less than joyous occasion.

"Oh, your mother, poor dear. I suppose she didn't realize evening weddings are more formal. But then, I guess consignment dress shops don't give out much fashion advice, do they?"

In spite of Sally's observation, Kimpe Ridell was the prettiest woman at the wedding. Even in her simple A-line dress, Kimpe had outshined the designer-gowned opposition across the aisle of the church. Jim Boykin had rested his hand along his mother's waist, further emphasizing her shapely attributes as he introduced her to friend after friend. The attention her father diverted from Sally and directed to his mother had evoked Sally's comment about the dress. Exposing Sally's jealousy would have been rude, but not doing so had been a mistake, a mistake he still regretted.

"Tim...hello!"

"Sorry, I was thinking of something else."

"Something important?" Yasnaya asked.

"It was at the time. I guess it doesn't matter now." If he lived a thousand years, the pain of not standing up for his mother never would leave him. The memory ricocheted off his brain and buried itself deep in his heart.

"Want to talk about it?"

"No, it was nothing."

Yasnaya studied the man in front of her. Handsome, dark eyes, full head of hair, tall, outwardly sinewy, but fragile within. There was no need to guess about his deepest weakness. Tim Ridell wore his vulnerability like a runt kid never picked for a team. His job with the Crown was his last source of pride. Removing him from the Crown had proved no more difficult than simply being overlooked by the cool kids at school. But this runt had spoiled the game and quit before it had even started. Yasnaya Polyana did not understand quitters, but she wanted the quitter to understand her.

"Tim, I want you to tell me what you've observed about me."

"Why don't we talk about something else, I'm really not good at observations."

"But I want you to."

"Yasnaya, if I do that, you won't like what I have to say."

"Try me."

If you can't say something nice, don't say anything at all. Remembering his mother's favorite admonishment wasn't a problem, but discarding it was.

"Okay…but remember you asked for it. Blueblood Bitch, with a silver spoon shoved up your butt."

Yasnaya smiled, then laughed, hard, before she spoke. "Well, you were right."

"That you wouldn't like it?"

"No, the other part…that you're not good at observations."

"Come on, I'm on the money. You reek of privilege."

"You really think that?"

"No, Miss Yasnaya Polyana, I know that. You see, I've had the unpleasant honor of knowing someone who comes from a similar background."

Yasnaya looked around the room and spied the waitress, then motioned for her.

"Yes, ma'am, can I get you something?"

"Yes, you may. I'd like a beer, Budweiser, no glass."

"I'm sorry, ma'am, we don't have domestic beer."

"Okay, Corona, but lose the lime." Yasnaya glanced at Tim, then added to her order, "And some pretzels from the bar."

"We only have nuts. Macadamia?"

"That'll be fine."

Tim glanced at the half-full bottle of wine, then back at Yasnaya. "You don't like the wine?"

"Of course I do. It's a wonderful bottle of wine. I'm trying to improve your powers of observation, revealing me to you."

"I'm a slow learner, remember?"

"Come on, at least try."

Tim shook his head and pointed at his face. "Hey, Yasnaya, how 'bout we just mime this out or use hand signals, it'll go quicker, trust me."

"What does a woman drinking a beer symbolize to you?" Yasnaya asked. "Certainly not the privileged class, right?"

"Maybe, but if you really want to make that point with a beverage and nuts, let me suggest a package of Lance peanuts poured into a Pepsi."

"Come on. What was your first thought when I ordered the beer?"

"You won't like it."

"Try me."

"Rich,   beer   swilling,   never-done-an-honest-day's-work   in   your life...Blueblood."

"I'll give you some subtle hints--working class, as in works hard for her money."

"You want me to guess what your job is? OK, supermodel. There."

"Nope, guess again."

"Stockbroker?"

"God, you are terrible at observations."

"Well, give me another hint."

"Topless dancer in Myrtle Beach."

"No shit?"

Chapter 6

Seconds after the driver's door closed on the white limousine, the first complaint on the thirty-minute drive from Newark to Manhattan crackled over the car's intercom. "Dammit, driver, I specifically ordered two things; ice and Oban. I see neither."

Making excuses was not the Baltic way. In the old country one was expected to suffer the consequences. Under Soviet control, suffering had been a national pastime. Three years as a Siberian prison guard had prepared Boris Yantikov for harsh consequences, but in America there was no fear of reprisals. Americans were soft, easy to forgive, and gullible, especially the New Yorkers. For as much as they were maligned for being tough, they were not. After the planes hit the towers, New Yorkers had become like family to one another. The world had responded to the tragedy with prayers and aid and the tough city had responded to generosity with random acts of kindness.

Nothing outwardly suggested this passenger would be any different from other New Yorkers. But the edge in her voice and a slight accent hinted that his passenger might not be one of *the family*. Boris glanced at his trip log and noted the Upper East Side destination, Fifth Avenue. Good, she was a native, which meant she would be soft and understanding of the deceit he was about to employ. Yes, she would hear his sad story and reward his lies with a big tip.

Before responding to the complaint, Boris mouthed his reply carefully, shaping each word and listening in his mind's ear, until his Slavic accent was barely noticeable. "A thousand pardons, mother, but my little girl is sick. It was necessary for me to get her medicine."

Ganna Mae lowered the privacy glass that most New Yorkers would have used as a shield to hide behind while they berated an oaf like Boris. In spite of her intense hatred of her redneck roots, two traits had remained; an affinity for iced drinks and direct confrontation. Denied one remnant of her past, Ganna Mae was now free to expose the remaining bonds to her heritage. "Driver."

Boris eyed the rearview mirror and acknowledged his passenger with a nod.

"Yes, mother."

"First, driver, I'm not your mother, and second I didn't just fall off a turnip truck. I want Scotch and ice, and I want it now...and just so we understand one another--if you try to sell me the Brooklyn Bridge I'll kick your balls up into your throat."

Turnip truck? Boris rolled the unfamiliar phrase over in his mind and came to the realization that this woman wasn't a native. Nor was she about to be part and parcel to his attempted petty larceny. German, or perhaps French, but one thing he knew--she wasn't an American--too aloof. This foreigner would challenge the $100 charge for the Oban on her credit card, no doubt about that. Even if the charge had been to help the daughter he didn't have, the charge would be contested. Nothing to do now but try to salvage his tip. Horns blared as the limo crossed three lanes of traffic to make the last Newark exit, and within five minutes Ganna Mae was sipping Oban and crunching ice.

While Boris entertained himself with thoughts of tossing this alien from the bridge she never would buy, Ganna Mae remembered the first time her affinity for iced beverages had embarrassed her. The fiasco had occurred at the Hotel Principe di Savoia in Milan. When asked how she preferred her tea, Ganna Mae had not understood the offerings of cream and sugar placed before her. Instead she had asked, in her thick Carolina accent, for ice. The charming laughter of her suave Italian lover, Adolfo, had done little to hide the gaffe of a bona fide Redneck woman.

Fifty-five years, and nearly as many lovers, had passed since that night in Milan. Anorexic, heroin-chic, hollow-eyed waifs did not dominate modeling in those days. Women were curvaceous, full-figured, even plump by today's standards, but those were different times. Men dressed in tuxedos and women wore gowns to dinner, even for cocktails, and no woman filled the clothes better than Ganna Mae Ferguson.

Sewing had been the one skill she'd learned on the farm, a skill she would turn out not to need to conquer the garment district of New York. Adolfo Barozini was forty-five years old, thirty years her senior, when he spied the magnificent redhead on 34th Street. Males and females alike, turned to look at the striking young woman as she passed by them in her homemade dress. Oblivious to the stares and salacious remarks, Ganna Mae was captivated by the brick and mortar buildings scraping against the blue sky. Wilmington's buildings were dwarfed by the freighters and tramp steamers that stopped in the sleepy port town to offload goods and the occasional seafaring visitor. Even two ships, stacked lengthwise, could not reach the heights of the sweat factories in the garment district, much less compete with the two colossal Midtown edifices, the Chrysler and Empire State Buildings.

"You must wear this. I made it for you." Before Ganna Mae could move away, Adolfo Barozini had pasted a low-cut beaded tulle dress and matching heels to her body. "Ah, and the color! Just as your eyes--perfect."

No doubt the ensemble was perfect, but the man holding it had interested her much more. Nothing about the man standing in front of her resembled the men from back home. Adolfo was tall and blessed with a complexion that bordered on angelic, rather than the leathery, sun-browned skin furrowed with fine lines that came from men squinting at fields all day

Ganna Mae was used to. This man's olive tones ran deep, and, she suspected, all-over. His white linen suit striped with powder blue lines and matching blue shirt set him even further apart from any man she had ever known.

"Ah can't wear 'at." In 1940's Wilmington her response would have sounded normal, but in New York, to a man whose lineage included Italian aristocrats, the words sounded nothing like the English he had learned at Eton.

"I beg your pardon?"

"It's purdy and all, but I'd be showing my backside to all these folks." Ganna Mae gestured at the crowd milling along 34th Street.

"But, Madame, such a lovely backside should reside only in a dress like this. Please, you may change in my fitting room." And thus began the education and refinement of the rough-as-a-cob Ganna Mae Ferguson.

"Damn, driver, can't you see the curb? I've spilled Scotch all over my outfit. It's ruined, you idiot!"

"Sorry, it was a tight turn, moth...ma'am."

"Tight, my ass. A real driver could have made that turn on a truck. Who's going to pay for this dress?"

Tight my ass. Ah ha! "Canadian," Boris muttered to himself, then fell silent and stared at the Hudson River that ran parallel to the West Side Highway. The Hudson, and to a greater extent, the East River were dumping grounds for the bodies generated by gangland killings. Surely, no one would notice one more.

"What is that god-awful smell in here? Smells like Pine Sol"

"It's pine tree." Boris looked at the fir shaped cardboard air freshener dangling from his rear view mirror, then back at the river; yes, one more body, no one would notice.

"I've smelled all the damn pine trees I can stand. Throw it out!"

Fifth Avenue was crowded and the residents of the townhouses that lined the street across from Central Park had filled the available parking spaces. Double parking only added to the congestion, not a concern for a limo driver cursed with the fare from hell. Boris opened the door for his passenger and exposed an open palm for his tip, a wasted effort.

"Up yours! Get my bags."

"But, mother...."

"You heard me, shyster...my bags."

With one hand Boris grabbed the large garment bag; with the other he opened the valise and spied a zippered leather notebook. Even on a quiet night the light thud of the book hitting the back of the carpeted trunk would have been hard to detect. On the busy Manhattan street the theft went completely unnoticed.

"Take them to the stoop, driver."

Boris smiled and nodded but did not reach for the bags. Instead he stretched his towering frame over his former fare and responded in his best New York accent. "Screw you, Canuck!"

Without responding to Boris, Ganna Mae turned toward the alcove in front of the brownstone. On warm nights, security guard John Mallory sometimes used the area to sneak a smoke, and no doubt a drink...he was Irish, after all. Ganna Mae thought for a moment. The alcove was empty, and she was alone with an obstinate Bolshevik. Emboldened by the busy street, she flipped the ogre off, and then lugged her bags toward the double flight of steps.

"Get me my Scotch...I paid for it."

Boris opened the back Limo door and grabbed her bottle, then took a long smooth drink. "Wasted money, old woman...you should have gotten vodka."

"Piss off, Commie."

Tires of the limo squealed as Boris sped off into the night. Alerted by the noise, John Mallory rushed from the nook below the steps and headed for Ganna Mae. "Top of the evening, Miss Ferguson...would you be needing some help with those bags?"

"No, I figured I'd wait until they grew legs, and God knows I've waited here long enough for that to happen. That man could have attacked me for all the good you are--security guard--my ass!"

"I'll get the bags, ma'am. Sorry you had to wait."

Relaxed by the Scotch, and ready for a bath, Ganna Mae opened the valise for her favorite reading material. A leisurely search though the bag turned into a frantic hunt. She dumped the contents of the valise onto the floor and scattered the pile of clothes across the apartment. Dressed only in a robe, Ganna Mae traced her steps from her door to the street, and back again. With each step the realization of her loss sank in further; her planner was missing. Worse than that, a blueprint of the perfect crime may now be in the public domain. "The scene." Ganna Mae moaned at the thought of returning to the pine forest she hated. The book had to be there. It was the only place it could be if it wasn't in the luggage.

The phone ringing interrupted her thoughts. *The Commie.* Maybe he had found the planner? Fat chance he would return it, even if he had...maybe. "Yes..." Remembering the scene with the driver Ganna Mae softened her greeting. "Good evening."

"Just wanted to let you know, we have the boat."

"Moole?"

"Yes, we have the boat."

"Good. Has he made contact with the other party?"

"Not yet. He's still in the harbor trying to fish out his suitcase."

Ganna Mae smiled at the thought of Wyatt Kincaid floundering in the water. "I wish I could see him. Maybe he'll get a cramp and drown."

Phillip Moole also savored the thought, "Wouldn't that be wonderful?"

"Well, I must admit, Phillip, I didn't think you had the nerve. Congratulations. Was he much trouble?"

"He gave me a little lip, but once he saw I meant business, he gave up."

"How did his suitcase get into the water?"

"I tossed it overboard."

Phillip Moole had not spent enough time on boats to know that privacy on a yacht came at the discretion of the crew. Clark Guilford shook his head at the lies he had just heard, but Moole was in charge of the boat, now. That entitled him to tell his lies as he saw fit. Still, not to give credit to Yvette and the Bahamian police squad for removing the Bossman seemed mutinous.

Liquor laws in New Jersey prohibited the exchange of retail for wholesale bottles. But Michael Fitzpatrick, brother-in-law of Boris Yantikov, was no fool. A nearly full bottle of Oban for a half-empty bottle of Popov was a deal too good to pass up. He did forego the offer of the gold-embossed leather planner for $100.00. Not that the price was too steep, the case was worth at least ten times that much, but becoming involved in one of Boris's robberies made the deal cost-prohibitive.

"Hand-tooled by Bulgari. Buy something nice for my sister--cheapskate!"

"Come on, Boris. It's a knockoff. You can buy them in the city all day long for half that. Besides, your mother's birthday is coming up, why don't you give it to her?"

"No knockoff. Look, real gold." Boris pointed at the gold lock midway down the cover. "I find it on Fifth Avenue."

"Yeah, well, if it's real maybe you should check the papers. I'm sure there will be a reward for it." Michael Fitzpatrick's eyes darted from the expensive planner to his brother-in-law. "Hell, Boris, they may even have a reward for the petty thief who stole it."

"Ah...cheapskate."

Boris grabbed the book and headed for a table in the back of the bar to examine his booty. Marked by a silk swatch of cloth were pages titled *The Last Kincaid*. Boris Yantikov read the entire volume of Ganna Mae's vendetta against the Crown and Wyatt Kincaid. Little of the old woman's plan interested him until he read a familiar name from his Siberian past, a name and a secret that would give him access to billions.

Chapter 7

Phillip Moole watched as Wyatt Kincaid struggled with his water-logged leather bag. Faced with drowning or saving possessions no longer worth having, Wyatt seemed to be making the wise choice and swam for shore.

"Well, so much for your cramp wishes. He made it out. I'll call you when we get back to Miami, Ms. Ferguson."

Ganna Mae's hopes for Wyatt's demise were too civilized for Phillip, who had envisioned a more violent end for his former boss. As Wyatt treaded water, Phillip had scanned the harbor for fins, or least one huge fin.... No such luck. Only in Hollywood would a monster shark show up on cue. *Chum*? Surely there was something on board to attract predators, but asking for it would have made him an accessory, and the Harvard-educated Moole was too clever for that.

Standing in a puddle of water left from his unplanned dip, Phillip leaned over the rail of the *Crown Jewel* and spied the Bahamian guards surrounding the boat. Good. Rene Jacobs was a man of his word. Wyatt wouldn't attempt to board the boat with the guards in place. "I need a towel. Get me one, Captain."

Clark Guilford had captained many boats and Phillip Moole had been his first encounter with a breach of protocol. Mates and stewards saw to the needs of passengers, chefs provided meals, and captains made sure those duties were performed without a hitch. "I'll get that taken care of for you, sir." This jerk needs to know that, Clark thought as he headed for the crew quarters to find the second mate.

Jim Williams handed Moole the towel and waited for his next request from the guest, as there certainly would be a next request. Months as a second mate aboard the *Crown Jewel* had given Jim a new respect for the ultra-rich. The truly wealthy knew the difference between manners and protocol, and the ten-cent millionaire guests Wyatt brought to the boat almost weekly, would never belong to that class.

"Young man, I'll need some clothes. I wish to visit with Mr. Denton next door. Is anyone on board close to my size?"

"In ego or stature, little man?" Jim mouthed, in a barely audible whisper.

"What was that?"

"Just the Bossman, sir--"

"That name is not to be mentioned on this boat from now on, is that understood, young man?" Bossman...sounded more like a name for a plantation owner than that of a businessman--ridiculous.

"Yes, sir. The gentlemen who left earlier might have something you could wear."

Moole thought of the size difference between himself and Wyatt. "There's no way I could wear his pants. They would be much too long."

"His uniform is shorts, sir. I don't think the length would matter that much."

"Wyatt wore a uniform? I don't recall that from my last visit."

"Oh yes sir. That gentleman took great pride in setting an example for the crew. Shall I get one for you?"

Phillip Moole looked at the hideous attire worn by the crew. Only Wyatt could have come up with such vulgar dress. "The shirt? It's different from yours. Don't you have one without the writing, or something with a collar?"

"No sir."

Moole read the bons mots across the shirt. **To hell with a Slice, I got the whole pie**. Then asked the obvious, "What's the meaning of this?"

"The meaning of what, sir?"

"The phrase on the shirt. Are you dense?"

"I have no idea, sir. It seemed to please the Boss--er--the other *gentleman.*"

Wyatt Kincaid had been unable to secure Jarek Denton's business, but that didn't surprise Phillip Moole. Wyatt was crass and uneducated. The man hadn't even finished college, much less attained a professional degree. No wonder Denton had refused to do business with the Crown. Once Denton discovered the company was being run by a Harvard man, that would change.

"Captain?"

Clark Guilford bit his lip so as not to laugh at the out of shape man dressed in the wife-beater shirt and frayed jean shorts. "Yes sir, Mr. Moole."

"I intend to visit Mr. Denton next door. Must I ask permission to come aboard? Wouldn't want him to think I didn't know my way around the yachting world.... Oh, and by the way I think you should have a talk with the cabin boy. He's a bit snippy."

"Jim is a mate, sir, not a cabin boy...and I'll have a talk with him." *You arrogant, prick.* "As for permission to come aboard.... Well, we're pretty informal down here. But asking would be proper etiquette."

"Very good. Once I meet with Mr. Denton I plan to ask him to join us for dinner. Have the chef set another place."

The joke had gone far enough. Regardless of his feeling for the man, Clark Guilford had a duty to protect Phillip Moole. "Sir, that might not be a good idea. Mr. Den--"

"I didn't ask for your opinion, Captain. I gave you an order. Please see that it's carried out." Rebellion and insolence. Two problems he would have to overcome when he took over at the Crown. No problem, Phillip thought. He would handle employees the same way he was handling the crew of the *Crown Jewel*, without mercy. Sure, there would be resentment to start with, but soon everyone would fall in line and learn to appreciate his iron hand…. Maybe they'd even give him a nickname: *Iron Hand Moole*, a damn good name.

"Iron Hand." Moole mused aloud.

"I'm sorry, sir?"

"Oh, I was just thinking of my old college nickname, 'Iron Hand Moole,' they called me. I was quite fond of it." Moole glanced hopefully at Clark Guilford.

"Another setting for dinner. Anything else, *Mr. Moole?*" Guilford was having none of it.

"Ahoy!" The greeting sounded foolish, but was perfectly acceptable in nautical circles, Phillip Moole surmised. Cramer Joseph, second mate on the *Slice of Life* poked his head from the pilothouse. "Can I help you?"

"Yes, I'm Phillip Moole from next door." Next door? Perhaps he should have said adjoining berth? No, the captain had said they were informal down here. "Your neighbor." *Neighbor.* Yes, much better-friendlier. "Please, inform Mr. Denton that Phillip Moole, the new CEO of the Crown Kincaid Development Company, wishes to come aboard."

Cramer Joseph looked at the shirt Phillip Moole was wearing. Life on Chub Cay was slow, laid back, but this little man was about to change that. "Yes sir, I'll get Mr. Denton for you."

"What time can we expect your guest, Mr. Moole?" Clark Guilford asked with a straight face.

"Mr. Denton won't be joining us. Er--is he on medication?"

"I'm sorry, sir. I don't understand?"

"He threatened to shoot me if I didn't vacate his dock. Surely he can't be all there."

"I wouldn't know, sir. Would you like me to ask the chef to stand down on your last directive?"

Wyatt Kincaid sat in the darkened gazebo at the entrance to Chub Cay harbor, staring at the well-lit yachts. The confrontation between Moole and Denton had played out less than one hundred yards from his airy refuge. Parts of the conversation had been muted by the distance, but there had been no mistaking Phillip Moole's crew attire, nor Jarek Denton's threat to shoot the slovenly mutineer. For a few minutes, Wyatt had forgotten his situation, even pulled for Jarek Denton to follow up on his threat. Now his damp clothes and swarms of hungry mosquitoes reminded him of the plan he was yet to formulate.

How to get back aboard? His first option was crushed as soon as he realized the Bahamian guards had set up a perimeter around the *Crown Jewel*. The two small splashes after his suitcase had entered the water were, no doubt, his phone and wallet. Left with no clothes, money, or communications, his options were definitely limited. Staring at two empty berths on either side of the *Crown Jewel* and *Slice of Life* deepened his dilemma. Both the *Inhognito* and *Bacon in the Sun* were owned by a couple of North Carolina pork barons. Either owner would be glad to take him aboard. But, like many boats based in Chub, the two yachts had headed north to enjoy the moderate autumn temperatures of the New England Coast.

Late summer and early fall were slow times for the Bahamas because warmth could be found in abundance across much of the Northern Hemisphere. People of means weren't interested in plentitude. One of the perks of wealth was being able to relocate to more suitable weather. Which meant most of the part-time residents of Chub Cay were in the cooler climates far from the heat of the equatorial latitudes. During the height of the season, the eclectic Barry Island Club ran a shuttle from the harbor to its site tucked away on a point south of the airport. As business fell off, so did the frequency of the shuttle runs. A quick look at the luminous dial of his Roger Dubuis Sympathie watch showed the hour to be 8:15 p.m. and reminded him of the story behind the timepiece.

"Only twenty-eight of these were made. You have no idea how long I had to shop to find one, and all you can say is 'It's nice.' I swear, Wyatt, I should have just purchased a Timex. You wouldn't have known the difference."

Setai Gramerci, his most recent ex-wife, had been right about that. Time was time. Why pay thousands for it when hundreds would do the job? What had Setai really paid for the watch? Nothing. The bill had come in on the American Express Platinum Card--his card. Why hadn't she bought a Timex? That one was easy; Setai wouldn't dare be seen in a store that sold Timex watches. Besides, according to the credit card bill, she had found plenty of expensive distractions to provide relief from the drudgery of shopping for his birthday present.

Another of her distractions, Thomas Beauchamp, had provided her with a new lifestyle in her native Provence. The divorce had been nasty, but quick. Thomas Beauchamp was undoubtedly happy with his latest prize, for now. One day Beauchamp, like Wyatt, would add up the expenses and realize his *Petit Bijou*, Little Jewel, was way overpriced.

Thinking about the past wasn't getting him any closer to more suitable quarters. No need putting it off any longer. If he was going to make it to the Barry Island Club, he would have to walk. The distance was less than two miles, but the coral-crusted path against his bare feet would make it seem like ten.

A beam from a scooter headlight sliced across the runway and headed straight for Wyatt. Desperate to avoid the remainder of the trip on foot, Wyatt flagged the scooter down. "Whoa, partner."

"Can I help you?"

"I need a lift to the club."

"Sorry, mate. I'm late to meet a friend."

"I'll pay you," Wyatt said.

"So sorry, but--"

"Look here, I'm Wyatt Kincaid from the *Crown Jewel*, I'll--"

"I beg your pardon. Who did you say?"

"Kincaid. Wyatt Kincaid."

"I wish I could help you, Mr. Kincaid, but I must get to Miami tonight."

Miami? To hell with the Barry Island Club, Wyatt thought. "You're going to Miami, tonight?"

"Yes. Do you need a ride, Mr. Kincaid?"

"You're damn right I do. You flying?"

"No, I afraid I'm not much of a flyer. I'm a boater."

Boat? No passport. Might be able to duck customs, an option not available on a plane. Good. "When'd you say you were leaving?"

The power plants on the 42' Fountain Lighting would have been an aphrodisiac for a boating enthusiast, but Wyatt cared nothing about the two 800hp supercharged MerCruisers hanging off the stern of the boat. Go Fasts, as the boats were known to the Coast Guard, were common in the Bahamas. Daytrippers from Miami and Fort Lauderdale used them to make the hour long run to Bimini, but the boats were less common in the waters of the outer islands. A trip to Miami on the *Crown Jewel* would take hours, but the sleek silhouette of this boat suggested a quicker ride. "How fast does this thing go?" Wyatt asked.

"Oh, about 170."

"Hell, I thought you said you were afraid of flying?"

"Funny. That was a good one, old chap."

"170...some of those little puddle hoppers don't fly that fast, do they?"

"I was speaking of kilometers."

"Oh yeah, kilometers." Wyatt scratched his head. Speed limit signs in Europe had always confused him; big numbers...slow speeds. "How fast is that in American?"

"In miles per hour? Oh, just a tad over 100."

Wyatt tried to remember the miles to the mainland from Chub; 150, maybe a little more. Less than two hours. Good. "Hell, yeah."

Wyatt's last comment was lost in the deep rumble of the engines. Rather than repeat it, he searched the harbor for the *Crown Jewel*, and spotted her. Moole was on the aft deck and Wyatt yelled his threat as they passed. "Don't move that boat Moole. I'll be back with the police...and your ass is fired!"

Busy below deck, searching for new clothes for Moole, second mate Jim Williams could not hear Wyatt's remarks, but the unmistakable sound of the throaty MerCruisers caught his attention. Jim glanced at his watch, then quickly jotted down the exact time in the log over his bunk.

The seas were light and the boat planed out, quickly reaching top speed. Lights from the Chub Cay harbor faded as the Fountain raced for the open sea. "There is something I should tell you. I'm sorry, I didn't catch your name, friend."

"I am John Smith, Mr. Kincaid."

"Well, John Smith, I'm pleased to meet you, and I appreciate the ride. But there's something I need to tell you." Wyatt waited for a question-- none came. "Anyway, as I was saying, you need to know I don't have a passport, or wallet for that matter."

"Um, you did mention something about paying me?"

"I will, but I just can't pay you tonight... Well, I can pay you if you leave me your address--"

"Then there is the little matter of Customs. I'm sorry, old chap." John made a wide sweeping arc with the boat.

"Hold on...where are you going?"

"Back to Chub, I'm afraid I can't risk running into Customs without compensation....unless you." John Smith stared at Wyatt's watch.

"Unless what?"

"I couldn't help but admire your watch."

Wyatt looked at his expensive watch. Sure, all the watch did was tell time like any watch, but it cost a helluva lot more. "Well, you see, my daddy gave me this watch. I'm afraid I couldn't bear to part with it. Sentimental value, you know?"

"Too bad."

"Hold on a minute. You get me to Miami and I'll call my pilot. He can bring cash--$5000"

"You have a plane?"

"Yeah, a jet. He can be in Miami in an hour and a half."

"Well, in that case." John Smith steered the boat back on course and powered the big Fountain back to full speed.

Lights from the *Baltic Queen* were barely visible on the horizon. She was making 22 knots, a respectable speed for a rusting, old freighter, but no match for the Go Fast Fountain. Within thirty minutes the men on her deck were visible. Heartened by the sight of the mothership, Smith leaned hard on the throttles and raced toward his destination.

John Smith picked up the ship-to-shore radio microphone and spoke to the *Baltic Queen* in perfect Russian. Three packages wrapped in yellow polyurethane were tossed from her deck. "Mr. Kincaid, get the gaff." Wyatt did as instructed and gave the handled-hook to John Smith. "Help me get them onboard, Comrade."

Comrade...what the hell happened to *"old chap?"* Wyatt wondered as he grabbed a package.

After the last package was aboard, John Smith radioed the *Baltic Queen*, and again conversed in the foreign language that was beginning to put Wyatt Kincaid on edge. Two minutes later a life raft with a line attached sailed from the deck of the freighter.

"Your watch, Comrade."

"Say what?"

"Your watch. I will have it," John Smith said as he shoved a Soviet-made Tokarev pistol into Wyatt's ribcage. "The watch, now!"

"I thought we agreed on cash?" Wyatt released the catch on the band and let the watch fall into his palm. "What are you, a damn pirate?"

"Quite right, old boy.... Now, into the raft, Mr. Kincaid."

"The hell I will. I just paid for a trip to Miami!"

John Smith moved the Tokarev to Wyatt's forehead. "You will get in the raft, or you will die, Comrade."

"Let me ask you a question, Comrade. You planned this, didn't you?"

"No, Mr. Wyatt Kincaid, owner of the Crown Development Company. That honor belongs to someone else. I'm simply following orders."

"Look, whatever Phillip Moole is paying you I can pay--"

"Phillip who?"

"That boat-stealing son of a bitch, Moole, the one you work for, that's who. I'll pay you double--"

"Moole, Phillip Moole." John Smith rolled the unfamiliar name around on his tongue then pointed the pistol back at Wyatt. "An interesting proposition for a man who doesn't have a wallet, Mr. Kincaid. In the raft."

Chapter 8

Traffic on Hwy 74 West was light. Blue-collar commuters, most bound for the lower rents and cheaper homes in Columbus County, had long since made their rush hour exodus from Wilmington. Lights from the fringe developments of starter homes and double-wide land home packages, tagged with littoral monikers like Gull Way and Atlantic Cove, shone dimly against the bright backdrop of Greater Wilmington. In spite of the less-than-prestigious reputation of inland Columbus County, Tim Ridell welcomed the darkness and anonymity.

His life with Sally had been lived under the glaring light and myopic scrutiny of Wilmington's new elites. Land Fall, Figure Eight Island, and dozens of other new gated developments clamoring to become the latest "best place to live" were familiar haunts during his three years with Sally.

In coastal cities, east or west, the distance of anything to the ocean determines pecking order. West Coast cities like Los Angeles define the zenith of upper crust with expensive cars. Unlike Los Angeles, cars were not status symbols in Wilmington, but the RESIDENT stickers affixed to windshields were. Treadwell's Mobile Home Park, Tim Ridell's domicile, had no manned gatehouse or windshield sticker with which to brand its owners and renters. Wilmington was different. Even in the few mobile home parks that remained, stickers, usually in the shape of a shield with an oversized MHP in the center of the logo, perpetuated the lunacy of the New Hanover County caste system.

Still skeptical of Yasnaya's claim to be a commoner, Tim scanned the windshield of her pickup for a telltale symbol that would disprove her story. Other than her South Carolina inspection sticker, the glass was clean. Maybe she had been honest. If that was the case, then he had to take her entire tale at face value. Phillip Moole had prepared documents and credited him as the Attorney of Record. Moole's act could have been a mistake or an oversight, but Phillip Moole was not renowned for making either. "Yas, I've been thinking--"

"I thought I smelled smoke."

"Funny. I guess when you're not dancing you headline at the Comedy Shop?"

"You didn't hear? Comedy is passé...magic, that's the new in thing. You should give it a try; I understand lawyers are really adept at smoke and mirrors."

"Why do you hate lawyers?"

Yasnaya took a quick look in the rearview mirror, then shot Tim a glance. "What on earth gave you that idea?"

"I think 'Scum of the earth' was my first clue." Tim shrugged his shoulders, "Maybe I just have thin skin?"

"Thin skin…that's not so bad. You should try being a *'beer-swilling, never-done-a-day's-work-in-your-life, blue blood'*. Now there's a condition your average dermatologist wouldn't touch with a ten-foot pole."

"I knew it! You women kill me. First you want honesty…then, bam!"

Yasnaya looked at Tim. No need to let him score points. He was right, but why concede. "You were thinking?"

"Oh, no you don't. That was earlier. Now I'm making a point."

"Ok, but first things first. I believe you asked why I hate lawyers?"

"Let's skip that and get back to my point."

"Nope, I demand the opportunity to respond to your question. The answer is they're condescending…and arrogant." Unlike the battle royals he and Sally had waged over most of the town that was becoming a small dot in the rearview mirror, this jousting was actually engaging and almost enjoyable…almost.

"Yas, how can you say that? I'm not condescending or arrogant…far--"

"Don't give me that. Ever since I told you I was a topless dancer, you've been looking down your nose at me. You should have seen that holier-than-thou look!"

"I'm a Baptist, for Christ's sake--and it wasn't a holier-than-thou look--it was shock."

"Shock? Is what I do for a living so horrible that it shocks you? Well, excuse me for dirtying your pristine world, Mr. Ridell. "

"Yas…I'm sorry." Tim Ridell did not savor constant foot-in-mouth moments. "I didn't mean it like it sounded. It's just that you look like an angel. Not that you aren't…I mean…what I'm trying to say is, you're the most beautiful woman I've ever seen." Tim Ridell thought about Rosalyn, his Santee-Cooper girl, and her tenure in the world's oldest profession. In spite of her prostitute status, Rosalyn was the best friend he had in his "pristine" world. "My best friend is a prostitute. That's worse than a topless dancer," Tim blurted out.

"Well thank God for prostitutes and lawyers--"

"I didn't mean worse—I meant—nothing. Can you just drop me off at my office?"

Good, he was on the defensive. No points, Yasnaya thought. "Why didn't you think of that before we left Wilmington?"

"What you said about the paperwork, and Moole, it got me to thinking. I'm quitting the Crown…who the heck am I kidding? They are going to fire me, but just the same maybe I should do a little checking before I leave. And…I'm sorry."

"Did you mean it?"

"Sorry? Heck yeah."

"Not that. When you said I was the most beautiful woman, did you mean it?"
Suddenly Yasnaya didn't seem so brash and confident. Even a person this beautiful needed validation. Human, she was human just like he was.
"Yes, and I know an honest answer will come back to bite me, but I meant it. You are beautiful, and you hear it all the time."
Yasnaya bowed her arms against the steering wheel, "You're right, I do hear it a lot, but never when I have my clothes on. Thank you, and I mean it."
Tim smiled as Yasnaya turned off the exit and headed back toward town. At least now he wouldn't have to lug his personal belongings across the parking lot under the stares of all the Crown Loyalists.
"You could have just put me out."
"Thought about it." Yasnaya furrowed her brow. "Guess I'm a sucker for a compliment."
"You're a lot of things lady, but sucker is not one of them."
The hum of the truck tires settled into a rhythm with the imperfections of the heavily-traveled beach route. For the moment the problems of two strangers faded behind the soft jazz floating from the dash speakers. Miles passed before Yas finally broke the silence. "Men are different in public. There they find me intimidating. At the club it's almost as if they have purchased the right to boldness. It's a place where they feel entitled to grab, poke, and probe me like I'm livestock, not a person."
"I know you will take this the wrong way...and it has nothing to do with your job or mine, but for the last few miles the music, the effect of the wine, the realization that a stranger is being nicer to me than my wife ever was--"
"Whoa, that's kind of heavy.'
"I didn't mean for it to be. It's just that I don't want to know everything about your past...not that there's anything wrong with it." Tim pressed upward on the pressure points above the bridge of his nose, an acupressure method for relieving stress. "I don't want to think about the past...at least until we get to the Crown...can we be the only two people on earth—no baggage, no history?"
Yasnaya nodded, "I'd like that.'

The tinted glass and brick edifice known as the Crown's Head reminded Tim of Yasnaya's earlier description of the legal profession, smoke and mirrors. The dual beams from the pickup's headlamps reflected off the hundreds of glass panes and gave the illusion of an invading army descending upon Wyatt Kincaid's corporate fortress. Security at the ultra-modern building was provided by a high-tech monitoring system, and though the late night visit was no doubt being recorded, Tim wanted to tone down the spectacle. "Kill the lights."

"Why? There are cameras all over the place."

"I know...I know, but--" Tim eyed the surplus of motion-sensitive Cyclops resting on gleaming aluminum poles, then thought of the infra-red images beamed to the entrance security desk. "You're right. Leave them on."

"What are you worried about? You still work here, right?" Yasnaya, usually cool under fire, was shaken by Tim's nervousness. "I mean, they won't arrest us, will they?"

"No, but someone's bound to ask why I was here."

Yasnaya glimpsed the dark outline of the chiffonier. "Why don't we leave the furniture here? You were supposed to pick it up, right?"

Surprised by the suggestion, Tim shot Yasnaya an inquisitive look. "You won. Why would you want to leave the spoils of war at the enemy's encampment?"

"Trojan Horse."

"Trojan Horse? What the heck are you talking about?"

"Look, Tim. Picking up the furniture was only part of my task...getting it to Wyatt Kincaid was the big problem." Yasnaya squirmed in her seat. "Don't you see this is perfect...you know, killing two birds with one stone?"

Tim flipped the cargo bed light on for a better look at the furniture. "Have you ever been inside this building?"

"No, but--"

"Yas, nothing in this building matches this." Tim thought of the art-deco furnishings inside the swanky digs of the Crown's headquarters. "This abomination will stand out like a g-string at a convent--I mean--"

"There you go again."

"Like a sore thumb. I swear, I meant like a sore thumb."

"Oh, hell! You did not! You wanted to remind me of my social standing. Well, Mr. High-and-Mighty Lawyer, I made 300 grand last year...how'd you do?"

Tim Ridell rolled the number around in his mind, then thought of the twenty-five-dollar bonus check. "Yas, I--"

"Well, how much did you make, Snob?"

Snob? Go ahead, Ridell, let her have it with both barrels. Don't hold back. "How much money did I make? Glad you asked...not even enough to cover my bills. Not even enough to pay for an attorney to enforce my parental visitation rights. I haven't seen my son in three years. I'm afraid to go home at night because there's a high probability that my landlord has evicted me." Tim locked eyes with Yasnaya. "And, when I'm not worried about the lot rent I worry that my home has been repossessed..... That's part of the reason I wanted you to bring me here...I didn't want you to know I live in a trailer. That's right. Mr. High and Mighty, Snob lawyer, lives in a trailer, and you've seen my car. The fiasco at the restaurant--that's normal--not a mix-up, and you want some *real* dirt?"

"Tim, I--"

"No! Please, let me finish. Social standing? Not one person in Wilmington will give me the time of day. Even the homeless shun me, because they, as bad off as they are, are in better financial shape than I'm in."

Yasnaya watched as tears welled in the corner of Tim Ridell's eyes and felt the seat shake as anguish racked his body. "Sore thumb...I know you meant sore thumb," she said softly as she patted his shoulder. "It's OK, everything will be OK."

"God, I'm sorry...it's, um I--"

"Shhh, shhh. Things will be better, I promise."

"Yas, you don't understand. Today was the last straw.... I've screwed up again. This time they'll fire me...I don't have a job. This is it for me."

Yasnaya looked up at the imposing building, then back at Tim. "Can you get us inside, and more importantly, can you get us to the company archives?"

Tim wiped at his eyes and swallowed hard to stifle his pitiful blubbering. Both barrels, huh? Good shot, Ridell...hit yourself right in the heart.

"Tim, can you get us to the archives?"

"Why...what is this fascination you have with the Crown's history?"

"Look, this isn't part of the plan...but then destroying you wasn't, either."

"Plan?"

"That's right, a plan. And I'm changing it. Let's get the furniture inside."

Any good lawyer knows there is a time to talk and a time to listen, and Tim Ridell was no different. What he was about to learn of the plan would not come from interrogation, he was sure of that. He was also sure that he, for better or worse, was now part of the plan.

"Where are you going? I can't move this by myself."

"There's a dolly in the maintenance room. You untie the rope and I'll be right back. When you have to move as much as I do, you learn to do it the easy way."

Yasnaya finished untying the rope and waited on the pickup tailgate. Ganna Mae would not be happy about the change in plans, but she was wrong to trust Phillip Moole. Yasnaya had met Moole once in Ganna Mae's apartment in New York. There, Moole had been sharp, impressive, and the perfect Southern Gentleman. Her second encounter with Moole in the *Club on the Strip* at Myrtle Beach had left a very different impression. Scantily clad, hell...naked, and wearing a black wig, Moole had not recognized her, nor had he tried to impress her with his courtly manner. *Courtly? Ha...slimeball, son of a bitch!*

"You're not still mad at me, are you?" Tim asked.

"No, of course not, why would you ask that?"

"Well, you look like you could bite nails...want me to get some from the maintenance room? They have some 10-pennies in there."

Yasnaya wondered about Tim's mood swings, but if she lived with his stress would she be any different? "I was just thinking about a customer I had once--bastard."

"I'm not putting down what you do. I mean it's really a good job. But could we not talk about it? I don't see you that way. I, uh--"

"It's OK, Tim. I know what you mean. It's sort of weird, though."

"How's that?"

"Well, most men fantasize about me without clothes. I think you're the first one that has ever wanted me clothed. Thanks."

"Dang Baptist background probably ruined me for life."

"I don't know. I'm really starting to like the Baptist in you."

Tim jumped up into the bed of the truck and worked the dresser to the tailgate. "I'll let it down, and you guide it on the dolly. Let me get this out first." Tim laid the smallest of three top drawers in the bed of the truck. "Hey, Yas, there's some writing on the bottom of this drawer," Tim said as he moved the drawer under the cargo light to read the chicken scratch scrawl.

"What does it say?"

"It says:*100 bushels new-ground*
: Tobbacy-- fifty cents.
: Hogs .75.
I think it's a ledger of some sort...Odd, huh?"

"All numbers are odd to me," Yas said. "I hate math, accounting, and taxes for that reason. Let's just get it inside."

After finding that Tim's office was too small to hold the dresser, they decided to store it in a storage room in the basement. "I bet this thing won't last a day in this building." Tim said.

"Why, it's not that bad--"

"It's French, and Wyatt Kincaid hates anything French."

"Oh yeah? The war in Iraq?"

"No, he started hating French stuff way before Freedom Fries. After his last divorce he cleaned the whole building out of anything that even vaguely resembled French. We had a yard sale right here in the parking lot. He must have lost thousands. Women from the office were snatching things up for a dime on the dollar."

"Now, that's odd."

"Yeah, it is...sort of like your plan. What gives?"

Yasnaya wrinkled her brow. "I've been thinking."

"Yeah, I saw the smoke--"

"No, I'm serious. I can't tell you what you need to know. If I do, I'd be in big trouble. But if I gave you clues and you figured things out..."

"Yas, we tried this earlier in the restaurant. Let's face it; I'm not good at it."

"Corporate minutes?"

"There're in Moole's office. Probably locked away."

"Where's his office?"

"Yas, whatever I'm supposed to find--Moole is too clever."

"Come on."

Phillip Moole's corner office overlooked the Cape Fear River. Framed in the center of his office windows was the battleship U.S.S. North Carolina. The view gave the impression that Moole alone was responsible for the war memorial that had become a permanent symbol of Wilmington. In fact, a half-century ago, school kids, thousands and thousands of them, had forked over their milk money to bring the *Gray Lady* "North Carolina" home. A fact, Tim Ridell was certain Phillip Moole never quoted to the hundreds of clients who had surveyed the ship through his office windows.

"Great view. Looks almost like a picture. Too bad all you shyster, sorry lawyers don't have the same view," Yasnaya said.

"Oh, all the shysters have this view. This is what I saw, too, before I was demoted to the pond-scum floor." No need to keep belaboring the point. Yas understood his position with the Crown; his double-barrel statement had insured that. No more pitying himself, and no more crying. Jeez...*crying*. Besides, the less time he spent talking, the sooner he could leave Moole's office, a place that made him nervous even without its owner's presence. "Come on, Yas. Let's get this over with. You check the bookcases. I'll look in his desk."

Within ten minutes the office had been searched, and, as expected, the two had found no corporate books. "I told you, Moole's too clever to leave anything around. Let's go."

"What's behind this door?" Yasnaya asked.

"I don't know. I think it's a closet, let's leave."

"Tim, why would someone lock a closet?"

"He wears expensive suits. Heck, I don't know, but I feel sure he wouldn't keep important papers in a closet. Let's go, please?"

"Let's open it."

"Yas, that's criminal...we have to leave. If you know something, just tell me, but I'm not breaking into his closet."

From her shorts, Yasnaya pulled a Swiss army knife clipped to mace spray. "I'm not leaving until I see what's in there."

"God, come on. Let's go."

Before Tim could leave the office Yasnaya had unscrewed the first screw from the closet doorknob. "Wait one more and we're--"

"Yas, don't--"

"Oops, too late We're in."

"You're in. I'm outta here."

"Corporate minutes." Yasnaya yelled from the closet, "Don't be such a baby, let's--"

"Baby? I'm a law-abiding citizen and a lawyer. That means I know breaking and entering when I see it, Christ."

"And I'm a stripper with the corporate minutes. Get your ass in here, now!"

Tim Ridell moved like a man on his way to the gallows, a place Moole would have no problem sending him if he found him in his office. "God, Yas, it would take all night to read this; look, there are volumes for each year."

"Find the meeting when the new board was established. It's all we need."

"Those would be the same papers Moole recorded, and we've seen them already--"

"No, there's more. The board can't vote," Yas insisted.

"The heck they can't. Trust me, they can vote."

"No, what's it called when someone else votes for you?"

"Are you talking about a proxy?"

"Yes, that's the word. Proxy. That wouldn't have been in the buyout papers, would it?"

"Maybe not, but those shares were $100,000,000 a share. Why would anyone invested that heavily not want input?"

"Because the board didn't pay for the stock."

Tim Ridell's mind raced. Four shares, $400,000,000. No one paid almost a half-billion dollars to buy proxy rights. "Yas, are you telling me the board is a front?"

"I don't know, but I know *proxy* was part of the deal."

"Who has the proxy?"

"I can't tell you. Read the minutes...the name would be in there, wouldn't it?"

Tim turned to the stock certificate issue page of the minutes and scanned it. "Yas, according to this the board owns the stock and the voting rights, and no proxy statements, sorry."

"No, I know what I'm talking about...what's this?" Yasnaya picked up a fireproof file box and flashed it toward Tim.

"We use them for important files, one copy here, and the original in a records vault we rent down town."

"Open it."

"Yas, I can't open it. I don't have a key, and you can forget about your little army tool; these things are secure."

"Do you have a key?"

"Yes, but it won't work. All the locks are different. Moole has a duplicate to all of our file boxes, but no one has a key to his."

"Maybe the key is here, in his desk, huh?"

"Forget it. Let's go. Moole wouldn't leave something like that here."

Yasnaya went to the desk and pulled out the drawers. "No key here. Look in the file cabinets."

"Yas, for Christ's sake, Moole is too smart for that. Where are you going?"

"The desk out front, who--"

"Janice Farrior, Moole's private secretary."

Before Tim could finish his statement, Yas was rummaging through Janice Farrior's desk. "Does this look like the key?" Yasnaya said as she dangled a key in front of Tim.

"Yeah, sort of, but we have hundreds of these boxes. No one key works on the same box, I'm telling--"

"Try it," Yas said as she tossed the key to Tim.

Normally, Tim Ridell's reflexes were right on, but being in Moole's office always brought out the worst in him. Instead of snatching the key from midair, Tim swatted it into Moole's prized 120-gallon aquarium. "Nice going, Ridell."

"Sorry...I'll find a net--"

"A net? Just reach in and get it."

Tim shook his head. "I don't think that's a good idea."

"Oh, get out of the way...for Christ's sakes--"

Tim grabbed Yas before she could get to the aquarium. "Yas, don't! You don't understand. Moole feeds those things live mice, and believe me, it's not a pretty sight."

"Geez, what kind of freak is he? And is it legal to keep this species?"

"I don't know," Tim said. "All I know is I'm not putting my hand in there."

"Where's the net?"

The net, like the corporate books, wasn't easily found. "Maybe we could use a coat hanger?" Tim suggested.

"I've seen about as many of those as I have nets. Got anymore bright ideas?"

"No, just that one that was it."

"Christ!... I'm getting that key. Turn your head."

"Why?"

"Because," Yas said as she grabbed a pointer underneath Moole's project board. "When people see the tools of my trade; they pay for the privilege. Now, turn your head."

With her lacy bra and the pointer Yas fashioned a makeshift net and retrieved the key, then handed it to Tim. "This time, try to be a little more careful--"

"Is that a bra? What size it that flopper-stopper anyway?"

"The right size! Try the key, pervert."

With both eyes glued to Yas's blouse Tim fumbled with the key.

"You might find the slot a little easier if you look at the lock--sicko."

"Sorry. Well, I'll be...it works--master key!"

One file folder labeled *Ferguson-Kincaid Plan* caught Yasnaya's eye. "That one. Read that one."

As Tim Ridell pulled the folder out, a slip of paper fell from the file. Yasnaya grabbed the paper from the floor and skimmed over it. "You might want to look at this first."

The paper turned out to be a check from the Crown Kincaid Development Company to Tim Ridell in the amount of fifty thousand dollars. It was stubbed "bonus check" and replaced check # 13887875. "That son of bitch! This was my real bonus check."

"Maybe he was going to surprise you?"

"Well, Yas, if that was the case, he put it off for a while. Look at the date. This check is almost four years old."

Tim folded the check and put it in his pocket.

"Won't he miss that?"

"I don't care if he does, this is my check. If he fires me, I'll at least get severance pay--bastard!"

"Good for you. Read the file."

Tim pulled one paper from the file. His shaking hand went unnoticed as he read it. "Yas, you set me up. Why?"

"I didn't set you up, what are you talking about?"

"This." Tim held the paper for Yasnaya to see.

"I don't understand."

"Well, let me help you. It's a proxy agreement that gives Phillip Moole the right to vote your two shares of Crown stock. *Two shares*---two hundred million bucks--topless dancer my butt."

"I've never seen that paper in my life--I don't even like Moole--I don't own any stock....Ganna Mae! She must have bought this when she bought the other stock."

"Ganna Mae bought the board's stock?"

"Yes, that's what I was trying to tell you."

Tim sat at Moole's desk and read the agreement. The proxy rights covered stock certificates 0002 and 0003. Wyatt Kincaid's stocks began at 0004, so even without looking at the original certificates, the truth wasn't hard to figure out. "Yas, you owned stock in this company before Wyatt Kincaid. Don't lie to me. What's going on?"

"I swear I don't know."

"But you know Moole, don't you?"

"I met him…but I don't know him, I swear."

Tim read the next paper in the folder, this time his hand shook so violently even Yas noticed.

"This can't be--no way."

"What is it?"

"It another proxy agreement, signed by Wyatt Kincaid."

"To Moole?"

"No, Yas…. It's assigned to me!"

Chapter 9

Drink in hand and wrapped in a thick terrycloth robe from the Ritz Carlton, Phillip Moole plopped down in one of the two identical Italian leather club chairs in the main salon. Wyatt, no doubt, was pleased with the Italian décor that ran throughout the *Crown Jewel*. In fact, the Italian leather was from France or Germany. True, the full-grain leather had been tanned and aniline-dyed in Italy, thus the nomenclature, but the high quality of the material screamed French.

It was easy to picture Wyatt with the interior boat designer, demanding the best but insisting on nothing French. Moole could hear him now. "You sure it ain't French, right?"

"Oh no, Mr. Kincaid, this is the finest Italian leather. No one does leather like the Italians."

Some little prissy designer could snow Wyatt, but the hoaxer wouldn't get over on Phillip Moole. By researching the furniture in his own home, Moole had discovered the well-kept secret of the origin of full-grain Italian leather…French or German and on occasions Scandinavian, but rarely Italian. "How the hell did an oaf like Wyatt accumulate so much?" Moole wondered aloud. His father. If it wasn't for his old man, Wyatt wouldn't have a damn thing, Moole decided.

Wyatt Kincaid Sr., according to the stories told by Wyatt, was a visionary and a man who had looked down Interstate 95 and seen the future. For days the old man had sat in the rest areas of I-95 and watched as the snowbirds flocked to rudimentary facilities carved into desolate stretches of loblolly pines. A lesser man would not have noticed the crowded picnic tables and associated the common activity of hungry travelers with an unfulfilled need. Trash barrels in the rest areas overflowed with discarded wrappings of sandwiches; ham, corned beef, and salami on rye. Cold food. Northern food. The rest areas fulfilled the traveler's biological needs, but no option existed to replace the soggy meals packed on slivers of ice in tin buckets. Restaurants located in the small towns close to the interstate offered hot meals, but many also provided speed traps and greedy justices of the peace. Federal funds used to build the interstate system provided security from the extortionate tactics of crossroad communities hell-bent on supplementing anemic town budgets with Northern tourist dollars. A few brave souls ventured from the safety of the interstate and paid dearly for their mistake.

Farmers, whose land had been divided by the interstate, were eager to rid themselves of the ruined acreage at cheap prices. The Crown had never been a company to pass on a chance to exploit opportunity, and Wyatt Sr.

had bought, at bargain prices, acres and acres of land located at interchanges along the road.

North Carolina, south of the hard winter line, was the halfway stop for most Northerners headed for the sunshine and warmth of Florida. Thus came the cornerstone of The Crown's immense real estate portfolio, land at intersections along the highway. Fast-food joints had been the first to realize the potential, then motels, and finally, outlet shopping malls.

Once the I-95 travelers had stopped to enjoy the food and shopping, many had noticed the subtropical climate and nearby beaches. Now, instead of passing through, rich retirees came in droves to live and play in the subtropics. And to give Wyatt Jr. credit, all his old man had done on I-95 Wyatt had done on I-40. Southern Pines, host of the 1999 U.S.Open, suffered as Wilmington and Myrtle Beach sucked duffers from across the country into the championship golf courses along I-40 and Hwy 17.

Like it or not, the Crown had changed the demographics of North and South Carolina. Though the masses had been happy to come, the traffic and lack of infrastructure to move them was raising cries of overdevelopment.

To circumvent the criticisms and traffic jams, the Crown had changed directions. Four-lane highways with high-access interchanges dominated the company's future plans. Large upscale houses would be built among bucolic settings; private golf courses and commercial projects would follow. That was the plan, but there smack dab in the middle of the Crown's first mixed-use development was Ganna Mae's forty acres.

What a break for Phillip Moole and what luck that Ganna Mae had chosen him to implement her *Last Kincaid* plan. She, like Wyatt Sr., was a visionary, and had seen the benefits of choosing a Harvard Man to upstage the Crown.

Still, it wasn't fair. He had graduated ninth in his class at Harvard Law and here he worked for Ganna Mae, a high-school dropout even less educated than Wyatt. At least Wyatt had spent some time on a campus, though mostly at keg parties--hence, no degree. But at least Wyatt had gone to college, and as much as he hated to admit it, Wyatt did have pedigree. Ganna Mae Ferguson, of the sharecropper Fergusons, was just plain white trash. "The whole damn lot of them," Moole growled, as he remembered the mud dauber family who had kept goats and chickens in their front yard. "Lowlifes... ruined the whole neighborhood."

Yet, Wyatt and Ganna Mae made the big bucks, and he, a Harvard man, worked directly for one and indirectly for the other. That little oversight had now worked its way out. Finally, the years of hard work had paid off and he, Phillip Moole, was at the top of the food chain. And Wyatt? Where had the old woman banished him? No, no need to think about it. The less he knew the better--deniability.

Too bad Wyatt's abduction was temporary...a man could get used to this life. But one day Wyatt would be back, back at the top, and Phillip's chief counsel job would be history. No doubt about that, but with the money he would make on this deal, a job would be the last thing Phillip Moole would ever need.

Sure, someone would take the fall, even go to prison for a few years, but Tim Ridell was young and he would still have a life when he got out. Moole thought about his own age, sixty. Too old to start over even if he got out in five years. Besides Ridell would have some money with which to start his new life. Two-hundred-thousand dollars would still be money in five years.

Ridell was a milquetoast. Four years without bonus checks, and Tim Ridell never complained once about the oversight. Accounting had replaced the first check, to balance the books, and after that it had just been a matter of replacing the company checks with certified ones. Phillip Moole had asked himself the same question for four years, "Why pay a bonus to a man who evidently knew he didn't deserve one?" Hiding the checks from Ridell wasn't a problem, but keeping them hidden from Wyatt after his order to issue--ah, only a Harvard Man could have pulled that one off. One thing was certain, there would be no bonus check for Tim Ridell once the plan came to fruition. Just like Kincaid to stick his nose where it didn't belong, ordering a bonus for a bonehead, Phillip fumed. Legal affairs were his responsibility, yet, each year Kincaid had admonished him for saving the company money. "Hell, Moole, the boy's car spends more time in the parking lot than on the road. Give him the bonus. The Boykins shafted him good--And another thing, lose the pickle screen saver. That damn Sally has punished him enough."

"Wonder how old Wyatt will feel about Ridell once he knows how bad he screwed him?"

"I'm sorry sir, were you speaking to me?"

Phillip Moole looked at Yvette. "No, I--I was just saying how screwed up Wyatt's clothes were--hideous. That's why I changed." Moole twirled around to give Yvette the full view of his robe. "I found this in the bathroom. Not bad even if it is Wyatt's."

"The robe belongs to Ms. Dubois, sir."

"Oh--uh, does Wyatt have one?"

"No sir, he walks around in his boxers."

Moole checked the robe over for any lace or pink. "Why does that not surprise me? Uh, the robe, does it look OK?'

"It's unisex and it looks fine on you, sir."

"Thank--"

"Sir, the reason you couldn't see Mr. Denton?"

"Yes?"

"It's a long story, sir. If I may?"

Yvette gave all the reasons for the Kincaid-Denton feud, as well as the misery caused by her former employer.

"Did the captain know about the uniform, Yvette?"

"Yes, sir."

"The young kid...the mate?"

"He's the one that came up with the *Whole Slice* idea."

"I see, and Mr. Denton, I suppose he views--"

"Redneck Royalty aboard the *Crown Jewel*..." Yvette paused for effect, "...were his exact words, sir."

"Is there a clothing store on this island?"

"Across the harbor, but I'm afraid the selection is limited, sir."

Phillip Moole was faced with his first executive decisions--firing the captain and the second mate would be his first choices. The decision was easy, but replacing the crew? If the clothing was limited on the island, surely the employment pool was even more in short supply.

"Yvette, I want you to get all of the clothing sizes for the crew--" Phillip Moole paused and thought of what Wyatt would do in the same situation....Compromise? No, Wyatt was not a man of compromise. In spite of his hatred for Wyatt, Moole had to respect the man's convictions. "If I fired the crew--can they be replaced?"

"No sir, but if you could drive the boat--"

"No...no, I can't--could Wyatt?"

"Yes sir, but if he comes back--I quit."

"The clothing store? Do they have outfits like Mr. Denton's crew wears?"

"They keep *Slice of Life* uniforms in stock, sir--I can sew *Crown Jewel* logos over them."

"Perfect." Ah, compromise--the difference between a gentleman and a buffoon.

"Suits, does the store carry suits?"

"No sir, but they have a nice selection of linen shirts and pants--and boat shoes."

"Good, good. Here are my sizes." Phillip Moole hurriedly scribbled the numbers on a pad. "Oh, Yvette. The mate, where can I find him?"

"In his quarters, sir--I can get him--"

"No, that won't be necessary. I'll wait until he comes up."

Phillip Moole walked to the aft deck and observed Denton's potted plants--a green barrier between him and Denton's money. Making the first move had been costly. Denton had threatened to shoot him, but still, someone had to make a move--compromise safety for profit--Ridell? Yes, Ridell he'd take a bullet for the team.

Moole, had never been a player on the Crown team, but for now he was quarterback, a stealth quarterback. Any profits generated by the Crown, from now on would belong to him. Turning Denton around would be worth hundreds of millions, millions that would be in his personal bank account long before Wyatt Kincaid re-entered the game. Stockholders voted on bonuses, and now the board votes were in his pocket...what a plan!

Wyatt had prided himself for thinking fast on his feet and once accused Moole of having to make a plan to go to the bathroom. The remark had drawn laughter at the last board meeting. "You were right, Wyatt. I am a planner, but who's laughing now?"

Moole thought of Ganna Mae and her ridiculously titled *Last Kincaid* plan. True, he didn't know all the details of the plan, but he had made one of his own. The Tim Ridell proxy assignment was brilliance, ah, but the Yasnaya proxy assignment was a stroke of genius. As long as Wyatt was out of the picture, Ridell could be manipulated. The lost bonus checks would see to that. The girl would be kept in the dark--Ganna Mae assured that. "She must never know how or why she owns the stock, never! Do you understand?" Moole shook his head to clear the cobwebs. Why alter only parts of the plan? Why not change the whole scheme? For that matter why not change the benefactor? This was the good life and who had worked harder to be more successful than he? Wyatt's good fortune came as a matter of birth; the old woman's, a lucky break. But he had earned this life more than either Wyatt or Ganna Mae.

Phillip Moole toasted the bright tropical moon. "Sorry Ms. Ferguson, but you know what they say: 'The best laid plans of mice and men often go awry'…. Even the very best plan, old woman!"

Chapter 10

Boris Yantikov finished reading the *Last Kincaid* plan for the second time and then stared at his brother-in-law Michael Fitzpatrick, behind the bar. *Petty thief.* Damn Irish Mick calling someone a petty thief. Who stole more than the Irish?

"I show you petty thief, Mick," Boris muttered.

"What was that, Boris?"

"Nothing."

"Yeah, nothing. Get out of my bar, and take your stolen loot with you-"

"I leave--When I come back, maybe I buy this place--turn it into nice vodka bar."

"Yeah, yeah, just leave before I call the cops."

Boris Yantikov jabbed the numbers into his limo phone and waited for an answer.

"Hello."

"Fyodor?"

"I told you, never call me that. John Smith--John Smith, do you understand?"

Boris stared at the receiver then slapped it. "John Smith? I spit on John Smith! Fyodor Yantikov--you understand?"

Fyodor Yantikov, younger brother of Boris Yantikov, had chosen an American name, a common American name, not for the love of his adopted country, but for anonymity. Thousands of men named John Smith lived and worked in America. Most of these men were decent and respectable citizens, a fact that provided excellent cover from law enforcement agencies searching for one John Smith slaved to the criminal element.

John No Middle Name Smith typed into an internet search engine brought thousands of results. *Fyodor Yantikov*, fed into the same field, yielded one result: "Fyodor Yantikov, Miami, Fl., suspected Russian Mafia activities, International fugitive, contact INTERPOL."

"John Smith or I hang up."

"Da, Da--John Smith." Boris slapped at the receiver again. "I find something, something worth much money."

"How much money?"

"Big Money--Fyodor, I swear--"

"Shut up--meet me, Friday at noon." John Smith said, then added in Russian, "Mama znayet myesta" ("Mom knows the place.")

John Smith snapped his phone shut and fumed. Boris Yantikov had never been smart, not even smart enough to remember a simple alias like

John Smith, but he had always been street savvy. He also had an uncanny ability to stumble onto big deals and, luckily for John Smith, was never smart enough to pull them off on his own. Nor was Boris smart enough to figure out the lopsided 90-10 splits his younger brother passed off as 50-50 deals. "Probably won't even remember who Mom is," John Smith whispered under his breath in perfect King's English.

Fyodor Yantikov had spent ten years in London before coming to America. In those years he had watched hundreds of British movies and imitated the actors' speech until his Baltic accent had vanished. Boris had stayed behind and his years as a prison guard in Siberia had fine-tuned his expertise as a master con man. Prisoners, desperate to make life more bearable, had traded prize possessions and even their dignity for the favors Boris could provide. Even now Boris used the secrets of the damned to extort money for his silence. But Boris's methods were crude, as crude as his immigrant's accent.

"Nice watch."

John Smith turned to face the man who had made the statement. A pair of clear blue eyes, framed by a youthful face sporting a five o'clock shadow that could best be described as week-old peach fuzz, stared back at him.

"Thank you." Remembering Wyatt Kincaid's story of the watch, Smith relayed it to his new acquaintance, "My father gave it to me."

"May I?"

"Certainly, old boy." Smith said as he shoved the watch under the bar lights at the Barry Island Club.

"Wow. A Roger Dubuis. Must have cost a bundle."

"I wouldn't know. As I said, it was a gift. How do you know so much about watches?"

"My father was a jeweler in Atlanta, so watches were sort of my hobby."

"I see." John Smith motioned for a refill and the bartender complied. A jeweler--might not be a bad connection. "Can I buy you a drink, my young friend?"

"Sure, thanks. I saw you come up on your boat. Fountain--Lighting, right?"

"That's right."

"Dual 800's?"

"Yes--"

"What's the top speed? Wait...let me guess--100 knots."

"Right again." John Smith eyed his companion. College student, or newly graduated—rich, innocent...and, therefore a mark. "Let me guess, your other hobby was boats?"

"Yes sir, I love boats." Sure he does, probably here on one of the yachts at Chub Cay. Delivering Kincaid would pay big bucks but Fyodor could always make time to squeeze in one more con...and conning this peach-fuzzed kid would be no harder than stealing books from the blind.

"I go to Atlanta quite often. Perhaps I would recognize your father's store--"

"We sold it a few years ago--after my father died."

"I'm sorry to hear that...I'm John, by the way."

"My name is James, but my friends call me Jimmy. Pleased to meet you."

"My pleasure. May I call you Jimmy?"

"Sure, Mr.--?"

"Call me John, please."

"Man, my Mom would kill me if I did that. I'd feel better if I called you by your last name, sir."

"Ok, Jimmy, if you insist. Smith, John Smith."

"You here on business, Mr. Smith?" Before Smith could answer, the policeman who removed Wyatt from the boat bumped into them. "Sorry," Jacobs said as he glared at Smith.

"No problems old chap." Smith turned back to Jim. "Sorry, you were saying?"

Jim watched as Jacobs faded back into the crowded bar scene in front on him. "Do you know him?" Jim asked.

"Never seen him before. No harm done." Smith scanned the room and turned back to Jim. "Ah, to answer your original question; I'm here on holiday and a little fishing. The same for you I imagine?"

"I wish.... I'm working. Helping my mom with tuition money, but the season ends in a few days." Jim Williams peered over the deck at the sexy Fountain sitting low in the water. "I'd love to get a closer look at your boat. Would you mind?"

"No, as a matter of fact I have to make a call. Perhaps we will meet again." John Smith pulled his phone from his pocket and called out, "Oh, Jimmy, don't go on board--I just washed it, you know."

John Smith watched from the deck of the Barry Island Club as the kid ogled his boat. OK, no con here. The kid was a working stiff...still, a man with an eye for jewelry could always be useful in this line of work--quick appraisals. Smith cupped the phone to his mouth. "What's the big deal bumping into me like that?"

"I told you to keep a low profile not hang out in a bar...and lose the watch."

James Tidwell waved goodbye to John Smith and headed for the pay phones at the Chub Dinner Club. Before calling, Tidwell walked around the building to check for late night diners. Seeing none, he made his call. "This is Tidwell. I have a report and a request."

"Is your line secure?"

"It is if the commo guys did their job--"

"They did. Go ahead, Tidwell."

"From: Special Agent, James Tidwell, Operation Peregrine; I've made contact with a John Smith. Subject has a British accent, but speaks fluent Russian, claims to be on a fishing trip. I've checked out his boat, no fishing gear, and no sign the boat has ever held a rod. I think he may have transported the missing package from Bahamas State Police. If he did, the cargo wasn't in sight. I'll go back later to check in the storage areas. I've observed Smith meeting with a Bahamian cop named Rene Jacobs twice on the beach here. They seem very well acquainted, but tonight Smith denies he knows Jacobs, even though he saw him face to face. See if we have anything on Jacobs and I'm certain "Smith" is an alias. End of report."

"And your request?"

"First, I'll need a list of everyone who owns a Sympathie model Roger Dubuis watch--"

"Tidwell, unlike firearms, we don't have a National Registry of watches. Do you know how long that could take?"

"Not long. There are only eleven Roger Dubuis authorized dealers in the U.S. and better than that, there are only twenty-eight of these watches in the world."

"Damn, must be expensive--"

"Very. About 225 grand per--and I've seen two today. Odd, don't you think?"

"What kind of watch was it again?"

"Roger Dubuis, Sympathie Window Perpetual Calendar Minute Repeater--"

"Is that the name or the description?"

"That's the model, here's the description: ivory dial, 18K Red Gold with tang buckle."

"OK, got it. What else?"

James Tidwell checked the hour marked on his bezel when the big Fountain rolled back around the point at Chub. "Let's see, subject's boat has a top speed of 100 knots. He was gone for two hours and six minutes. Give me all the landmasses within a 100-nautical-miles area east of Chub Cay."

"Why didn't you notify Eagle Eye?"

James Tidwell thought of the squadron of Citation and Falcon jets, his old squadron, used by the Coast Guard to patrol the 12-mile maritime ADIZ (Air Defense Identification Zone) and smiled. "Tell the guys I was a little busy with a needy passenger, but I'll get them in this game, and soon. In the mean-time I'm going back for a better look at Smith's boat.... Encode this to the Miami office."

Lights were out at the Barry Island Club by 3:00 a.m. and Smith's boat was still tied to the guest dock. Special Agent James Tidwell leaned against the Fountain to listen for any signs of life aboard the boat. Other than the bilge pump, there were none. "No air conditioning--no passengers--logical," Tidwell whispered as he remembered the acronym of the logical reasoning course he'd had at Quantico R.E.A.L.: Reliable + Evidence + Assimilated = Logic.

Other than a few changes of clothes and a Soviet-made pistol, the boat was clean. Firearms on boats were the norm. Even in these days of Global Positioning and digital communications, few boats ventured onto the high seas unarmed. Even well-appointed ocean going yachts came equipped with gun safes and a crew qualified to use them. But not many firearms in these waters were Russian-made, James Tidwell thought as he hopped from the boat and made his way to the path leading back to Chub.

Less than a hundred yards down the path, a hand grabbed Tidwell by the shoulder. Tidwell spun from the grasp and assumed a Karate stance. "What the...Clark! What are you doing here?"

"The same as you, but you beat me to it."

"Beat you to what?"

"The Fountain...I saw you board her. Did you find anything?"

Damn, Clark Guilford was DEA. Man, we gotta get better coordinated. "No, I didn't find anything."

"I didn't think you would. He rinsed the boat off when he came in. I figured maybe he was washing it to get rid of the evidence."

"Drugs?"

"No, evidence from Wyatt. I figured the Bossman was catching a ride to Nassau, but then they headed west. The boat was gone only a couple of hours...not enough time to make it to the mainland and back."

"Does Bossman know Smith?"

"Who the hell is Smith?" Clark growled.

"The guy who owns the Fountain--are you sure Wyatt was on the boat?"

"Yeah, I saw them when they left the harbor. Wyatt threatened Moole when they were leaving...you didn't see them?"

"No, I--"

"Well, if you didn't see them...what were you looking for on the Fountain?"

Damn good question and it deserved a good answer, but if he told Clark of his suspicions it could reveal his identity. "Clark...I was just curious. You know I'm a boat fanatic, I just wanted to get a closer look."

"At this hour and in pitch dark? Bullshit." Captain Clark Guilford grabbed James Tidwell by the arm. "Come on. You're coming with me."

"Clark, what are you doing?'

"I thought you were a good guy, that's why I hired you. But I won't tolerate a thief. I'm taking you to that Bahamian policeman."

"Clark, I--"

"Nope, no excuses. Future doctors don't steal, and neither does my second mate--"

"Clark." --Tidwell thought about knocking Clark out and letting the agency deal with the aftermath, but how could they replace Clark as captain without raising suspicions? A mistake now could negate five months of undercover work...definitely not worth the risk. "Clark, I've got a confession to make."

"Tell it to the policeman. I'm going to tell him about Wyatt.... Something's wrong here--"

Agent James Tidwell had not had time to put all the pieces together, but one thing he knew for sure. Rene Jacobs was involved with John Smith...and John Smith wasn't likely to turn up on the list of Roger Dubuis watch owners. Furthermore he now had an eyewitness who could put Wyatt on the Fountain. The agency couldn't run interference before Clark Guilford did what he thought was the right thing, so Tidwell took the gamble.

"Clark, I heard the engines when they came by the yacht. I figured it had to be the Fountain. I made contact with Smith, the owner. That's when I discovered he may have Wyatt's very rare watch. I was just trying to verify what you've told me, that Wyatt Kincaid was on board the Fountain."

"Bullshit, you're just making that story up because I caught you. If what you're saying is the truth you would have told me sooner."

"What I told you is the truth, I swear."

Clark shook his head. "I want to believe you, but I'm calling Inspector Jacobs. He is qualified to sort this out, not me,"

"You talk to Jacobs and months of undercover work are gone. Not only that, but you may be jeopardizing national security.--" Tidwell reached in his pocket and pulled out his badge.

"Jim, stop it. You think I don't know a fake badge when I see one. You're not old enough--"

"I'm thirty, with a baby face. I know it's hard to believe."

"Damn right, it is--"

"Let me make a phone call. I can prove it."

"Do you think I'm stupid? You call one of your college buddies and he verifies you're a spy. Ain't happening...I'm calling Jacobs. He left his card on the boat."

"Clark before you do that, let me prove to you that I'm telling the truth."

"How?"

"Let me make a call. Within fifteen minutes a Falcon jet with Coast Guard markings will fly over us at 200 feet. Then bank south and pour on the coals."

"Make your call. That happens and I'll eat the badge."

"Let's sit on the dock."

Fourteen minutes after the call was placed a Falcon jet at 200 feet rocked its wings flashed the landing light, and banked hard to the south at full throttle.

"Umm, I hate that," Clark Guilford said as he watched the jet roar off.

"Why?"

"Well, 'cause it's going to be damn hard to eat that badge with nothing to wash it down."

Chapter 11

Sounds from the streets below drifted up to the terrace, playing gently off the brick walls of her tenth-floor apartment, and Ganna Mae bear-hugged the sweet melody of urbanity. Central Park, like a great peacock, spread its plumaged silva against the amethyst dawn sky. Real trees--paper birch, white walnut, and scarlet hawthorn...ah, and the best part--not one damn pine tree to mask the smell of warm bagels and fresh baked pretzels. Nothing made Ganna Mae appreciate the wonders of the city like a trip back home. *Home*--pine trees, rednecks, grits, and damn Kincaids.

The quick trip down memory lane reminded Ganna Mae of the scene and her lost day planner. Quicker than an express elevator, she rose from her utopian perch and found her mobile phone.

"Oh God, what time is it?"

"6:30, my pretty...time to rise."

"Gan, could you not be so chipper? I'm not a morning person, and you know that!"

Neither had Ganna Mae been a morning person when she was in the entertainment business...not that Yas's occupation could be classified as entertainment. Men were much more excited at the illusion of sex than they were at being smothered by it. Exotic dancing sprang from the strip tease. Now, lap dances and complete nudity replaced the tease portion. Change was good, but not all good should be changed, Ganna Mae thought as she remembered one of Adolfo's favorite adages. "One day when you hang up your G-string...oh, I forgot, you don't use those, do you dear?"

"No Gan, they went the way of pasties, and feather fans...I'm surprised you could remember back to those days before gravity sagged your ass--sets."

"Funny...and that may be the truth. May I remind you, once I danced for royalty and--"

"I know, I know, and the heads of the politburo--"

"Mock me if you will, but my connections saved you from being a little street urchin in Russia. Never forget that."

How could she forget it? Even her name, Yasnaya Polyana, paid homage to the Russian bureaucrat who made her adoption possible. Not that she remembered the adoption. Her recollection was only of the story Ganna Mae told, and told often.

According to Ganna Mae, the official was a fan of Tolstoy. To gain favor she had agreed to name the orphaned infant after Tolstoy's home, Yasnaya Polyana. Familiar with bribing men, Yasnaya was certain the name change wasn't the only concession Ganna Mae had made to gain favor.

Even after the adoption was finalized, Ganna Mae never pretended to be her mother. In fact, one of the earliest words Yas had learned was "adopted", and just like now, she was constantly reminded of it. "No, Gan, I'll never forget that…and, I'll never forget that I can't pay you for saving me from the Commies, whatever the going rate for Commie saving is these days…But, thank you, my gracious benefactor, a thousand times, thank you."

"Ingrate!"

"I'm not an ingrate--but how many more times must I hear the story? Believe me, Gan, I get it."

"Do you? I sometimes wonder why I even bothered."

"Well, let me help you. Because at the ripe old age of forty, you realized you were alone, and it scared the hell out of you. My adoption wasn't about me, Gan, it was about you."

"Enough! Or I may--"

"Or you may what? Send me back to Russia? That worked when I was a child, but not anymore."

"Yasnaya, let's not argue. Not today, I'm upset enough."

"What's wrong?"

"My day planner--I think I left it at the scene. The whole *Last Kincaid* plan is in that book."

"I'll pick it up for--"

"No! …I mean that won't be necessary. I have to meet with Moole soon; I'll pick it up then." Great, just what she needed, Yas snooping around the scene. What if she did find the planner? How would Yas feel knowing Kincaid DNA was half her genetic make up? And more importantly, would she still be OK with the surgery? Or, would she think there were ulterior motives involved in the decision?

"But if you're so worried about it, I could be there in a couple of hours--"

"No, forget it. That's not why I called. Did you pick up the chiffonier?"

Yas explained the events of the past evening, but was careful not to mention the stock certificates in her name. "Tim feels--"

"Tim? You used him to get the furniture to Wyatt? Quick thinking, by the way, but we have no more use for him now."

"Maybe I like him. It's not unheard of to like a person even if you can't use him, is it?"

"Yasnaya, men, women—people in general--are all a means to someone's end. I'm not the only person who has figured that out; I'm just one of the few who will admit it." Ganna Mae gave Yas time for her pearl of wisdom sink in. "And now it's time for you to follow the plan. Forget him, we don't need him."

Rather than use Ganna Mae's dramatic pause to ponder the wisdom of the old woman's analogy Yasnaya asked the question that had been bugging her for days, "I'm glad you mentioned that, I've been thinking about this plan. Why didn't you make me a board member? Why strangers?"

"You a board member? Fat chance! The corporation is privately held and the Kincaids never have been politically correct, especially that oaf, Wyatt. Let me assure you, my dear; a female won't ever sit on the board of the Crown."

"So a female can't even own stock in the Crown?"

"Never, the Crown is a bastion of testosterone."

Ganna Mae had spent years studying the Crown. Tim Ridell had not been aware of the available stock split. Yet Ganna Mae knew the numbers, even explained them to her, so how could she not know about Yas's two shares?

"I see...interesting...but I still think Tim has a point."

"And his point?"

"He doesn't think Wyatt will keep the chiffonier in his building...and why is it so important than Kincaid have it?"

Ganna Mae thought back to the day her father salvaged the furniture from the roadside, victim of a moving mishaps no doubt. He worked weeks to restore the piece and finished the project just in time for her mother's birthday and the day Caleb was born. Though it was meant for a bedroom her mother had shared it with the family and placed it in the living room where her dad turned it into his desk.

"It was the only nice thing we ever owned. When they died I couldn't get Caleb away from it. You wouldn't believe how happy that chest of drawers had made my mother and how proud that made my father...I want Kincaid to have some understanding of what his family took... It's personal and you wouldn't understand!" Just thinking about those times made her sick and only vengeance held the cure.

"What if maintenance has standing orders to remove anything French? After hearing Tim's stories I could see that."

"Let me worry about that, Yasnaya. Besides, Wyatt Kincaid will be gone for sometime. The furniture is safe for now."

"How can you be so sure he won't come back?"

"I'm sure, that's all you need to know. And forget this Tim."

"Maybe I--"

"You will forget him, and you will not stand in my way. I've spent my life waiting for this moment. Don't cross me, Yasnaya Polyana, or there will be hell to pay, do you understand?"

Rarely did Gan use her full name. Only twice in her youth could Yas remember when she had--and both times, there *had* been hell to pay.

"Yes, Gan. I understand."

"Good, now go back to sleep. You're grumpy in the mornings."

Yasnaya kicked back the covers and padded into her kitchen to make coffee. Once the aroma of fresh brew filled the house she opened the door to her guestroom. Tim Ridell was snuggled up to his pillow like a child to a teddy bear. For a moment she wondered about his story of exposing Santa. Even at thirty-seven, Tim Ridell had the look of youthful innocence. Not as handsome as many of the men she had dated no doubt about that. There was something about him that was different, better, yes, better than the hunks. Tim Ridell had moral fiber. "Dang Baptist background," Yasnaya murmured into Tim's ear.

"Oh boy--where am I?"

"In my bed, Mr. Ridell."

"Man, this is terrible."

"Why?"

"I've spent the night in your bed and I don't remember any of it. Fill me in on the details--was I any good?"

"You were an animal."

Light from the doorway silhouetted Yasnaya's naked body against her sheer nightgown and Tim Ridell soaked in the view. "God, you're beautiful."

"Bed head, no makeup--oops." Yas looked down at her gown and realized her mistake. "Pervert...I'll put some clothes on and we can have coffee."

"No coffee for me, just a big helping of raw red meat--us animals have to keep up our strength."

"I'm a gatherer--you want raw meat, you hunt it. Bathroom is on the right, towels are in the closet."

Smells of bacon and eggs mixed with the aroma of the coffee greeted Tim as he left the bathroom. Ah, the scent of breakfast, a simple thing really, but so meaningful to someone who hadn't shared that pleasure in a long time. To think that someone cared enough about him to prepare food, real food, made him feel warm and welcomed. Yes, no doubt about it. Life for the moment, was good, and it was about to get a lot better, he thought, as he patted his wallet.

"Smells great, I'm starved."

"Oh, this is for me--your hunk of raw meat is in a forest somewhere."

"Come on, Yas, feed me."

"I did last night, remember?"

"I do, and as soon as I find a bank I'm going to repay you in spades."

"Tim, I was just kidding."

"I wasn't. I owe you. If it wasn't for you--I wouldn't have this check. Glad you decided to change the plan."

Yasnaya remembered her earlier conversation with Ganna Mae.... *Forget him...no female will ever be part of the Crown...there will be hell to pay.* "Yes, the plan, I'm sorry I've gotten you involved, maybe we should forget what we found last night?"

"Yas, when you first decided to change the plan, I thought from that moment on, I was part of the plan--it's not that way. I was a part of this plan long before last night."

"No, I spoke to Gan this morning. She said to forget about you because we have no further use for you."

"No further use? Have you forgotten about Wyatt's proxies? Get my name off them and I'm out of here. I'll leave on my own, and you don't have to throw me away." Tim's remark reminded Yas again of the kid on the playground never picked for a team. There was just something about this man that made you want to cuddle him and keep the cold hard world at bay...strange.

"That's what she thinks. I don't want you to go away. I--"

"Then tell me the plan. I'm involved and I have the right to know."

"I can't."

"Can't or won't, Yas, which it?"

"I don't know the plan. I'm like you, a pawn--but I know how we can find out."

"How?"

"Ganna Mae has this day planner. She left it somewhere by mistake, and I know where. Her entire plan is in it."

"Well, let's go."

"Right now? Don't you have to work?"

"Nope, I worked late last night. Besides I finally have enough money to take a little vacation. Let's roll."

Hints of cool autumn air were nipping around the edges of the summer's record heat. Soon the long hot days would be little more than memories and conversation starters. In the Piedmont, away from the moisture of the coast, the day was turning delightful. Yasnaya opened the sunroof and the pickup's cab filled with fresh air. Neither Yasnaya nor Tim spoke of the changing weather, but both were captivated by it as they rolled along.

"Yas, Ganna Mae...is she your mother?"

"In a legal sense, I guess she is, but she never treated me like a daughter. She adopted me when I was a baby, but we don't share the same last name."

"That's strange?"

"My name was a condition for my adoption, or so she claims."

"Never heard of that before."

"I'm a Russian baby."

"That explains your breath-taking beauty, but not your name." Tim said. "I just don't see that being a condition for adoption."

"Yeah, me either, but that's what she claims. And another weird thing, she never treated me like a child. She always treated me with...with...."

"Abject indifference?"

"No, she cared for me. I mean she dressed me up and took me to dinner or plays, occasionally. For some reason our times together always reminded me of a little girl playing with her doll. As soon as playtime was over I went back to school or to my nanny. I never wanted for anything. I was sent to a boarding school, then college at DePaul. Don't feel so bad about her not liking you; she has always hated it when I got serious with a guy. It's strange, all my life I've felt like Gan was grooming me, like her own Femme Nikita for a purpose."

"Such as?"

"I never could figure it out when I was a kid—and lately, you'll really think this is crazy. I think sometimes maybe I'm like a sleeper cell; just waiting to be brought online when Gan flips the switch."

"You mean as a player in the plan you keep talking about?"

"Yes, she calls it *the Last Kincaid*."

The *Last Kincaid*, Tim Ridell thought. That's exactly who he would be facing when his proxy to vote Wyatt's shares was revealed. Not a confrontation he looked forward to if his choices failed to please the Bossman. What crazy plan would give him, The Scourge of Legal such power? Why hadn't Moole retained the proxy?

He had the proxy and that meant that he, Tim Ridell, Scourge of Legal, would have to exercise those rights at the board meeting...and that made him an integral part of the plan, no matter what Yas thought.

"Yas, you said Ganna Mae said to forget about me, right?"

"Yes, but remember she said that not me."

"I know, but think about it. Wouldn't she have to meet with me to tell me how to vote Wyatt's stocks-- I mean that's the reason someone gives proxy rights--to vote them."

"I don't know much about corporate rules, but how about my shares of stock? Why didn't Gan tell me about them?"

"Maybe she doesn't know about them. I mean I'm a lawyer there, and I didn't."

"No, Tim, you don't know Gan. She researched the Crown for years. If there were any blanks, I'm sure Moole filled them."

"Moole has your proxy, maybe he didn't tell her about the stock?"

"No, she knows. I could tell this morning--she was lying."

"The signature on the proxy to Moole--was it yours?"

"It looked like it. But I don't remember signing a paper when I saw Moole--"

"Sign any for Ganna Mae?"

"Yes, but I don't remember those agreements--though it's possible."

"Then Ganna Mae must know that Moole has your proxy."

"I guess we'll find out soon enough." Yasnaya slowed the pickup and turned down a long red-clay path. "We're home, honey."

"Ganna Mae lives here?"

Even the single-wide trailer at Treadwell's Mobile Home Park looked more inviting than the building Tim Ridell saw before him. Any charm the shack might have had had been lost to years of neglect. What had once been a white picket fence was now a gray, snaggle-toothed remnant of the past held upright by a wisteria vine. The fence slats that once protected the yard were scattered about the grounds along with broken branches and a layers of leaves and acorns. Tucked under the shade of two giant red oaks and surrounded by a pine thicket, the scene looked completely inhospitable.

"No, she doesn't live here. But the inside is kind of cozy. I helped Gan stage for the visit."

"Visit?"

"Yeah, this is where she completed the deal with Mr. Kincaid."

"Why?"

"I don't know. It's like everything else she does--part of her plan." Yas turned the doorknob and kicked the bottom of the door. "Shall we?"

In the living room, a print of an old man sitting alone with a loaf of bread and a slice of cheese hung on the wall. Bright blue and white curtains covered the windows. A lone sofa, covered by a handmade quilt, completed the furnishings. In spite of the Spartan décor, the house, as Yas promised, was indeed cozy. "Where do we start?" Tim asked.

"You look in here. I'll try the bedroom. Knowing Gan, she read it every night before she went to bed."

Fifteen minutes later the search was over, and Yasnaya made her report.

"Nothing. Did you find anything?"

"Just this." Tim said as he held up a partially full bottle of Early Times. "Yours?"

"No, and certainly not Gan's. She only drinks Oban it's probably a prop."

"Prop?"

"Yeah, Gan is a stickler for staging, she even called this place *the scene*-- and check out the horseshoe. Only my mother would believe in the power of a horseshoe," Yasnaya said, as she wiped their footprints from the linoleum floor. "I'm going to check the bedroom for tracks--you tidy up in here, and make sure you put the whiskey bottle back where you found it-- *exactly* where you found it." Yasnaya admonished.

Tim fiddled with the bottle placement until it was finally dead center of the table, exactly where he had found it. As he scanned the room for any signs of their entry, he noticed the upside down horseshoe on the windowsill. "She won't ever get luck if she leaves it like that," he said as he flipped the talisman into the good luck "up" position, then joined Yas in the bedroom.

"No day planner--what now?" Tim asked, as Yas finished wiping up the last of their prints.

"I think we have to go back to Moole's office." As dismal as the cabin scene was, thoughts of returning to the glaring austerity of the Crown headquarters sent Tim Ridell into a panic. He would not be making a trip back to Moole's office, and Yas could put that in her pipe and smoke it…or do whatever beautiful women do when they don't get their way.

"Oh, no we're not. We had a reason to be there last night--"

"You work there, and don't tell me lawyers don't burn the midnight oil--"

"Sure I do, but you don't. How am I supposed to keep bringing you in the building? Moole knows you! Dang, I hadn't thought of that--the security tapes…what if he looks at them?"

"I'm sure Phillip Moole has better things to do than look at security tapes."

"Yeah, but still you don't need to be seen in the building. He works late, too."

"Good point. You'll have to get back in his office. I want to know when my stocks were issued."

"Yas, I'm not a burglar--"

"Well, neither am I."

"The heck you're not. You even have burglar's tools!"

"It was a Swiss Army knife and a can of mace--and a Phillips screwdriver, for Christ's sake!"

"Whoa! Not so fast, I need to think about this."

"THINK? All we know about this plan--is that we are pawns in it. We have a chance to improve our positions--and you have to THINK. What kind of man are you?"

The uneasy quiet of the ride back to Wilmington was made more enjoyable by the rolling countryside of the Piedmont. Yasnaya's accusatory statement kept jabbing against Tim's manhood until he could take it no more. As soon as they passed over I-95 and were back in the familiar flatlands of the coastal plain Tim broke the silence.

"You were right…I know we have to go back to Moole's office--"

"Well, duh."

"Yas, being bold, that comes easy for you. But I'm not like you. All my life I've had to carry the banner for a family that never had a college graduate. Choices were always easy for me. Right was right, and wrong? That's something I never considered, not because I was a saint or anything like that. I never had to work while I was in school, my parents saw to that. But I saw what they went through to give me a better life. My father worked in a textile mill and my mother worked at a bank. Overtime for them wasn't an inconvenience; it was an opportunity for them to give me more. When I graduated from law school, a local one by the way, you would have thought I'd been elected President. My mother must have at least a thousand pictures from that day."

"Tim, I'm sorry I yelled--"

"I know, and I know I'm talking too much, but let me get this out."

"OK."

"I've never stood up against anyone...that's one of the reasons I work for the Crown. Heck, that's probably why I'm divorced...or married at all, to be honest. Last night, when we broke into Moole's office, I almost ran out on you."

"Why didn't you?"

"Because you were putting yourself on the line for me and no one has ever done that, except my parents. You said destroying me wasn't part of the plan, and you made a choice to do wrong, because it was right. I thought about that before I went to sleep. I had more time to think about it today. It's time for me to stand up like you did."

"Well...oh, boy...."

"Are you crying?"

"Well, yeah..."

"Why?"

"Why? Because that's the first time a man has noticed me...admired me...for something other than my body. Geez, I can't stop cry--"

"Stop!"

"I'm trying to stop--"

"No, not crying.... Stop the car, now. There's a Farmers and Maritime Bank."

"What?"

"I owe you a drinks and dinner. Pull into the drive-up. I want to cash this check."

The plate glass window of the drive-thru was obscured by the reflection of trees surrounding the small white building. Not until the chrome speaker in the window crackled with static could they see the heavyset woman inside as she leaned against the roll-out drawer.

"May I help you?"

"Yes ma'am, you may. I'd like to cash this check."

The teller looked at the $50,000 check, then pressed the talk button. "I'm sorry, sir, we don't have those kinds of funds."

Those kinds of funds...how sweet it is!

"OK, give me $5000 in cash, the rest in a certified check to Tim Ridell-- here's my license."

"One moment, Sir."

"So what are you going to do with all that money?" Yas asked.
Again Tim Ridell turned into a kid before her eyes; she could see him as an eight-year old making out his list for Santa at the family's Formica kitchen table.

"I don't know...I mean it's been so long since I've had money to spend, I haven't thought about it...well, other than just now, I mean."

"Well, don't you think it's about time you did?"

"Dinner first, I know that. Then an engine for my car...my trailer...I'll pay that off, and the rest for a good lawyer. I want to see my son."

"Why don't you spend some on yourself? Just a little? I mean, there must be something you want?"

"You're right!" Tim beamed like the last kid standing at a spelling contest. "I want some new socks."

"Socks?"

"Yeah.... Well, this is kind of embarrassing to admit, but all my socks have holes in them. Do you know how uncomfortable it is to walk on socks with holes--here she comes."

"Sir."

"I forgot to tell you, I'm sorry. I want the money in large bills--wait, maybe a couple of hundred in small--"

"Sir, I'm sorry but, I can't cash this check."

"It's good. It's drawn on the Crown Kincaid Development Company; they own stock in this bank. It's good. I know it is."

"Sir, it has nothing to do with available funds; a stop payment was put on the check almost four years ago. That's what took so long, I'm sorry."

Suddenly the alchemy process had come to a screeching halt; the paper check would not be turned into gold and the crushing news came as no surprise to the bearer of the now worthless note.

"That's OK...it's OK, really... thank you." Tim Ridell slipped down in the seat to avoid the teller and Yasnaya.

"Tim, I'm so sorry."

"Just take me home... Please, I need to be alone."

Chapter 12

Wyatt Kincaid grabbed the accommodation ladder attached to the hull of the *Baltic Queen* and lifted himself from the raft. Warm Caribbean water washed over the platform and floated him up the steps and under the raft being hoisted back onto the ship. Swim for shore, why not? He was a strong swimmer and a floater…only a few more hours to daylight, someone would spot him.

A voice from above interrupted his thoughts.

"Go ahead, comrade. Try it. Swim. Maybe you will make it around the sharks." Captain Yuri Kozlov laughed, and then said, "But I think not."

"You the man in charge?" Wyatt yelled.

"I am."

"Well, I'm Wyatt Kincaid, and I demand to know--"

"You make no demands aboard this ship Mr. Kincaid. You take orders just like everyone else. Come aboard now." Captain Kozlov said, as he grabbed the lever on the crane securing the A-comp ladder. "Or, I decide your fate."

Wyatt stepped onto the deck and leaned down until he was eyeball to eyeball with Kozlov. "I want off this damn ship--you hear me?" Kozlov ignored the comment and, without breaking eye contact with the big American, gave an order in Russian to a pair of seamen beside him. The two grabbed Wyatt as directed.

"Git ya damn hands off me! Commie sons--"

A thin veil of water reeking of sewage seeped along Wyatt's side and woke him. Light from a dim bulb covered by a dingy glass dome illuminated the room. He sat up to survey his surroundings. Steel sheeting painted gunmetal gray formed the walls, overhead, and floor of the berth. Two bare pipes ran vertically down one wall and terminated at a stainless steel lavatory. Adjacent to the lavatory was a porcelain head supplied by a small copper line from one of the lavatory pipes. Two metal bunks, each no longer than six feet, were bolted to the back wall.

Wyatt stood and smashed into the metal overhead. "Damn, what is this, a boat for pygmies? Ahh crap!" Wyatt felt the two pop knots on his head and shuffled to the lower bunk. From the bunk he opened one of the rusty faucets. A steady drip of lukewarm water dribbled into the basin. Still seated, he cupped his hand together and filled them with water, and then sloshed the liquid on his face. Traces of red and dark brown slid down his face and splattered onto the floor. "Crap, I'm bleeding."

Mindful of the low overhead, Wyatt stooped in front of the basin. A mirror, fogged with layers of overspray, revealed the extent of his injuries. Bruises around both eyes made him look like a raccoon. Two threads of blood curved down either side of his nose and mixed with the dried blood congealed on his lips. "Sons of bitches knocked me out and let me fall like a sack of potatoes," Wyatt grunted, as he remembered the hostile reception of the boarding party.

Sounds, similar to those Yvette had made while in the galley of the *Crown Jewel,* emanated from the area outside the oval hatch door in front of the bunks. Wyatt pressed his ear against the door and heard muted sounds of two Russian voices, a man and a woman. The male voice, was that of the captain. The voice of the woman had the tone and timbre of Yvette's. "Don't tell me they captured her, too. I'll kill her--"

Before Wyatt could finish, the center bolt of his door spun in a counterclockwise direction. The Captain stepped inside the berth and leveled a Tokarev pistol at Wyatt's chest. "Sit," Kozlov said as he motioned toward the bunk. "I've brought you some food. You eat, Mr. Kincaid, while I explain the rules."

Wyatt grabbed the bowl offered by Kozlov and sat on the bunk. Kozlov rested one foot on the head and propped his firearm on his knee. "Borscht. Try it," Kozlov said. Wyatt spooned a mouthful of the liquid into his mouth, winced, and then swallowed.

"Good, eh?" Kozlov asked.

"Hell no! Tastes like someone pissed in a bowl of beets. That woman out there…her voice reminds me of someone. Her name ain't Yvette, is it?"

Kozlov drew small circles in the air with the barrel of the gun. "Let me get the rules out of the way first, Mr. Kincaid. First rule, you don't ask questions. Second rule, I, and only I, give the orders on this ship."

"I don't take orders from kidnappers, you son--"

"Kidnapper? We haven't kidnapped you, Mr. Kincaid. You are our guest."

"In that case, I 'ppreciate your hospitality. Now put me ashore."

"That sounds like an order to me, Mr. Kincaid." Kozlov raised the pistol and slammed it into Wyatt's face. "Never forget rule number two again, do you understand?"

Wyatt slumped on the bunk and spilled the borscht. "You son of a bitch, you said I was your guest. Hell of a way to treat a guest."

"You are our guest, Mr. Kincaid, but when you don't act like one--" Kozlov raised the pistol again. "I think you get the message. Don't you, Mr. Kincaid?"

"Yeah, I get the hell beat out of me, right?"

"Exactly." Kozlov backed to the door. "Too bad about breakfast," Kozlov said, as he looked at the spilled soup on the floor. "Perhaps you will be more careful with your lunch."

"Wait--please."

"Please? I like that, Mr. Kincaid. You are starting to sound more like a guest."

"You said I was a guest--how long will I be a guest?"

"Is that a question, Mr. Kincaid?" Kozlov stepped toward Kincaid and raised the pistol. "Must I remind you of rule number one?"

"No--sir, I--"

"*Sir.* Very nice, Mr. Kincaid. Since you seem to be behaving better I will forget your breach of rule number one. I will even answer your question."

"Thank you...sir."

"We have been hired to--shall we say...*entertain* you for a period of time. I will be notified when your stay with us is over."

"But, who hired--"

"Careful, Mr. Kincaid...rule number one, remember."

"Yes, sir. Sorry Captain."

"Very good! Mr. Kincaid, very good indeed."

Wyatt spent the remainder of the morning searching his accommodations, a place he now called *the cell from hell.* The first search, a general one, had yielded only one find of any significance. On the narrow wall at the foot of the bunks was a porthole painted in the same gray theme that apparently ran throughout the ship. A stub of metal protruding from the bottom of the porthole was all that remained of the locking latch.

Later in the day he conducted a more intense search. Like a building inspector, Wyatt checked for seams, cracks, or gaps within the cell that could be pried open, but found none. Certain that a rusting bucket like the *Baltic Queen* could not be that solid, Wyatt began to check the rivets and bolts. A small circular metal plate, about the size of the porthole, was situated approximately a foot from the top of the hatch. Six bolts, roughly 5/8 inch in diameter, held the plate to the hatch. One bolt was loose enough to unscrew by hand.

The bolt hole provided a laser-view of the adjoining cabin, and, as Wyatt had suspected, the space was the ship's galley. Standing next to a crudely fashioned metal stove was a tall, disheveled woman. Streaks of gray highlighted a shock of raven black hair twisted into a bun and pinched at the top by a bone-colored clip. Feathered wisps, too short to reach the clip, flittered along the sides of her pale neck. A smock hung lopsided on her shoulders, added to her frowzy haute couture. Protruding from the uneven hemline was a pair of equally pale, but shapely legs. "What the hell?" Wyatt pressed his eye closer to the bolt-hole to get a better look at her footwear.

"Well, I be damned, if that don't beat all," Wyatt said as he viewed her yellow, bunny rabbit slippers.

"Kofi--,syka!" [Coffee--,bitch]

Startled by the gruff voice, the woman turned to face a young sailor, glared at him, then reached for a coffeepot hanging on the rack above the stove. Her actions caused the dress to rise and expose the cup of her buttocks. Eager to see more, the young sailor squatted and craned his neck upward. With one hand on the grab rail the sailor leaned over and smacked the exposed cheek.

Baestad!" [Bastard] the woman shouted as she swung the coffeepot at the miscreant. Satisfied with his cheap thrill, the sailor retreated laughing to the top deck.

Wyatt watched as the woman filled the strainer with grounds of coffee broken from an ebony brick. Before filling the pot with water the woman looked around, then placed the pot under her dress and drained her bladder.

"No coffee for me," Wyatt mumbled from behind the steel wall.

Svetlana Andreevich drew little satisfaction from her disgusting act of culinary sabotage. As a distant descendant of Prince Aleksandr Andreevich Bezborodko, such a petty act of revenge was beneath her. In the days of Catherine the Great, no one would have dared to insult a member of the Andreevich family. And if they had, lead or steel, not urine, would have been the choices for weapons of vengeance.

Not that Svetlana Andreevich could personally remember the heady days of history. Woeful stories of her vanquished ancestors, told by her father in their two -room, cold water flat, somehow lessened the misery of their own existence. And though she lived the suffering vicariously, Svetlana Andreevich hated the host of Bolsheviks and Communists who had diluted the power of her once proud family. Such a pity she thought, that a descendant of royalty should be forced to use peasant tactics to avenge her honor.

Imperial Russia had ended with the deaths of Nicholas II and Alexandra Romanov and their five children. But even the Bolsheviks and their successors, the Communists, had seen the value of the beauty and culture of the White Russians. Many of the Imperialists had fled Russia, but for those left behind choices were few. Men once entrusted with great power were executed or forced into prison. Many of the royal women had suffered the same fate, but others had gained favor by exploiting their refined sexuality. Like rare jewels of the monarchy, Leninist fanatics hoarded White Russian women in secrecy. Then Lenin himself realized the waste of such a valuable natural resource. Peasant women could not hold court or gain the attention and favor of foreign dignitaries. Many noblewomen, including

Svetlana's grandmother, were summoned from the prisons and offered jobs as hostesses or as trainers of peasant women for the task, and those who refused had been shot.

When faced with the unsavory choice of her ancestors, Svetlana had not rebelled or embraced her father's code of honor. She, like her mother and grandmother before her, to her everlasting shame, had offered her virginal blossom to the state rather than face death.

Thirty years had elapsed since the nineteen-year-old beauty had been shipped off to Washington for duty at the Russia Consulate. The early 70's were tumultuous times for the United States, especially in Washington. Encouraged by the party to participate in the chaos and anti government demonstrations, Svetlana had tasted, for the first time, the power of the people. When the American President, Nixon, had resigned, hope sprang in her heart that the Kremlin could change, too. And so, as the snow that reminded her of Moscow melted and the cherry blossoms hailed the arrival of spring, Svetlana's thoughts turned to love. Against the warnings of her handler, and her hopes that the harsh rule of the USSR would soften, Svetlana began an affair with an older American. Retribution had been swift, so instead of imported Beluga caviar, champagne, and posh hotels, she had been deported to Siberia, where a meal of potatoes and beef fat was a delicacy. But none of the deprivations of prison compared to the sacrifice of her heart and soul. She was sure the loss was final, but then thirty years later, the letter had come with the promise of a reunion, and she had booked passage on the *Baltic Queen*--servitude class.

Captain Yuri Kozlov brushed past Svetlana and grabbed the steaming pot of coffee, poured himself a cup and took a long sip. "Ah...your cooking leaves much to be desired, but your coffee." Kozlov smacked his lips in a rapid-fire motion. "Wonderful, wonderful."

"Thank you, Captain. I'm glad you like it," Svetlana said without a hint of a smile.

"Svetlana, prepare another cup for our guest."

"We have a guest?"

"Yes, he's in the quarters behind--"

"And is he a *guest* like me?"

Kozlov spread his hand across the swollen face of Svetlana Andreevich.

"Questions, eh?...Have you forgotten rule number one so soon?"

"No captain...please," Svetlana mumbled as she cringed against the wall.

"So you haven't forgotten. Very good, very good. Now, prepare the coffee and follow me." Svetlana poured the coffee and followed Kozlov into Wyatt's quarters.

Wyatt stepped away from his peephole and stuck the bolt in his pocket.

"See what our guest thinks of your cooking, Svetlana." Kozlov said as he pointed to the remnants of Wyatt's morning meal. "Coffee. Much better than her borscht, I promise you, comrade."

Wyatt took the cup of coffee from Svetlana and nodded. Kozlov turned to Svetlana and said, "You may go now."

"Nice looking lady." Wyatt said, as he smelled the coffee he had no intentions of drinking. Intrigued by a familiar aroma rising from the cup, Wyatt sniffed the liquid again. Memories of his signature postprandial drink aboard the *Crown Jewel* flooded his thoughts. Wyatt had mused in those days that it must have been the Kahlua, that accounted for the odd smell of the coffee. No…the acrid scent in this coffee was the same smell of his drink. It hadn't been Kahlua at all! "Yvette--Bitch!"

Kozlov gave Wyatt a puzzled looked. "Bitch…do you mean Svetlana?"

"Who?"

"Our cook, Svetlana. You said 'Yvette--bitch--'"

"Oh, I was thinking of a dog I once knew…Yvette. Not your cook. She is a nice-looking lady. Sorry." Wyatt said, as he set his cup on the lavatory.

"You may be right on both counts, Mr. Kincaid. Svetlana is a bitch…and yes, for her age, nice looking."

"Yeah, I bet she was a smoker in her day."

"It has been said that, in her day, she was one of the most beautiful women in all of Russia. Pity to waste such beauty in Siberia." Kozlov sneered as he remembered the file on Svetlana Andreevich. "But those were the days before Russia became a great democracy."

"Yeah well, seems like y'all are voting over there. Now maybe you can work on human rights--"

"Careful, Mr. Kincaid--"

"Not a question or a directive, Captain--just a comment."

"You would do well to keep your comments to yourself, comrade," Kozlov said as he patted the Tokarev. "Besides, I have decided to give you a job. There is an old saying in Russia, 'Tired men don't talk.' It is one of my favorite sayings."

Wyatt thought of his beatings and the swollen face of the cook, Svetlana. "Well, we got an old saying in America, seems like it might suit you better."

"What it this old saying, Mr. Kincaid?"

"If I want any crap out of you, I'll beat it out of you."

Kozlov's face turned as red as the beets in the soup. "Rest today, comrade. Tomorrow I will work you hard, then maybe your tongue will wag more…productively." Kozlov slammed the hatch and spun the handle.

Wyatt watched Kozlov through his peephole until he disappeared, then scanned the space for the cook. The galley was empty. Alone, he lunged against the hatch--solid. Quickly he ran his hands over the remaining bolts of the peephole cover checking for loose bolts. One bolt gave a quarter of a turn and then stopped. Wyatt pulled off his *Slice of Life* tee shirt and twisted the hem of the garment around the bolt and ratcheted the bolt a half turn more before the cloth ripped. "Son of a bitch!" Wyatt screamed as his knuckles scraped against the center bolt in the door peeling back flesh.

"I gotta get out of here." But where would he go, and where the hell was he? With his good hand Wyatt retrieved the bolt from his pocket, and turned his attention to the porthole. Using one side of the hex-head bolt he began to scrape away at the paint. Within fifteen minutes he had cleared a three-inch square of glass. The ocean was calm except for swirling catpaws moving westerly with the prevailing wind. Wyatt scanned the sky and saw the early afternoon sun in the western sky, confirming his notion that the ship was on a northerly course. Good…nothing to the north but the USA and Canada. Wyatt tapped the thick glass with the bolt--no use. Even if he could break the glass, he was too large to fit through the hole. But maybe he could use the mirror to signal a ship or a pleasure boat. Had to be someone out there--had to be. Wyatt peered across the vast ocean-- "Nothing, not a damn thing but water. Son of a bitch," Wyatt moaned.

Chapter 13

Fyodor's fears were unfounded. Boris Yantikov did remember Mom, but this mom looked nothing like the one who had given him life. The chasm between Mom and mom was more than deep and wide.

Liliya Yantikov, mother of Boris and Fyodor, looked like the p*easant woman* in Van Gogh's painting with the same name. Though Liliya had tried hard to fit into Western society for the sake of her children, and especially for her grandchildren, few people in her new homeland viewed her as anything but a relic of Stalinist Russia. Despite her drab outer appearance, the inner soul of Liliya Yantikov glowed with the brilliance of Saint Peter's halo. While most in Russia, during the Soviet era had apostatized against the Russian Orthodox Church, Liliya had held fast to her faith. In America, lauded for its religion freedom, the path to salvation would be easier, or so she had thought. But America, the nation most blessed by God, had proven to be a hostile land for the pious Liliya Yantikov.

God, it seemed, was not welcomed as much as He was tolerated. School prayer was forbidden, and even the Ten Commandments found a hostile reception in government buildings. Separation of church and state coupled with free speech had provided the ACLU with enough firepower to blast God's word to the basement and elevate pornography to the narthex of public art museums. Flummoxed by such policies, Liliya Yantikov held on to the old ways and prayed fervently every night that her extended family would one day see the light. So far they were unanswered prayers.

Mahts Al'abinochka, now known as Matb "Mom" White, came from the same village as Liliya, but had not been conflicted by the looser values of his adoptive country. Like a greedy sponge, Mom had soaked up everything Western. Resplendent with tattoos and body piercing, he looked more like the new All-American Male than those who had a legitimate claim on the look. While others had chosen the Punk Funk look in order to stand out, he had chosen the style to blend in. Born an albino, Mom was thankful for the fad that had made his orange-blonde hair and pink eyes chic. Some in his group had even copied his outlandish look by utilizing pink contact lens and bottles of Sunset Orange hair dye #133.

Determined to separate himself from his Eastern European background, *Matz Al'abinochka*, shortened his surname yet still retained his heritage. Dropping the last four letters only served to remind him in English of his affliction, so Albino was changed to White. Mom, his unusual nickname, had come from his fellow immigrant classmates. Mahts, which closely resembled *Matbh*, the Russian word for mother, became Mom and to Al'binochka's everlasting dismay, the name stuck.

Double-cursed with a sissy nickname and a complexion from hell, Mom was not a pleasant man, and being reminded of either only made him nastier. Boris, fascinated by the anomaly before him and oblivious to the consequences of commenting, unwisely pushed both buttons. "Mom, your eyes...they look just like pig eyes."

Mom put on his shades and grabbed a switchblade knife from his drawer, snapped the blade and parked it inside Boris's nostril. "Pig nose. That's what you will have if you say one more word," Mom said, as he snuggled the blade against the blood-rich snout of his antagonist. Boris's eyes watered as the blade drew blood. "Comrade, I was only loud thinking, please--"

"Think to yourself, and thank God you are the brother of Fyodor Yantikov, fool."

"Yes, thank God for Fyodor," Boris said, as he lifted his nose from the knife. "Nice blonde hair, you have though--"

"Shut up, Boris," Mom said as he reached in his drawer for a thick manila envelope. "This is for Fyodor. Tell him he gets the rest when he makes delivery, understand?"

Boris felt the envelope. "Money?"

Mom stabbed the switchblade between Boris's first two fingers, spread on his desk. "Do not open that, or your next job will be rooting for truffles in France, I swear."

Boris sat down and stuffed the envelope in his shirt. "That was funny. The pigs find the truffles with their noses...good one, comrade--"

"Shut up or that will be your last laugh. Now, do you know how to find New Bern?"

"New Bern, why would I find this New Bern?"

"Because that's where you will meet Fyodor, idiot!"

Boris stared at Mom. Oh, for the good old days in Siberia. No one had ever called him an idiot in Siberia. Except for that woman Svetlana. She had called him a fool, and she had not paid the price. But fate had given him one more chance to extract justice from the snooty White Russian, and she would pay dearly for her arrogance. The pig-eyed albino across the table would pay. One day they would *all* pay, when Boris had the billions from the *Last Kincaid Plan*. "New Bern...is that in Switzerland?"

Directions to New Bern, North Carolina were less familiar to Boris than directions to Siberia. Though separated by the vast Atlantic Ocean, Berne and New Bern shared commonalties when past and present were considered. Both were, or had been, capital cities, but there the similarities ended. Berne had maintained its capital city status and evolved into a major European city. New Bern, once the capital of colonial North Carolina had long ago relinquished its title and taken on the less-storied moniker of county seat. Geographic and cultural comparisons further separated the like-named entities. Berne, located in the foothills of the Alps and divided by the Wohlensee River was a chiefly Nordic city. New Bern, situated on the iron-flat coastal plain of North Carolina at the confluence of the Neuse and Trent Rivers, was originally inhabited by a diverse mixture of English, Scotch-Irish, and African Americans.

Boris Yantikov had no interest in the history or cultural differences between Berne and New Bern except for one obscure footnote about his favorite non-alcoholic beverage. Pepsi, the soft drink giant, was born in New Bern. Unlike its competitor, Coca-Cola, who had established corporate headquarters in Atlanta, its place of origin. Pepsi, feeling a little tony after a little national recognition, hightailed it out of rural New Bern and established corporate offices in New York.

The move had undoubtedly kept the town from becoming a corporate enclave and left it to continue as a sleepy village supported mainly by timber and tourism.

In spite of the misfortune brought on by the Pepsi abandonment, New Bern had crated its natural beauty and navigable waters into a welcome mat for seafaring travelers from around the world. German, Dutch, and even French conversations were not uncommon in the local cafes. Even the almost-pigged nose Boris Yantikov was impressed with the continental flair of the place he had first viewed as a world-class backwater.

Boris discovered interesting historical tidbits about New Bern by accident. Fyodor, on the other hand, learned of the town's history through intense research. The international press release mentioning the discovery of the pirate ship *Queen Anne's Revenge*, flagship of the buccaneer Edward Teach, better known as Blackbeard, caused Fyodor to scrutinize the Crystal Coast. The intracoastal shoreline of North Carolina, excluding the populated outer banks and coastal barrier islands, was still sparsely populated. A perfect situation, thought Fyodor, for a modern-day smuggler tired of doing battle with the heavily patrolled coast of South Florida. One look at a local map and Fyodor had seen what Blackbeard had seen hundreds of coves and inlets that could serve as hideaways. Millions of wooded acres owned by large timber companies and the military lined the rivers for mile after desolate mile, insuring that the area would not be developed any time soon. One flight over the area in a small plane and Fyodor had seen his future.

From the window of the commuter flight that served the Craven County Regional Airport, Fyodor surveyed his forest of dreams and smiled. Eager for the money Boris carried and to hear the latest con from his older brother, Fyodor sprinted from the terminal and grabbed the first available cab.

"Hurry! That damn bridge will open soon."

Cab driver Taylor Averette ignored Fyodor's comment and timed the stop perfectly. He turned to engage his passenger as the bridge opened. "How long y'all down--"

"I told you to hurry...damn bridge."

"Ten minutes, tops. Keep your shirt on, pal." Damn, blew my cover, Averette thought as his New York accent echoed through the cab. "Sorry, sir, *suh*-- but it won' be long." Special Agent Taylor Averette, assigned to Homeland Security, had jumped at the chance for a Southern duty station when he volunteered for his latest assignment although he had envisioned a *Miami Vice* lifestyle in South Beach with its throngs (and thongs) of beautiful women. Instead, he had drawn Eastern North Carolina and the role of a grungy Southern cab driver. James Tidwell had landed the juicy Miami plum and an assignment on a luxury yacht. A suave New York sophisticate in a backwater town and a country boy in the big city, how stupid was that? The mix-up in assignments was typical of the agency Tidwell spoke flawless grits and ham hocks and he spoke fluent upper crust--go figure. But here he was, "Smack dab in the middle of the nowhere" as the locals said. Remembering the colloquialism, Averette engaged his passenger again. "Y'all ain't from around here, are you?"

"Hardly," an agitated Fyodor Yantikov snapped from the back seat. "Haven't you noticed--I move at normal speed."

Happy with his recovery, Taylor Averette again engaged his passenger with his best Southern speak, "Yeah, folks 'round here move 'bout as fast as molasses on a cold day. Got business here, do you?"

"Yes.... Mine."

Averette took the hint and spoke no more to Fyodor Yantikov until they reached the Sheraton Hotel. "Want me to carry your bag for you?"

Fyodor Yantikov clutched the valise. "No, but pick me up in one hour."

Averette nodded and headed for the bathroom. Once inside he snatched off his fake beard and doo-rag, then reversed his windbreaker and tailed Fyodor Yantikov into the hotel restaurant.

Boris stood and greeted his brother. "Fyodor, how are you?"

"John Smith.... Understand?"

"Da, da, but it's just us--ah--" Boris averted his eyes from Fyodor's cold stare, then complied with his wishes. "John, how do you like the table? Quite a view, eh?"

"Boats and water. I see it every day, Boris. Did you bring my gift?"

Boris, peeved by his brother's lack of appreciation for his claiming a table with a view, lit into Fyodor's soft underside. "Da, I brought your gift, but did you get your own mother a gift for her birthday? No. And did you even bother to call her? Such a fine son you are--"

"Boris, I did bring her a gift." Fyodor Yantikov reached into his valise and removed a small package. "How is she?"

"Why should you care? Go see for yourself."

How could his brother be so stupid? Why would John Smith visit with Fyodor Yantikov's mother? And if he did why wouldn't the police be waiting for him? But one day, a big hit would come his way, and he could move to Argentina. For years, criminals had flocked to Argentina where a few well-placed bribes would guarantee anonymity in one of the few countries on earth that had no extradition treaty with the United States.

Over eighty now, and in failing health, his mother probably wouldn't make it to the reunion in South America. Acknowledging that his mother's time was short only put more pressure on finding the big hit. Life would mean nothing if his mother died before they could reconcile. Even so, he had tried to be a good son by sending her money. She had always returned it. *Devil's money*, she called it.

And so on his last visit Fyodor had given $25,000--money too dirty for his mother-- to the priest. The priest had not rejected it, though he was well aware of Fyodor's reputation. Instead, the holy man had blessed the giver of the Devil's money with the same ardor reserved for respected members of the church who donated. But then Fyodor made the mistake that had separated him from his mother. "Father, I give you this money in the name of Liliya Yantikov." Why he did such a thing was no secret. Hadn't he heard the snickers and taunts made toward his dear mother when he was a child? Didn't he want to let them all know that Liliya Yantikov was a queen, not a peasant?

No good deed goes unpunished, and so it had been with his grand gesture. Liliya Yantikov, in front of the whole congregation, had slapped his face and disowned him. The thought sent a pain through the cold heart of Fyodor Yantikov and he reached for the hand of the only family member he had seen in five years. "Boris, I love you, and I love my mother and my sister--" Moisture welled in the eyes of the Devil, Fyodor Yantikov, and he kissed his brother's hand, the same hand that had probably touched his sweet mother this very day. "One day, when I make enough money, we will be together again. I promise you that."

Boris looked at his younger brother and for the first time realized how lonely he must be. Then with a grin on his face he pulled Ganna Mae's day planner from his own valise.

"That day may be sooner than you think, my brother.... Read this."

As Fyodor read the *Last Kincaid* plan, Boris Yantikov thought of the promise his brother had made. A reunion...the family together again...his mother, brother, and sister, just like the old days. Thoughts of his sister, as always, made him think of his brother-in-law, Michael Fitzpatrick. "This day--when we are all together...no Irish Mick, nyet?"

"Boris, I don't like him either, but he is the father of Katarina's children."

"I will be the father...Russian tradition--"

"Only if the father is dead--"

"I will kill the Mick--then I will be the father."

Fyodor Yantikov, deep into the *Last Kincaid* plan, ignored his brother's ranting. Boris, lucky Boris, had found the score that could provide that reunion--and so much more, if they could pull it off. "I know this person." Fyodor said as he tapped the pages of the day planner.

"You know Svetlana Andreevich? How?" Boris asked, as his eyebrows crowded the bridge of his nose.

"No, but I know this one." Fyodor said as he pointed to the names of Phillip Moole and Ganna Mae.

"Ah, the old woman, I know her, too. We should kill her, Fyodor--Canadian--"

"No this man--Phillip Moole." Fyodor Yantikov ran his fingers over another name on the page then tapped it as before. "And this one, Wyatt Kincaid--ah!"

"What is it, brother?"

"Wyatt Kincaid, he is the big fish. I had him and let him go."

From the corner of his eye, Fyodor noticed a man behind a potted plant lean in their direction. "Such a lovely view," Fyodor said as he pointed toward the boats in the marina. "Come on, old chap, let's walk on the dock."

Boris had not noticed the man at the table behind the plant. He did question his brother's sudden interest in the scenery he had dismissed earlier, but said nothing and followed Fyodor to the docks. Neither man spoke as they walked the narrow wooden pier crowded with boats on either side. At the end of the pier, a good thirty feet from the nearest occupied berth, Fyodor sat on the dock and dangled his feet over the water. "Join me, brother. I want to discuss this," Fyodor said as he flashed the day planner at Boris.

"Worth much money, eh...John?"

"You can call me Fyodor here." Fyodor gave a quick look around the dock. "No one will hear us."

Boris, in an attempt to impress his brother, doubled-checked the dock, then sat down beside his brother. "Is clear, I checked." Though Boris was eight years older than his brother, he had always sought Fyodor's approval and respect. To show more concern for their privacy, Boris lowered his head and scanned the waters beneath the dock.

"Boris, what are you doing?"

"Checking for people...good idea, eh?"

Fyodor shook his head, and discarded his thought of insulting his brother. No need to remind Boris of his room-temperature IQ. Besides, loyalty was more valuable than brains and Boris would always be loyal. "Yes, good thinking. I must be slipping."

Beaming from the unexpected compliment, Boris patted his brother on his back. "Don't worry, Fyodor, I will always be there when you are slipping."

"Boris, this woman Svetlana, how do you know her?"

"Syka!"

"English, Boris, always speak English, until it is perfect. That is the language of money, understand?"

"Da, da...English."

"This woman, tell me about her."

"It was a long time ago, when I was a guard in Siberia. Oh, I miss the motherland like I miss my heart."

Fyodor Yantikov shook his head again. Only his brother could miss the gloom and cold of Siberia. "The woman, Boris--just tell me of the woman."

"She came to the prison--ah, you should have seen her, Fyodor." Boris mapped the curvaceous figure of a woman with his out-stretched hands. "And her face, like an angel--but she was a cold princess, as the Americans say--"

"Ice Princess--ice, not cold," Fyodor admonished.

"Is not ice cold?"

"OK, Boris, have it your way--cold princess, go on."

"She came to the prison and the nights get cold in Siberia." Boris jabbed Fyodor in the ribs. "A woman like this could--"

"I understand, finish."

"The guards...we all wanted her, but she would have nothing to do with us. I slipped her beef fat and sometimes even Vodka--for a favor." Boris circled finger and thumb on one hand and poked it with his finger. "But she would not do the favor. She told me 'not for all the riches of Russia, or even the return of her lost treasure would she do--" he gestured again.

"Da, da." Fyodor shouted, ignoring Boris's crude hand symbols. Remembering the pieces of the plan he did not know Fyodor soften his voice and started over.

"What was this treasure she lost, Boris?"

"I don't know, Fyodor, you know how the White Russians are, always crying about the jewels and palaces taken by the party. All of them have lost jewels and palaces--ha, if we could find all that they have lost Russia would not be big enough to hold their treasures--the liars."

"Boris--"

"Da, da, I finish." Finally the center of his brother's attention, Boris paused to enjoy the moment before continuing his story. "Coats...coats in Siberia are worth more than jewels, so I use all my savings to buy Svetlana a nice fur coat--Russian fur, the best. When she came in from the mine, she was wet and so cold. I gave her the coat. She pulled off her clothes and wrapped the coat around her. A gift for a gift, eh? That's what I thought, so I grab her beautiful breasts and squeeze--like an orange. Mother's milk, I swear, mother's milk came from them. I tried to suckle, but she slapped me and called me a fool--Syka."

"Mother's milk, are you sure?"

"Yes, the pregnant women in the prison always had one teat for the *pebyonok* [baby] and one for themselves. If the pebyonok died they would sell the milk--ah, Fyodor, nothing like milk from a warm breast." Boris smacked his lips.

"This woman, she had a child with her?"

"No, and her shape was not that of a mother." Boris made the gesture for a well-stacked woman with his hands. "No mother fat."

"Maybe her baby died?"

"No. In the prison, the mothers would not kill the babies, but they prayed for them to die--for the milk money. And when they die, the mothers would wail and carry on--such a lie. But Svetlana was not like that, and she never spoke of a child."

"Uh-huh. I think I know what this treasure was, and maybe who," Fyodor said as he tapped the day planner. "Now, the old woman. You said she came from Canada. Are you sure?"

"I think so."

"No, Boris, do not tell me what you think--only what you know for sure."

Boris closed his eyes and tried to remember his ride with Ganna Mae. This was important, and another chance to impress his brother. "I can tell you for sure where she did not come from. She told me this from her own mouth."

"Where?"

"From turnip truck."

"Turnip truck?"

"Da, Fyodor, she said, 'I did not just come from turnip truck'. Then she wanted to kick my balls in my throat--"

So did Fyodor Yantikov. At least with his balls in his throat, Boris would have a hard time making a fool of himself.

Taylor Averette looked in disgust at the two men on the end of the dock. Too risky to try and get within earshot. Nothing to do now but make his report while the details were still fresh in his mind. With no more need for cover, Averette rose from the table obscured by the potted plant and returned to his cab. As he dialed the agency's Miami office he adjusted his fake beard.

"Operations. How may I direct your call?"

"Agent James Tidwell, and if he's not in, I'll take his voice mail." Averette listened to the voice mail instructions, and then followed them. "Jim, Taylor Averette. We had quite a touching reunion here. Smith is definitely Fyodor Yantikov, but I'll have forensics check the back seat of the cab just to make sure. I also have more names for your file--Svetlana Andreevich, probably a Russia National, and a Phillip Mule--or Phillip the mule...he could be a carrier. Then there is an elderly lady, possibly a Canadian citizen. I didn't get her name, but she could be in danger because Boris Yantikov made a threat against her life. Sorry to bring this up, but looks like you've screwed up...again. Your friend, Wyatt Kincaid, isn't in any danger. He's the Kingpin. Whatever is going on down there--Kincaid is in it up to his eyeballs. Call me."

Chapter 14

Sounds of marital discord from neighboring lot 148 roused Tim Ridell from his alcohol-induced slumber. Separated by a mere ten feet, family secrets from the adjoining units at Treadwell's Mobile Home Park would soon become common knowledge of any resident who cared to listen. And the secrets of lot 148 were loud and chronic. Both parties involved in today's argument were presenting their cases with the fervor of two Philadelphia lawyers. "Don't tell me that's not purple lipstick…and I know where it came from, you bastard!"

"Woman, you're crazy, it's from a grease pencil, I swear."

"Grease pencil? You expect me to believe you marked your pecker with a grease pencil?"

"Yeah, it was in my pocket at work…must have rubbed off on me."

Thuds from an angry search bounced off the thin walls of lot 148 and reverberated on the paneling of Tim Ridell's 10 X 14 bedroom.

"These pants? Not a mark on 'em, and look at this blonde hair in the zipper, 'at rub off on you at work, too?"

"You keep talking, bitch, and I'll put something on you that won't rub off."

"Go ahead, hit me, big man! I dare you!"

Tim Ridell covered his head with his pillow. The scene at lot 148 was about to escalate, as it always did, from words to violence. Lisa Cox, the woman of the house over there, had been a pretty girl in high school, more than pretty, really. Her exotic blend of Cherokee Indian and Scandinavian ancestry had produced a raven-haired beauty with ice-cold blue eyes and high chiseled cheekbones, a rare combination in Eastern North Carolina. So rare, and so desirable that the usually shy Tim Ridell had asked the head cheerleader of Uniondale High School to the senior prom. Her reply was more a lesson in life than a rejection, and for that reason, Tim Ridell never had forgotten Lisa Stratton.

A chance meeting at the park's community mailboxes and a hackneyed question had initiated the twentieth-year reunion of the two Uniondale High alumni.

"You don't remember me, do you?" she asked him. Tim Ridell flinched inwardly at the overused icebreaker, especially since he felt no hint of familiarity about her. One look at the woman and Tim had relaxed with good reason. Nothing about this woman was even vaguely familiar. "I'm afraid you have me confused with someone else. I'm certain we've never me."

"You're Tim Ridell, the lawyer, right?"

"Yes, but I--"

"I'm Lisa Cox--Lisa Stratton." Without answering Tim Ridell studied the woman standing beside him. Bloodshot blue eyes surrounded by dark circles separated by a flat, off-kilter-nose stared back at him. "Stratton," Tim whispered and then aloud, "Yes, you're Mrs. Stratton. I'm sorry I didn't recognize you. How is your daughter—wasn't her name Lisa, too?"

Tears welled up in the woman's eyes, and Tim Ridell realized his mistake. This poor creature standing in front of him was the once strikingly beautiful Lisa Stratton, not her mother. Not until several weeks at the mobile home park did he realize why her looks had changed so drastically.

"You dare me?" Charles Cox's voice slammed Tim back to the moment. "Just remember you asked for it, bitch." It was clear if he didn't do something right away Lisa's looks, or what was left of them, would certainly change again.

"Oooh, not my face, don't hit my face."

Tim tossed the pillow and cranked open his bedroom window. "Stop right there! Don't hit her again or I'll have you in jail before lunch."

"Say what?"

"You heard me. Don't hit her again."

"Well, how about I just come over there and hit you, asshole?"

A hot surge shot down Tim Ridell's spine as he snatched on a pair of jeans and a tee shirt. For thirty-seven years Tim Ridell's adrenal glands had always failed him, now he was teeming with the nectar of courage. Before the barrel-chested Charles Cox could make it to his trailer, Tim was waiting for him. Cox rounded the corner and tossed a lit cigarette onto the ground. "You a law man?"

"Nope."

Cox maneuvered in close to the lanky Ridell, a tactic favored by short men with even shorter reach. "Well, in that case, neighbor--I've done brung you her ass-whumping."

"You might want to think about that. I'm an officer of the court."

Cox backed off and hissed through clenched, yellow-stained teeth, "Thought you said you won't the law."

"I'm not. I'm a lawyer."

"A lawyer...living in a trailer? Hell boy, you ain't nothing but a damn liar and a nosy som-bitch!" Cox, filled with blood-red rage, ignored the fancy footwork being displayed by his adversary and lunged at Tim.

From the access road into Treadwell's Mobile Home Park, Yasnaya saw the two men maneuvering like fighting cocks, a scene she had witnessed many times between alcohol-fueled patrons in the parking lot at the Club on the Beach. With little time to plan a proper attack, Yas stepped into the slipstream of air blowing between the trailers and unleashed a short blast from her pepper spray. As the burning, choking, cloud of gas assailed her nostrils, Yas realized her tactical error. Downwind and higher ground were required components for a successful attack, and she foolishly had chosen neither.

"Why, you little bitch!" Cox growled, as he smashed his backhand into Yas's face. "Bet you won't ever try that shit again." Blood spurted from her nose and sealed the spray of gas against her skin. Panicked and disoriented, she stumbled closer to the hulking figure. Cox, like a wild beast sated only by the kill, clenched his fist for the final assault. Tim Ridell, crouched in a boxer stance, moved between Cox and Yas.

"Get out of the way, boy. I'm going teach this little bitch a lesson, then I'm going--"

Tim's left hook slammed the unfinished sentence back into Cox's throat. Before Cox could groan, Tim fired a right cross into the big man's fleshly jowls, and then quickly tattooed two body shots into his solar plexus.

Applause from the surrounding trailers erupted as Tim straddled the terror of Treadwell's Mobile Home Park

"Don't kill him, you bully!" Lisa Cox screamed as she pushed Tim away and cuddled her husband's head in her lap. "You didn't have to hit him."

Tim looked at the remnant of the once-beautiful girl he had known. Gone were the high cheekbones and aquiline nose of her mixed heritage. Now the prized features of the exotic beauty melded into a horrid mask of twisted cartilage and bruised flesh.

During a field trip in law school, Tim had met a bandaged policeman at the Dunn, N.C. Police Department. Curious about the cop's injury, he had inquired about the wound's origin. "Domestic dispute-- a wife stabbed me for clubbing her husband. Thought I should have asked him nicely not to choke her...weird, huh?" At the time, Tim had been certain there was more to the story...no one would attack their savior. Now, faced with the icy stare of Lisa Cox, he nodded to affirm the officer's response. "Yeah-- weird."

"What if he can't work? How are we going to pay our bills? Just look what you've done!" Lisa Cox screamed. Tim turned to Yas and steadied her with his arm around her waist. "Are you OK?"

"Water. I need to wash my face...burns."

"Come on, I'll get you fixed up," Tim said.

"How about my husband. Who's going to fix him--"

"Lisa," Tim said as he stood in front of the woman. "You don't have to stay in this. There are shelters for abused women--"

"He don't mean it. It's only when I make him mad--don't you see? It's my fault."

"Lisa, if he lays a hand on you, I'm going to file charges. If that doesn't work, I'm going to beat the hell out of him. You tell him that when he wakes up, and if you decide you want help, you know where I live."

Lisa Cox looked at her husband then back at Tim. She had become numb to the pain of the beatings long ago; now, even her fear of death had waned. Charles Cox would find her and kill her. Tim was wrong--there was no safe place to hide. The risk of leaving, she decided, was worth the serenity the few days or weeks without Charles would provide. She would use the time to prepare for death, and make things right with her family and her God.

"Thank you," Lisa whispered. "I want to leave--before he wakes up."

"Pack your things and come over here." Tim looked at the incapacitated man on the ground. "He'll be out for a while, but hurry."

Yasnaya moaned softly as Tim flushed cold water on her face from the kitchen faucet. "Damn, that guy packed a wallop--is my nose broken?" Tim ran his fingers down the bridge of Yas's nose. "No, I don't think so. Looks like your lips cushioned the blow...split both of them."

"Great, I have to work tonight."

"Let's put a cold compress on there. If the swelling doesn't go down you might want to call in sick."

"That bad, huh?"

"Pretty bad. Might need stitches. We can go by the emergency room after we drop Lisa off at the women's shelter--if you don't mind...I did offer--"

"That was nice of you--and where did you learn to fight like that, by the way?"

Tim Ridell ignored Yas's question and crammed ice cubes into a plastic baggie then placed it on her bruised face. "Does that feel better?"

Yas pulled the pack away from her mouth. "I want to know where you learned to fight like that."

"Lucky punch, I guess."

"Unh uh...I've seen a lot of fights at the club and I've seen lucky punches. What you did was quite a display of pugilistic skills. How--?"

"Shh....Put this back on your lips."

"Tim Ridell, are you trying to shut me up?"

"Yes."

Chapter 15

Lot 147 was abuzz with activity and Tim Ridell, despite his rusty skills, was proving to be a gracious host. Yasnaya, no longer bleeding, stood in front of the living room mirror and moved the cold compress from her nose to her lips and back. Lisa Cox, crying and confused, sat at the kitchen table clutching her cardboard suitcase covered in a frayed paisley cloth. Ten years with Charles Cox had been stuffed into a suitcase many women would have used for an overnight bag. Incredulous that even a hard life like Lisa's provided so little, Tim Ridell parted the curtain over the kitchen sink and surveyed the still motionless Charles Cox. "Lisa, get your other things. He's out cold."

"No, this is all I need. Can we just go?"

"There has to be more. How about a winter coat? It'll turn cold soon," Tim prodded.

Lisa shook her head and slowly rubbed the worn valise. "No, this is all I need. He won't miss this stuff." Tim tugged at Lisa's bag. "May I?" Reluctantly, Lisa released her grip on the bag, and allowed Yas and Tim to check the contents. Five changes of clothes and a mismatched assortment of undergarments attested to the Spartan life Lisa Cox had lived under her dominating husband. Yas, aware of a woman's need for privacy, deftly tucked the undergarments inside a cream-colored blouse and removed the bundle from the case. Five Barbie dolls, prone but lined in a military-type formation, stood sentinel over a wood framed photograph of a man and a woman Tim Ridell recognized as Mr. and Mrs. Hamp Stratton.

"What happened to the dolls?" Yas asked in a soft voice. Tim, still fixated on the photograph of the smiling older couple, shifted his gaze to the dolls. Facial features of the once-perky figurines had been crushed into an unrecognizable blob of plastic heap. Even Ken, Barbie's ardent suitor, would have had a hard time identifying his lifelong partner. Only the cobalt blue eyes remained as symbols of Barbie's beauty. "Charles said that's what he'd do to me if I ever left him." Lisa stood and faced the mirror. "Guess it couldn't get much worse than this," she said as she fingered her swollen, distorted face.

Yas pressed her cold compress to Lisa's face. "You know, if we could get this swelling down a little." She snapped open her purse and retrieved a compact. "...and with a little of this--"

"You're nice, but we both know all the makeup in the world won't help. I should have left the first time he hit…"

"How would you feel about plastic surgery? My moth--a woman I know--has this great plastic surgeon in New York--"

"I could never afford that. I don't even--"

"Why not let him do a consultation? He won't charge for that. Besides, with all the work--this woman has had...she's bound to have accumulated some frequent-tuck miles. It wouldn't cost you much if she's willing to redeem them."

Lisa Cox smiled and thought of the Mason jar hid behind the heating unit in the trailer that held her life's savings, barely $200. The money was earmarked for removal of the wisdom teeth that kept her in constant pain. Plastic surgery, what a dream! But for the moment a dream was all she needed. "Do you think he could fix my cheekbones--and my nose?"

"Yes, and more. I'll call him as soon as I get home."

Tim Ridell eased beside the two women and grasped Lisa's arm. "In the meantime, you and I are going to get some more of your things."

"No!" Lisa Cox wrapped her arms around Yas's waist and hung on. "Please, I don't ever want to go back in that trailer."

You'll need some things for winter--"

"I'll go, but only if you come with us."

"Sure," Yas said as she opened the trailer door. "Let's go."

Before the trio could leave, the phone rang. "Let the recorder get it." Tim said as he moved for the door.

"Tim, this is Phillip Moole--are you there? Hello...."

Tim Ridell, still flushed from decking Charles, snatched up the handset. "Ridell. How can I help you?"

"Tim.... Phillip Moole. I'm just back from the islands, and, ah--" Moole floundered for words as he absorbed the out-of-character brashness in Tim Ridell's voice. Obviously, the boy hadn't recognized the caller. "This is Phillip Moole, head counsel for the Crown."

Something, perhaps the adrenaline high or maybe the glow of liberation that Lisa Cox was giving off, had changed Tim Ridell. No matter the source, Tim Ridell had been awakened. No longer would he be a lackey for the Crown. From now on, Tim Ridell would be his own man, just as Lisa Cox would be her own woman. "I know who you are. How can I help you?"

"I--ah--we...have some things to discuss--"

"If these things have anything to do with Crown business, I guess you should know something, Moole--I don't work for the Crown anymore."

Yas fired a look at disbelief at Tim Ridell then mouthed, "You have to get back inside, don't --"

Tim shrugged his shoulders, and listened to Moole's hurried response. "Tim, now don't make any rash decision."

"Rash? No, Phillip, trust me, this isn't a rash decision. I'm tired of the view from the pond-scum floor, and I'm pissed off. Pissed off at being the only attorney in the firm who gets paid in cents rather than dollars. Twenty-five dollars! That's how much bonus I've received in the last four years.

Twenty-five hundred cents...Moole--for four years. So don't tell me I'm rash, you--"

Phillip Moole pondered his predicament. Only days in charge, and already a main component of his altered *Last Kincaid* plan was rebelling. Hardly a worthy adversary, yet Ridell had him back pedaling...but not for long. "Tim, I don't blame you for being, to use your words, pissed off. But you're mad at the wrong guy. For years I've gone to bat for you--"

"Gone to bat for me? You mean for years you beat me down with a bat--"

"No, it was Wyatt who blocked your bonus."

"Wyatt? *You* handle the bonuses for legal, Moole--"

"That's true, Tim, but Wyatt..." Has to be some way to blame Wyatt, Moole thought. "He did it because of Sally, I'm sure."

"Come on, Moole, we both know Wyatt was never that crazy about Sally." That much was true, Tim thought, even Sally would admit her relationship with Wyatt had more to do with similar DNA markers than TLC. But why the charade? Moole had tried for years to find reasons to fire him and with the bogus Polyana deed, he had gotten his grounds for dismissal. The mistake was so monumental there was no potential claim for wrongful dismissal. Moole had devised a brilliant stroke of deception that had cleared the way to fire the only non-Ivy in legal, but why delay the cleansing? "Are we done?" Tim looked at Yas and Lisa huddled in girl talk. "I got better things to do than listen to this bull."

Moole's mind raced. His argument wasn't working. Logic had no place in this conversation. Throw the dog a bone and take charge, damn it!

"Listen; there is some immediate compensation involved. If that doesn't interest you then, yes, I guess we are done."

"What kind of compensation?"

"Two hundred thousand dollar bonus--and I'm obligated to make you a more lucrative option." Moole poured his next words like ice water, "But I need an answer, today."

Tim Ridell calculated his tax liabilities, even after taxes he would net well over a hundred thousand dollars--a hundred thousand badly needed dollars--*obligated?* The non-Ivy purge wasn't taking place because Moole wasn't pulling the trigger--assassins were obligated to kill--not obliged to make lucrative options. "This money...it's mine even if I decline the option?" Tim asked.

"That's the way I'd play it, if I were you. Take the money and run--forget the option."

"Not so fast, Moole. What are the terms?"

"I can't discuss it in detail, not over the phone, but generally it concerns an employment option."

"You mean a job?"

"A position." Moole cringed. "Job sounds a little pedestrian."

Rather than feeling warm and fuzzy from the security a *position* at the Crown provided, Tim remembered the hoopla over his first position with Crown. Big Jim and Sally--correcting his misguided ambitions--saving him from the pitfalls of public service. But what had the position done for him? Nothing. Not a goddamn thing.

Tim looked at Lisa Cox, then remembered how she had automatically defended her piece-of-crap husband...defended the hand that suppressed her...defended the hand that smashed her dolls...defended the hand that may very well take her life.... Crazy, but no crazier than his defense of the Crown. How different was the Crown from Charles Cox, really? Why should he be any different than Lisa--seize the opportunity, like she had done. Moole was right...take the money and run, and never look back.

"Tim, we need to get back inside Moole's office." Yasnaya looked deep into Tim's eyes, past the contented surface reflected by the clear pools of brown. Somewhere, deep inside this man there had to be a battle raging, a will to win, a need to know the rest of the saga—but she could spot nothing. Couldn't he see that Moole and Ganna Mae would win, and they would lose everything--without even knowing what everything was? "Don't you think you owe us that much?"

Owed? Sure he owed her, and half the credit card companies in America. If he had to pay back every thing he owed he'd have to out live Methuselah. Why couldn't she just forget about the Crown stuff and enjoy the food and drinks he could finally afford? What was so wrong about live and let live, forget and move on? Besides, Moole would play him like Nero's fiddle. "I think I should just take the money--"

"You need to bury this...I understand."

"Do you mean that?" *Bury?* For whatever reason, Tim though of the epitaph on Harmon Ridell's tombstone: *He fought the Good Fight.*

"Yes." Yas nodded. "It's OK."

"Ridell, I need your answer," Moole demanded.

Yasnaya was nothing like Sally, she believed in him no matter what...and damn if he was going to let her down. "Moole, I'm prepared to discuss this offer."

"Thank you." Yas beamed.

Tim reached for her hand. "But right now my life is about as good as it gets. So whatever your offer is, it can't top what I have at this moment."

"As I said, I'm obligated to make the offer, and hopefully you'll decide that it can't enrich what you have. Let's get this over with--Harbor Bistro, lunch...if that suits you?"

"It suits. I'll be there at twelve."

Live oaks, thick with Spanish moss, bordered both sides of Modello Street. Stirred by an off shore breeze, the fluttering leaves wagged like green tongues gorged with nature's truth--temporal order-- acorns to oaks, caterpillars to butterflies. Mesmerized by the shadows cast by the gnarly limbs against the sun-split sky, Tim mumbled the lesson learned, "logic." Something sorely lacking in his conversation with Moole. Why the money and why offer him a job--*position*? Moole's words, but not Moole's actions. *Logic*, would dictate that his malfeasance earn a termination—not a reward.

The entire conversation was illogical, something not usually associated with Phillip Moole, he concluded as he turned onto River Road. *"Obligated to make you an offer."* Obligated by who? He was starting to regret his hasty decision to meet Moole. He should have postponed the meeting--talked it over with Yas some more.

No time for that now...think. Wyatt's proxy--sure that had to be part of the reason for the offer. They had to keep him around to exercise the proxy. Ganna Mae had lied to Yas; they needed him to make this *Last Kincaid* plan work.

Slowly the realization sank in, Moole and Ganna Mae couldn't force him to play the game. Only one person could insure his participation and that was Yas. *You owe me that*...four words spoken by the only person that could keep him around. Man, talk about a coordinated strike...

Ganna Mae, Moole, and as far as he knew, Yas and Lisa Cox were all players in the *Last Kincaid* plan. It was time to devise a plan of his own, time to think about Tim Ridell, he thought as he drove past the Harbor Bistro parking lot. Finally, after thirty minutes of driving up and down River Road his plan was formulated. *If*, always the largest word in any plan, Phillip Moole's offer of the money became reality, then he would take the money and run. Yas had two shares of Crown stock. Two hundred million, more than enough to make up for the debt he could never repay. Lisa Cox had no payback coming. He had saved her from her husband and Yas had offered Lisa a shot at plastic surgery. They were even discussing Lisa moving in with Yas...could this plan be elaborate enough to involve the Coxes? Satisfied his cynicism was in tact, Tim Ridell strutted into the Harbor Bistro.

Phillip Moole had arrived at the restaurant early to find strategic seating. Staging was everything, according to Ganna Mae Ferguson, and in spite of his dislike for the old woman, Phillip agreed. Framed by a window was a view of the Battleship North Carolina. Moole admired the staging that would tame the newfound brashness of Tim Ridell. Remind him of the posh office of the Head of Legal and of the powerful man who occupied it. "Advantage Moole," Phillip gloated to himself as he slid a little too the left to improve Ridell's view of the battleship's signature 16-inch gun battery.

More symbols of power, and phallic symbols to boot--the boy would be overwhelmed.

Satisfied with the scene, Moole mulled over his tactics. How could he justify his offer to Ridell when so many more lawyers in the company were more qualified for the position? How could one pass over Harvard, Yale, and Duke Law graduates in favor of a Campbell man…if there was such a thing? Ridell's family had no business background either. His mother was a bank teller, and his father had been a janitor in a factory. A janitor, for Christ sake! Ridell was simple, but not stupid. He'd smell the rat; surely he had that much sense. Why had he told Ridell the lie about Wyatt blocking his bonus checks? Simple--Ridell had caught him off guard when he had threatened to quit. Phillip Moole stood and waved to Tim Ridell as he entered the restaurant. "Take him down, take him down" Phillip whispered to himself.

"Good afternoon." Phillip Moole said as he extended his hand to Tim.

"I believed you mentioned you had some checks for me?" No need to drag his plan out. Either the money happened or it didn't.

"As promised." Moole pushed the checks across the table turned and gestured at the view of the battleship. "Quite a sight isn't it--powerful, virile."

Tim recognized Moole's ersatz office view and the corporate gamesmanship Moole was employing. With the checks safely tucked away in his wallet, Tim thought of one base that hadn't been covered. Why let Moole off so easily? The job--*position*--would be some bogus Assistant to the Head of Legal title to keep him around to exercise Wyatt's proxy, no doubt about that. So why not torture the bastard before he served notice that the *Last Kincaid* cabal would have to recruit a new boy?

Get you some of this, Tim thought as he stretched his 6'2" frame over the shorter Moole. "More like a paper tiger, if you ask me. Her guns don't work and she's sitting in a bed of mud--neutered, impotent."

"A matter of opinion, I suppose," Moole said as he quickly sat down to take away Tim's height advantage. "So, how have you been?"

"Oh, about the same. The wind blew away the underpinning from my trailer, my car is sitting out in a field, and I'm behind on most of my payments. Not so good, but thank you for finally asking."

"Sorry to hear that. Maybe I should have brought cash?"

"Nah, the checks are fine--as long as they don't bounce," Tim said, as he remembered the check-cashing fiasco at the bank.

"Certified checks--I don't think that will be a problem, do you?"

Tim ignored Moole's question, and began to have second thoughts about torturing Moole. What if he stopped payment on the checks before he could get to the bank? Could you even stop payment on certified checks? Stay calm, lie if you have to, but just get the money in hand.

"Tim, when I told you earlier about Wyatt blocking the checks--"

"That's not important, Mr. Moole. You saw a mistake and you corrected it."

"Call me Phillip. I insist. But as I was saying, it was hard for me to understand at first, as it was for you, I'm sure." Moole paused to look at the face of Tim Ridell...no visible emotion, only a nod. Not even a thank-you for the money he knew damn well he didn't deserve--cretin. "But the truth is, Wyatt made it hard on you for a reason. I'm sure he never expressed this to you, but Wyatt thought of you as a son."

Tim Ridell could not hide his amazement at the lie he had just heard. Wyatt Kincaid couldn't even remember his name and, Tim was certain, surely never thought of him as a son. "Tom, you know I've always thought of you as a son." Tim smiled as he tried to imagine Wyatt Kincaid making the same pitch Moole was making now. Why Moole felt the need to explain still wasn't clear, but at least he knew why he was dealing with Moole rather than Wyatt. Not even the great bullshitter Wyatt Kincaid could make this pile smell good. Bull, Tim thought. But, he had to admit, the two hundred grand was certainly making the stinky-pile tolerable.

"Phillip, to be honest, I find that hard to believe."

Moole glared at Tim Ridell, and quickly softened his stare. All of the rewards he so richly deserved, the yacht, the private jet, and more money than he could ever spend were separated from him by this damn lowlife. Maybe it was time to end the meeting and give Ganna Mae a call. Her background and Ridell's weren't that far apart, and she would know how to handle someone of her own class. Anxious to hide his hatred, Moole turned to look at the battleship and was rewarded with a government issued epiphany. Time to bring out the big guns, the 16-inch guns, Moole thought as he surveyed the silhouette of the warship. To hell with Ganna Mae and her ilk.

"I found it hard to believe too, but bear in mind that Wyatt made me do this. I told him there were dozens of people more qualified for the position than you. And while we're being honest, you know I don't think too highly of anyone who doesn't have an Ivy League degree. So you can imagine how shocked I was when Wyatt suggested--hell, we're being honest here, *demanded* that you be given the position."

Yeah, old Wyatt demanded that I be given the Whipping Boy position, Tim thought as he executed an exaggerated-I'm-buying-this-crap-nod to Moole.

Phillip Moole intentionally changed his tone. Ridell was hooked. A worthwhile lie, Moole thought, works every time. "Understand this, Ridell, I wanted no part of this. But for reasons I can't even fathom Wyatt Kincaid wants you to take over as president of Crown Kincaid Development Company."

In spite of his efforts to remain calm, every facial muscle scattered out from the center of Tim's face and divulged his slack-jawed amazement.

"Look at you, Ridell. Even you recognize the fallacy of such a request." Moole let the statement sink in before he set the hook and reeled like hell. "That's why I wanted to have a personal meeting with you. We both know you're not qualified for this job. By God, man, we have two Harvard MBA's on staff. Take the job…just for a few days. Then write a letter of resignation, for the sake of the company. I'll call Wyatt and tell him you couldn't handle it." Moole, ever the sportsman, pressed harder. "I'll see to it that you receive a decent severance package. With that, and the money I've just given you, you can go back to that great life you touted earlier."

Tim Ridell hailed the waitress as she passed by. "Excuse me, miss, I'd like a Scotch, neat…and make it a double."

Phillip Moole covered his mouth as if he were in deep thought, and used the only camouflage he had to cover his smile. Ridell needed the drink now, the same one *he* had needed earlier.

"I--I, don't understand. If you didn't want me to have the job why didn't you let me quit--"

"Because if you don't take the job--You have to take the job just long enough to resign--"

"Wait a minute, if I take the job, Wyatt's job, would I be your boss?"

"You would be the president of the Crown Kincaid Development Company…but surely, you can't be serious about taking this job? Face the facts, man! You have neither the skill nor the tools for this position; it's beyond your abilities."

"Well, that's your opinion, Mr. Moole, but obviously someone higher up thinks I do. So, I won't be needing that drink. My mind is made up. I'll take the job, and you can't fire me, right?"

"Of course not. Only Wyatt Kincaid can fire you--"

"Good! In that case you, and all of your Ivy League cronies can clear out of the Crown. Your services are no longer needed."

"I was afraid of this." Moole said. "But there is something I didn't tell you. Before I agreed to this idiotic blunder, I made my staff and myself untouchable by you. With Wyatt's blessing, I control the board of directors. You will have Wyatt's proxy, but you will vote the stock as I direct, Mr. Ridell."

Tim Ridell massaged his temples, the *Last Kincaid* plan was alive and well, Moole still had control. "Something is screwy here. If I don't take the job, you lose big time. But if I *t*ake the job, which you obviously don't want to happen, you lose even more, right?"

"Very perceptive, Mr. Ridell. More perception, frankly, than I thought you possessed. Touché."

"Sorry to disappoint you...so, do you want to deepen my perception?"

"Ok, I'll lay it all out for you. Wyatt Kincaid is a devious man. Not a smart man, but devious. His offer is this. Unless you take the position Wyatt brings in outside management to run the company--God knows what subpar talent that would be." Moole shook his head. "But if you take the job and fail, which you will surely do, Mr. Ridell, then I not only control the board, I can bring in my own management team. A cruel irony, don't you think? I have to recruit you for a job I know you can't possibly do, to make sure the job gets done."

Tim Ridell smiled--finally some logic. "So that's why you were so quick to hand out the two hundred grand?"

"Precisely, and you might note the dates on the checks. They go back over a four- year period, except for one check that I apparently misplaced."

Ridell's heart rate sped up. The restaurant stilled like an old E. F. Hutton commercial and everyone in the place seemed to be listening. His breathing became deeper and he was sure Moole could hear his heart pounding against his chest. Maybe the bank had called the Crown to let them know someone was trying to cash a check with a stop payment on it? He glanced at Moole, who seemed almost disinterested. He had to know if Moole was on to him. "Why did you hold them so long?" Tim forced the words out hoping Moole didn't detect the quiver in his voice. Moole settled back in his chair and stared directly into Tim's eyes. "I held them even after Wyatt insisted I give them to you. It's important that you know that."

"Why?"

"Are you sure you want to know, Tim?"

"Yeah, this is the best part of the story so far."

"I held them because you have never deserved a bonus. And as soon as you fall on your face everyone else will know you never deserved--"

"If you weren't so old, Moole, I'd take you outside and--"

Moole leaned within easy reach of Tim Ridell. "And beat the crap out of me?"

"Something like that."

"That's exactly why you will fall on your face, Ridell. An Ivy Leaguer would handle this situation like a gentleman. But you choose to handle the problem like--like a janitor. It's as they say, I suppose. 'The fruit doesn't fall far from the tree.' Right, Mr. Ridell?"

Tim Ridell stared at Moole and thought of the janitor he had alluded to, Hartman Ridell. No doubt there was a time when the ex-middleweight-boxing champion of the XVIII Airborne Corps would have resolved the dispute with Moole by resorting to fisticuffs. But that time was before he met and fell in love with the vivacious Kimpe Ridell. Never once in the couple's thirty-year marriage had Hartman Ridell ever used his skills in anger. But neither had his father let those skills atrophy. Each evening after work, Hartman Ridell, with his young son in tow, had practiced the sport that had almost made him famous.

In spite of his mother's complaints, Tim Ridell had punched and jabbed until he became a contender worthy of his father's admiration. Eager to display his talents, Tim Ridell had asked his father over dinner to schedule a match. Rather than answer, Hartman Ridell had retreated to the makeshift gym and burned their boxing equipment. Not until two years later, as his father lay on his deathbed, did Tim understand why. "Lead with your words, counter with your brains. Box when you run out of both." Hartman Ridell was a good father and teacher to the end.

Tim Ridell remembered his father's last words and responded to Moole's comment.

"Phillip, that tree I didn't fall too far from? You won't understand, but he's the reason I won't fail, and he's also the reason you won't be visiting a hospital today…. But, back to business. The directive from Wyatt. I assume you have the original?"

"I do indeed."

"I'd like to see it, if you don't mind."

"I knew you would, Mr. Ridell, so I took the liberty of making a copy." Phillip Moole shoved a file folder across the table to Tim. "Along with the directive you will also find an employment contract in duplicate. You'll need to sign the originals and return them to me."

"I'll look the terms over, and if I decide to take the job…position, then I'll sign and return them." Tim Ridell took a sip of his freshly delivered drink. "I'll also need to verify the signature on the directive is Wyatt's."

"That can be arranged. Is that all, Mr. Ridell?"

"One more thing, Moole, where is Wyatt? Why isn't he here to enjoy this little game?"

"I suppose." Moole shrugged, "He's traipsing around the world in the lap of luxury and dancing the night away serenaded by sounds of his minions bashing each other's brains out--the cruel bastard."

"So you don't know where he is?"

"No, truly I do not." For the first time in this meeting Phillip Moole had made an honest statement, a statement Tim Ridell believed to be a lie.

Chapter 16

Tim Ridell's first stop was at the main branch of the Farmers and Maritime Bank on College Road. In case the checks didn't work this time, at least he could suffer the embarrassment alone.

"Cash...are you sure, sir?"

"If you don't mind." Tim watched as the teller punched numbers into the machine in front of her and worried that Moole had stopped payment.

"Sir, this may take awhile. Would you follow me, please?"

As the teller left the booth, Tim Ridell's mind raced--something was wrong, just like before--Moole had set him up. The checks were stolen or forged--damn.

"Mr. Ridell, you can wait in here. Can I get you a beverage? We have Cokes and coffee or, if you want something, else I'll be glad to get it for you."

"No...I--is anything wrong?"

"No, sir. Nothing is wrong. It's just that your transaction has exceeded my authority. Someone in management will be right with you," the teller said as she opened the office door. "Please make yourself comfortable, Mr. Ridell."

Tim's last visit to this bank had been to a sparsely decorated office to discuss his delinquent account. The office, by design, had been furnished in a décor that screamed *CHEAP!* From the pressboard desks covered in faux wood grain vinyl, to the hard plastic customer's chairs, the bank's message was simple--cheapskates not welcome. But Tim Ridell had missed the message. Not until his Personal Account Partner, Jada Wynn, checked the box titled *Trash Bash* did he understand the décor and his status.

The space he found himself in today was of an altogether different décor...*opulent, lavish, moneyed*...Tim ran the adjective choices through his mind in an effort to tag the bank's message for this office. Appointed in deep-grained rosewood office furnishings with like-paneled walls, the room definitely had a theme. *Affluent, luxurious*... Tim touched the window treatments *(velvet)*, then tried to lift one of the leather office chairs *(hefty)*. The bank's message was coming through, and unlike the "trash bash" meeting, this time no one would have to spell it out. As he moved toward a credenza laden with a sterling silver serving set and three lead crystal decanters etched with the Farmers and Maritime's logo, the message became clearer. Like a psychic divining for vibes, Tim picked up the decanter full of fine Scotch whiskey. "Heavy," he declared, as the room revealed its secret message.

"Let me get that for you." Before Tim could explain, a tall slightly balding, gray-haired man relieved Tim of the heavy container. "Good idea, by the way. Don't mind if I join you, do you?"

"No--ah, no sir."

The man turned his back to Tim and plopped two ice cubes into each glass.

"I usually don't drink during business hours," the man said, as he handed Tim a glass. "But then again, we don't usually get visits from major clients during lunch hour."

Tim took the glass, *heavy*. No *heavyweights*...the theme was heavyweight, as in Big Dogs.

"Sir, I afraid you have me confused with someone else. I'm just here to cash some checks--"

"Indeed you are, and I must admit that upsets me."

"Why?" Tim asked, as he thought of the trouble he was in, and his unfulfilled threat to pummel Moole, the weasel who had caused it.

"Perhaps we should get something straightened out before we continue," the gray-haired man said as he moved behind his desk. "I'm L. Robert Lee, president of the Farmers and Maritime Bank." Lee removed a note from his pocket, scanned it and looked back at Tim. As Lee stuffed the note back into his pocket, Tim reassessed his earlier assumption of the room's message. Somewhere scrawled on a file, or maybe on the note L. Robert Lee had in his pocket, were the words *deadbeat*, he was certain. And like Yas's hints, he'd missed it.

A sheen of perspiration covered Tim's palms as he eyed the closed office door. If the president of the bank was here and concerned about the checks, then the police would be entering the door very soon.

"Mr. Lee, I didn't mean to upset you...and I'm not a major client... I'm--"

"I know very well who you are, Mr. Timothy Ridell, and though our motto here at the Maritime is 'the customer is always right,' I must respectfully disagree with you. And let me assure you, Mr. Ridell. There is no client more important to us than the new C.E.O. of the Crown Kincaid Development Company." L. Robert Lee clinked Tim's glass, then took a long sip. "Congratulations."

Tim Ridell emptied his glass in one gulp and contemplated L. Robert Lee's words as the hard liquor burned a path to his stomach. C.E.O.-- Crown Kincaid--Timothy Ridell. The unfamiliar word grouping, unlike the liquor, had not yet made it to his brain.

"Th...thank you--but how did you know?"

L. Robert Lee refilled Tim's glass and patted him on the back. "There are no secrets between the Crown and our bank, Mr. Ridell. I suspect I knew shortly after you."

Before, Tim thought, definitely before. "But you said you were upset about the checks--I don't understand."

"It's simple really, Mr. Ridell. By cashing the checks rather than depositing them, it's logical to assume you don't intend to bank with us. That's certainly your choice, but I'd like to remind you of the history that the Crown and the Maritime share. The Kincaids are charter members of this bank. For over fifty years we have serviced both the corporate and personal accounts of the principals. We'd like to maintain that tradition, and whatever offers you have been made by other banks, we can top them."

"Well, to be honest, Mr. Lee--"

"Robert, please," L. Robert Lee said, as his finger hovered over the talk button on his intercom. "Excuse me for just one second, Timothy.... Or do you prefer Tim?"

"Tim's fine--"

"Tim it is then--good name." Lee held one finger in the air. "One second, Tim." Then made his request into the intercom. "Margaret, bring me that account summary for Mr. Ridell, please." Within seconds the file was on his desk.

*Trash Bash...*Soon L. Robert Lee would have full knowledge of why no other banks were clamoring for the Tim Ridell accounts. Probably best to soften the blow. "My account--ah--I was a little late on some payments...uh, Robert."

L. Robert Lee ignored Tim's comment and concentrated on the report in front of him. "Good thing I checked this report," Lee said, as he slashed a red X across the first page of the file.

"Yeah, that's what I was trying to tell--"

"Seemed like we made some erroneous charges for some late payments," Lee continued. "And some NSF charges."

Tim Ridell's face flushed with embarrassment, he'd forgotten about the non-sufficient funds--Sally's secret bank raid. "I--was going to--"

"To complain, Tim," Lee said. "And well you should have. This is an outrage. The fault was ours. I apologize." Lee added the column of numbers on his calculator. "Let's see--um...bank error in your favor--" Lee paused. "Of exactly one thousand three hundred six dollars and forty-two cents."

Bank error in your favor. Tim suppressed a smile as he remembered what he had always considered to be a fictional notice on the yellow Community Chest cards of his Monopoly game.

"Does that figure correspond with your records, Tim?"

"I guess--I mean--ah. Yes, to the penny."

"Great." Lee winked. "Nothing like a balanced balance sheet as we say at the bank. Now, let's talk about our checking account proposal." Lee pulled the proposal from the folder. "This is our 'Privileged One Club' account. With this account, you have automatic overdraw protection up to fifty. Interest bearing, of course, and free checks--" Lee marked out a figure and wrote in another. "Let's make that seventy-five on the overdraft...unless you think you may need more?"

"Well, maybe a hundred...I mean if that isn't a problem?"

"Not a problem." L. Robert Lee scratched out his latest figure and wrote in another. "OK, that's one-hundred-thousand on the overdraft. Anything else?"

Tim Ridell had just learned his first lesson in high finance speak. The word *thousand* was silent. He would learn later that *point* denoted millions, as in ten point two million, the cost of the *Crown Jewel.* "No that's fine. Thank you, Robert."

"No, thank you, Tim, and welcome to the Privileged One Club--as soon as you sign." Lee pointed out the signature line. "Right here."

Tim Ridell floated out of the Farmers and Maritime Bank, despite being $1,306.42 heavier. Flush with the warm feeling of success, that only a hard liquor drink and a wad of cash could provide, Tim snuggled into the deep leather seat of Yas' truck and called his new best friend.

"Yas, have I got some good news for you."

"Great. I could use some good news," Yasnaya sighed.

Tim marveled at the phrase and delivery Yas had used. Except for her accent, she sounded exactly like his mother. Familiar with such pretext, Tim deliberately postponed the obligatory question that would undoubtedly kill his buzz.

"Tim?"

"Yeah, I'm here.... What's wrong?" Tim asked, as he braced himself for bad news.

"It's my mother, Gan," Yas moaned. "She's coming down. Tomorrow."

"That's it?" Tim choked. Amazed that his euphoria was still intact.

"Tim, trust me. When I say my mother is coming--it doesn't get any worse than that. What's the good news?"

Good news? The only way to keep good news was to keep it to yourself Tim decided, as he invented some other good news. "Car...new car--"

"New car?"

"Yeah, that's my good news. I won't have to borrow your truck anymore," Tim said as he composed himself. "I got the money and I'm getting a new car--"

"I thought you were going to get a lawyer--so you could see your son?"

"I am, but you said I should spend some money on myself," Tim said. "I'm just taking your advice. I'll have the dealership deliver your truck--and I have a few loose ends to tie up, so I won't be able to see you for a few days, OK?"

"OK, but stay in touch."

"I'll call you. Bye."

Socks. What happened to the socks, Yas wondered as the phoned clicked.

L. Robert Lee had a call to make, too. Phillip Moole checked his caller ID and picked up on the first ring. "Robert, how'd it go?"

"Mr. Tim Ridell is the newest member of our Privileged One Club--"

"And the freeze stipulation?"

"Secretary-Treasurer, or Head Legal Counsel of the Crown can freeze his account if Mr. Ridell is suspected of any corporate malfeasance." L. Robert Lee laughed. "Think that might happen, Phillip?"

"I suspect it already has, Robert." Moole laughed. "*Suspect*--get it?"

Chapter 17

Ganna Mae waited, and as the third ring turned into the fourth, she transcribed the number just dialed into a new day planner. "Damn, stupid me!" She fumed as the ever present thought of the lost day planner circled her mind for the millionth time.

Phillip Moole checked his caller ID, and unlike the call from L. Robert Lee, was in no hurry to answer. His good news would no doubt appease the old woman, but why not let her wait? Wyatt Kincaid's dip had been too good not to share, but his victory over Tim Ridell was something he wanted to savor--alone.

"Moole," Ganna Mae snapped into the recorder. "Call me. We have a problem."

No, old woman, we don't have a problem. We don't have a problem because Phillip Moole, *Ironhand Moole*, has everything under control.

"Tim Ridell is not to be put into play, do you understand? No play on Ridell," Ganna Mae stressed. "No play."

Moole snatched the handset from its cradle. "Mrs. Ferguson, sorry--"

"Did you get my message?"

"Part of it--something about--"

"You can't put Ridell in play--find someone else--"

"Er...ah--I--" Moole fumbled his words like a reluctant quarterback facing a two-hundred-fifty-pound linebacker. "I've already--"

"Replace him, Moole. Do you understand?"

Moole thought of his list of replacements for Tim Ridell, all Ivy League boys, except for Hal Winters, the Duke graduate. All of them, including Winters, were from wealthy families. Families that were well-versed in payback, and even worse, families that were plugged into political powerhouses capable of running the country for decades. No, Ridell was the right choice--powerless, not even enough juice to trip a ten-amp breaker, Moole thought as he digested Ganna Mae's directive. "But, we discussed this--"

"Discussed, Moole...but we did not agree--"

"Mrs. Ferguson, Ridell is the perfect choice--he's vulnerable, a loser of one."

"No, Moole, not anymore. If my guess is correct, he's picked up a powerful ally." Ganna Mae thought of the rebellious girl she had raised. The ingrate who was forever attaching herself to lost causes. Yasnaya, the protector of the damned, savior of dogs, cats, and even a jewelry-stealing raccoon—all strays, just like Tim Ridell. "One that I can't control."

"That may be, but I can control Ridell. I know how he works--"

"You know how he works, but do you know how he works when he's been inspired by my daughter?"

"Your daughter?"

"Yes, Moole. My daughter, the balance of power in our little *coup d'etat.* How will you handle her?"

Moole thought of his toast on the aft deck of the *Crown Jewel*.... *She will never know.* "You said yourself--she doesn't know--"

"Moole, Ridell will have access to company records--before he met Yasnaya, her name would have meant nothing to him--but now?"

"No, I can handle this, I--"

"We...Mr. Moole. We will handle this--my way. Don't put Ridell into play--"

"I can't. It's done."

"Then undo it!"

"I won't jeopardize my freedom. Any other option is too risky."

Ganna Mae remembered Adolfo's words of wisdom. "Persuasion is best practiced in person, my dear." Phillip Moole would have to be persuaded, or be replaced. In either case, Adolfo was right; the task would have to be handled in person. "Moole, we must meet. Too much talk over the phone is not good."

Phillip Moole fought back a barely discernible, but familiar feeling. A feeling much like the one Wyatt Kincaid evoked when he had suggested a meeting. Bad vibes, Phillip thought as he tried to ignore the jitters balled in his gut. But why, why should a man of his intellect and talent feel nervous about a meeting with either Wyatt or Ganna Mae?

"Moole, are you there?"

"Yes, yes...but I don't think a meeting is wise."

"I do. Miami on the boat, day after tomorrow," Ganna Mae directed.

Miami, Moole winced, as he thought about the *Crown Jewel* still berthed in the Bahamas. "Why don't I just come up to New York? The humidity is--"

"Because there is a little matter in Wilmington I have to deal with tomorrow, and besides, I want to spend a little time planning what to do with my spoils of war."

Ironhand Phillip Moole swallowed the rusty taste in his mouth. He would have to explain why he had not followed Ganna Mae's directive to bring the boat back to Miami. No, call the crew and have them move the boat. Yes, call the crew.

"Let me guess, Moole. Right about now you're trying to figure out how to get the boat to Miami, since it's still in the Bahamas, right?"

"Yes. No, I, er--"

"Don't lie! Is the boat in Miami?"

"Mrs. Ferguson, let me--"

"Yes or no, Moole,. Answer me, dammit."

"No...but I can explain," Moole said.

"Explain away, Moole, but this better be good and it better be fast."

"Well, you see...ah," Moole searched his vocabulary for words that would baffle yet satisfy his inquisitor. "Ah, the boat is...strategically placed, by that, I--"

"I don't have time for this lawyer crap, explain faster, Moole."

"Ah, yes, as I was saying, the boat's present location is vital to--"

"Faster, Moole, cut the crap."

"Jarek Denton," Moole rushed.

"Jarek Denton. Cheesy Pleasy Jarek Denton?"

"Yes." Moole relaxed. "You've heard of him, then?"

Heard of him? Ganna Mae mused, No, but I've loaned him money--pulled his ass out of the fire a few times and screwed his eyeballs out, and hell yes, I've heard of him! "Vaguely, but what does Jarek Denton have to do with this?"

God, Moole thought, how could she be so stupid? If the old woman knew Denton, didn't she know how important he could be to the Crown? Idiot! My employer is an idiot. "Mrs. Ferguson, Jarek Denton could be key to our plan." Moole rolled his head around on his neck. "And Jarek Denton and I have become fast friends. A few more visits and Denton will be begging to do business with us."

"So, you're telling me that you've done something even the great Wyatt Kincaid couldn't do?"

How did Ganna Mae know about Wyatt's failed attempt to get Denton's business? Yvette had relayed the story to him, but who had told Ganna Mae? Moole did a recap of his cursory investigation of Denton; crude, self-made, no formal education. Only one other party had knowledge of the feud, and that was Denton. Did Ganna Mae have a link to him? Time to test the water. "Ms. Ferguson, Wyatt Kincaid was a fool. Mr. Denton is a man of culture, and I suspect, a man with an extensive formal education."

"Is that right? Well, you'd know better than I."

Moole, who had tossed the bait and Ganna Mae hadn't bitten--cast again. "Yes, and I suspect Wyatt and Denton share no common ground." Moole waited for a nibble, and then tried again. "But I think Jarek Denton and I are carved from the same stock."

Jarek Denton cultured and formally educated!--what a stretch, Ganna Mae thought as she remembered her first meeting with Jarek Denton. Denton's culture had more in common with the grit in oysters than the cultured pearls it became. The only degrees Jarek Denton could lay claim to were the honorary ones bestowed upon him by beleaguered backwater colleges in exchange for his fat cash donations. But Moole was right about one thing--he and Denton were carved from the same stock--Devil's wood.

"Well, in that case, I suppose we should exploit your friendship with Mr. Denton. I may need two days in Wilmington, and then I'll join you on the boat. In the meantime, you consider a replacement for Ridell. "

In the meantime I'll do that, old woman--that and conduct a little fishing expedition, Moole thought.

Ganna Mae packed as she formulated her itinerary. Boots and slacks for her trip back to the scene. Black, double-breasted-power-suit for her talk with Yas. Linen and silk ensembles for her stay on the boat, and, she thought with a smile, this little number for Jarek, as she folded a silk charmeuse kimono. Memories of Jarek Denton reminded her of the call she needed to make. Giddy with schoolgirl anticipation, she dialed the number to *The Slice of Life*.

"Slice--Captain Martin, go ahead."

"Yes, Jarek, please," Ganna purred.

"One moment Ms. Ferguson."

"Jarek, *up* for a little company?"

"Will be soon as I choke down some Viagra. When will you be down?"

"Naughty man...this is a business trip."

"Sex, business--it's all the same. Ganna Mae Ferguson shows up, somebody's getting screwed. Do I know 'em?"

"How positively insightful," Ganna Mae cooed. "Perhaps.... His name is Phillip Moole. I understand he's your new best friend, but I find that odd considering he doesn't know a damn thing about you, Jarek."

"Moole...umm, never heard of him."

"*Crown Jewel*, paid you a visit--"

"Oh, yeah--the one Wyatt tried to feed to the sharks. Damn, that was funny--I miss Wyatt...in a good way. But you gotta admit--he makes life interesting."

"Made, darling. He *made* life interesting."

"Is he...you know...?"

"Dead? Hardly, but I'm sure he wishes he was."

Poor Kincaid, Jarek thought. Getting screwed and not knowing why--must be driving him nuts. Jarek Denton knew the entire *Last Kincaid* plan, but it had taken him thirty years to complete the mosaic of Ganna's total destruction of Wyatt. Snippets revealed during pillow talk after he and Ganna Mae had made love. Tidbits gathered during the drunken nights Ganna Mae had been fortified enough to revisit her childhood. Shards and morsels tossed out during her fits of rage and rare moments of vulnerability.

Thirty years to learn of a plan that made no sense at all. Revenge against a man whose only crime was being the son of his father. Like any of us had a choice in the matter of our parents. Logic lost on Ganna Mae, and, as much as Jarek tried to understand, he could never square it. Punishing a man for his father's sins. Sins? Depended on the way you looked at it. Good intentions gone awry, maybe--but sins? Only Ganna Mae could see it that way. Call it what you will, see it any way you like, but after almost fifty years, did it even matter? Punishing a man for not being a bastard--oh, well. Good thing about it, one day Wyatt would know, but like the mouse trapped by a playful kitten, he would never see it as a game. "You know, Wyatt's disappearance has caused a stir down here. His crew really liked him except for his chef. She's been beaming like a cat who ate the Reddy Kilowatt man. Kincaid should have fired her. Did you know she used to piss..."

"My idea, darling. And speaking of my crew, how do they look now?"

"Like my crew, spiffy. Guess that was due to, ah…what's his name, again?" Jarek asked.

"Moole, Phillip Moole, and the reason I called actually. When I see you, I want you to pretend that we've never met."

"I don't think my crew on the Slice will buy that--"

"They don't have to buy it. They just have to go along with it, dammit!" Ganna Mae barked.

"Hold on, don't get all fired up. I'm just saying, they may slip up, it's not like they don't know you."

"See that they don't, Jarek, or those juicy little pizza locations the Crown has been buying all these years could go poof."

"Don't threaten me, Gan. I could have dealt with Wyatt, you know?"

Ganna Mae cringed at the thought of Jarek Denton betraying her. Of all the men she had ever seduced, more then three times the number of her fingers and toes, Jarek had been the only one she trusted enough to share her Kincaid final solution plan.

"Don't ever say that again, and don't ever forget who made you. You damn--damn--ah--"

"Go ahead, say it! Gigolo," Denton spelled out the insult. "Capital G-I-G-O-L-O."

First Moole, and now Jarek. Sensitive little egotistical men, so easily crushed, Ganna Mae thought, but then, lucky for me, so easily placated. "Jarek, I've never thought of you like that. You're a giant among men. You know I could have never faced Wyatt Kincaid without your strength. Forgive me?"

Giant among men, yeah that much was true, but still, Denton thought, you don't threaten me, bitch. "Nice that you remembered that we're on the same side, and I forgive you."

"Jarek, I apologized and you accepted. Let's don't cloud this wonderful adult moment with juvenile puffery."

"Puffery?"

"Call it what you will, darling, but the bottom line is money, money that we won't have if we don't stick with the plan. And the plan is this: When Moole calls you, and I'm certain he will, you make concessions, but don't agree to do business with him. Moole must know that without me the whole plan will fail. Once Moole tries and fails, I will then arrange a meeting with you. You will agree to do business with the Crown, but only if I control the company."

"Sounds like you've run into a little problem, already. Doesn't Moole--"

"Jarek, I can handle Moole. But if Moole gets egotistical and believes he can arrange a deal Wyatt Kincaid couldn't pull off, he may be inclined to overstep his bounds."

"Roughly translated: Moole has *already* overstepped his bounds. What gives?"

Ganna Mae paused before she confirmed Jarek's suspicions. In theory, Tim Ridell was the perfect patsy, but Yasnaya had a way of disrupting theory. Until she could meet with her wayward daughter and reel her in, the plan was in jeopardy. But was this information she wanted to share with Jarek? "Jarek, the plan has developed a little kink, but that will be taken care of before I see you."

"Hey, I'm in this up to my neck. If this '*Last Kincaid*' plan doesn't work--"

"It will work!" Ganna Mae snapped.

"So you say, but I want to know what's going on. We slip up and Wyatt Kincaid buries us. Tell me about this little kink, Gan."

Ganna Mae thought of her problem, Tim Ridell. Who took the fall had not been important, and for that reason she had not done due diligence on Tim Ridell. Moole was certain Ridell couldn't cause a problem, but how much did she trust Phillip Moole's judgment? Not much. If only she and Jarek could meet Ridell, satisfy themselves that he would work for the patsy part--yes, meet Ridell. Ah, the perfect solution. Meet Ridell, and get a feel for his relationship with Yasnaya. "I have a better idea; I'm going to introduce you to the kink. In the meantime, get that dirt-digging army of yours to find out everything they can about one Mr. Timothy Ridell."

"Who the hell is Timothy Ridell?"

"Why Jarek, you disappoint me. Surely you know the new president of the Crown Kincaid Development Company."

"The patsy?"

"Exactly, contact L. Robert Lee with the Farmers and Maritime. He can get you started on Ridell. But check him out thoroughly."

"Not to worry. I'll know Timothy Ridell's thoughts before he does."

"Jarek,"...such a shame not to trust your own cabal, Ganna Mae thought...but. "Do a little digging on Phillip Moole while you're at it. I've checked him out, but let's face it; no one turns the dirt better than Jarek Denton."

"Ain't that the truth."

Chapter 18

The antiseptic scent of pine trees wafted through the open window and grated against Ganna Mae's raw nerves. To hell with Rents-for-Cent's no-smoking policy...surely the rental company would prefer a hint of stale cigarette smoke to the gagging stench of pine-induced puke she was about to hurl? One more whiff of pine and the rental company would have both fumes and vomit to deal with, and her fifty-dollar environmental deposit wouldn't cover the damage. "Big damn deal," Ganna Mae snarled as she tamped the smoldering butt into the never-used ashtray. Banished to a pine forest for being forgetful! A stiff sentence for such a common malady and trouble Father Time would regret stirring up if she ever got her hands on him.

No sooner had the car come to a stop when the reluctant visitor leapt from the seat and streaked, like a GPS guided missile, to the bedroom located in the rear of the cabin. After a quick check in the obvious places, Ganna Mae stooped to look under the bed. Still on her knees, as at prayer, Ganna Mae strained to recall the last time she had used her day planner. Kitchen...had to be, and yet she was certain the planner never left the bedroom.

One look at the kitchen table and Ganna Mae forgot about the smell and dread of being back in the piney woods. In the center of the table, label facing away from the window, sat her bottle of Early Times. Twinges of doubt crept into her thoughts as she retraced her actions after Wyatt's visit. She had been careful to center the bottle, but couldn't remember if she had double-checked the label's position, then cursed herself for not marking the bottle's content. Remembering the two drinks she had taken from the bottle, Ganna Mae retrieved two tin cups from the pie safe and poured her customary four-fingered drink into each cup. Careful not to spill a drop, she poured the water back into the bottle. As the last drops dribbled from the cup her suspicions began to wane. The level was exactly equal to the distiller's full mark--nothing was out of place. "Except," Ganna Mae muttered as she lifted her gaze from the bottle, someone had reversed the position of the horseshoe she had used to hex Wyatt. Someone had been in the cabin, and only one suspect came to mind--"*Yasnaya.*"

As the tree lined path shaded out the reflection of the cabin in the rearview mirror her spirits lifted. Utilizing a mental exercise suggested by her psychiatrist Ganna Mae began to systematically replace unsettling thoughts with peaceful scenes. The exaggerated image of Wyatt Kincaid roasting on a spit over a fire made with the last pine trees on earth gave her the most pleasure.

Her next stop, a pilgrimage she had made twice a year for thirty years now, was not a place she wanted to spoil with bad vibes. Only once had anyone shared the trip and the visitation with her. Yasnaya had been a small child and the visit had upset her so badly that Ganna promised never to bring her again.

The exclusive and private hospital was located near the plush resort town of Southern Pines. A perfect cover if she ever needed an excuse to explain her presence in the area. In years past she had even managed to squeeze in rounds of golf at the Pine Needles Golf Resort that would soon host the next Women's US Open. Not that she was good a golfer, or even enjoyed the game for that matter. The ruse of duffer aided in the concealment of her most prized treasure, Caleb.

Lombardy Poplar Trees stood like sentries along the winding road leading to the hospital and Ganna Mae rushed to make herself presentable. With one hand she fished a cigarette from the pack and ignited the lighter with the other. This defilement of the car's interior was not an act of vengeance against the deposit stealing rental company, or even pine trees for that matter. Caleb, like all the Ferguson children, had learned to love the herbal aroma of flu-cured tobacco at an early age. Not that stale cigarette smoke compared to the sweet musky smell that layered eastern Carolina from July to September, but it was similar enough to remind Caleb of his brief happy childhood. No perfume, no matter how expensive, could do that; and that made her rebellious act worth a hundred "environment" deposits.

There were only two types of days that could keep Caleb cooped up inside the hospital's glorified atrium/dayroom; frigid raw days, a rare occurrence, or boiling hot ones, not so rare. Today was not a day of extremes. Caleb would be hunkered down under his favorite weeping willow tree, staring into the dark waters of the Lumber River. The temperature was perfect and the cool breeze off the water felt invigorating. A pang shot through her heart at she got her first glimpse of him. In spite of the clubfoot and teasing for being the "runt" Caleb looked just like their father. Massive arms protruded from the bib overalls and his wide shoulders stretched the tee shirt until it conformed to the shape of his muscular body.

Like a wild animal sensing prior to seeing its prey, Caleb sniffed at the traces of tobacco floating from the path and sprang to his feet. At the same time Ganna Mae rushed into his crushing embrace. For a moment, she was back in her father's arm. "Oh, and I've missed you too, my darling." Around and around the giant turned and then gently placed her on the river bank. How wonderful it would be to have a brother to share her dreams, plans and hopes...

"Mule did it. Mule did it. Mule did it."

Always the same words, and always the same urge to flee this place and never come back to be reminded of what Caleb would always be.

"No darling. The Kincaids did it, remember?"

Damn them to hell for what they've done to you. But don't you worry. Soon they will be no more. "Walk with me to the hospital darling I want to speak with your doctor."

As they walked she could feel the power emanating from his body. Such a shame she couldn't toss Wyatt into a cage with Caleb and let him deal with the *Last Kincaid*. But Caleb needed protection, a need she had provided for exceptionally well. Kincaid's army of lawyers had spent millions searching, leaving no records unturned. But they would never find Caleb, just as they had never found Yasnaya.

A brief visit with Caleb always left her in an emotional mess. On the one hand she felt guilty for not visiting longer, but the doctors assured her Caleb, like a dog, had no sense of time. In his mind, her last visit, over six months ago, seemed like yesterday. As she crossed the Cape Fear River, the last natural barrier separating her from Wilmington the air was suddenly awash with the salt-laced vapors of the Atlantic Coast. Ganna Mae dropped her window and inhaled deeply to cleanse her lungs.

Wilmington had changed, but not until I-40 turned into College Road did she realize how much. Bumper-to-bumper traffic and strip mall after strip mall. "Progress," Ganna Mae snorted. "Damn gridlock, is more like it." She'd never make it to Yasnaya's apartment on time, Ganna Mae thought as she reached for her phone. "I'll be late--damn traffic--"

"Where are you?" Yasnaya asked.

"In this damn four-lane parking lot--College Road--how do I get out of it?"

"You don't. Just find Highway 17 then grin and bear it."

Two hours later and Ganna Mae finally rolled to a stop in front of the apartment. From her window Yas marveled at the agility the older woman displayed as she got out of her car. As much as she hated to admit it, Ganna Mae still cut a striking figure, enough so that she could easily pass for a woman in her mid-fifties. If her plastic surgeon could work this miracle, what could he do with you, Yas wondered as she looked at Lisa Cox. "Lisa, why don't you go into the bedroom--I want to find out what kind of mood she's in before I ask her to help you."

As Lisa left the room, Yas contemplated the best way to determine her visitor's dispositon. Ganna Mae burst through the door and slammed her purse down on the coffee table. A quick glance confirmed the expected diagnosis: shitty, no surprise there.

"Grand Strand, my ass! They should have named it Grand Stranded," Ganna Mae grunted as she made reference to the Myrtle Beach Chamber of Commerce preferred travel brochure name for the region.

"Why didn't you fly into Myrtle Beach? It's a lot easier than coming through Raleigh-Durham."

Sure it is, Ganna Mae thought, but it's a helluva lot further from the cabin and Caleb. "I know, but you know how I hate those commuter planes...what happened to your face?"

"Occupational hazard--slipped off the pole."

"Have you seen a doctor? That looks serious?"

"It's mostly swelling--Oban and ice?" Yasnaya queried as she changed the subject.

"Why thank you, dear, but I really feel like some bourbon."

Commuter planes and bourbon--hates one likes the other--strange, Yasnaya thought, and news to her on both accounts. "I thought Oban was your drink of choice? I bought the bottle just for you."

"I drink bourbon sometimes. Don't you remember the bottle of Early Times at the cabin?"

Yasnaya wondered if Tim had followed her instructions to replace the bottle exactly as he had found it. Ganna Mae seldom asked questions without knowing the answer. "I don't remember." Yas rummaged through her bar. "How about some Jack Daniels?"

"No." Ganna Mae grunted, pissed that Yasnaya had sidestepped her reference to the cabin. "But you should really pay attention to your staging, especially the props. I've told you that a hundred times."

"Mother, I do remember the props, just not what type of bourbon it was. No big deal, OK?"

"Do you remember what I put over the window?"

"A horseshoe, a painting of an old man, and a bottle of Early Times--props accounted for. Happy now, Mother?"

"Good, though I'm surprised you remembered the horseshoe." Ganna Mae said, as she hoped her reminder would turn the conversation to the day planner she was certain Yas had picked up.

"How could I forget such a dumb idea--and you had it upside down anyway."

Had it upside down? "Must not have been such a dumb idea. If you could ask Wyatt Kincaid, I bet he'd tell you an upside down horseshoe can cause a powerful headache."

"Only if the broom-riding-bitch who put it up there dropped it on his head."

"Watch your mouth--"

"I said *witch*, Mother."

"Sounded like--oh, never mind." Ganna Mae said, as she buffed her nails against her silk blazer. "But the next time you go to the cabin pick up the horseshoe for me."

"Why on earth would you want a horseshoe, and why would you think I would go to the cabin?"

Ganna Mae looked at Yas and regretted not taking the drink she had been offered. Dealing with Yas always made her want a drink. "Well, first off not many stores in New York carry horseshoes, and I thought since I mentioned I left my planner...you might take a little initiative."

"Nope, I'm fresh out of initiative. I don't make any moves without getting orders directly from the top," Yasnaya said, as she rolled her eyes toward the overhead.

Enough of this, Ganna Mae thought, and waited for Yasnaya to make eye contact. "So you don't have my planner?"

"No," The question reminded Yas of Ganna Mae's childhood interrogation tactics: First a direct question and then checking her pupils for dilation. "But I'll be glad to get it for you...and your horseshoe," Yas said, as she widened her eyes to make it easier for Ganna Mae to see the truth.

"Forget it; I'll pick them up after I meet with Moole." *Moole*, the next most likely suspect, but had she even mentioned the loss of her day planner to him?

"Speaking of the devil, do you really trust him?"

"I trust no one," Ganna Mae snapped. "Not even you."

"No kidding, Mother."

"Oh, don't take it so personal, Yas. I've told you since you were a child."

"I know, I know. 'Trust no one, not even your lying ass eyes.' Well, tell me *mother*--did my eyes lie?"

"What are you talking about?"

"Oh, come on Gan; the direct question--looking at my pupils. Did I lie?"

Ganna Mae moved in front of Yas and stared deep into her eyes. Did you lie, or will you lie? Let's find out. "Tim Ridell. Did you forget about him, like I asked? Or did you find some of that initiative you claimed not to have?"

"No."

"No you didn't forget about him, or no, you didn't find any initiative?"

"No, on both counts."

Ganna Mae gritted her teeth. "I warning you, Yas. You screw up my plan and--"

"And Tim isn't a part of your plan?" Yasnaya asked remembering the proxy assigned to Tim Ridell.

"Absolutely not." Ganna Mae turned both palms up. "I thought I made that perfectly clear."

Nothing was absolutely clear anymore. Yasnaya had been certain Tim was right when he assessed Wyatt's proxy and its importance to the plan. "He's never been part of the plan, ever?"

Sure Ridell was part of the plan, but that mistake would be corrected as soon as she met with Moole. *The Last Kincaid* was constantly evolving, and for that reason she updated her notes religiously. But had she noted Ridell's involvement, and had Yas discovered it when she stole the day planner? No, she had never updated that portion of the plan--or had she? Ganna Mae fumed. Damn old age and this forgetfulness! "You *will* forget about him, and if you have my day planner I want it back."

"I don't have the planner and I will choose who I see, not you, Gan."

"Then why are you insisting that Tim Ridell is part of the plan?"

"I'm not. I just want to make sure he's *not* part of your plan."

"Why?"

"Because I like him, Mother. But if he's knowingly involved with you or your plan." Yas pulled her fingers through her hair and fluffed her thick mane. "I want nothing to do with him."

Ganna Mae smiled to herself. Oh my little darling, I wish you hadn't told me that...problem solved. "OK, OK, it's time for me to be honest with you. Tim is involved and I think he's using you to gain leverage. He's desperate, you know?"

"I don't believe you."

"It's true. Tim stands to make some money from his part in the plan, but aligned with you he can make a lot more." Ganna Mae studied the familiar facial expressions displayed by Yas since childhood. The upraised brow, flared nostrils, and pouting lips...all signs that she was losing faith in her newest project. "He abused his wife and, according to Phillip Moole, he's a very violent man. That's why I'm here, frankly; I'm concerned for your safety."

"Get out of my house!" Yas screamed as she grabbed Ganna Mae's bag and headed for the door.

"What are you doing?"

"What I should have done a long time ago--divesting myself of you. I know what you are doing!" Every time I like someone the tiniest bit, you have to destroy them to prove that I'm a horrible judge of character. But this time I'm proving you wrong. That's right *wrong*! I deem you a horrible character. Now get out!!!"

First, Moole and now her own daughter. Both determined to ruin her plan. No way, Hell No. *The Last Kincaid* will be implemented and they can all get used to that! "Now, Yas--"

"No, I mean it. Get out!"

Ganna Mae sat down on the couch and did something Yasnaya never had seen before. She starting crying, loudly. "All I ever wanted was what's best for you. I know I haven't been a good mother, but I've always tried to be."

"How could you be a good mother? It pains you when I say the word. The only reason I call you Mother is because it pisses you off. And whether you believe me or not, I don't have your planner, and I haven't read your plan, either. But I know you, and I know that anyone involved in your plan will be destroyed. Wyatt Kincaid, Phillip Moole and even me. Maybe we all deserve that, but I won't let you destroy Tim. He's a good person, and he'd never hurt anyone. I know that much about him, so dry up and get out!"

Ganna Mae grabbed her chest, slumped to the floor and closed her eyes. "Oh, my heart. Oh, Yas, I think I'm dying. Somebody help me, please!" Lisa Cox rushed from the bedroom and grabbed Ganna Mae. "Are you all right, ma'am?"

Ganna Mae half-opened one eye and looked at Lisa. "My God, what happened to you?" Ganna Mae asked. "And don't tell me you slipped on the pole, too. What going on around here?" Lisa covered her face with her hands and sobbed. Ganna Mae put her arm around Lisa and whispered, "It's OK; you can tell me. Was it a customer or management?"

"Gan!" Yasnaya yelled.

"Oh, please Yas. I was in the business for a long time. Do you think I don't know abuse when I see it? Who did this?"

"She's not in the business," Yas said. "And congratulations on a miraculous recovery, by the way."

Ganna Mae ignored Yas and cradled Lisa's battered face in her hands. "Then who did this to you?"

"My husband," Lisa Cox mumbled. "I made him mad."

"You made him mad?" Ganna Mae asked rhetorically, as she turned Lisa's face from side to side. "If he did this to me, he'd be dead, the bastard."

Just like Ganna Mae. The only way to solve a problem was with hate and vengeance, and she would never change. "Trust no one." For thirty years Yas had lived that mantra. Relationships where appraised according to family wealth or political connections, or as a means to an end.

There was no pleasing Ganna Mae. Even when Yas had dropped out of medical school to follow in Ganna Mae's footsteps, the old woman had not been pleased. The only thing that would make Ganna Mae happy would be waking up to the news that Wyatt Kincaid had died some horrible death. Even then she wouldn't be happy. With Kincaid dead, Ganna Mae would have no one to hate, and therefore, no reason to live. Time to put an end to this, even if Ganna Mae was acting like she cared about Lisa, and she didn't, Yas thought. "Gan, now that you're better, I want you to leave."

"I'm not better." Ganna Mae turned to Lisa. "Feel my heart, honey. It's racing, tell her."

Lisa placed her hand on Ganna Mae's chest to feel her heartbeat.

"Don't bother, Lisa--you won't find one," Yas said as she pointed toward the door. "Out!"

"Yas, don't do this...you're all I have. I'll be all alone...and in my condition--"

"Please, don't make her go," Lisa said, as she looked at Yas. "I know how it feels not to be wanted."

"You don't understand, Lisa. All I've ever been to her is a tool of vengeance. I didn't realize that until a few days ago." Yas looked at Ganna Mae. "I'm sorry you hate the Kincaids, but I'm done with this."

"The Kincaids have it coming!"

"That's all you ever say, Gan, but you never say why. Don't I have the right to know why I'm supposed to hate?"

Ganna Mae grunted as she rose and moved closer to Yas. "How do you feel about her husband?" Ganna Mae asked pointing at Lisa. "How do feel about someone who could do that to another human being, much less his wife?"

"I don't like him one bit, Gan. But I can't see where killing him would help. So I offered to help Lisa by giving her a place to stay. Provide assistance to the victim rather than kill the perpetrator--pretty radical idea, but it beats killing everyone who wrongs us." Yasnaya squeezed her mother's hands in hers. "I know its simplistic thinking, but it's a fix."

"What the Kincaids did to me can't be fixed." Ganna Mae pulled her hands away. "I bet you'd want vengeance if someone killed your loved ones."

"I would want justice, but not vengeance."

"And what if justice was denied?"

"Is that why you hate so much, Mother?"

Ganna Mae walked to the window and looked back into the past. Past the new and improved Wilmington, past the traffic jams on College Road, and past the fancy Bistros and high-end shops. Her mind raced as she fell through the dimensions of time and space. Memories from reality and dreams flooded her mind until she stood in the living room of the home Grover and Iris Ferguson had built with their hands. Warmth from the crackling fire and the aroma of green cedar logs filled the room. The smell, she remembered, had seemed pleasant at first, and she relayed that thought to the man standing next to her. "It smells wonderful...almost like a pine forest."

"Helps cover the smell; sorry we couldn't embalm them, Missy." The words jarred her back to the task ahead. She nodded to Gus Forester, the undertaker, and moved in front of the window. Goose-feather snow flakes fell from the sky, an unusual event in Wilmington. As the flakes silently covered the brown earth, her eyes moved to a small mound a few feet from the barn. A wooden cross propped up by the pile of dirt stood out from the whiteness of the storm. "The grave," she whispered.

"Yes, ma'am." Gus nodded. "I like to think of it as the final resting place. Hope the location suits you?"

Final resting place, she thought as she looked at the coffin holding the remains of her parents. How would they ever rest, and how would she? "I want a tombstone, black granite. I'll wire you the money as soon as I get back to New York."

"Yes, Ma'am."

Ganna Mae turned from the window and walked to the coffin. "Come here, Caleb. It's time to say goodbye." The towheaded boy crawled from behind the chiffonier that had been converted into desk. Every drawer had been pulled out and Caleb's hands were stained red. "What in the world?" Ganna Mae gasped. Gus Forester looked at the steady drip of blood oozing from the corner of the wooden coffin. "I'm sorry ma'am. I sealed it as best I could, but I've never dealt with a situation like this." Ganna Mae grabbed Caleb and began to scrub him clean over the kitchen sink. "Clean up that mess Mr. Forester."

"Yes, ma'am." Gus Forester shoved the drawers back into the frame and stuffed the hodge-podge of receipts and bills back into the drawers. He found two burlap sacks used to carry wood lying on the hearth and mopped up the blood as best he could. What a mess! If Wyatt Kincaid hadn't insisted, he never would have tackled this job, but the large payment made it worthwhile. "Miss Ferguson, perhaps it might be better to say your good-byes at the final resting place?"

"No, we'll say them now; we're not staying for the burial." Ganna Mae pointed at a kitchen chair. "Please put this by the coffin for Caleb to stand on."

"Missy, please, he's just a boy," Gus pleaded.

"He has to remember this day. He has to remember what was done to them."

"Yes, ma'am."

Gus Forester backed away from the open coffin and watched as sister and brother looked at the remains. Young Caleb grabbed his sister's arm and screamed, "Mule did it! Mule did it! Mule did it!" Ganna Mae leaned down and whispered in the child's ear. The boy shook his head and screamed again. "Mule did it! Mule did it! Mule did it!"

Ganna Mae wiped her eyes and looked at Yas and Lisa. "I don't remember much about the explosion. I was in shock. One minute you have parents and the next you don't." She turned from the window and went to the kitchen and poured a shot of Jack Daniels into a glass and slugged it.

"Do you remember visiting your uncle, Yas? I think you were three--maybe four?"

"I think I do. He was weird. I remember he grabbed me and kept saying the same thing over and over again."

"That's right, and do you remember what he said?" Ganna Mae asked.

"No, I just remember he was intense and he scared me."

'Mule did it. Mule did it,' Ganna Mae said in a low voice. "The first time he said that was the last day he ever saw his parents, our parents. Know what he saw that day, Yas?"

"Your parents, obviously."

"No, what he saw was what was left of our parents. He was five years old, and what he saw were their heads, hands, and chucks of flesh. Their hands were still clasped, as they always were when they walked together...and that's all we had to bury." Ganna Mae turned to Lisa and Yas. "Caleb is still alive. He's fifty five now. I visit with him twice a year. We always have the same conversation, but to him it is news. News that he thinks I've never heard--and you know what he says?"

Yas saw a changed Ganna Mae. Instead of the vibrant female of minutes earlier, a tired woman looking all of her seventy years stood before her.

"No," Yas whispered.

"He says the same thing, the only words he's spoken for over fifty years, 'Mule did it.' But the words he speaks are not what I hear." Ganna Mae wiped her eyes. "I hear the words I spoke that day when we saw our parents for the last time; *Kincaids did it. Kincaids did it. Kincaids did it.* I tried to drum it into his head, to snap him out of it. But Caleb, like my parents, is gone forever."

Neither Yas nor Lisa Cox spoke as Ganna Mae told the story of the demise of the elder Fergusons. For the moment, they were transported to the world of twenty-one-year-old Ganna Mae Ferguson. A world filled with misery and loss. A world rife with vengeance and hate--justifiable rancor.

Lisa spoke first, "Why would Mr. Kincaid do such a thing?"

"He did it for the land...but the way he killed them, why?" Ganna Mae said dully.

"Was he arrested?"

"No, never even charged. Rich people are above the law, I suppose. In a way, that's the last lesson my parents taught me. That day, at the funeral, I swore I would become wealthy, no matter what it took," Ganna Mae said. "An ambitious goal for a girl with no education--no skills." Ganna Mae traced the outline of her hips, then raised her chin and held her body erect. "This is all I had, my body. It's not what it was, but once.... but once, it was what so many men wanted--and they had it. Bankers, lawyers, actors, and rich businessmen. Some paid for my pleasures with money, others paid for what I knew, but they all paid, except...," Ganna Mae looked at Yas, "...the Kincaids. And they *will* pay. You have to understand that."

"But, that was then, and this is now. If Wyatt Kincaid killed your parents and you can prove it, why not let the police handle it?" Yas asked.

"I can't prove Wyatt Kincaid did it. He wasn't even born when my parents died."

"Then why punish him?"

Ganna Mae slugged another shot of Jack Daniels and picked up a cigarette. "May I?"

"I'd rather you didn't," Yas said.

"Fine, I'll smoke in the car." Ganna Mae started for the door. "You still want me to leave?"

"No, I want to hear more about Kincaid."

"Me, too," Lisa added.

"I have to eat," Ganna Mae twirled the cigarette in her fingers, "or smoke."

"I can fix you a sandwich or pasta," Yas offered.

"No, I want a meal. I'm starved. Have you girls eaten?"

Yas and Lisa answered at the same time, "No."

"Let's go have dinner. I can finish the story there."

"OK, but answer my question first."

Ganna Mae groped for a more plausible affliction than old-age-forgetfulness. "My blood-sugar...it makes me forgetful. What was your question?"

"Why punish Wyatt Kincaid?" Yas repeated unsympathetically.

Ganna Mae walked over to Yasnaya's latest pet project, Lisa Cox. "I know this surgeon in New York, he can work wonders...but we can discuss that over dinner, too." Fighting for the same cause, yeah, this will get Yas back on the team, Ganna Mae thought as she marveled at her ruse.

"My question, Mother?"

"Oh, sorry," Ganna Mae said, and then with the fire and brimstone of a born-again evangelist, "Nothing emboldens sin so much as mercy."

On the way to the car, Lisa Cox whispered to Yas, "You wouldn't think she could quote the Bible--I mean the way she cusses and all--"

"She didn't," Yas said. "It's from Shakespeare." Under her breath, Yas muttered another line from Macbeth, "Something wicked this way comes."

Chapter 19

The absence of engine sounds and screws stopping awakened Wyatt with a hopeful jolt. His view from the porthole verified his presumption. Barely visible on the horizon were outlines of buildings and houses sprouting up through a coastal haze. "Hey, we must be near a port I can see land." On the wall above the porthole he scratched a slash across the four vertical marks that represented the number of ports visited so far. "This makes five," he whispered to himself as he eyed the tally. To the left of the harbor entries were four vertical marks that represented the high-seas encounters with yachts or small speed boats like the go-fast Smith had piloted.

During the first weeks of captivity he logged the days and the direction of the ship's course. Rough seas and a severe bout of seasickness soon ended that endeavor and gave Kozlov and crew lots of entertainment as he spewed his guts out hugging a porcelain throne.

"Why do you count?" Svetlana asked as she observed her cellmate admiring his numeric log.

"To establish a pattern. Each time before we dock, Customs comes aboard to check paperwork or do whatever it is custom people do. This time, if we're docking, I'm going to get their attention."

"Kozlov will knock you out again, or lock you away, as he has every time before. Is all the punishment for these half-baked plans worth it?" Svetlana asked from the corner of her bunk.

Wyatt ignored Svetlana's negative comment, but found it impossible to ignore the woman. Days spent on the sun-baked deck had turned her once haunting pallor into a warm chestnut glow that accented her smoldering black eyes. Even her dark hair had lightened until the streaks of gray looked more like blonde highlights than harbingers of advancing age. Under her cotton print blouse, full, firm breasts strained against the flimsy material and made a convincing case for *au natural* after forty. In ways, the gangly brunette reminded Wyatt of the leggy and much younger, Jasmine Dubois-- Wyatt stole another look at Svetlana--*I've been on this boat too damn long...* Jasmine, despite being twenty years younger, could never compare to the aged perfection of Svetlana Andreevich. *Fifty! I'm falling for a woman my age?*

"Damn sure am," Wyatt muttered aloud as he tried to come to terms with this astonishing revelation. For a man who had believed in upgrading all things, even wives, at the first signs of age, this was radical thinking.

Setai, like most trophy wives accepted the unwritten rules of replacement, yet they all fought like hell for compensation packages; some settlements rivaled the Golden Parachute deals crafted by soon to be ex-husbands. Of course bloodsucking divorce attorney received sizable portions of the settlements, and if children were involved so much the better. Those little assets were worth their weights in gold in front of the right judge. And the cottage soak-the-rich-spouse industry didn't stop there. As soon as the settlement funds hit the law firms bank accounts, private investigators where retained to dig up dirt, even on happily married couple. He and Setai fell into that category. A few suggestive photos staged by some slime-ball private detective was all it had taken to plant the seeds of doubt. Once the divorce attorneys explained to Setai how they could pierce the prenuptial veil…wife number four packed up most of *his* belonging and moved to the south of France.

That part of his old world he didn't miss. In fact, the solitude of a captive's life was almost enjoyable in that sense. Maybe the best part was knowing that if Svetlana liked him, even a little, her feeling would be for him and not his possessions.

Kozlov's best efforts to keep them separated worked at first. But as Wyatt's injurious attempts at escape frequently landed him in the infirmary or brig he came to know Svetlana very well. Their bond formed from mutual respect for one another's rebellion. In addition to serving urine-laced coffee and laxative spiked brownies to keep Kozlov and the crew *occupied*, Svetlana also served salt peter laced meals to stem sexual desires. Wyatt appreciated her moxie and innovative cuisine…and he especially appreciated his own side dishes served sans *additives*.

In truth, the mutual respect was somewhat lopsided. While Svetlana's covert activities never resulted in punishment, Wyatt's failed antics almost always did. Each hair-brained scheme led to shared brig time due to Kozlov's mutual punishment doctrine. Through the obvious contention, somehow, they had managed to forge an alliance and agreed to disagree. Today would be one of those days when the alliance was strained, Wyatt surmised as he took in Svetlana's obvious disgust.

"You don't want to hear my plan?"

"No. I'm sure it will be another exercise in futility--"

"Well, we can't all dish out diarrhea, or shrink gonads--"

"Careful or you may lose your exemption."

Time to beg favor. Svetlana seldom made idle threats. "I'm just saying you have your ways and I have mine. But if my plan works--"

"And what if it fails, Wyatt?" Svetlana wrinkled up her nose as she remembered the feculent odor of the bilge water. "How can you be so quick to forget the "hellhole", as you call it?"

Mercifully unconscious for five of his six-day stay in the brig, he had been spared the full extent of the malodorous concoction sloshing beneath the deck boards of said hellhole. Svetlana, fortified with only a sachet of dried rosemary, had not been as lucky.

"Don't worry, we won't be making any more trips down there. I'm not going to fight them again," Wyatt said as he fingered the healing fracture on the back of his head. "Kozlov has bounced that damn pistol off my head for the last time." Wyatt smiled. "But you have to admit…I gave'em a run for the money."

Run for the money, Svetlana mused. Wyatt's last attack on three crewmembers had been ill planned and ill advised. Instead of taking them out quietly, one at a time, Wyatt Kincaid had leaped from atop the bridge, in plain sight of Kozlov, like John Wayne from a stagecoach. His *run for the money* had lasted right up until Kozlov had put his lights out with a crushing blow from the ever-present Tokarev. "Three minutes that will never make it into the annals of great battles."

"Ah, come on," Wyatt said as he punched the air. "If that old bastard didn't have eyes in the back of his head, we'd be long gone from this tub."

"Eyes in the back of his head?" Svetlana shook her head. "It was in broad daylight. You jumped them in front of the bridge--a blind man couldn't miss--"

"Well, how was I supposed to know he'd be on the bridge, huh?"

Svetlana laced her fingers together. "Peas in a pod, horse and carriage, captain and bridge--common sense, or you could have asked me."

"You weren't on the English-speaking program at the time," Wyatt snorted.

"*Speaky English?*" Svetlana laughed as she remembered Wyatt's first attempts to communicate with her. "Hardly a precursor to intelligent conversation."

"You could have stopped me before I embarrassed myself."

"What, and miss that world-class performance…how did it go?" Svetlana stood and placed her fist with thumb extended in front of her groin, then grabbed Wyatt's coffee cup. "No pee pee in coffee."

Wyatt groaned, as Svetlana emulated his plea for coffee--plain. "Yeah, well." Wyatt winced. "I swear, sometimes I can still taste that drink…Yvette--"

"Why do you lie about such things?"

"I'm not lying. I did have a cook and a boat…and a--"

"And a big jet plane." Svetlana finished Wyatt's statement. "Then how is it that the papers…" Svetlana picked up an old copy of the *Wall Street Journal* discarded by Kozlov and shook it in Wyatt's face. "…never mention the disappearance of such an important person as Wyatt Kincaid? How can the leader of such a huge company go missing and no one notice? Explain that to me."

Wyatt thought of Jim and Sally Boykin, his only living relatives. Why hadn't they filed a missing person's report? Why weren't the papers full of stories about the missing executive of the Crown Kincaid Development

Company? Months had gone by since he had hitched a ride with the pirate, Smith. Even Jim and Sally, despite their indifference to him, had to know something was wrong. "I told you, I don't have a very extended family, and besides, we were never that close."

"Surely you had friends, a child, or at least an ex-wife...someone would miss you, right?"

Wyatt marveled at the perfection of Moole's plan--the slimy worm had even convinced him to have all his payments automatically debited from his account, including Setai's monthly stipend. What a calculating bastard!-- Moole's *friendly legal advice* would ensure that no one would miss him until his money ran out, and no one would live long enough for that to happen. Fifty years of life and the only thing he had to show for it was his fat bank account, a prized asset that was turning out to be his worst enemy. "I told you I was set up--it's like I've been erased. You know--Poof!" Wyatt said, as he peeked out of the porthole and exaggerated a scan of the horizon. "What? It can't be!"

Svetlana ran to porthole. "What it is?"

"Oh, I figured there was bound to be some search parties out here looking for you... but nothing. Not a damn thing. So I guess that puts us in the same boat--pardon the pun." Wyatt grinned.

Svetlana ignored the wordplay, but the comment hit home. True, no one would miss her, but she was different than Wyatt Kincaid. Once she had had friends, and once, briefly, she had a family. Twenty years in a Soviet prison had taken everything she had held dear. Wyatt Kincaid had no such excuse. "We are on the same boat, but not in the same boat. I'm not like you, Wyatt. I had friends and..." Svetlana swallowed hard. "And once, I had a family."

"Well, hell, that's good to hear. Send out a smoke signal, dash off an SOS--let's get those friends and family on the stick...we'll be found within the week!"

Svetlana Andreevich gave Wyatt an icy stare, and then broke down into tears. "I said, *had*. Damn you."

"Whoa," Wyatt said, as he put his hand on Svetlana's shoulder. "I'm sorry. I didn't mean to upset you--I was shooting for a light moment--"

"Light moment? Your whole life, if you are telling the truth, sounds like a light moment. How could a man with so much not take the time to make friends or have a child?" Svetlana snarled. "You've squandered your life-- tell me one thing you've done to make the world a better place--*one* thing!"

Wyatt clenched his jaw as he remembered the last good thing he had done to make the world better. The image of four-year-old Princess Ho Ho drained the color from his face. The sneer on Svetlana's face deserved the story, but the memory of the little warrior's last battle was too painful.

"My daddy taught me two things. One, a true gift is given anonymously, and two, bragging about your good deeds cheapens them."

"Such convenient advice," Svetlana said. "Kudos to your father for providing you with a pass from honest scrutiny. Deniability-- the crutch of the wealthy."

Wyatt digested the familiar criticism. Everyone hated the wealthy…right up until they needed something. Fulfill every need for every cause…then it was OK to be rich. But miss one charity donation, one charity ball--let one little girl die--Princess Ho Ho…. He'd never spent much time with children until his encounter with the tiny four-year old leukemia patient on what Trent called an Angel Flight. Wyatt had agreed to let his jet be used to fly sick children to medical treatments. It was on a shared Angel Flight that he met the precocious little girl. "Mister, you think you could help me beat up cancer?" Since Wyatt was a grown up, she had asked him for help. This was before he had learned the rules of dealing with terminal children, and he had foolishly promised that cancer's "butt whooping" was in the bag. To make up for his blunder, he made sure he was on every Princess Ho Ho flight from then on. With the help of his international flight attendant, who volunteered her time for Angel Flights, he threw lavish tea parties…or, as the little princess used to describe them, "Parties, just like Alice in Wonderland." As CEO of The Crown, Wyatt had attended many elaborate functions, but none would ever rival those he shared with Princess Ho Ho.

Even all the Crown's resources and the latest experimental drugs couldn't save her. Little Honey Howard died on his jet at 41000 ft; the first leg of her journey to heaven. The medical team on the tarmac had to pry her from Wyatt's arms.

"You really don't know what you are talking about," Wyatt choked down his emotions. "I've done good things."

"Have you, now? Without your toys and money, you are nothing."

Out of habit, Wyatt patted his pocket for his cell phone. Just one phone call to the hospital—or a call to Princess Ho Ho's parents…. Let Svetlana ask them how they felt about Wyatt Kincaid…filthy rich Wyatt Kincaid. "Svetlana, I'm getting off of this boat one day…and I'm taking you with me, just so I can show you--ah, forget it."

Svetlana walked to the lavatory and rinsed her face with cold water. "Even if you have all the money you talk about, you have less than I."

"You're damn near a slave on a crummy boat, with an ass-grabbing crew and a captain from hell--give me a break. And what's your excuse for not having friends or a child--I might have had a miserable life, but at least I have a successful company to show for it."

"I'm not a slave. I agreed to work as a cook for passage to America, where I will meet my child, my daughter…irrefutable proof that my life has not been as meaningless as yours."

"Well, if that's the case you need to speak to someone in booking, 'cause it don't look like your ticket to America is going to be punched. We've been to four harbors, and as far as I can tell, none of them were in America--"

Svetlana glared at Wyatt. "I would have been there already, if you hadn't shown up."

"Well, excuse me for being kidnapped!"

Squeaks from the wheel lock spinning in the hatch signaled the arrival of the pair's common adversary, Kozlov. Wyatt and Svetlana moved to opposite ends of the cell from hell and awaited the now-familiar, pre-docking prisoner prep.

"Hands behind your back," Kozlov barked at Svetlana as he stirred the air with his Tokarev. "You too, Mr. Kincaid." Wyatt turned sideways and watched as the two crewmen taped Svetlana's hands behind her back with gray duct tape. As Kozlov turned his attention to Wyatt, the young ass-grabbing mate shot both hands under Svetlana's blouse and cupped her full breasts.

"Get your damn hands off of her--"

Before Wyatt could finish, Kozlov slammed his fist into Wyatt's face. "Rule number two, Mr. Kincaid. I give the orders on this ship."

"Well, why don't you order that scumbag to stop copping a feel," Wyatt muttered through bloody lips.

"Copping a feel?" Kozlov queried curiously in response to the unfamiliar phrase.

"Yeah, grabbing her butt and breasts--copping a feel. The little pervert can't keep his hands off her."

Kozlov looked at the mate standing behind Svetlana. The mate lifted both hands in the air to proclaim his innocence. "So tell me, Mr. Kincaid, have you never *copped a feel*, as you say?"

"I, um...ah." Wyatt sputtered as he remembered the cheap thrills he had inflicted upon countless waitresses and flight attendants. But his transgressions were different, at least he had tipped. "Yeah, I have, but I paid for the privilege."

Kozlov's smirk didn't bother Wyatt, but the hurt in Svetlana's eyes cut him to his soul.

"Nicholas, give me 100 kopecks." Kozlov ordered.
The mate reached into his trousers and produced the note. Kozlov, in return, stuffed the note into Svetlana's waistband. "Now, comrade, cop your feel."

With all eyes on him, the mate pushed his hand under Svetlana's dress until the dark patch between her thighs was exposed. Emboldened by the captain's order, Nicholas Gurov, did just as he was told.

Svetlana, as she had done as a child to make the monster in her closet go away, closed her eyes and hoped the men, like the monster, would disappear.

You som-bitch," Wyatt growled.

"Did he not pay for the privilege, Mr. Kincaid?" Kozlov teased as he waved another note in Wyatt's face. Funny how the capitalist pig squeals the loudest when confronted with his sins.

"That don't make it right--"

Kozlov signaled for the mate to stop then turned to Wyatt. "Perhaps you will remember that the next time you *pay for the privilege*, Mr. Kincaid?"

Wyatt's shoulders slumped as tears pooled in Svetlana's eyes, and as they fell to the deck, Wyatt Kincaid vowed to find every woman he had ever objectified and apologize--profusely.

Chapter 20

The clanging noise of the A-com ladder being stowed on deck confirmed Customs departure. Kozlov, true to form, had again concealed him in the brig to avoid notice by the officials...hard to get anyone's attention bound and gagged. But one little advantage didn't make Kozlov the winner. They still had to dock and that meant another chance at escape...this time he wouldn't blow it. As the ship got under way Wyatt wondered if Kozlov would keep him locked up the entire time the ship was in port, a depressing thought. As if in response to his musing, Konstantin and Gurov unlocked the door and shoved him roughly back up to the galley.

Svetlana remained bound and gagged in the fetal position as she had been since he was escorted to the brig. If he could just talk to her...explain things. He stroked her hair hoping for a smile, or some sign that things where ok between them. Svetlana rolled away from him and faced the wall. Probably best to leave her alone, but solitary time in the brig always made him eager to talk. If she would work with him they could probably remove their gags. But working together wasn't on Svetlana's mind, apparently.

In spite of the vulnerability Svetlana Andreevich displayed when Gurov molested her, there was no doubt about her toughness. Before he was hustled off to the brig and Gurov could tape Svetlana's mouth, she managed to shoot a question at the pervert in front of most of the crew. "Comrade, tell me. Do you know what defines a bastard?"

"No, grandma. Tell me," Gurov had sneered, and a calm Svetlana Andreevich had obliged. "A bastard is one who picks his nose with a four-inch finger and urinates through an inch less."

Even Kozlov managed a rare smile, Wyatt remembered as he licked at the thick tape across his lips. He and Svetlana had spent many days together and enjoyed many conversations, but he had never before wanted to talk to her as badly—to explain why his actions were different from Gurov's. "Ummm--ummm." Wyatt snorted in disgust, as he realized his explanation would have to wait until the ship docked. And what if they returned him to the hellhole without Svetlana, how long would it be before he could apologize? As if she read his mind, Svetlana faced him, aimed a "Go to hell with your lame excuses" look in his direction and turned away.

Who could blame her? A groper was a groper, Wyatt thought, as he positioned himself in front of his porthole. He could have lied, pretended that he had never defiled a woman, but Kozlov would have exposed his lie. Yuri Kozlov was not a long-time acquaintance, but he was definitely connected to a pipeline from Wyatt's past--probably Moole. How else could he know about the sexual harassment charges (false charges by the way) filed by a former employee of the Crown? "Careful, Mr. Kincaid. On the high seas I am the judge, not a panel from E.E.O commission. Now keep your distance."

Kozlov's remark had come when Wyatt brushed Svetlana's hair from her face. Brushed her hair—no where else! Where was that little speech when the ass-grabbing Gurov made his move? Two-faced som bitch!

A vaguely familiar spit of land appeared, and suddenly nothing mattered more than the scene outside the window. Behind the sandy beach and across the lush green marsh a very familiar landmark centered itself into Wyatt's limited view. "Old Baldy" Wyatt snorted against the adhesive backing of his gag. The Bald Head Lighthouse had never been more resplendent. After five port entries, Kozlov has finally done it...made a mistake, and landed in my backyard, Wyatt thought as he scrambled to the bunk Svetlana was holding down.

Ignoring her wide-eyed fury, Wyatt reached under the thin mattress and retrieved the shiny top to a #10 can. With hands behind his back and in a seated position, he positioned the lid toward the rays of the early morning sun and aimed them along the shores of Bald Head Island. Three quick flashes followed by three longer then three short flashes. Wyatt again repeated the process for several seconds then rolled over onto his stomach to see the results. Two golfers on the #3 tee box of the Bald Head Island course waved at the rusty freighter. Encouraged by the attention Wyatt again repeated the visual S-O-S then flopped to his stomach. The golfers, eager to work their way to the 19th hole, ignored the flashing light and teed off.

Bothered by the commotion Svetlana finally looked at Wyatt.

"Ummm--Ummm--Ummm," Wyatt grunted to Svetlana in an attempt to convey his discovery. With little effort Svetlana nudged the mattress back with her face and snuggled her gag against a spring hook in the bunk. Two seconds later, the gag and the silence in the berth were gone.

"What are you saying?" Svetlana hissed.

Wyatt followed Svetlana's lead and removed the tape. "Hey, smooth move! No more silence, great." The compliment made Svetlana smile. Wyatt quickly followed up on the opportunity. "Svetlana, I'm sorry that my past caused you trouble, but I'm about to make that up to you...WE'RE ON MY TURF!"

"Keep your voice down." Svetlana admonished. "Gurov is in the galley."

"Right," Wyatt whispered. "All this will be over soon. I'm home."

"Home?"

"Yeah. My home, Wilmington. I just saw 'Old Baldy,' the--"

"Who?"

"Not who, what, but that's not important. Hey," Wyatt said, as he eyed the can lid. "Take that lid and cut the tape from my wrists. Hell, I can swim to shore from here."

Svetlana moved across the room and stared at Wyatt. "I'm afraid."

"You don't have to be afraid of Kozlov or Gurov…hell you don't have to be afraid of any of them once I get to shore. Just get this tape off me."

"I'm not so sure they're the ones I need to worry about." Svetlana said.

"What…you're kidding, right?" Wyatt Kincaid exhaled slowly, almost as slowly as this lesson was sinking into his gut. "Svetlana, I know what I did to those women upset you, but you don't understand. In America, women want the guy with the money and the power--"

"Is that how your last girlfriend, an employee half your age, felt? Or did she just want to keep her job, Wyatt?"

Wyatt thought of Jasmine, and how their relationship had started. Sure he had doubled her salary, but for good reason. Jasmine was a damn good paralegal *and* really easy on the eyes. Any C.E.O. with half a mind and one good eye would have done the same thing. "It wasn't like that. Jasmine liked me and besides I wouldn't have fired her. She was worth every cent I paid her and then some." Might not have given her a big bonus if she turned out to be less friendly, but I'd a never fired her.

"So she was treated like any other employee--no gifts, no special favors?"

Wyatt remembered the new Jag convertible he had given Jasmine to replace her VW--a little favor for an employee. "A car—hers was a cheap little number called a 'bug.' I upgraded her. What's wrong with that?"

Svetlana nodded knowingly. "Something you would have done for any employee who needed a better car?"

Wyatt thought of the kid in legal…*Ridell with the junker from hell.* He needed a car, and yes in a round-about way he had helped him get one. Moole and Big Jim were screwing with the kid's bonus and he put a stop to it. "That's exactly right…any employee!"

"Liar! There were employees you wouldn't help."

"Name one!"

"Tim Ridell," Svetlana blurted out.

Wyatt thought of all the conversations he'd ever had with Svetlana. Not once had he ever mentioned the kid's name. The information pipeline, Moole's pipeline, was connected to Svetlana as well as Kozlov. No wonder she refused to help free him--Svetlana Andreevich and Yuri Kozlov were on the same team.

Wyatt looked at the #10 lid and back at Svetlana. If she was on the opposing team, it was likely she'd start screaming for help to stop him. Killing her was out of the question. But he could tie her up and gag her again. If he could just get over the railing and into the water he could probably make it to shore even bound and with his mouth taped. But with his hands tied behind his back there was no way he could tape Svetlana's mouth before she would yell to Gurov. Maybe stuff the mattress over her head and knock her out somehow? Options tumbled through Wyatt's mind like a vault's dial in a safecracker's hands. *Negotiate*! Hell, yeah. Why wouldn't one of the best in the business negotiate his way out of this mess? Wyatt sat up and looked at Svetlana. "How'd you know about Ridell?"

"Who?"

"Ridell, the kid with the bad car. How do you know about him?"

Svetlana's heart raced, Tim Ridell was not a name she should have used to prove her point that Wyatt was a liar and possibly a dangerous man. She had slipped, and now she had to regain her balance. "You told me about him--in the hellhole." Svetlana said, as she remembered Wyatt's rants during his moments of semi-consciousness.

"I said Tim Ridell?"

"Yes, he's a lawyer in your company."

"Liar."

"Phillip Moole, Jasmine, Setai, Heidi, Grace, Angelica, Monica," Svetlana repeated names Wyatt had spoken during their time in the hellhole and then lied. "And Tim Ridell."

Wyatt leaned toward Svetlana. "I'll give you the first group--hell I was married to half of the women, and I can see where Moole was on my mind. But I've never mentioned Tim Ridell." Wyatt pressed his face close to Svetlana. "And you want to know how I know that?"

"How?"

"Because I've always called him Tom, never Tim, not once."

"Tom--Tim...maybe I misunderstood?"

"Svetlana, maybe I took some inappropriate liberties with a few women, but those women were flirting and kidding around, too. I can tell you this; I've never touched a woman without her being a willing participant in the game. I'd never do that. What I did as an employer was wrong. I'm admitting that and it's time for you to admit that you're lying--because, you are."

"Admit to being a murderer and a crook," Svetlana demanded as she glared at Wyatt. "Then maybe I will admit that... I'm a liar."

"A *murderer*?" Wyatt leaned back on his bunk. "What the hell makes you think I'm a murderer?"

Svetlana fumbled with the tape on her wrist. To prove her accusation she would have to reveal her source--something she couldn't do. "OK, I am a liar!" Svetlana rolled away from Wyatt. "Now leave me alone."

Wyatt looked at Svetlana's trembling hands. Was it fear or anger that caused her reaction? "Is that why you wanted us bound and gagged when we were alone--because you think I'm a murderer?"

"Yes."

"Who told you I was a murderer…Kozlov--Moole? They're liars, I've never--"

"I know your intended victim, Wyatt, and I know the reason you have to murder."

"And that reason is?"

"Greed."

"Greed?" Wyatt echoed

"Yes. All you've talked about is how much money you have. I only pretended not to know you were rich. I know very well who you are, Wyatt Kincaid."

"Then tell me exactly who it is that I am."

Svetlana sat up on her bunk and faced Wyatt. "You are not a murderer, not yet. But you will be. It's part of your plan. My ticket to America would have been punched, as you say, if I hadn't learned of your plan. I'm here to make sure you don't kill the person that stands between you and full ownership of your company—dog that you are!"

"Svetlana, I'm going to beat the hell out of Phillip Moole and make sure that he goes to jail. But I'm not going to kill him--and what's your connection to Moole anyway?"

"Moole?"

"Yeah, Moole--the person you think I have to kill." Wyatt kneeled in front of her bunk, eyeball to eyeball. "If you know so much about me, it's only fair that I know who you really are? Tell me your connection to Moole, damn it!"

"Get away from me, or I will scream."

"Oh, don't even try to play that card. I'd never hurt you and you know that…" Wyatt rocked back on his haunches. "This is a long shot…but are you Phillip Moole's wife--his other wife?"

"No," Svetlana said as she pressed against the hatch. "I am the mother of Yasnaya Polyana."

Wyatt laid flat on the floor and exhaled a long slow breath. Yasnaya Polyana, the *enigmatic entity*, as his father's estate attorney referred to the Yasnaya Polyana in Wyatt Kincaid Sr's. Last Will and Testament. The shareholder without a paper trail, or any documentation recorded in the courts of America, wasn't a figment of the old man's senile dementia-- Yasnaya Polyana was a real person…the daughter of Svetlana Andreevich…really?

"Svetlana--we need to talk."

Chapter 21

Light reflected from the windshield of the pilot barge glinted around room. Wyatt, still on the floor rolled onto his stomach and crawled to the porthole. Through the square he had previously cleared he could see the harbor pilot reaching for the Jacob's ladder attached to the *Baltic Queen*. Oh, hell yeah! My ride's here.

Wyatt toyed with the can lid as Svetlana continued to ignore to him. Not that it mattered. As far as he knew she might very well be Phillip Moole's wife. And if she really *was* the mother of Yasnaya Polyana, that made her more closely connected to Moole and his crowd than to him. Good riddance...one less thing to worry about. Now all he had to do was figure out how to signal longshoremen on the port side of the *Baltic Queen* from his starboard side roost? Before he had time to formulate a plan, he felt the boat being pushed in the opposite direction. "Yesss!!" Wyatt whispered, as he remembered a scene he had witnessed hundreds of times from his office windows. Two harbor tugs, one fore and one opposite aft, were executing a 180° turn to reposition the freighter on a seaward heading.

Finally, the tables, like the boat, were turning in his favor. Kozlov would pay dearly for this mistake. Whatever game this was would be played, and played very soon, with the only rules that mattered...his.

Crazy from his first hope of possible freedom, Wyatt plastered his face against the porthole. Slowly, familiar haunts and landmarks he hadn't seen in months filled his little square of vision. Wyatt banged his forehead repeatedly against the porthole, then cursed the impenetrable window that separated him from his world, so close and yet, truly, so far away. Harbor Bistro, come on, come on! Cotton Exchange get out of the way.... "Stop." Wyatt grunted as the most beautiful edifice he ever had seen came into his limited view.

Dappled by the morning sun and sparkling like a diamond-encrusted jeweled scepter, the tallest and most expensive building on the Port City Waterfront, his building, the Crown's Head, revealed its majesty. The initial proprietary satisfaction in his gut cooled like blood spattered against a cold steel blade. Not until the sharp outline of the C-K logo etched into the building's top center panels emerged from the bright eastern sky, did the pain subside. "C.K." Wyatt mumbled, as he admired the logo. "C.K, Moole--*Crown Kincaid--it's still Crown Kincaid* you dirty bastard!"

Wyatt stood and blood dripped from his forehead. "Moole, damn you. I'll have my life back today...and it'll be your blood I taste before the sun goes down. You som-bitch--"

"Wyatt." Svetlana backed away from the hulking tower of rage that now shared the brig with her. "You're scaring me."

"Svetlana, if your daughter really is the one who owns stock in the Crown...join with me. It's to her advantage I swear. Moole is trying to destroy the company don't you see?" Wyatt whispered. "For the love of whatever you hold sacred...help me get off this damn ship, please."

"No! You will kill what I hold sacred--"

"Your daughter, right?"

"Yes, Yasnaya Polyana"

"Svetlana, that can't be her name. Your daughter may exist but not by that name, I know." Wyatt moved his face closer and glared at her. "You got the name from Moole didn't you?"

Svetlana braced against the hatch. "She does exist, and once I know she is safe from you, I will go to her."

"You are quite the actress," Wyatt said as he watched the tears pooling in Svetlana's eyes run down her face. "For a moment there you had me going. I almost, *almost*...bought this mother role you're playing--"

"Do you think I'm lying?"

"No. Not lying...but you're confused." Wyatt exhaled another long slow breath to calm himself. "Svetlana, I don't know why my father gave shares of the Crown to this...this, *untraceable entity*, Yasnaya Polyana. Not even the best lawyers in the country--my lawyers, know why he added this stipulation to my inheritance. But what they do know, what they all agreed on, is that Yasnaya Polyana was a figment of my old man's imagination, one last jab at me before he died. She doesn't exist--never has."

"Liar," Svetlana hissed. "Your father hid her identity because he knew what you would do if you found her."

"Moole was lying. Maybe you have a child, and maybe, just maybe, her name is Yasnaya Polyana." Wyatt clenched his teeth and rammed the words through them. "But the Yasnaya Polyana I'm speaking of exists in name only on the corporate books of the Crown. She's a joke...a sick joke, my father devised--"

"Who is Moole?"

"Dammit, Svetlana, don't patronize me, the jig is up. You, Moole, and Kozlov are as thick as thieves."

"I do not know Moole. But I know this Mister Wyatt Kincaid the second." Svetlana's fiery eyes burned into Wyatt's. "My Yasnaya Polyana is bound to this inheritance, by blood, just as you are."

"Bullshit, I'm an only child--"

"No, my daughter is--" A pang of fear pierced Svetlana's breast. Already she had said too much. Any more and she would jeopardize her benefactor, not to mention the life of her own daughter. *Say no more.*

"Not real!" Wyatt shouted.

"No?" Svetlana swallowed her fear. "My daughter is the child of Wyatt Kincaid!"

"Say what?" Wyatt growled. "You're crazy…. I slept with you? No, no, I…I'd have remembered"

Svetlana tossed her head back and laughed, long, cold, and hard. "Don't flatter yourself. I never could have loved a pig like you."

"But you said earlier 'by blood'--"

"Yes, but the blood of your father runs through my daughter's veins…not yours."

A flood of relief surged into Wyatt's gut. Poor, damnable Moole. If this was the best help he could find…his plan was doomed. Wyatt Kincaid? Deacon in the church, married to the same woman for fifty years, Myra, Wyatt Jr.'s own mother? Wyatt smiled at Svetlana. Moole had given her a name but not even Moole knew the integrity of Wyatt Kincaid Sr.

Memories returned to him of late night runs with his father delivering food and clothing to a neighboring family "on hard times." Cold nights in his father's Cadillac stuffed with overcoats and pine crates of salted streak-o'-lean deposited on unlit porches…anonymously. *A man will accept a helping hand, son, but never a handout. To keep your good deeds good, keep them to yourself.*

"I take back what I said about you being an actress. A good actress would have researched her role. My father was a good man," Wyatt bristled with pride. "And he never screwed around in his life. You and Moole better go back to the old drawing board. True, the shares held by Yasnaya Polyana could tilt the balance of power in the Crown. But--ah, *this* is ridiculous!"

"It's true. Your father and I met when I was just out of college in Washington, D.C. My relationship with your father is why I was sent to Siberia."

"Svetlana, my father…. If you only knew, jeez. The man never looked at another woman." Wyatt shook his head. "And besides, I've paid thousands, hell maybe hundreds of thousands, to detective agencies to find this Yasnaya Polyana. I'm telling you, a person by that name does not exist. Your best bet is to throw in with me. I'll pay you more than Moole. You help me get off this boat and you will be a rich woman."

"I do not know Moole, and I don't want your money. I want my daughter. Who I will protect from you." Svetlana's eyes narrowed. "Even if it means killing you to save her."

Wyatt backed away from Svetlana to better assess her. No actress, not even an Academy-Award-winning one, could muster the maternal resolve being displayed at this moment. Svetlana's feelings, however misguided, appeared genuine.

And I know the reason you have to murder. Svetlana's words ricocheted like popping corn in Wyatt's head. *Your father's blood runs through her veins.*

Obviously two erroneous *facts*; he had no need to kill anyone, anymore than his father had a daughter. His escape hinged on his ability to convey those truths in a way that Svetlana would accept them.

"So, I have a sister, huh?"

Svetlana did not respond. Too much had been said already. Without looking at Wyatt she sat on the bunk and faced the wall.

"You know, when I was a kid, I used to pretend I had a kid brother; even had a name for him." Wyatt waited for Svetlana to engage...she did not. "Yeah, used to call him Sam. Kinda funny, don't you think? Sam, such a simple name, especially when you compare it to Yasnaya Polyana, who according to you is my real sibling." Wyatt spat out the name like a bad taste in his mouth, "Yasnaya Polyana. Weird name...what does it mean and why would you hang that on a child? She...er, your daughter. She must hate it."

Svetlana spoke to the wall in front of her. "Lubova. That is the name I gave her. It means *daughter of love* in Russian." *Lubova*, Svetlana had not said the name aloud to anyone in more years than she cared to remember. Not even the adoptive mother knew her name. The Russian prison guards would have seen to that. *Lubova*.

"Lou Bubba--not much better'n Yasnaya Polyana, but easier to spell I rekon?" Wyatt said, thankful that his putative sibling at least had a Southern-sounding name, though gender-conflicted.

"L-U-B-O-V-A ...Lu-**bova,** not Lou Bubba."

"Lu-bova," Wyatt repeated. "Means daughter of love, huh?"

"In Russian, yes."

"Where in the world did Yasnaya Polyana come from, and what does *that* mean?"

Svetlana turned around in the bunk and faced Wyatt. No need to let him think he could manipulate her, just because she was a woman. Men like Wyatt weren't hard to figure out. Women were toys to Wyatt Kincaid; once he tired of them, they were discarded. How else to explain so many wives and so few family and friends? During the past months Wyatt had revealed his life to her, and the plain truth was that nobody cared about him because he had cared for no one.

"Wyatt, I know what you are trying to do with this conversation...and it won't work. Who I am and what I am doing has to come out, but not now."

"Look, I think you believe with all your heart that what you told me is the truth. But if I can hear the rest of your story, I think I can prove it false. I don't know what you were told about Yasnaya Polyana. You say Moole didn't tell you. I believe you. But all this is nothing but a cruel hoax. You are being used. They are using your need for revenge to help execute a crooked scheme--"

"No. What you yourself have told me validates what I was told. Look at you." Svetlana pointed to Wyatt's forehead. "You hurt yourself, and then promise to taste another's blood. Only a murderous person could do such a thing."

"Svetlana, I've never thought about killing anyone in my life. Now, that may change if I get my hands on Phillip Moole. But he has it coming...has for a long time. I told you why I haven't been missed but that was Moole's doing. He made sure that I wouldn't be missed. The connection I have to people is my money. Moole made sure the flow of money wouldn't stop, and unless it does, no one will know I'm gone--"

"How sad. You know this about yourself...and yet, you have done nothing to change it."

"Well, in Russia, if that's where you're really from, that may be a bad thing. But in America...well, it's the ways things are. People use you, and you use them back--"

Svetlana pressed her mouth close to the seal around the hatch so Gurov would be more likely to hear her when she called out. The conversation with Wyatt was going nowhere. The more she learned about her cellmate, the less she liked him. "I spent time in America. The people I met were not like that, especially *one*."

"My father, right?"

"Yes."

"You were what...twenty then--Washington, right?" Wyatt shook his head. "Come on...that's proves it couldn't have been my dad. He would have been over fifty--"

"You." Svetlana rolled her eyes. "You, of all people find *that* hard to believe? How old was your last wife--thirty?"

"Her next birthday. But you're also forgetting I was never a deacon in the church. My dad was old school. One woman, childhood sweetheart, *my mom*, and he would have told her about you. He didn't kept things from her--"

"How about your secret, Wyatt? The secret that destroyed your family? The secret that almost caused your father to commit suicide? That's when we met. I stopped him.-"

"Liar!" Wyatt glared at Svetlana. "We had our problems...you don't know what you're talking about."

Svetlana stared at Wyatt until his eyes met hers. "You are the liar. You say you never killed anyone--"

"That's right! I'd swear to it on a stack of Bibles ten stories high with a lighting rod in each hand during a thunderstorm."

"Your father told me about the abortion, and..." Svetlana looked deep into the darkest corners of Wyatt's soul. "I know the girl died, Wyatt."

Wyatt closed his eyes and hung his head. For more than thirty years he had avoided the truth. A secret he had always assumed his father had carried to the grave had been shared with his *lover*? But never his wife...Poor guy...It must have been too much of a burden to bear alone. "He..." Wyatt choked on the words. "It bothered him that badly?--Suicide? It wasn't like that...I--" Wyatt shook the image of his tortured father from his mind. "I could never make him understand. I paid for her, Jenny's, abortion, but I didn't kill her. It wasn't his fault. He.... Ah, Dad...Jenny, I'm so sorry."

Svetlana, so sure she could twist the knife once it was buried, now felt only pity for the man she had wanted to destroy. Wyatt was not a good-for-nothing jerk. She had judged him too harshly. Only a man with a heart could suffer like he obviously was at the memory...poor Wyatt. "He forgave you--"

Wyatt nudged his face against his shoulders to wipe the tears from his face. "He told you that?"

"Yes. But he could never forgive himself."

"It wasn't his fault. He gave me the money, but," Wyatt forced himself back to the last day of closeness he had experienced with his father. "He told me I'd make the right decision, I--"

Wyatt looked into Svetlana's eyes. "I didn't. That's why Jenny died and why I could never make him love me again. Svetlana, the reason I never had a child...never wanted a child--"

"You don't have to explain."

"No." Wyatt swallowed. "Let me tell you another family secret. A secret that only I know. The girl, Jenny, she came from a big family and her family...they went through--hard times. They had nothing, but I was envious of them. Only children are lonely children...I guess that's why I wanted what Jenny had. She was beautiful and I was determined to have her, but she wanted nothing to do with me. She had plans, big plans. She wanted to go to college and become successful so she could help her family. Me, I just wanted to have fun. I knew I'd get a degree. With my father's donations some school would oblige me. There was never any doubt about that.

"Jenny couldn't abide a lazy person, and God help me...I was about as lazy as they came. We dated a few times, and I fell hard for her, but she wanted someone with drive, ambition." Wyatt fumbled again with the lid. "Then something happened, something bad--"

Svetlana waited as Wyatt struggled for the words.

"Wyatt," Svetlana said. "Your father, as you said, was conventional. He couldn't understand how you could...abort your own child--"

"No, that's what I'm trying to tell you. Jenny's baby wasn't mine." Wyatt gritted his teeth. "She found someone with drive and ambition, an older guy--a prick. When she told him she was pregnant, she thought he would be happy. He wasn't. He told her there was no way he could marry someone without pedigree, 'white trash', he called her." Wyatt stared at the floor. "That's when Jenny came to me for help. I offered to marry her--" Wyatt laughed. "But Jenny had her pride...she wasn't about to marry a deadbeat like me. Besides, she'd had it with rich boys. The abortion was her idea. In those days abortions were illegal and expensive, a thousand bucks...more money than my dad was willing to give me for no reason. So--" Wyatt shrugged his shoulders. "I told my father that I had gotten a girl in trouble...and that I needed a thousand dollars. He never said a word, just walked over to his safe and put the money on his desk. When he handed me the cash he said, 'You have a choice to make. I trust you'll make the right one'."

Wyatt turned to the porthole and stared into the dark waters of the Cape Fear River hoping they would wash away the painful memory. "Jenny found this guy...I thought he was a doctor...he wasn't. I took her to a gas station--" Wyatt looked back at Svetlana. "I thought that's where we were meeting the doctor.... The guy used a coat hanger." Wyatt's face paled. "Jenny bled to death before I could get her to the hospital. I...ah, wrong choice. I guess you could say I loved her to death."

"Wyatt, you never told your father this story?"

"No."

"Why? "

"Jenny was dead. And whether my father thought so or not, I was convinced I had made the right choice and performed a good deed. 'To keep good deeds good, keep them to yourself', his words, Svetlana, his code: my code."

"But if he had known--"

"It makes more sense if you know the rest of the story." Wyatt waited for an interruption...none came. "The abortionist was arrested, and the story made all the papers. The creep, the guy Jenny fell for, was a young lawyer. I was a witness. Before the case came to trial he contacted me. I'm sure he knew his name would come out at trial. He assured me that if it did he had several friends that would admit to having sex with Jenny. They would paint her as a whore, a scheming gold-digger who got what she deserved." Wyatt exhaled his anger and turned to face Svetlana. "Jenny lost her virginity to the creep, she told me that, and I believed her...still do. So in the judge's chambers, who happened to be the creep's father, by the way, in front of my father--I did what any gentlemen would have done."

"No, the girl was dead. The truth--"

"Her family, that big beautiful family was still alive and all they had left was Jenny's memory. I wasn't about to destroy that. With my admission and substantial compensation to the victim's family, the judge agreed to seal the records."

"But your lie, it--"

"Was exactly what my father would have done. If he'd have been in my shoes--if you knew him, you'd know that."

Svetlana moved over to Wyatt and removed a small paring knife from her skirt. No words were spoken as she cut the tape from Wyatt's wrist and feet. With her eyes Svetlana told Wyatt everything he needed to know. Her act was nothing more or nothing less than an honorable young man had done thirty-two years earlier. Svetlana Andreevich's courage proved a truth Wyatt Kincaid could no longer deny. She was the mother of a sister he never had known. "Wyatt, one question. The creep, who was he?"

"Phillip Moole."

Chapter 22

Trent Rayle watched as the hospital attendant tugged down the last pocket of the fitted sheet. More than hour had passed since Cheryl's body had been released to Simpson's Funeral Home. Slowly, his eyes scanned the checklist in Cheryl's looped cursive writing:

1. Call Simpson Funeral Home 910-555-3323.
2. Pay hospital bill (Finance Office, 1st floor)
3. Deliver funeral instructions, dress, and jewelry (box in bedroom closet, marked Simpson) to funeral home.
4. After burial contact Granite Monuments (prepaid)
5. Contact Life Insurance Company (policy in your desk). You will need medical certificate from hospital. Ask for it after you pay medical bills.

Trent turned the list over in his hands. As promised, Cheryl had left no affectionate note, and worst of all, no instruction on how to live life without his soul mate. "Closure," she had said. "is for people who are apart. I'll always be with you."

In the room where his wife had breathed her last breath, Trent Rayle searched for signs that Cheryl had fulfilled her promise. Flowers, cards, a collage of snapshots of their shared lives, all the way back to kindergarten, but no Cheryl. Undaunted, he closed his eyes and visualized the image of the only woman he had ever loved.

"Sir." The attendant gently touched Trent's shoulder. "You want me to get a cart to put this stuff on?" The image of his wife so full of life faded, and was quickly replaced by the young black face of a sympathetic stranger.

"I'm sorry?" Trent asked.

"A cart...I can get you a cart." The attendant gazed at Cheryl's cheerleading picture.

"Pretty lady...nice, too."

"Yes." Trent pressed the picture to his chest. "She...she was--." *Was.* Past tense--dead. "Is...is." Trent rose, then wobbled on unsteady legs. Before he fell the attendant caught him and held him upright against his chest. "You OK, mister?"

Sobs, deep and convulsing, shattered the silence of the room. For a moment, through the compassion of this stranger, Cheryl Rayle was sending a sign. "My Grandma says," the attendant interjected, "they always with you."

Always with you. Strengthened by the affirmation, Trent Rayle stepped away from the young man and smiled. "I knew that...I just forgot for a moment--thanks. I'll take that cart now."

Trent ignored the stares of the administrative workers on the first floor and pushed the cart, laden with the remnants of Cheryl's month-long hospital stay, in front of the door labeled Finance Office. "May I help you?" the young woman behind the desk asked in a cheery voice.

"Yes, I'm here to pay the bill for my wife, Cheryl Rayle."

Without a word the woman typed the name into the computer in front of her. Rayle, Cheryl popped up on the screen. Under patient status, in red, blinked the word: *Deceased.* "I'm so sorry, Mr. Rayle. I didn't know that--"

"It's OK," Trent mumbled. "She..ah, we...ah--could I just have the bill, please?"

The woman nodded and turned back to the screen. "Did you want a printout?"

"Yeah--no, just the amount I owe." Trent pulled the list from his pocket and read the last line. *Life Insurance.* "Not unless the insurance company needs--"

"I'll send them a copy, and the medical certificate if you want me, to."

"Thank you." Trent laid the list on the counter and checked off items 1,2, & 5. So like Cheryl to put her last instructions in the format all pilots could relate to...a checklist.

The mechanical click of the laser printer broke the uneasy silence. Quietly, the woman highlighted the amount due column in yellow and slid the document in front of Trent. "Zero--that can't be right. The doctor said, experimental stuff wasn't--"

"Your bill has been paid in full, Mr. Rayle. No payment due."

"Who...who paid--"

"Anonymous?"

"Anonymous?" A flush of anger spread across Trent's face. "No, that's not good enough. Who paid, dammit!"

Frightened by the outburst, the woman turned the screen toward him. "See, Payee: Anonymous."

"I don't care what it says." Trent looked at the door behind the woman. Hospital Administrator. "I want to see the Administrator."

"Yes, sir."

Seconds after a brief, whispered conversation at the office door, Trent Rayle was face to face with a statuesque, well-coifed brunette. "Phyllis Barnum, Hospital Administrator. How may I help you Mr. Rayle?"

"I want to know who paid my bill." Trent fumed. "If my brother thinks he can make me into a charity case, he can forget it."

"The payee wishes to remain anonymous, Mr.--"

"It's my bill. I have a right to know who paid it. I'll sue if I have to."

Phyllis Barnum looked at the familiar address in the payee information box. "Do you and your brother share the same last name, Mr. Rayle?"

"Of course, and what--"

"In that case." Phyllis removed her glasses. "I can assure you that your brother did not pay this bill."

"Then, who? I have a right to know, don't I?"

"Mr. Rayle, you have a right to know. But we, the hospital, have to both consider your rights and comply with the wishes of your benefactor." Phyllis Barnum gave her most dazzling smile. "I'm sure you can understand our predicament."

"I don't care about your predicament. I want to know who paid my wife's bill, now!"

"Please keep your voice down. You're causing a scene--"

"I'll be causing a lot more than that when I come back with my lawyer, lady." The document in Trent's hand quivered like wings on a horsefly.

"Very well, Mr. Rayle." Phyllis moved the cursor over the payee box and hit the reveal function button. Then she turned the screen back toward the counter.

Instead of Trey Rayle, the name Trent had expected to see, a name he wouldn't have guessed in a million years filled the payee box.

"Satisfied, Mr. Rayle?"

"But, but...why would he pay?"

"That, Mr. Rayle," Phyllis said coolly. "Is information you can't sue us for. I'm so sorry about your wife."

As Trent Rayle pushed his cart out the door, Phyllis entertained another request.

"Can I see who it was, Ms. Barnum?"

"Sure." Phyllis Barnum hit the hide and replace function buttons then turned the screen toward her young assistant. "Be my guest, Mary."

Mary Larsen scanned to the bottom screen and read the name in the payee box--*Anonymous*.

"And that satisfied him?"

Chapter 23

Condolences…confirm flight availability for May 1… the C-K Aviation Department, memo read. Eight months had passed since Trent had taken a leave of absence from the Crown to be with Cheryl. To the company's credit, no one, not even the Bossman, had bothered him. Two weeks had passed since the funeral, a respectable time. Eager to get back in the saddle, Trent fired off his response to the memo with a text message…Y E S.

Contract flight crews from Raleigh had handled the few trips the Challenger had flown since Trent's last trip to Chub with Bossman. New charts, currency checkride, and refreshments…Trent mentally checked the items off as he headed for the corporate hanger at the New Hanover County Regional Airport. Two days was scant time to prepare for the upcoming trip, but that was not the reason he was in a hurry to get back to the hanger. Even before the two giant halogen lamps had reached max power, Trent was in the office thumbing through the trip log. *Ridell, Tim--*"So the littlest lawyer finally makes it to Chub, good for you kid…umm, and *Moole, Phillip--*prick," Trent said as he read the names under flight manifest. "*Ferguson, Gan and Polyana, Yasnaya,* guest--women, light load, good." *No Bossman,* Trent thought as he snapped the ledger closed. *He's probably already on the boat.*

As the massive pile of clothes disappeared into the bags on the bed, Yas asked Tim, "Aren't you excited? Your first executive perks since you took over the company."

"Some perks. President of the company, and I have to take two people who can't stand me," Tim mouthed as he latched his bag.

"I don't like Moole, either. But he is head of legal and you know this Denton guy will have his lawyer there."

"OK, that punches Moole's ticket, but why does your mother have to--?"

"Two reasons, dear." Yas held up a new teddy. "You like?"

"Second largest stockholder." Tim ignored Yas's question. "And remind me what the second reason is."

"She's my mother."

"Mother! Eight months ago you wouldn't even give her that courtesy, the old--"

"She's changed, Tim, and besides if it wasn't for her you wouldn't be getting this opportunity with Denton."

That much was true. Moole had begged for the Denton meeting but Ganna Mae had nixed the deal. Still the old woman hated him--he could feel it. "Yas, I've heard stories about how Denton feels about the Crown. He hated Mr. Kincaid. The only reason they want me to meet with Denton is so I will fall on my face. Don't you see? This is just what Moole has been waiting for--proof that Mr. Kincaid made a bad choice."

A pang of guilt hit Yasnaya--Tim still had no idea that Wyatt Kincaid was the last person who would have ceded power to him. Ganna Mae had revealed that part of the plan, but not the location and only a vague explanation of Wyatt's condition.

"Mother, please tell me you didn't kill Wyatt."

"Suicide, not homicide, will end the Kincaid Dynasty." Ganna Mae smiled. "It's part of my plan."

"But...he's not dead, right?"

"As good as. But not quite yet, dear."

"Yas...yo, Yas." Tim snapped his fingers. "Why do you drift off into Never-never land when I mention Mr. Kincaid. Do you know something I don't?"

"No." Yas turned to hide the lie on her face. Other than the details about Wyatt, she had been completely honest with Tim. But, as Ganna Mae used to say, 'Sometimes the truth just absolutely will not work.' If Tim Ridell knew that Moole's story about Wyatt wasn't true, he would go straight to the police and ruin everything even his new posh life. "And that," Yas whispered, "will absolutely *not* work."

"What won't work?"

"These shoes with this outfit." Yas tossed a pair of slides into the closet then zipped her bag. "I'm done, let's go."

Lisa Cox parked her car in front of the corporate hanger, grabbed a file and ran for the plane. Her new job as assistant to the president of the Crown Kincaid Company consisted of odd jobs like the one she was doing now. Tim Ridell was a good man, but memory was another story. "Tim," Lisa yelled at the boarding party standing outside the plane. "You'll need this." Lisa waved the Denton file over her head.

Crew and passengers, as well as every line boy and transient pilot on the ramp, looked at the vivacious woman sprinting toward the plane. Ganna Mae's surgeon had proved to be more than skilful, the man was as masterful as Picasso. Gone was the hideous mask created by the fists of Charles Cox. In its place was a face that would have been at home on any big screen in America. Lisa Stratton's beauty had been restored.

Tim pulled his laptop from the pile of bags on the tarmac. "No, I put it--left it on my desk. Thanks, Lisa."

Ganna Mae grabbed Lisa's arm and turned her face toward the sun. "You'd think with all the money I've paid that quack he could make me look half this good."

"Not all the money in Fort Knox--" Tim mumbled to Yas, who quickly punched him in the ribs before he could finish.

"What did you say?" Ganna Mae asked Tim.

"He said the plane goes 400 knots, Mother. He was answering my question."

"Actually," Trent Rayle piped in. "We be doing closer to 500, ma'am."

Ganna Mae ignored the exchange and turned to Lisa. "Why don't you come with us, dear? God knows," Ganna Mae sneered at Tim, "he'd forget his head if you didn't remind him."

"Can she?" Yas asked, excited with the prospect of having a woman her own age on the trip.

Tim looked at Trent. "Do we have enough room?"

"I'd have to rework the weight and balance and edit the flight plan." Trent picked up on the disappointment on Lisa's face. "Wouldn't take but a minute, though."

"But I don't have any clothes, or--"

"You can wear some of mine...I packed enough for two--"

"And," Ganna Mae added, "we can buy the rest in Nassau."

Chapter 24

A quick stopover in Nassau turned into an impromptu evening at the luxury resort of Atlantis. Trent feigned some in-flight glitches and requested a solo maintenance flight to Chub, the place he would spend the night. The request was made of Moole, but the permission was given by Tim. Things at the Crown had changed.

The flight would be fifteen minutes in stealth mode. Trent grinned as he switched off the dual transponders in the Challenger. He had advised the tower of the problems with the plane's Mode C and requested an altitude of 1000'. Less than eight miles off the coast, radar contact was lost with Nassau Air Traffic Control.

Vortices from the Challenger's wingtips stirred the calm surface of the Caribbean as Trent busted his assigned altitude. Not since his time in F15's had he enjoyed this variation of TFO, Terrain Flight Operations. Ten feet above the ocean, watching sea spray mix with his jet wash, Trent Rayle was back in an element he loved. For the brief time it took to reach Chub, the demands of the intense flight took his mind off Cheryl--a welcome respite.

Six miles from Chub Marina, Trent nudged the big jet upward and leveled at 150'. This buzz job would be one the Bossman would love. Clark Guilford and Jim Williams dove for cover on the upper deck of the Crown Jewel as the roaring jet passed within 100' of the communication mast. The two looked at one another, then shouted in unison--"*The Bossman?*"

"Gotta be," Clark Guilford said. "I guess that blows your theory about him hanging with the bad guys, eh?"

"Doesn't matter," Jim Williams said somberly. "I still have to take him back to Miami. He's got some explaining to do."

"That's bullcrap. He was probably stranded on one of these islands. I hope he sues the whole damn bunch of you for not initiating a search--"

"Clark," Jim said and stressed the words. "*Credible Threat* and it came from an agent in the field. If he's lucky they won't declare him an *Enemy Combatant.*"

"And if they do?"

"You read the papers--figure it out."

"That's crazy!" Clark yelled. "He loves America."

No need to argue without ammunition, Jim thought. Terrorists were having a hard time cracking the increased security on the mainland. Soft targets like the Bahamas provided the best chance for terrorists to shoot down an American airliner. How hard would it be to launch a

MANPADS (Man Portable Air Defense Systems) weapon at a slow-climbing plane from the Nassau airport? Nor was the target threat limited to commercial operations. According to recent intel, corporate jets laden with some of America's most valuable assets, corporate CEO's whose demise could wreak havoc in the financial world, had also been targeted.

Valuable information, but not information to be shared with the general public. More disturbing was the established link between Chechen Rebels and terrorist elements from the Gulf.

Subversive radicals from the Gulf States had financed the attack on the Dubrovka Theater in Moscow. It had also been that learned, Mosvar Barayev, the Chechen leader of the attack, had plans to flee to the Gulf after the attack.

Most disturbing of all was a verified report that a shipment of weapons from the Caucasus region had made its way to the Caribbean. The likely destination, many experts believed, was to recently established terrorist cells in the Bahamas. Smack dab in the middle of the plan were members of the Russian Mafia, a group that had loyalty only to the highest bidder. Fyodor Yantikov, alias John Smith, fluent in Russian, and, blessed or cursed, depending on your side, with European features and an impeccable upper-crust British accent, could easily facilitate the union of the two groups. Whether Clark wanted to acknowledge it or not, Wyatt Kincaid had been tied to Yantikov.

"Guess I'll go meet the plane. Want to come?"

"No," Clark said. "I don't want the big man to think I had anything to do with this disaster. You can have the credit when you find out the truth, and you will--"

"Clark, there are things I know that I can't tell you." Jim looked Clark in the eyes. "I need to know I have your trust?"

"You got that the night you called down the thunder." Clark remembered the night the Coast Guard jet buzzed the island. More awe-inspiring was the fact that the young man sitting beside him could have just as easily requested a fully armed fighter jet--open for business. "Jim, I gave you my word. Far as I'm concerned you're my mate. That's it."

Jim Williams nodded his thanks, stopped by his berth and collected his Glock and badge, two items he was never to carry undercover unless he was in imminent danger or going to make an arrest. He crammed a pair of flex cuffs in his shorts, pulled his shirttail over his Glock, and headed for the field.

Before Trent Rayle had cleared Customs in the small shack on the field, the boat's mule rolled to a stop by the plane.

"No tie downs, no hangers." The Bahamian Customs Agent stated the obvious. Overnight stays by corporate jets were a rarity. Most dropped off their passengers and returned home or went to Nassau to rent a hanger. "Not a problem. I'll be leaving in the morning." Trent answered the unasked question.

"What time?"

"Seven?"

"Make it nine, man." The officer shook his head and looked at the big jet. "Too much noise, and…" the man wagged his finger in Trent's face, "not so low."

Trent smiled. In the States there would have been no polite reprimand for his ear-splitting arrival. "Sorry about that."

"Long time no see," Jim shouted from the mule. "Who's with you?"

"Solo for now. Party of five will be here tomorrow morning. Thought I'd shoot over here and give you guys a heads up. According to the log, it's been awhile since you've had guests."

"You got that right. Is the Bossman in the party?"

Trent had guessed a flight two weeks earlier carrying one unnamed passenger had been the Bossman--not the case. "No, I was kinda hoping he was already here. I need to speak with him."

Yeah, so do I, Jim Williams thought as he swung the mule next to Trent. What the hay? Very seldom did a suspect fly right into your arms, anyway.

"How's the wife?"

"Dead."

"Sorry, Trent," Jim said. "We're out of the loop. No one tells us anything since Moole took over. Other than some talk about moving the boat to Miami, we've had no contact--"

"Moole? What happened to Wyatt?"

Apparently, Jim thought, everyone at the Crown was out of the loop. Head Knocker in charge disappears and no one in management cares. Wyatt's disappearance seemed almost planned. "Latest mystery of the Bermuda Triangle. I was hoping you knew something…and I'm really sorry about--"

"Ended her suffering. I suppose that was good."

"Yeah, but somebody should have told us down here, we could have sent--"

"Can we not talk about it?" Trent grimaced. "It's…it's…hard."

Every condolence, each heartfelt apology put him right back at the foot of Cheryl's empty hospital bed reliving the worst time of his life. Only memories of happier times eased the pain. No topic the young mate could bring up would lead down that path. Jim had never met Cheryl. Too bad for him. He'd missed out on a world-class woman.

The remainder of the ride to the Crown Jewel was made in an uneasy quiet. Only the mating call of a male Magnificent Frigatebird broke the silence. When the female bird answered from her nest in a nearby sand pine, it reminded Trent that life goes on.

Clark held his arm high over his head and waved in a continuous slow motion. As soon as Trent's eyes focused on the movement, Clark folded all of his fingers but one, the middle one.

"What was that for," Trent yelled from the mule before it stopped.

"It's an old nautical salute for jet jockeys who make boat captains soil their whites. You crazy bastard!"

"Guess that explains that god-awful odor." Trent pinched his nose, and looked at Jim. "I thought it was you."

"You thought right." Clark said as he bounced down the gangplank. "That wad in his britches ain't his manhood. You scared the crap outta both of us."

Three Kaliks and a half-ass apology from Trent later, the conversation turned to Wyatt. "I don't get it," Clark said. "Moole was here with a Bahamian police force telling Wyatt and anybody else who would listen that the boat didn't belong to Crown-Kincaid, but, my pay check looks the same to me."

"So does mine, I guess that's why all these changes get to me," Trent added. "Did Moole ever mention Tim Ridell?"

"Who's Ridell? Never heard of him before."

"No one said for sure, but I got the feeling he's the Big Dog now. The execs used to call him *little pickle*--never got that one," Trent said as he retrieved another Kalik from the cooler.

"I can help you out there," Jim said as he dropped down from the upper deck. "Jasmine, Bossman's girlfriend, put this screensaver up on her laptop one night. A picture of this guy, Ridell, and his wife--"

"You never messed with her did you?" Clark scowled. "I told you about that mess."

Jim smiled. "I didn't fraternize with her, Clark."

"That wasn't the F-word I was thinking of…she sure had the hots for you."

"Come on, Clark, you know I couldn't jeopardize my position on the boat."

That was true enough, Clark thought. Second mates generally had a hard time keeping it zipped up, but a federal agent wouldn't have that problem. "Yeah, guess you couldn't risk your position."

"Come on Clark, position? When'd a second mate become a *position*? Sorry, Jim." Trent said.

"Nah, you're right," Jim said as he opened a bottle of water and handed it to Clark. "What's that old saying you Navy guys have--*loose lips sink ships*?" The hint was subtle, but, pointed enough that the slightly drunken Clark set his beer down and sipped on the water.

"So, Trent, nobody mentioned Wyatt on the way down?" Jim asked.

"No, and I didn't ask. I assumed he was already here, but I plan to ask about him tomorrow."

"If you find out anything, let me know, will you?" Jim looked at his watch. "Guess I better go find Yvette and get ready for tomorrow. Good night."

Trent waited until Jim disappeared down the spiral staircase connecting the main saloon to the staterooms below deck. "Damn, I feel like I'm in the Twilight Zone."

"What do you mean?" Clark tossed his empty bottle into the trashcan.

"I don't know." Trent shrugged his shoulders. "It's like I've come back to the same job, but not to the same place. Sort of like a parallel world where all the players have changed places."

"Ah hell, Trent, you're just drunk." Clark said as he reached for another beer.

"Three beers...I don't think so. Even you've changed, Clark,"

"How's that?"

Trent stood on the divan and peered onto the top deck. "Well, unless I missed something a while ago, you where just chastised by the second mate. I've known you a long time. Never seen that before--"

"Naw." Clark took a long sip. "The kid's on edge...that Moole's a real prick."

"That's another thing. You say Moole's in charge, but my money's on Ridell."

"Better not let old *Ironhand* hear you say--"

"Who the hell is *Ironhand*?"

Clark tipped his hat back on his head. "It's a long story. Stick around tomorrow I'm sure Moole will tell it to you."

"I'd rather hear the story about what happened to Wyatt. That's another thing that's screwy. Wyatt leaves with a stranger and you haven't heard from him in months, yet no one calls the police?"

Jim Williams pressed his ear tighter against the vent from the aft deck to the engine room. Don't mess this up, Clark.

"What gave you that idea?"

"Damn, Clark, you *must* be drunk. You said earlier that you didn't call--"

"I said, I didn't call the Bahamian Police," Clark looked around for Jim. Hell let the undercover guy tell the story.

"So who did you call?"

Clark fumbled with his hat. "I can't tell you."

"I know why you didn't call anyone." Trent bent down beside Clark. "Because I know for a fact that Wyatt Kincaid isn't missing."

"He isn't?"

"Nope"

Clark poured his beer overboard. "How do you know that?"

"Because three weeks ago Wyatt Kincaid paid Cheryl's hospital bill, that's how I know."

Chapter 25

Agent Jim Williams scrambled back to his bunk and grabbed his log. Half the Peregrine task force was conducting covert operations to find Wyatt Kincaid and he's walking around paying hospital bills? Impossible! Surely someone had bothered to check his residence in Wilmington--major snafu. No way, someone screwed up that badly. Maybe before the Homeland Security Act, but not now. Local, state and federal agencies were connected. Information was flowing, and even information from U.S. Customs and the Internal Revenue Service was finding its way into law enforcement databanks.

Williams slipped on his shoes. It couldn't hurt to check. A young Bahamian on the secure landline at the Chub Cay Dining Club was having an extended, and amorous, conversation. "Oh, no, girl, it's only you--what?" The would be Don Juan looking around and saw Williams. "Hey, Jack. A little privacy, please." Jim faded back into the shadows of the building but continued to watch. Satisfied he was alone, the islander made kissing noises into the phone. "OK, OK." Once again the man looked around. "I love you.... How much? Oh, girl, it would take me all night--"

"Damn," Williams whispered. "All the world loves a lover, pal...but not a long-winded one." Without thinking he patted his pocket and felt the badge he had forgotten to hide in his cabin. "Ah, what the hell." Williams reached in his pocket, pulled out the badge and held it up to the phone booth. "Federal Agent--I need this line." Useless if the guy knows international law, golden if he doesn't.

Staring at the badge then back at Williams, Lover Boy managed a hasty "I'll call you back, girl. I have to go," and hung up. Rather than rush off into the night the guy studied Williams, taking in all his features, and formulating a positive ID. "Later, Jack."

Williams waited until the local was clear of the area and then called the Miami office. Properly coded in, he made his request. "Any activity on Wyatt Kincaid's financial accounts? Specifically, a hospital payment made three weeks ago?"

"Hold, please."

In less than three minutes the voice was back. "Which ones?"

"Which ones? You mean the guy is writing checks and we haven't nailed him?"

"Not checks. He's using debits, and there are a boatload of them."

Debits? Sure, Wyatt was that smart, no paper trail leading back to him.

"Anything suspicious?"

"Oh, yeah."

"What?"

"It's the damnest thing," the voice on the end said. "He pays bills, not just medical either, for a lot of people."

"I meant suspicious, suspicious."

"This is the suspicious part. None of these people are related to him, some are employees. The rest are people he doesn't appear to have any connection to at all...and none of them are tax deductible. You'd think a rich guy like Kincaid would funnel the money through a charity and take the deduction. Not to, now *that's* suspicious."

"Any foreign nationals in the mix?" Jim asked.

"Umm, no,. Other than some alimony payments going to France, the rest are standard bills. Oh, and no credit card activity, no cash withdrawals. If the guy is active, it isn't showing up."

"Thanks."

Agent Williams, passing and recognizing the young Lothario from earlier, gave a nod. "It's all yours."

The Bahamian glared at Williams and returned to the phone booth to place a call.

"Inspector Rene Jacobs, please."

Tim Ridell rushed back to his Atlantis hotel room, out of breath. "They're here on Paradise Island. I just saw them and little Jim's with them."

"They and Jim who?"

"Sally and Celestine Bryce...and my son, Jim--"

"Jim," Yas repeated. "Do you know that's the first time you've ever called him that, usually it's just 'my boy'--"

"Jim Boykin Ridell. My son's named for Sally's dad, Big Jim Boykin--not exactly my favorite name in the world. So, I call him Boy...you know, just shortened his middle name. Anyway, Jim and Sally were talking to Moole. I could have sworn they mentioned Wyatt and dead."

"Wyatt's dead?" Yasnaya asked, "That lying--."

"Who's lying, Moole?"

"No. Gan."

Tim held his hands out like a traffic cop stopping traffic. "Whoa, let's start over."

"How do they know Wyatt is dead?"

"They don't. He's not...that I know of. Is he?"

Yas took a deep breath. "No, or at least that's my impression. Tell me what you heard. My source is unreliable."

"OK. I found a booth in the casino restaurant...I just had to see little Jim; it's been so long. But I couldn't let Big Jim and Sally see me. You know how Sally is...until I get papers little Jim is off limits--"

"That'll happen soon enough." Yas smiled. "I can't wait to meet your son...I'll bet he's just like you.... But what were you saying about Wyatt?"

"From my vantage point I could sort of hear Big Jim, Sally, Celeste and Moole talking. The Boykins are pressuring Moole to have Wyatt declared dead, I think. But they could have said they *wished* he was dead. I can't be sure."

"Why would they want Wyatt dead? That doesn't make sense."

"Didn't I tell you this already?"

"Tim," Yas sighed. "You haven't told me *anything*, yet. That makes sense anyway."

"Jim and Sally Boykin are Wyatt's relatives."

"So?"

"His *only* living relatives."

"Oh, boy," Yas moaned. "Can they do that?"

"There's some rule about being lost at sea. I thought I'd do some research when I got back to our law library. But Big Jim is sure it applies to Wyatt, and here's the kicker. Moole is all over it." Tim grasped Yasnaya by her shoulders. "That part of the conversation I clearly heard. So, if Wyatt isn't dead they are planning to kill him, or make it look like he's dead. We have to find Wyatt--or call the police. Moole led me to believe that Wyatt was gallivanting around the world, and clearly that's not the case."

In the crowded lobby between the casino and the upscale shops in Atlantis, Phillip Moole whispered into Big Jim Boykin's ear, "Follow me, we have to talk--in private." From the casino through the labyrinth of fake caves and passageways bordered by walls of glass holding back millions of gallons of water filled with tropical sea life, the two walked without talking. All around them tourists oohed and ahhed at the more adventurous guests dropping sixty feet down a clear acrylic tube atop a mock Mayan Temple into a shark-filled lagoon. Phillip Moole struggled with a heart rate increasing to that of the first time riders of the Leap of Faith slide.

On the bridge crossing the Paradise Lagoon, Phillip turned to Big Jim. "What in the hell are you doing here?"

"Vacation. We've had it planned for months."

"Months?" Phillip snarled.

"OK, weeks. Since we found out about the little get-together on Chub."

"How did you know I'd be here?"

"I didn't," Big Jim drawled. "That part was an accident--maybe fate. What difference does it make?"

"Plenty. What if the old woman gets wind of our plan--"

"How's she going to do that?"

"You were detailing it in the restaurant. What were you thinking?"

"Well." Big Jim hung his head. "Just wanted my little girl to know who came up with the idea...before you took credit--"

"Look, having Wyatt declared dead doesn't make him dead. He'll be back and your inheritance will be short-lived--"

"And you'll be in prison. You know he'll find you. Wyatt's not one to give up."

"Not if he can't prove we're involved. We simply have to tip the preponderance of the evidence. It will take years to sort things out. Ridell looks guilty as hell already and, as soon as L. Robert Lee manipulates some Farmers and Maritime documents, we'll home free."

Big Jim laughed. "Your patsy has some powerful insurance. Did you see him and that girl at the Heart Ball?" Big Jim made a heart symbol with his hands. "They're in *love*. That old woman will feed someone to Wyatt." Big Jim pointed to a large dorsal fin slicing through the Predator Pool. "But it sure as hell won't be Tim Ridell."

Phillip scanned the apron around the shark pen. Ganna Mae had fought against using Ridell, even warned him not to put him into play, for the very reason Big Jim explained so clearly.

"I say we declare him dead. At least we'll be rich." Big Jim wiped sweat from his forehead.

"No, you would be temporarily rich...then in the poorhouse. Like you said, Wyatt's not one to give up. Besides, if Wyatt is declared dead there will be an investigation, or worse, a search to find him. Either way we lose." Phillip waved to a man on the far end of the pool. "But I have another idea."

"What's that?"

"Rather than declare Wyatt dead; let's make Wyatt dead. It's the only way we can both win."

Big Jim used both hands to wipe the sweat from his eyes, and then searched Moole's face for a hint of frivolity--nothing. Moole's eyes were as dead serious as the barracuda's eyes swimming before them. "Don't we have to find him first?"

"I already have." Phillip extended his hand to the man he had waved to moments before. "Big Jim Boykin, meet Mr. John Smith."

Chapter 26

Sooner or later, Tim Ridell figured, he would have to tell them of his decision to opt out of *The Last Kincaid* plan and the meeting with Jarek Denton. The news would be a minor inconvenience for Ganna Mae and Moole. As quickly as they could convene the board, the good life, for him, would be over. Once the news of his demise hit the street, Big Jim Boykin, Sally and Celestine Bryce would celebrate long into the night. As soon as one of them could draw a sober breath, a full-page announcement in the Wilmington Star Business Section,   along the lines of--**Gherkin Blows Another One: Loses Son and Beautiful Girlfriend, Forever!**—was bound to follow.

Sure it would be hard to give up the corporate perks, and fat salary, but those losses and Sally's revelry seemed insignificant compared to how Yas would react. Ironically, the chiding Yas had given him for not paying more attention to the corporate minutes had provided his logic for distancing himself as far away from the *Last Kincaid* plan as possible.

During his spare time at the office he had delved into the corporate archives, and what he had found out was disturbing. Yasnaya Polyana, the vivacious and caring woman he had fallen in love with, did not exist. Wyatt Kincaid had employed an army of private investigators to comb thousands of deed vaults, search hundreds of newspaper announcements and on a hunch, spread enough greenbacks around Russia to paper Red Square for any proof of the existence of Yasnaya Polyana. No rocks had been left unturned, no tidbit of information unchecked, and still his troops had found nothing. Yet, the most elusive fugitive since Osama Bin Laden had popped out of nowhere to become the most significant person in the life of the Crown's newest top executive. Only in the personal files of Wyatt Kincaid Sr., files he had no business reading, had the name, Yasnaya Polyana, appeared. And even in the sacrosanct files of the company founder, there was no explanation as to why a person who didn't exist had been issued a large chunk of Crown Kincaid stock.

In the tender minutes before they made love, when a man is most vulnerable and accepting, Tim had cajoled, hinted, and damn near begged Yas for a half-ass explanation. Apart from being abducted by aliens, he would have accepted any explanation, and at the height of ecstasy, even the alien story would have worked. Yas, however, as she had done from the beginning, ignored the opportunity to set the record straight. Now it was clear, painfully clear, that unless Yas came clean, their relationship was over.

So what if she was pretending to be someone else? And who the hell really cared if Wyatt Kincaid, killer of a young pregnant woman and the son of a murdering father, never made it back from wherever he was? Why should the former laughing stock of the Crown Kincaid Development Company lose everything to save such a scoundrel? *If a fight is fought well--it's fought fair, son.* The words of the long-dead Hartman Ridell dinged like a round ending bell in Tim's head. Fair meant balanced--equality balanced the scales held by Lady Justice. So far, only one side of the story had been presented. For the fight between Ganna Mae and Wyatt to be fair, Wyatt had to have an opportunity to present his side, didn't he? Justice demanded it, and more importantly, Hartman Ridell's simple rules of fair play demanded it.

Tim put both hands on Yas' shoulders, "Some days when I wake up and see you lying beside me I wonder if what I'm seeing is real. That's why I touch you, and that's why I squeeze you so tight sometimes that I wake you--to make sure you're real." Tim cupped Yas' hands in his. "But you're not real--"

"What are you talking about?"

"I took your advice, Yas. I read the company archives...and Wyatt's personal files." Tim let Yasnaya's fingers sift through his before freeing himself from her touch. "So, now that I know your secret am I going to disappear, like Wyatt?"

"What secret?"

"The secret that you and Ganna Mae were sure I would never see--give a hungry dog a bone, and why should he care where it came from--that was the logic, wasn't it?"

"Tim, I honestly don't know what you're talking about."

"Come on, Yas, admit it. All of this success was suppose to go to my head--blind me to the obvious--Sally and Boy in Atlantis--brilliant. A great reminder of what would happen if I didn't go along with *The Last Kincaid* plan--"

"Stop it!" Yas screamed, "I had nothing to do with that. Yes, I pushed for you to get the job over Moole, but only because I knew--"

"That I was too dumb to figure out there is no Yasnaya Polyana? Wyatt spent a fortune trying to find her--I spent considerably less, a few calls to DMV, a check of the tax records--but my results were the same. You're not who you claim to be. There is no Yasnaya Polyana--"

"It's my stage name." Yas tugged at the waistband of her thong. "When men cram a few sweaty dollars in here I smile and give them a longing look--it's part of the act. Most men get it--but some don't--I'm an entertainer--not a whore." Yas covered herself with a towel. "I've been felt up in department stores, groped in restaurants, and fondled in church by a deacon who recognized me. Can you imagine what would have happened if one of these men found out where I lived--who I really am?"

Tim squatted beside Yas and brushed away the tears beaded on her cheeks. "I'm not like that, and I'm sorry that those things happened to you. But I have to know the truth, the whole story. Tell me who you really are...and tell me what really happened to Wyatt Kincaid."

"I know only part of the story," Yas began as she looked at Tim, "and the part I know...you won't believe."

"Try me. Unless there's a third eye and a Roswell zip code involved, I'll probably buy it."

"Wyatt Kincaid is safe aboard a ship accompanied by the woman who gave me my real name--Lubova Diacnik--"

"Whoa, don't tell me anymore. This woman is the long lost heir of Alexis or Anastasia Romanov...sound about right?

Lubova Diacnik," Yas said with the same confident resolve as an expert witness who had just revealed an irrefutable fact. Why should she act otherwise? Hadn't he believed every scintilla of bullshit associated with *Last Kincaid?* From Moole's outrageous claim that Wyatt Kincaid had turned the reins of the company over to a man he knew as "Tom" Ridell, to the instant line of credit so readily given by the Farmers and Maritime Bank--bullshit--every last bit of it. Rather than question the obvious, he had believed, even Moole and Ganna Mae's weak explanations for Wyatt's disappearance.... Why, indeed, would Yas act any differently?

Tim grabbed a pen from desk, "Could you spell that for me?"

"Why?"

"Sounds like a Russian name to me. President Reagan had a saying...I think it was an old Russian proverb--*trust, but verify.* That'd be hard to do without the correct spelling."

"Verify?" Yas twisted her face in disbelief, "*Who* I am--or *whose side* am I on? That's what you really want to know, isn't it?"

"Yas, come on." Tim twirled the pen in his hand. "Lou Bubba, and a surname you can't spell with can of alphabet soup. Really? That's the best you can do?"

You don't believe me?"

"No more than I believe in Santa. That's the sad part about growing up, Yas, we become pessimist. We grow until we lose the Tooth Fairy, the Easter Bunny, and finally Santa. Then we grow some more until we realize that just because we can see a person, touch a person, fall in love with a person--that doesn't make them *real.* I ask for the truth and you give me some fake name, and I'm supposed to believe you? Well I don't, and, until I have proof, I'll never believe, or trust you." Tim grabbed her shoulders and pinned them against the wall.

"I agreed to listen to the story, Yas, and I did. But I see it a whole lot different than you do. To you, the story is the gospel according to Ganna Mae, for me, it's one side of the story. I want to hear the other side--and that comes from my legal, not my religious background, by the way."

"Tim, let go. You're hurting me." Yas struggled against Tim's tightening grip.

"Not before you tell me the truth." Tim swallowed hard, unsure if he wanted to hear the answer to the question he was about to ask. "The *Last Kincaid* plan...does it involve killing Wyatt Kincaid?"

Yas wriggled free from Tim and faced the full-length mirror at the end of the room. Tim's question, like the reflective surface before her, had brought her face to face with her own doubts. Was the mother--daughter bond she had finally forged with Ganna Mae real or role-play? Would Ganna Mae do whatever it took to make the plan work, even manipulate her? Could even the great Ganna Mae pull off such a convincing display of maternal devotion? And even if she could...did it mean she was also capable of planning and carrying out a *murder*?

"I don't know." Yas crumpled to the floor. "I don't know."

"Yas." Tim softened his voice. "Sometimes doing what's right is hard." Tim gestured around the plush room. "I like living like this, getting a fancy room, jets, yachts...and probably most of all, respect. I didn't tell you this at the time--at the Heart Ball." Tim waited for Yas to recall that evening. "Remember how Sally, Big Jim, and Celeste were crowded around the four topper Boykin & Boykin table with three other people? I kept staring at them. You called it gloating, because we were at the biggest damn table in the place--the Crown Kincaid Table, and I was at the head with the most beautiful woman at the Ball." Tim shook his head. "You were partly right...I guess I was gloating. Forgive me for the petty self-indulgence. Seeing the envy in their eyes was worth every embarrassing moment that family had ever caused me.

"But then," Tim knelt beside Yas, "I realized that without you, none of it would have meant a thing. I felt proud, Yas, not because you were the most beautiful person in the place, but because you had the courage to do what was right." Tim stood and helped Yas to her feet. "Deep in my heart I knew Moole was lying about Wyatt giving me the company. But I got so caught up in the trappings, the power, that I made myself think it was OK. When we find Wyatt, all this will go away. Maybe even the best part...you."

"Tim--"

"It will. Wyatt's never going to let me keep his job. And you need a man with money. Ganna Mae would settle for nothing less. But that's not important. What's important to me is that you have the same feeling I had that night. I can take going back to where I was.... If I know you're as proud of me for doing the right thing as I was of you. But with or without you, I have to make this right-- it's that Baptist thing."

Yas smoothed the folds of her skirt. "I guess converting to another religion is out of the question, huh?"

"Which one?"

"The Ganna Mae Ferguson Church of Misanthropy."

"Nope. That one's definitely off the table."

Chapter 27

Finding a way to give Yas and Ganna Mae time alone meant spending time with Lisa. Tim looked at the beautiful woman strolling confidently by his side and admired the changes, both inside and out, since the showdown with Charles Cox.

"You know by the time the personal injury lawyers finish suing me, I'll be lucky to have enough money to get home."

"Why are they suing you?" Lisa asked defensively.

Tim laughed. "Don't tell me you haven't noticed. Every guy in Atlantis is breaking his neck to get a better look at you. The first thing their lawyers will argue is that I contributed to their clients' injuries by not keeping you under lock and key."

Lisa put her arm in Tim's. "Not to worry. We find a woman judge, draw her attention to the under-lock-and-key statement and...poof, you win." Lisa looked at the berthed yachts straining for freedom against the mooring lines that kept them from the open seas. "I see things so differently now. 'Under lock and key,' not so long ago, would have meant *me*. I guess sometimes even a caged animal needs a mirror to see its predicament." Lisa squeezed Tim's arm. "Thank you."

"Have you seen him?"

"Not since the protective order." Lisa smiled. "I think the cop that caught him in the office parking lot put the fear of God in him. He's cute."

"Charles? Are you nuts--"

"The cop. Robert Miller. He's cute."

"Sounds serious. Has he asked you out yet?"

"No, we've talked over the phone." An uneasy look settled on Lisa's face. "I don't want to date until my divorce is final. Charles said--" Lisa's voiced faded to silence.

"He said," Tim made a rolling motion with his hand. "*What?*"

Lisa whispered, "He said he would kill me if I dated."

Tim stiffened. "He threatened you. Did you report him?"

"No. If I do, that will just make him madder. There's no telling what he might do."

"Lisa, he'll go to jail. You can't let him intimidate you. Charles is a bully. He wants no part of anyone who fights back. You saw that."

"I know. That's what Robert said, too." Lisa's body trembled. "But, if I leave Charles alone, he'll forget about me.... Let me do it my way, please?"

Obviously the cop had put the pressure on her to bag her ex...good. "I'm sure you know what's best. Let's talk about the cop some more."

"Let's not."

"Why?"

"Because, if I don't fill the blanks in correctly," Lisa said, "A file folder, as thick as a honey bun, detailing the life and times of patrolman Robert Miller will turn up on my desk, and you know I'm right."

Tim nodded. "OK, I was going to have him checked out. So what's wrong with that?"

"Nothing." Lisa winked. "And nothing is wrong with making sure I get to my car safely, or riding by Charles' trailer at two in the morning, or--"

"How'd you know that?"

"Robert told me you called the police when Charles was in the parking lot, and he saw you at the trailer park, too."

"What's a Wilmington cop doing in Columbus County?"

Lisa smiled. "He was off duty...and he's a good man. I don't need a private eye's report to tell me that." Lisa stopped and faced Tim. "I appreciate all that you've done for me, taking care of Charles, watching over me, my job." Lisa touched her face. "And this, especially this."

"That was Yas." Tim beamed.

"And Ganna Mae." Lisa nudged Tim. "Come on, say it. *Ganna Mae.*"

"And...Ganna Mae," Tim mumbled.

Nothing more was said until they reached a bridge spanning The Lazy River Ride. The couple stopped on the bridge and watched as tourists floated underneath in brightly colored rafts. Tim pointed at the spectacle below. "Sort of like life, isn't it?"

"Just keeps rolling along, you mean?" Lisa asked.

"No. More like delivering us to our destiny, whether we want to go there or not."

"Are you saying you don't like being where you are?"

"I like where I'm at...for the moment."

"Me, too. My life, my friends, my job...I love my life, all of it." Lisa added.

Tim savored Lisa's contentment. Of all the things he'd ever done in his life, this was the best—and possibly the worst. "Lisa, that's why I wanted to have this time alone with you. There's something I need to tell you."

"Is it bad?"

"It could be." Terrible for me, Tim thought. "But, it could also be an opportunity.... I want you to start taking some classes, and start preparing yourself for a career."

"Why, am I not doing my job?"

"Whoa." Tim grabbed Lisa's hands. "It's not like that. Heck, you're the best executive assistant in the world, I bet."

"I'll take a pay cut, or work for free...almost." Lisa pleaded. "Just let me stay."

"I can't guarantee your job and I can't go into details. Not now." Tim gave a weak smile. "Trust me, things will work out."

Lisa nodded. "You've gotten me this far...if it all ends tomorrow, it was worth taking the chance." Lisa frowned. "Will it end tomorrow?"

"I don't know, Lisa. But there is one thing we can always count on."

"What's that?"

"Our friendship."

Chapter 28

Ganna Mae returned from the bathroom surprised to find the room empty, except for Yas. "Where's Lisa?" Ganna Mae snapped a diamond bracelet onto her wrist and admired the sparkling trinket against the warm tropical sky draping the balcony. "We've got a little shopping spree planned. I thought I'd buy her a few baubles."

"You're really taken with her, aren't you?"

"Jealous?"

"No." Yas smiled. "Proud, Mother. Proud of you for doing something kind--with no strings attached."

Proud, Ganna Mae thought. Finally, after more than thirty years, she had done something that made Yas proud and, more importantly, made her admit it. Why not? It was, after all, part of her plan. Rallying around a common cause. Working together as a team. "So, I'm not such a horrible person after all?"

Yas joined her mother on the balcony and kissed her on the cheek. "Actually, you can be quite wonderful when you want to be...thank you."

"Yas." Ganna Mae brushed away real tears. "You haven't done that since you were a little girl."

"You haven't done anything nice since then--"

"Yasnaya Polyana--"

"I was joking--sort of...." Yas tilted her head and put her chin in her palm. "What was the last nice thing you did?"

"I gave you that flea-bitten--"

"*Rowdy*, and you loved him."

Ganna Mae winced. "He grew on me. He grew on everyone, the big hairy mutt."

"That was when I was six. Do you have anything more recent?"

"You were eight."

"Six."

"Eight...that's the year you learned the truth about Santa. Don't you remember? The mutt wouldn't shut up, so I gave him to you a week early--"

"I was eight. Umm--" Tim hadn't been so gullible after all, Yas thought. "I could have sworn I was younger when I figured that out."

"Curse of only children. Always the last to know,. No support group. Your psychiatrist told me that."

"Dr. Carmel?"

"Dr. Quack.' Ganna Mae grunted. "Three years, and who knows how many dollars, but we finally rid ourselves of that invisible playmate of yours. Something, something...*Diddy Doo*?"

"*Callahan B. B. Ditty Doo*, and he wasn't my playmate, he was my older brother."

Ganna Mae snapped her fingers. "That was something nice...and you were eleven. Then there was the time...." Ganna Mae stalled as she tried to think of another good deed--nothing. "What did *B.B.* stand for, anyway?" Ganna Mae asked, hoping the good deed subject would be forgotten.

"Bad Boy."

"Ugh, how could I forget that? God knows you've had enough of them--including this last one, I might add."

"Gan, he's a good guy—don't start."

"Let's not talk about him. We were having such a good time."

Yas remembered Tim's threat. "I think you'd better sit down, Mother."

Gan walked to the bar and poured her customary four-finger highball. "Why do I get the feeling that I've just been fattened for the kill? Sincere compliment, kiss on the cheek, a little trip down memory lane."

"I meant every word of it, but--"

"But, now I have to stab you in the back. Spit it out, Yasnaya Polyana!"

Many times Yas had considered ending the fractious *mother/stranger-daughter/stranger* relationship with Ganna Mae. She even relished the idea some days. Today she was as far away from those feelings as the distant past they had recalled moments earlier.

Gan, despite her faults, was capable of doing good. Coerced good deeds--but good deeds nonetheless. Lisa and Rowdy, regardless of Ganna Mae's denial, were prime examples of her occasional humanity. Revealing Tim's intentions would invariably lead to a demand that she choose between a man she hoped to marry and a mother she hoped to keep...unless.

Yas's mind raced to formulate a plan that could circumvent the unpleasant options facing her.

"It's about him isn't it?" Ganna Mae asked as she lit a cigarette.

"Yes." Yas plunged head-first into troubled waters without checking the depth.

"Tim has some demands."

"Demands! Where does that trailer trash get off demanding anything--he's living better than he's ever lived."

Yas ignored the urge to remind Ganna Mae of her own less than stellar lineage. "He wants to know that Wyatt Kincaid is safe--and he wants to be assured that Wyatt wants him to run the company."

Ganna Mae tossed the cigarette over the balcony. "He has that, in writing, and I have a copy."

"I don't think Tim trusts any document produced by Moole."

"Well, you might remind him." Ganna Mae drained her drink, "that the document is part of the corporate minutes. Minutes approved, unanimously, by the board that made him president."

Yas, determined not to be bullied, continued, "and, as I was saying, he doesn't trust Phillip Moole, and if you knew what I knew, you wouldn't trust him, either."

Ganna Mae circled Yas slowly, like a predator searching for a soft spot. "Do you really think that trust is the reason I chose Moole for this job?" Ganna Mae snarled.

Yas matched Ganna Mae's movements, refusing to lose eye contact. "Then why did you?"

"History. History between Moole and Kincaid. History that you know nothing about. Let me tell you about this man that you and your boyfriend are so worried about." Ganna Mae poured another drink. "Years ago, Wyatt Kincaid got a girl pregnant, but the girl was Phillip Moole's girlfriend, the love of his life. That was bad enough, but then Wyatt did what Kincaids have always done--dodged his responsibility. He took the girl to a backroom butcher for an abortion, and the girl died. Phillip Moole drug Wyatt, kicking and screaming, before his father, Judge Moole to answer for his actions." Ganna Mae sneered. "Wyatt admitted what he had done. The Kincaids paid restitution to the girl's family, but that didn't satisfy Moole. He's hated Wyatt Kincaid ever since." Ganna Mae lifted one finger into the air. "A common goal, Yas. Phillip Moole and I share a common goal, the destruction of the Kincaid family, that's why I picked him for this job."

Yas could feel her sympathy for Wyatt turning to hate, raw and fierce--*cowardly slime*. But as bad as the story was, it still didn't explain Ganna Mae and Moole's shared goal. "You told me that the Kincaids killed your parents...but never exactly how?"

Ganna Mae moved back to the balcony and looked out at the ocean. "I keep that bottled up, in here." Ganna Mae pointed to her stomach. "The hate feeds my drive, and I'm afraid if I let it out, I'll lose the nerve I need to finish the job."

"Mother, Tim intends to go to the police. If I tell him Moole's story that may stop him--*may*. But if he knew the whole story, if we knew the whole story, we could help you get what you want." Yas grabbed the last of her mother's drink and downed it in one gulp. "As long as Wyatt's death is by his own hand."

"If you meant that," Ganna Mae dabbed at her eyes, "you've just made me the proudest mother in the world."

"Tell me the story." Yas gently rubbed Ganna Mae's back.

"It took me years to piece together the truth and that's the way I'll have to explain it to you. My father bought a mule from Wyatt Kincaid Sr. to replace the mules we lost during a horrible heat wave. He was so proud of that mule and very thankful for the deal Kincaid gave him. So thankful, that each night at supper, he always included Wyatt Kincaid Sr. in his blessing for the food we were about to receive."

"Why would Kincaid do him a favor if he hated your father enough to kill him?"

"Kincaid never hated my father. In fact, he was quite fond of him. Every year my father struggled to find enough money to buy seeds for the next year's crops. Kincaid was rich, and he always had more seeds and fertilizer than he needed. He always gave us the surplus."

"Gan, you're making a good case for not killing Kincaid." Yas said.

"Yas, if *hate* was the reason Kincaid killed my parents--I would have killed him long ago. *Last Kincaid* is not about *hate*.... It's about *love*."

"Love?"

Ganna Mae choked the balcony railing. "Yes, *love*. Love for a worthless tract of land is what orphaned me."

"Wyatt loved your land?"

"No, Kincaid only *wanted* the land. My father *loved* it. We never had one good crop on that land. It was a worthless farm. My parents died for nothing, until--"

Yas finished her thought. "You sold the land to Wyatt?"

"That's right, for the love of my parents. I had to give some value to my father's misguided passion."

"I still don't understand why Kincaid killed your parents?"

"For the land--"

"But, Gan. You said the land was worthless, then."

"It was--for farming."

"I don't understand."

"Quail," Ganna Mae sighed.

"Quail...like the birds?"

"Yes."

"Are there more pieces to this story?" Yas shook her head. "I'm confused."

Ganna Mae took a deep breath, determined to finish the story. "Wyatt Kincaid Sr. was a quail hunter, and for some strange reason the quail loved our farm. Maybe they knew they would be safe there. Papa didn't believe in killing for sport. He didn't allow hunting on the farm, even by the man who kept him farming.

"Kincaid's land had birds, but the coveys were scattered, so Wyatt took to hunting quail on horseback. The horses proved to be too skittish for the job. That's where Demon, the mule my father bought from Wyatt, came into the picture. Demon was perfect for the task except for one small quirk. He sat down each time a gun was fired and threw the rider, Kincaid--"

"So that's why your dad got such a good deal, and that was a good thing, right?" Yas asked.

"On the face of it. But Papa had a pine stump in the middle of his field. You wouldn't know this, but pines have deep tap roots. Each fall, after the harvest, when work was slow and during quail season, Papa tried to remove the stump. He tried digging it out, and pulling it out with the mules we had before Demon, but it wouldn't budge. Demon loosened it a little each year, but even he couldn't get that thing out. Then someone suggested dynamite, probably Kincaid. I wasn't on the farm then so I'm not sure--"

"Dynamite...wasn't that dangerous?" Yas interrupted.

"It was, but it was also an accepted method to clear land. Bulldozers were far and few between in those days. On the day of the accident..." Ganna Mae corrected herself, "*Murder....* Papa, Mama, and Caleb headed off for the stump. I'm not sure how it happened, or why the dynamite was wired to the plunger or why Papa and Mama were by the stump. But, according to the sheriff, Demon sat on the plunger and set off the charge--"

"How could the sheriff know that? Were there witnesses?" Yas asked.

"The sheriff found Demon's hoof prints all around the plunger--" Ganna Mae struggled not to cry. "I saw them myself, but Caleb, your uncle, was the only eyewitness."

"*Mule did it, mule did it,*" Caleb? Yas questioned. But still, he was a witness."

"Not one the authorities wanted to take a chance on in court."

"But, Gan, if all the evidence pointed toward Demon, then how--"

"Wyatt Kincaid was hunting the adjoining land that day. I can't prove it, nor can anyone else. But he knew that mule. With my parents gone, he could buy the farm, and he tried many times before he died. That tract of land has been an obsession with the Kincaids--"

"That's speculation," Yas said. "It could have been an accident."

"I thought that, too. Until I talked to a man who was hunting on the other side of our farm. He told me there were two blasts in rapid succession, one small blast like a shotgun and then the big one."

"Kincaid saw the mule over the plunger and fired his gun because he knew what Demon would do, right?" Yas asked.

"That's the way I see it."

"Gan, who was the other hunter?"

"Judge Henry Moole, Phillip Moole's father. The second reason I wanted Phillip for this job."

Yas breathed a sign of relief. "Good, then I don't feel so bad about what Tim told me about Moole."

"What did he tell you?"

"Nothing. I thought it was important at the time. I thought it might derail your *Last Kincaid* plan. But after hearing how close you and the Mooles are--"

"What did Tim tell you?"

"He told me that Moole and Wyatt's only living relatives, his ex-wife and her father, Big Jim Boykin, wanted to have Wyatt Kincaid declared legally dead."

"That son of a bitch!" Ganna Mae shouted.

Chapter 29

Fyodor Yantikov ran his fingers through his newly permed and bleached yellow hair. Not even Liliya, his own dear mother, could pick him from a lineup. Hiding in plain sight was not a risk he would have taken if Boris had even an inkling of good judgment. Fyodor tossed the empty container of Sunset Orange # 133 dye into the trashcan and marveled at his brother's stupidity. The only thing less conspicuous than his glowing new hair color would have been a neon fugitive sign and a boom box playing *"Man on the Run"*. Items, thankfully, not stocked by any of the stores of the Atlantis Resort Boris had scavenged for disguises.

"It's the Canadian, I'm sure," Boris whispered as he adjusted the binoculars aimed at the balcony across the courtyard. "Have a look, Fyodor."

"John Smith," Fyodor growled, "and you are Bo Smith, my brother, don't forget."

"Fyodor, John--Boris, Bo--what is a name, as long as we are brothers, eh?" Boris wrinkled his forehead, perplexed. "Maybe I buy more dye." Boris looked at Fyodor's fluorescent mane. "Brothers should not look so different."

"Idiot," Fyodor managed before he was completely consumed by the beguiling image of Yasnaya Polyana. With the hum of the telescopic lens motor humming to him, Fyodor Yantikov sank deeper and deeper into the LCD monitor of his digital Nikon. Like a fashion photographer inspired by perfect lighting, Fyodor snapped frame after frame. "Aah, such a beauty -- just as you described her, Boris"

A beauty? "Nyet, nyet," Boris protested. What did Fyodor see to compliment in Ganna Mae?

Fyodor switched the camera to playback mode and shoved the monitor in front of Boris' face. *"Beauty!"*

Boris grabbed the camera and studied each picture. "Svetlana Andreevich...so young...how did you...?"

"No, Boris." Fyodor smiled. "Yasnaya Polyana, *daughter* of Svetlana Andreevich, and maybe the keystone to the *Last Kincaid Plan*."

"But she had no daughter...I told you--"

"And I told you--tell me only what you know. She had a daughter. You guessed wrong. No more guessing, Boris."

"Who told you this? Moole?"

"No, old chap. You did." Fyodor tapped the monitor. "Just now."

"Ah yes. Two peas in the soup--"

"*Pod*, Boris. Like two peas in a *pod*. Make no mention of this to Moole, or anyone else--do you understand?"

Telling Boris anything was a mistake, but without his input, Yasnaya's identity would still be in question. The meeting with Moole had led to more questions than answers. His promise to Moole to eliminate Wyatt Kincaid, a debatable tactic, had provided much-needed resources. Fyodor eyed the room safe containing the $50,000 advance from Moole. Even if Kincaid promised to double Moole's offer of $100,000, which he could surely afford, the money would fall woefully short of the billions involved should the *Last Kincaid* plan came to fruition. But the old woman, the Canadian, what would *she* offer the brothers to keep her plan intact?

Fyodor weighed the latest facts of the *Last Kincaid* plan. Moole, undoubtedly, knew less of the plan than he did because Moole had admitted he had no idea as to Wyatt Kincaid's whereabouts. Unless Kincaid was no longer aboard the *Baltic Queen*, Fyodor was one up on Moole. The old woman had devised the plan, so she would know Kincaid's location. But, if he moved Kincaid to an undisclosed location, no--*when* he moved Kincaid--he would have the upper hand with Moole and Ganna Mae. Ah, but snatching Kincaid would lead to a confrontation with Yuri Kozlov, not a pleasant prospect.

Kozlov, a member of the *Odessa*, the Chechen branch of the Russian Mafia, had been instrumental in the attempted sale of a Soviet submarine to Colombian drug dealers. Only photographs from an American spy satellite had thwarted the plan, an act that had deepened the organization's resolve to destroy the superpower.

Crossing Kozlov was not an option, even for millions of dollars. Hiding underground from Interpol was one thing--hiding from the gatekeeper of the underground, was quite another. Definitely a wrinkle in the plan that needed to be ironed out.

"Boris, Svetlana Andreevich...does she speak English?"

"How did you know--?" Boris pointed his index finger to his head. "Ah--I get it. I told you again, just now. Pretty smart, eh?"

"Brilliant."

"But what does it matter, Fyodor?"

Fyodor explained Kozlov's ties to the *Odessa* and his trips to the *Baltic Queen*. "My first time on the ship, I spoke in English with Kozlov so his crew could not understand--he stopped me when the ship's cook delivered us coffee. The cook was a woman, who despite her age, bore an uncanny resemblance to the beauty on the balcony." Fyodor jerked his head toward the building across the courtyard. "And I'm sure this woman was fluent in English."

"You think this woman is Svetlana?"

Fyodor mulled over Boris' question. Logically, there was no reason to think that was the case. Yet, in the plan, all of the players had to be in the same place at one time, even Kincaid. But why would the woman on the boat, biological mother of the adopted heiress of the rich Canadian, work as a cook on a bucket like the *Baltic Queen*?

"According to the plan...it makes no sense. But--," Fyodor gave Boris a blank stare. "But Kozlov is not mentioned in the plan, either. Why do you think that is, Boris?"

"You said he was part of the *Odessa*. Maybe they needed an expert in one field?"

"What do you mean?"

"The *Odessa* are nothing but kidnappers and smugglers. Even in New York, the ones from the old country still hire them for such jobs. Maybe--"

Fyodor snapped his fingers. "Maybe Kozlov is in the plan by the luck of the draw. Of course!" Fyodor's excitement was short-lived. Even if Kozlov was involved by chance, merely as a kidnapper, not only would he have Kozlov to worry about if he double-crossed him, but all of the *Odessa* as well.

"Fyodor," Boris said. "Why do you worry about Kozlov if he has nothing to do with the old woman's plan?"

The *Last Kincaid* plan, whether the old woman realized it, was falling apart. The meeting with Moole, confirmed the *Odessa's* involvement. Boris was right about them; kidnappers and smugglers for sure. Traits shared with any of the criminal elements in Russia, or the world for that matter. What concerned Fyodor most was the skill that made the *Odessa* the most feared segment of the Russian Mafia--assassination. Fragile governments in many of the newly formed republics of the former Soviet Union were kept in constant turmoil by supposed "terrorist acts." While the republics dedicated all army and police forces to fighting the terrorist problem, the *Odessa* had free reign to kidnap and kill for money.

The *Odessa* had encouraged and helped suicidal martyrs in any way they could, reinvesting a small percentage of their profits in support of the terrorists. As the *Odessa* had expanded into other countries, so had the doctrine of "turmoil-for-dollars". Terrorism was a godsend that was making minor criminals invisible to law enforcement. So far, the *Odessa* had not aided terrorists in Western countries like Spain and the United States, but that was about to change--Fyodor thought of the bundles of polyurethane weapons he had smuggled into the Bahamas, and the innocent lives they would take.

Fyodor felt a paper-cut of guilt, so he reminded himself of the happy family reunion his shameful acts would afford. If he could get the *Last Kincaid* money into his pockets, he would save the innocents, and God and Liliya Yantikov would love him again.

But how could he make the plan work now? The old woman was a fool--only a fool would involve such a no-account creature as Kozlov in any plan--and only a bigger fool would knowingly take on the *Odessa*.

"What is it, Fyodor? You look troubled."

Fyodor sighed. "No, Boris, I am not troubled--I am a fool.... What I am about to tell you must remain between us. If you say one word of this to anyone, we will die. All of our family will die."

Boris squirmed in his seat like a little boy anxious for the bathroom. "Maybe you shouldn't tell me--you know how I talk when I drink."

Fyodor nodded. "You're right, I will tell you the plan at the last minute."

"Good," Boris sighed. "We are safe."

"Boris, one more thing."

"Anything, my brother."

"When you talk to our mother again...ask her to pray for us."

Chapter 30

Svetlana watched Wyatt as he flexed his ham-sized hands back to their normal color. "Phillip Moole...how did he manage to—you know?"

"Take over my company?" Wyatt interjected, arching an eyebrow at her.

"Yes, you told me yourself you hired him. Clearly, he was a subordinate."

"I didn't hire him." Wyatt slammed his fist into his palm hoping to kill the pinprick feeling caused by lack of circulation. "He was part of a package deal that a group of investors made--long story.... Let's just say I sold half of my company to have a shot at Phillip Moole. In my eyes, he killed Jenny and destroyed my relationship with my dad. I had this grand plan to destroy him, but apparently he had a better plan. " Wyatt looked around his dismal surroundings and then turned back to the porthole. "A much better plan...Hey! What the hell?"

"What it is?"

"That's Eagles Point." Wyatt banged against the glass. "We're past the port--they're not docking." Like a trapped tiger, Wyatt paced against captivity. "Gotta get out of here--Svetlana, can you swim?"

"What?"

"Can you swim?"

"Yes...but--"

"Look, I know you still have doubts about me." Wyatt pointed to the strips of duct tape Svetlana had cut from his wrist. "If we can get out of here, I can prove that I don't have plans to kill your daughter."

"I'm listening."

"One Crown Kincaid bank account, the Yasnaya Polyana Contingency Account, is an account that was set up by my father. To be on the safe side, I funded the account with her stock earnings after his death. If I intended to kill her--"

"But you said she didn't exist."

"And she hasn't for over thirty years. When we get on shore, you'll just have to present the proof you have that she is who you say she is. The bank will--"

"Funding a bank account hardly proves you had no plans to kill her."

"Svetlana, only two people know this account exists. L. Robert Lee, president of the Farmers and Maritime Bank, and me. With the money in that account you and your daughter can buy as much security as you and she will ever need. Trust me, if I meant to harm Yasnaya Polyana... I'd have never given her that kind of leverage."

"Even if what you say is true, I can't leave the ship."

"Why not?"

"Once you arrived, I was ordered to stay with you."

"Who are you working for?"

"Wyatt, I'm starting to believe you don't want to kill my daughter. But if I don't do what I'm told, I will never see her again. I can't take that chance, and I can't answer your question."

"And you won't help me escape?"

Svetlana shook her head. "I can't."

Wyatt gathered the pieces of tape from the deck and gave them to Svetlana, then placed his hands behind his back. "Guess you better tape me back up...wouldn't want old Kozlov to think you were giving aid and comfort to the enemy."

Svetlana slowly wrapped the tape around Wyatt's wrist, and then suddenly began to undo the bindings. "How can you be so sure my daughter is who I say she is" She asked

"582681."

"582681--I don't understand." Svetlana said.

"Neither did I, until I remembered the pass code for the account my dad opened for me when I was a kid."

"582681?"

"Nope, 99288. Spells Wyatt if you use a telephone keypad."

"And 582681?" Svetlana asked as she tried to picture a western style phone.

"582681 is the pass code for the Yasnaya account. Spells L-U-B-O-V-A, best I can figure."

"Lubova," Svetlana breathed. "He *did* know." The note had been hastily scribbled and sealed in an embassy envelope. *It is a girl her name is Lubova.* Whether or not the message had been delivered was a question the prison guard, Boris, refused to confirm. Svetlana's gut churned as she remembered the payment made to Boris for mailing the note. Her cell's iron bars had prevented physical contact, but the violation of her nude body by the piercing eyes of the guard she would never forget, and the memory still sickened her.

"I spent 20 years trying to figure out his reason for that code. If you hadn't said the name--"

"Is that how long he's been dead--20 years?" Svetlana asked.

"Pretty near."

"I'm glad he knew her real name." Svetlana patted Wyatt's shoulder. "I wish he could have known the real you, your story."

Wyatt sat on the bunk and put his head in his hands. "Yeah, me, too. Maybe if he had I wouldn't have gotten myself in this mess trying to get even with Moole."

Svetlana reached into her pocket and retrieved the paring knife. "Take this."

"What for?"

"Kozlov has a pistol. You will need a weapon if you have any hope of escape."

"What about your daughter?"

Svetlana lay face down on the bunk. "Tie me up. I will be your decoy."

Wyatt jammed the knife through the material in his shirt pocket and double wrapped the blade in duct tape. "I want you to come with me."

"Hurry, Wyatt, before I change my mind."

Wyatt loosely knotted the bindings then pressed his mouth into Svetlana's thick black hair and whispered, "I'll make things right, I swear."

Svetlana shook her head and screamed, "Gurov!"

Nicholas Gurov was barely six feet and a stone under 200 pounds-- no match for the rampaging bulk of Wyatt Kincaid. Head down and at full speed, Wyatt slammed into Gurov's ribcage and smiled when the sternum of the bird-breasted sailor cracked. Before Gurov could gasp for air, Wyatt slammed his limp body onto the steel deck.

Footsteps clanged to a stop at the head of the galley ladder well. Wyatt grabbed an iron skillet from the stove and choked the long handle with a baseball grip. Hidden from the ladder well, Wyatt counted the descending footsteps of his next victim. A perfectly timed swing splattered blood from boatswain mate Kirill Petrov's face over most of the lower third of the galley's dry storage bin.

Wyatt dragged the body into the cold storage locker at the base of the steps and waited for more footsteps. Only the soft sounds of Svetlana struggling against the bunk mattress filled the space. Skillet still in hand, Wyatt returned to check on his decoy.

"Are you OK?"

"Yes." Svetlana eyed the sprawled body before her. "And him?" "Out cold...I'm not to sure about the other one--I may have hit him too hard."

"He's dead?"

Wyatt shrugged his shoulders and headed back to the locker. Foam and bloody bubbles covered Petrov's nose and mouth. Relieved for the signs of life, Wyatt raised Kirill's eyelids and found the pupils sluggish but functioning. The steady supply of bubbles and shallow but rhythmic breathing were also good signs. Kirill would live, but when he wakened he'd have a hellish headache.

"Wyatt, you've had medical training?" Svetlana asked as she stood over the young sailor.

"Naw, played football at ECU. Concussions were pretty common. He'll make it--hey, you better get back on your bunk. Kozlov will be here soon…it's coffee time."

"Why do you have to wait for him…can't you just leave?"

"He'd shoot me before I ever made it to shore." Wyatt lifted the skillet. "Gotta pop him one. Insurance." Wyatt guided Svetlana away from the damage he'd done to Kirill Petrov and back toward her bunk. "Svetlana, one thing before I go."

"Yes."

"Yasnaya Polyana--if my father knew her as Lubova, why this name?"

"Hours before I wrote your father the note to tell him of his daughter and her name" Svetlana closed her eyes "They took her…. Only months ago…did I myself, learn she was still alive--as Yasnaya Polyana. I will learn the rest of the story as your father did—but only if I stay on this ship. That's why I cannot help you."

"How old was she when you last saw her?"

"Three months."

"Who took her--?"

Sounds on deck sent Svetlana scurrying back to her bunk while Wyatt repositioned himself by the ladder well. Wyatt fixed his eyes on the opening.

Yuri Kozlov took two steps down the ladder well before he spied the bloody splotches on the dry storage bin at the bottom of the steps. Quietly he retreated to the deck and motioned to Konstantin Nikolayev and Vitya Baranov. Konstantin was a man of Wyatt Kincaid's height but with considerably more girth--a giant. Vitya was a man of Kozlov's stature, and, as luck would have it, the exact same shoe size as Kozlov. "Vitya," Kozlov said as he untied his boots. "Put these on and walk slowly to the galley."

Kozlov and Konstantin lagged behind the unsuspecting Vitya. Wyatt immediately recognized the steel toe boots of Kozlov. As many times as they had been buried in his ribs the boots were hard to forget.

"Svetlana, kafi," Kozlov called out.

Wyatt gripped the skillet and aimed at the now-visible kneecaps on the ladder well. Like a limb cracking under the weight of freezing rain, Vitya Baranov's leg snapped, as he tumbled forward, Wyatt slammed the skillet into Vitya's back.

"I would not do that again Mr. Kincaid," Yuri Kozlov said, as he pointed his Tokarev at Wyatt. "Not if you value your life."

"Kozlov--you som bitch!"

"You will have names better than that for me once I am through with you," Kozlov sneered. "Much better than that, Mr. Kincaid.... Konstantin, take Mr. Kincaid to the brig and tie him up. I will join you shortly."

Kozlov called for Svetlana.

"In here. Captain."

"Come out, so I can see you."

Svetlana eased from behind the hatch. "Yes, captain."

"Where are Kirill and Gurov?"

"Gurov is in here...I don't know about Kirill."

Kozlov followed the trail of blood from the bin to the storage locker. One look at Kirill Petrov and Kozlov made a beeline for Svetlana. "What happened here?"

"I don't know, Cap--"

Kozlov slapped the unfinished words back into Svetlana's mouth. "Perhaps that will refresh your memory."

Rather than remember the events Kozlov's slap was intended to jog, Svetlana thought back to the days when beauty had spread a protective aura around her. So much of her early life had been governed by events linked to her exquisite beauty. Events such as her job at the embassy, where she had hobnobbed not only with high-ranking Soviet leaders, but with world leaders as well. Men had fawned over her, showered her with gifts, money, and promises of never-ending bliss.

She had rejected all for a man twice her age. Not for his good looks, or even his wealth. She had fallen for Wyatt Kincaid, Sr., for a very simple quality--respect. Not once in their time together had Wyatt the elder pressed her for what others had so overtly demanded, sex.

Days with him were spent in museums or small coffee shops, on walks in the park. And always, always, she had been cared for with the tender and gentle strength of a man who wanted nothing more than her company. How he would suffer if he could have seen the abuse she had endured since they had parted.

"Svetlana, answer me--" Kozlov pulled the heavy leather belt from his trousers belt loops. "Or I will beat it out of you, I swear."

"Kincaid forced me to yell out for Gurov." Svetlana held up her bound hands. "I had no choice, he had a knife."

"Knife? I saw no knife." Kozlov dangled the belt in front of her. "If I find no knife, Svetlana...I will be back, and what happens to you then will not be as pleasant as a beating."

"It is in his pocket." Svetlana moved to the corner of the berth and squatted. *Please forgive me Wyatt.* "In his shirt pocket...I would not lie, Captain."

Kozlov sailed down the ladder well using only the rails as young sailors often did. Not in years had he felt as invigorated as he did at this moment. "An eye for an eye, Mr. Kincaid!" Kozlov shouted as he entered the cell from hell.

"Stand him up, Konstantin."

With one powerful tug, Konstantin Nikolayev snatched the hog-tied Wyatt and set him on his feet.

"This is probably a bad time, but I'd like to remind you that I am a guest. If you damage the goods...your employers might not be happy, Captain."

Kozlov ignored Wyatt's comment and tore the pocket from his shirt. The paring knife bounced on the grated decking and then disappeared into the bilge below.

"Did Svetlana give you the knife?"

"Svetlana hates me." Wyatt drawled. "The only knife she'd give me would be sticking out of my back."

Kozlov smiled. "Too bad for you, Mr. Kincaid. Before I am done with you--you will beg for the kindness of Svetlana's knife.... Konstantin, secure him to the hook." Kozlov pointed at a hook, like the ones used to hang sides of beef, that was bolted to the overhead. "Then fetch the deck hose."

Chapter 31

More than an hour had passed since Kozlov had given Konstantin his orders. Time and the weight of his own body became the first instruments of torture Wyatt suffered. The soft cotton ropes securing him to the hook in the ceiling above his head tightened the more he struggled against them, until the bindings again shut off the circulation to his hands.

Wyatt pirouetted to ease the 240-pound strain on his darkening hands. Pain in the tips of his fingers transferred to dorsal muscles of his back and finally the searing pain burned into his calves. Cold sweat beaded on his forehead and ran into his eyes. Bleary peripheral images funneled into an intense laser beam and finally bleeped off.

"Oh, no you don't, Mr. Kincaid." Kozlov motioned for Konstantin to start the flow from the deck hose. Wyatt lapped at the water as it hit his face.

"Brackish water. Drink at your own peril, Mr. Kincaid. This water may or may not kill you. But when we are on the open sea…the salt water will finish you."

"Why?" Wyatt struggled back to consciousness. "Why back to sea?"

Kozlov bristled at the question and Wyatt's apparent indifference to rule number one. "Dissappointed, Mr. Kincaid?"

"Very." Wyatt muttered, as he turned away from the potentially lethal water.

"You should be proud--new Homeland Security laws have saved the day, yet again. It seems we have triggered what may or may not be a glitch in some security software. At any rate, we are being escorted to international waters by the Coast Guard for *our* safety."

"Will they allow us back in?"

Kozlov took the deck hose from Konstantin and shut off the flow. "Was that another breech of rule number one, comrade?"

"Go to hell, Kozlov. I don't care about your stupid rule…just let me go!"

Kozlov rammed the metal tip of the hose into Wyatt's abdomen muscles cutting the CEO some pure raw pain. "Ah, Konstantin, look… we have damaged the goods…our employers will be so unhappy." Kozlov clucked his tongue like a disapproving parent. "Perhaps we should use something less damaging--eh, Mr. Kincaid?"

"Good idea," Wyatt groaned.

"What would you suggest, comrade?"

Wyatt twisted in Kozlov's direction. "How about a pair of those little fuzzy handcuffs I saw in your locker--AAAAAH!"

Kozlov inspected the second gash below Wyatt's ribcage. "Konstantin, go get your gloves and come back." With a violent yank, Kozlov sent Wyatt twirling, as the ropes tightened, thin trails of blood and sweat spiraled down his arms. "Kozlov," Wyatt panted. "If that was meant to get my attention--it worked, you can stop now."

"Oh, I'm sure a tough guy like you needs more.... What is the word I'm looking for--'softening'?" Kozlov send two body shots into Wyatt's solar plexus. "The word for making the meat less tough?" Kozlov kicked the question into Wyatt's gut. "Help me, comrade."

"Tenderize?" Wyatt gasped.

"Tenderize. Yes, that's the word...thank you. Konstantin," Kozlov said, as he tied the 16-ounce boxing gloves to the giant's hands. "Tenderize our guest."

"Whoa--don't I get gloves, too?" Wyatt asked.

"I don't think it would be a fair fight, Mr. Kincaid. You see, Konstantin was an Olympic boxer--until.... Perhaps," Kozlov teased, "that is a story better left untold."

"Until what?"

"Until," Kozlov sneered. "Konstantin ruptured an opponent's spleen with a low blow."

"No low blow," Konstantin growled.

"I stand corrected." Kozlov smiled at Konstantin. "A low blow according to a crooked American referee. Show Mr. Kincaid what you did to the American thief who stole your title, Konstantin."

"I hit him." With the fire-power of a rocket propelled grenade, Konstantin Nikolayev destroyed the metal locker with a 1-2 combination. "Like that."

"Damn!" Wyatt grimaced and spun from the raging oaf. "Keep him away from me...a shot like that could kill a man."

"Did! Did kill a man, actually."

"The boxer?" Wyatt whispered.

"No, the boxer recovered." Kozlov smiled, sensing the terror in Wyatt's voice. "The thief was not as lucky, and poor Konstantin was sent to prison. Which of course ruined his career...I suppose that's why he hates Americans--"

"Look here, Kozlov." Wyatt's eyes pleaded for sympathy. "You turn him loose and he'll kill me."

"Konstantin," Kozlov barked. "Body shots!"

With measured force and a yeoman's work ethic, Konstantin the Giant pounded every square inch of Wyatt's torso. Each numbing thud piled ache on top of ache, until even the involuntary act of breathing became an effort. "Stop," Wyatt labored the words. "I'll pay you--just stop...please."

"*Ostahlaveet*! (Halt)" Kozlov held his palms up in front of the wheezing Konstantin. "Stop before you have a heart attack." Kozlov pointed to Konstantin's flabby gut. "The good life of a sailor has spoiled you...you fat pig!"

"Thanks Kozlov. Thank you," Wyatt moaned.

"I did not stop for your sake, Mr. Kincaid." Kozlov looked at Konstantin slumped against the wall. "I can ill afford to lose another member of my crew." Kozlov slapped Wyatt across the face. "Thanks to you!"

"Let me go. I'll give you money, lots of money."

"Money? You have nothing."

"No?" Wyatt leaned his head toward the Crown Kincaid headquarters building. "Did you see that big building in the harbor--the one with C.K. on it? That's my building...Crown Kincaid Development Company. I swear, ask Svetlana."

"Konstantin, go get Svetlana." Kozlov grabbed the deck hose. "For your sake, her story better match yours, or I will finish you myself."

Svetlana recoiled at the bloody mess before her. "Wyatt! I didn't think he would go this far! I would not have told him about--"

"Not have told me about the knife you gave him, Svetlana?" Kozlov glared from the shadowed recesses of the cell. "Do not think I believed your lie for one second." Kozlov smacked the rubber hose against the deck. "I will deal with you later, Svetlana. But before I do... tell me what you know about this Crown Kincaid Company."

Svetlana shot Wyatt an inquiring glance. "No, look at me, *syka*!" Kozlov placed the hose against Svetlana's face. "Tell me what you know. Is he wealthy?"

Svetlana Andreevich was no stranger to *Odessa* or the tactics they used to extort money or information from their hapless victims. No one retained wealth or life once the *Odessa* sank their blood-sucking fangs into the victim. Wyatt, no doubt, had thought he could trade his wealth for his life. Svetlana knew he would keep neither once Kozlov discovered what he wanted to know.

"He rambles on about such things." Svetlana pointed to Wyatt. "But it is just talk--only a hard worker gets so big and strong."

"Damn it, Svetlana! Tell him about my yacht and my plane." Wyatt looked wide-eyed at Kozlov. "Go up on deck. You can still see my building. I'm rich as hell, I swear."

Kozlov stroked his chin then bounced the hose in his hand.

"Call the bank," Wyatt screamed. "They'll tell you I'm rich."

"What bank, Mr. Kincaid?" Kozlov asked.

"Farmers and Maritime...ask for L. Robert Lee. He's the president and a long time friend. He'll verify my claim."

"Enough!" Kozlov shouted. "Konstantin, take care of him. I am going to the bridge.... Maybe the harbor pilot has a phone I could use."

Kozlov made small talk with the harbor pilot before he made his request. "So, my friend, are you from Wilmington?"

"Born and bred, as they say. Where's home for you?"

"The sea is my home. I know no other." Kozlov said. "I couldn't help but notice the big building on the waterfront, the one with C. K.--"

"Crown Kincaid building," Ray McDonald said with a smile. "Pretty impressive for a small town, huh?"

"Very--this Crown Kincaid...I imagine he is wealthy?"

"Name's Wyatt Kincaid.... I've never known where the Crown came from...might have been a partner at one time."

"Wyatt Kincaid...you know him?" Kozlov asked.

"Met him a time or two. But we don't run in the same circles. Hell, his yacht the *Crown Jewel* is bigger than most of the commercial fishing boats around here."

"Yacht? Wyatt Kincaid, he has a yacht?"

"Yacht, jet, and anything else money can buy, he's loaded."

Kozlov nodded. "He must be very old to be so wealthy?"

"Old man Kincaid is dead. His son, Wyatt--umm, I'd say he's late forties, early fifties."

"A little man?"

"Hell no, Wyatt must be 6' 5" or better--he ain't fat neither--hold on." Ray McDonald picked up the latest edition of the *Wilmington Star News*. "Here's a picture of him."

Kozlov scanned the caption below the picture, **Court petitioned to declare Kincaid dead: Lost at Sea,** then read the first lines of text in the article. *Local attorney Jim Boykin has petitioned to have Wilmington's most prominent and reclusive businessman, Wyatt Kincaid II, declared dead....*

"How long has he been missing?" Kozlov asked.

"To tell you the truth, I haven't had time to read the paper, yet-- what does the article say?"

"I speak English...but reading, ah, that is another matter--it would take me a while to read the whole article."

"I guaran-damn-tee you, your English is better'n my Russian--you're from Russia, right?"

Kozlov smiled. "Close enough. May I buy this paper...maybe I can brush up on my English?"

"You can have it, captain. I'll get another."

"And for your kindness, I will get you a bottle of the finest Vodka in the world." Kozlov said as reached under the ship's control panel and poured 2 fist size shots.

"Stolichnaya Elit, only the best for you my friend."

McDonald held up his hands in protest. "Now, Captain you know I can't be drinking on duty."

"OK," Kozlov said as he tilted the highball glass over the bottle's neck. "Perhaps when you are off duty?"

"Whoa, let's not be so hasty." McDonald said, "I said I couldn't be drinking." McDonald winked at Kozlov "Didn't say nothing about sipping, besides no ones going smell this on me. That's the good thing about fine vodka."

"Fine Russian Vodka." Kozlov said as the two new best friends clinked glasses.

Svetlana opened the hatch to the brig hoping to dissipate the stifling and rancid air. "Wyatt." she whispered. "You have to convince him you are only a worker, not rich. Kozlov is more than a sea captain--he is a killer. Trust me." Svetlana squeezed Wyatt's arm. "Do as I say or we die."

Svetlana tried to lifted Wyatt's bulk. "Konstantin, help me. He will die if he stays like this. Help me, please." Svetlana cupped her mouth to Wyatt's ear, "If he knows you have wealth, he will not stop until he finds a way to take it all. Then he will kill you, the *Odessa* know--"

"The who?" Wyatt mumbled.

"I will explain, later. Convince him you are a worker, Kozlov is short-handed. Make him see that you have value as a crew member. You told me you piloted your own boat--offer yourself as a replacement for Gurov."

"OK, OK! God!--I hurt all over."

"Konstantin, help me. We must take him down, now!"

Wasted words: The giant could hear nothing but the insults of Kozlov- *Fat Pig, low blow.* "Nyet!" Konstantin bellowed as he shadow-boxed his way back to the dangling Wyatt Kincaid.

Wyatt used the rope to swing from the wild roundhouse punches Konstantin threw. But as the rope twisted so did the distance from the potentially crushing blows. Waiting for his target to comeback in range Konstantin crouched into his Olympic boxer's stance. Unlike the earlier wild swings he drummed, crisp, short jabs in the methodical cadence learned on a heavy bag.

Dull thuds like the ones Konstantin had learned to love as he sparred with sides of beef in the slaughterhouses of the state run farm he worked on as a boy, pleasured his ears.

"Get him off of me Svetlana...he's breaking my ribs!" Svetlana pulled at Konstantin slapping, begging only to be pushed aside before the former boxer powered another series of frenzied jabs into Wyatt's exposed gut.

Svetlana spotted and grabbed the deck hose, then held it, full blast, against Konstantin's face. Stunned the big man rushed forward knocking her against the wall. The hose whipped helter-skelter around the room chipping paint, teeth, and gouging flesh. Rather than take cover Konstantin went back to the task at hand only now the beating became more savage as his blood and broken teeth reminded him of tough ring bouts.

Out cold Wyatt's dislocated joints looked to Svetlana as if his arms were pulled away from his body. With no thought of the punishment Kozlov would inflict on her, Svetlana raced toward the bridge. Had she taken time to listen before she barged in, she would have heard the slightly slurred voices of two old salts becoming fast friends.

"Captain, you must come Konstantin is killing Wyatt. Come now!" Kozlov ignored Svetlana wide-eyed excitement. Nothing to be gained from this unless the situation could be diminished. "Svetlana, for the last time, not every little fight on this ship requires the urgency you attach to such things." Kozlov smiled at the harbor captain. "It is this way on your vessel, too? Or do you Americans have the good sense not to include females into your cadre?"

"Captain, please you must..."

"Svetlana I will go, but at my choosing." Kozlov said, "You do remember rule number two, Svetlana?"

"Yes, but you have to stop..."

"Have to? Must? Tell me, comrade do such words remind you of directives?" Kozlov asked of Ray McDonald.

"I've got a female at my house, captain and if there is one thing I know, a man shouldn't get in the middle of an argument between a man and his woman."

Ah, better Kozlov thought. A tiff between lovers. Kozlov pulled Svetlana to him as a domineering husband would a misguided wife. "Tell you what, dear. Get the captain here a cup of your world famous coffee and then we shall go see what all the fuss is about, *syka* [bitch]."

Svetlana hand-surfed the stairwells as deftly as any accomplished seaman on her pell-mell trip to the galley. Weapons, not coffee were on her mind. Images of Konstantin and the magnitude of the equalizer required to dispatch him boggled her mind. Nothing short of a cannon was a sure bet and even if that were available cannonballs were in short supply. Long-handled pans, knifes, tenderizing mallet, nothing could stop the giant with one blow and one-shot was all she would have. Certain, Kozlov was the only weapon aboard who could stop Konstantin, Svetlana grabbed the simmering coffeepot, poured a cup and slapped a saucer over the steaming mug as she raced back to the bridge.

"Ah, and so your good manners have overcome your hysteria, my dear," Kozlov said as he motioned for the coffee to be placed on the control panel. "Enjoy, my Scottish friend. I must go tend to a crisis of unimaginable scope."

"Sure thing, Captain, and thank you ma'am," McDonald said as he noticed the wide-eyed woman staring at the picture and caption on the front page of the Star News. Even before the pair departed the bridge a thought lodged in Ray McDonald's head that would haunt him for days, "killing" *who*?

Chapter 32

Rene Jacobs thanked the informant for his tip then pressed the disconnect button. Foreign agents in Nassau and Freeport were common. Bahamas' alliance with the 130 other countries that comprised INTERPOL assured reciprocity between member nations. But an American agent on Chub, one of the smallest islands in the Caribbean Archipelago, meant only one thing.

Jacobs highlighted INTERPOL Red Alerts on his desktop and typed in Chub. **Fyodor Yantikov--John Smith: Last confirmed sighting Chub Cay Island Resort, Bahamas.** Rene Jacobs printed the results of his search and crammed the paper into his pocket then signed out on the status board located in the duty room.

Traffic on Bay Street, as usual, was heavy, nearly at a standstill. Horns blared as bargain-hunting tourists, eager to buy tropical standards--straw hats, brightly colored silk shirts, and laminated conch shells--darted from kiosk to kiosk that lined the street on either side. Not that the lean-to shops bundled together under low-slung verandas provided either variety or bargains.

For as far as the eye could see, the merchandise and the merchants who sold it were identical. Rene Jacobs shook his head in disgust at the shoppers' ignorance. Once, before rich foreigners had discovered Nassau, the island had been a true tropical paradise. Soon, Allah willing, the island would return to normal.

At the corner of Bay Street and Blue Hill Road, Jacobs turned on his emergency lights and siren, then coaxed his Toyota 4Runner onto the curb. Shopkeepers and motorists performed contortionist feats to accommodate his passage. Minutes later, the sights and sounds of commerce and chaos faded to the dull misery of inner-city desperation.

The thick scents of decaying conchs and net culls permeated the streets and shacks tourists would never walk or visit. Drunken Bahamians, soaked in urine laced with the sickly odor of stale beer and cheap whiskey, milled about lost in a haze of broken government promises. While the lucrative tourist trade had bought prosperity to some parts of the city, many more sections were plagued with the blight of poverty, Conch Town being the worst affected.

Though Rene Jacobs' government benefits entitled him to housing in New Providence South, an upscale domestic neighborhood, he chose to stay in Conch Town, not so much to remind him of how things were, but rather of how things shouldn't be. Drugs and alcohol, as far as Jacobs was concerned, had sickened his boyhood home, and only strict Islamic fundamentalism could cure it.

Two dope-smoking Rastafarians spied the marked police car and scampered into an alley like rats being chased by a ship's cat. Jacobs jumped from his car and fired a shot at the fleeing dreadlocks. If cleaning up the neighborhood took drastic measures, then drastic measures it would be, Jacobs concluded as he holstered his weapon. A drunk across the street got the message and stumbled out of Jacobs' line of fire. Empowered by the results, Jacobs again drew his weapon and scattered a young gang of Bahamian teens obviously up to no good. The law was a powerful tool in the hands of the right people, something his tourist-loving superiors would never understand.

Deeper into the misery of Conch Town, the road narrowed to a well-beaten dirt lane. Jacobs parked his SUV and walked the remaining distance. Discarded beer cans blackened with crack residue dotted the concrete slab at the entrance to the cinder block communication bunker hidden among weeds and transient's garbage--the building was undoubtedly the Bahamian Telephone Company's most forgotten asset.

Jacobs did a swift survey for vagrants then slid his master key into the locked steel door. The orderly layout inside the building contrasted sharply with garbage heaped outside its walls. Two uniform rows of cross-connection boxes lined the back wall and single fluorescent light fixture buzzed overhead. Jacobs grabbed a Butt-in-ski handset from the room's center stanchion and connected the clips to two terminals. Fyodor Yantikov answered his room phone on the second ring. "John Smith."

"My voice is my identity--do you know me?"

"Yes."

"Meet me at the box in one hour."

Fyodor Yantikov shot a quick glance across the vista beyond his balcony, half expecting to see the big Bahamian cop waving to him-- nothing. Calls from Rene Jacobs to his mobile phone were nothing unusual, but this call had come to his room. Jacobs' way of telling him he had been spotted, blond hair and all. "Boris, pack our bags, we are leaving. I'll be back in two hours." Before Boris could question his directive, Fyodor was out the door and on his way to Conch Town.

Meeting beyond the pristine confines of Atlantis and Potter's Cay made sense, but light skin in Conch Town would stand out like a geisha in a Miss Hawaiian Tropic bikini contest. Why hadn't Jacobs coded a message and contacted him after he was safely away from Nassau? Before Fyodor could entertain answers to his question the cab driver executed a U-turn and stopped. "Far as I go, mon."

Fyodor looked around for Jacobs' SUV and settled back into his seat. "Take me to the dead end...my friend is there."

"He may be, mon. But this is as far as I go."

"Dead end or no fare--"

"No fare--no problem, mon. Out!"

Before Fyodor closed the door the cab was burning rubber. Alone on the street, he slipped a set of brass knuckles over his fingers and began to run. Less than half a block later, four Bahamian teenagers fell in behind Fyodor, matching him stride for stride. A block further and the teens were less than a few meters away. Fyodor poured on the coals, but the teens only gained ground. "God damn you, Jacobs," Fyodor panted.

The pack was less than a stride behind him and from the corner of his eye, he could see the hand of the largest kid reaching out for him. Fear poured over him when the hand smacked his shoulder with a loud pop and hyena laughter erupted from the pack. The kid who made the touch shouted, "Tag, mon--you're it," and the four fell out laughing and bumping into each other and Fyodor as they circled, bent over at their prank. Then the howling laughter faded as the teens dashed off into the night, black on black. Fyodor raced once again toward the rendezvous spot, and not until he saw Jacobs' SUV did Fyodor brave checking the street behind him. Exhausted, he crumbled beside the police car and caught his breath.

"I believe, to play the game properly," Rene Jacobs boomed, "you're supposed to tag them back."

"You saw them then--and you didn't--"

"Saving you from some kids is not my job." Jacobs reached into his pocket for the INTERPOL report. "You have bigger problems than playful waifs--read this."

Fyodor scanned the text and looked at Jacobs. "What would you suggest I do?"

"Two things." Jacobs held up as many fingers. "First, go back to the hole you were in, and second, lose the hair. My man in Atlantis spotted you before he crossed the bridge."

"How did you know I'd be there?"

"Follow me. I will explain."

Rene Jacobs kicked one of the makeshift crack pipes and sent the can careening across the concrete slab. "Not only do the tourists bring us dollars," Jacobs growled, "they bring us this--drugs…. Decadence is the scourge of democracy."

Fyodor said nothing, but wondered about another decadent influence brought to the Caribbean, long before tourists corrupted the place--pirates. While Jacobs fished the key from his pocket, Fyodor studied the structure before him. One look and he instantly understood

Jacobs' name for the meeting place, *the box*. Until this moment, the street behind was as close to the box as he had gotten.

A rush of cool air filtered around Rene's broad mass, a tease of relief that made Fyodor anxious to enter the bunker. "So this is why you are so fond of this place. Nice."

Jacobs grunted, "I prefer the heat. This...," said Jacobs, as he pointed to a steel locker stenciled with the Bahamian Police Force logo, "...is why I am fond of this place." Jacobs fished another key from his pocket and snapped the lock from the door. "And this," Jacobs cradled one of the three yellow polyurethane containers Fyodor had delivered months earlier, "is why there is not a rock you can hide under in these islands--not even the fake rocks of Atlantis--where I cannot find you."

"I wasn't hiding from you, old chap. No offense, but the Bahamian Police Force and Interpol are hardly peers."

"Lucky for you." Jacobs glared at Fyodor. "If they were, you would be having this conversation in irons."

"Touché, old boy. But--"

"But comparison of police proficiency is not the reason for this meeting." Jacobs wadded a handful of Fyodor's shirt in one of his big hands and yanked the Russian close to his face. "Without the electronic components, these weapons are useless. We want the rest of our order." Jacobs smashed his other fist into Fyodor's gut.

From his kneeling position, Fyodor clutched at Jacobs' legs for support. With a powerful thrust, Jacobs buried a knee into Fyodor's thorax. Gasping for air, Fyodor rolled behind the pillar in the center of the room. The short reprieve was just enough time to grab a few gulps of air and clear his head. As Jacobs approached, Fyodor slipped the brass knuckles over his fingers and hammered a shot into the big man's shin.

Surprised by the assault, Rene Jacobs retreated to the locker and massaged the gathering pain in his tibia. Scared and filled with adrenaline, Fyodor somersaulted through the open door and scrambled behind the bunker. Chunks of concrete tore at his hands and feet. Aiming wildly, Fyodor slung two large pieces at the shadow looming behind him. A bone-snapping crack confirmed his success, and without looking back Fyodor raced for the SUV parked under a lone street light.

All Fyodor Yantikov wanted was safe passage from Conch Town and a few hours head start. Orhocht "Mom" White could deal with Jacobs' concerns over the rest of the shipment. An open window and the keys dangling from the ignition of the 4Runner proved to be an illusional panacea. Before he could turn the key, the long shadow of Rene Jacobs darkened the hood of the SUV. Barely able to steady himself on his mangled leg, Jacobs fired a round from his Glock into the windshield.

Splinters of glass exploded around Fyodor's head like spores from a barrel coral. White-hot lead seared down his arm and peeled the flesh away from his forearm. Oblivious to the pain, Fyodor fired the engine and lunged the vehicle at full throttle toward the limping cop.

Slowed by his injuries, and unable to avoid the full brunt of the speeding cruiser, Jacobs flew backwards. Ligaments and tendons snapped. The muscles in his legs furled like motorized sails. Rooster tails of sand and shell sprayed from the spinning tires of the Toyota as Fyodor reversed and positioned himself for another charge.

Jacobs, paralyzed from the waist down, rolled into a prone firing position. Rounds fired from his Glock thudded harmlessly into the lose sand of the vacant lot. With one last Herculean effort, Jacobs leveled his pistol at the 4Runner's grill and fired his remaining two rounds. Even with the well-placed shots, there would be no escape from the inevitable. But then, how many men were lucky enough to take their first and last breaths in the place they called home? Jacobs' last inhalation of Conch's wretched air blended perfectly with the mixture of steam and hot motor oil spewing from his own iron predator which had come to rest upon his body.

Hours later, officers from the Bahamian Police Force pieced together clues from the carnage that had claimed the life of fellow officer, Rene Jacobs. The INTERPOL text and the shoulder-fired missiles found in the box proved beyond a doubt that the inspector had died a hero's death. For three days, the funeral of the man who had given his life to save the country from a terrorist attack dominated the Bahamian airways.

Fyodor Yantikov watched the televised requiem in his hideout far from the bogus rocks of Atlantis, a drunken stupor his only medicine and Boris his only physician.

Chapter 33

Fyodor reached for the vodka under his cot and took a long swig from the frosted glass bottle. The combination of vodka, aspirins, and codeine-based 2-2-2's from the drug store in Atlantis provided welcomed relief from the throbbing wound in his arm. Boris had cauterized the gash to prevent infection. The painful procedure had eliminated the need for medical attention, but more important, was the suspicion such a wound would arouse. Fyodor studied the jagged line of blisters and scabs that extended from his hand to his elbow. Necessary, yes, but still...Boris could have been more delicate--idiot.

The steel bullet from Jacobs' Glock had left a tenable scar, but the butchery caused by Boris' white-hot metal rod left a permanent distinguishing mark, a detail, sure to be added to his growing INTERPOL file. "Distinguishing mark," Fyodor snorted. Nothing compared to the *Cop Killer* charge waiting to be pinned on him in Nassau.

Rene Jacobs eulogized as a hero in the "War on Terror." how absolutely preposterous! Even more ludicrous were the three cenotaphs the Bahamian government had planned for each of Jacobs' duty stations. Any more attention from the America press, and a monument to Jacobs could wind up on the Washington Mall.

Let it go. Even if the truth about the cop-turned-terrorist was exposed, there would be no accolades for the unknown assailant responsible for the hit. *Unknown assailant?* Fyodor mused. How soon would that description change once the DNA evidence from Jacobs' car arrived at the agency's lab in Washington--in days...hours?

With his good hand, Fyodor typed a text message into his phone-- Lat. Lon. Baltic Queen-- and sent the message to "Mom" White.

"How are you feeling, my brother?"

Fyodor shoved his mangled arm under Boris' nose and screamed, "How do you think I feel? Butcher!"

Boris rolled Fyodor's arm in his hands and looked for the telltale red marks of infection. No need to worry about tetanus. With the way Fyodor's tongue was lashing, the danger of lockjaw had passed. "I crank the generator and fix you breakfast. You rest and watch the news--"

"No more news," Fyodor sighed. "Please, no more news."

Boris sawed off four slices of bread and made two sandwiches of fried-yellowtails leftover from dinner. Remembering his mother's favorite side dish, Boris raked three foil-wrapped baked potatoes from the smoldering coals and removed the skins. Within minutes the aroma of fresh brewed coffee and potato pancakes floated across the still waters surrounding the deserted Cay five miles from San Andros.

Fyodor would never admit it, but life was good in the hideout. Fish were plentiful and the canvas cistern hanging between two palm trees overflowed from the rain of near-daily tropical showers. Provisions, enough to feed ten people for weeks, lined the back wall of the abandoned fish camp. With the comforts provided by the stolen Honda generator and television, life was more than bearable...it was almost perfect.

"Ah, potato pancakes--smells almost like Mama's kitchen."

Boris slid a plastic chair behind Fyodor and eased his brother into the seat. "I miss her, Fyodor."

Missing loved ones was nothing new to Fyodor Yantikov. Until now, he had placated himself and Boris with the fantasy of a family reunion. The stark reality of truth burned through the fog of drugs and alcohol--any hope of seeing Liliya Yantikov again had died with the prophetic Rene Jacobs. The Inspector had been right. There was no rock in the Bahamas that could hide a fugitive, especially one with a terrorist bounty on his head. Millions of dollars in reward money could entice the most committed members of the underworld to betray one of their own. The cheapskates of his ilk would sell him out for much less.

"Soon. You will see her again, soon, I promise."

"At our reunion?" Boris asked.

The text message alarm vibrated the phone on the table. Fyodor scribbled down the latitude-longitude, speed, and on course heading of the *Baltic Queen*. His quick thinking had paid off, obviously, and news of his pending charges had not found their way to the press. "Mom" White was no fool, and only a fool would have responded to a text from a *Most Wanted* fugitive. "Boris, get my chart, and bring my compass and divider."

Boris ignored his brother's command and sucked a mouthful of tender meat from the bones of yesterday's catch. "Eat first, you will need your strength."

Fyodor broke the crispy tail from his fish and scooped up a mouthful of warm pancake. "Ummm--just like Mama's--I'll finish when I get the chart."

Greasy smudges shone like uncharted translucent islands on the mylar map spread on the kitchen table. Once again, Fyodor twirled the divider from San Andros to the last known position of the *Baltic Queen*. If his calculations were correct, the ship would pass within seventy miles of the hideout at present heading and speed.

Fyodor circled the fix derived from his triangulation and divided the distance between present position and the fix by the ship's speed--ten hours--plenty of time to make preparations.

"Come on, Boris, we have much to do."

The remainder of the morning was spent transforming the flashy Fountain into something less noticeable. *Faux* resin patches, painted in dull gray primer adorned the once gleaming hull. No nosy kids, like the one on Chub who knew so much about watches, would want a closer look now, Fyodor figured, as he finished the last patch.

Later in the afternoon, under the shade of a copse of palm trees, the two brothers shaped putty-like charges of C-4 around remote detonators. Magnets attached to the explosives with quick drying epoxy finished the deadly project. After a quick meal of canned corned-beef-hash washed down with warm Kaliks, the two rested.

"Maybe now is the time to tell me the plan, Fyodor?"

"First," Fyodor grabbed two tins of Kiwi shoe paste and smeared alternating stripes of brown and black onto Boris' face. "We need to camouflage you, just in case Kozlov gets a look at you. I don't want him to see our resemblance. But, for our mother's sake, make sure no one on the ship sees you--and above all, Boris--do not board the ship for any reason--"

"But...what if you don't come back?"

"Blow the charges--"

"No," Boris shook his head angrily. "I will not kill my own brother."

"Boris." Fyodor snapped the tins closed and wiped his hands on his pant leg. "If my plan fails and Kozlov captures me, he will make me talk. If that happens our family, all of them, will die.... You must promise me--"

"Let's forget about this plan, and bring the family here." Boris spread his arms toward the cay. "With a little work on the house and a bigger generator--for air conditioner--mother wouldn't mind. You could fish...no one is better at it than you, Fyodor."

"Boris, once I am named as the killer of Rene Jacobs, there will be no place for me to hide."

"You said yourself, the cop was a terrorist. Killing him was good thing...they may even give you a reward, a big one."

"Didn't you watch the news? Rene Jacobs is a mythical hero, and the police will never let the myth die. No matter how much proof is thrown up against it." Fyodor snatched up two charges and headed for the boat. "Besides, who would believe me, a smuggler and a crook?"

"I believe you."

Fyodor turned toward Boris and smiled. "I'm afraid affirmation of my veracity from my brother, a petty thief, would mean little to the authorities." Boris hung his head and shuffled after Fyodor. "But," Fyodor nudged Boris with his shoulder. "It means a great deal to me. I love you, Boris. No matter how this day turns out, remember that. Always remember that."

"And that is why I cannot kill you."

"No, Boris…that is why you must."

Chapter 34

Merging the dual lives of an undercover agent was usually a challenge for agent Jim Williams/James Tidwell, but this trip from Nassau to Chub was a covert operative's dream. Other than Clark, who knew more than he wanted to know about second mate *Jim Williams*, no one else on the boat would be alert or sober enough to tell whether he was a government agent or a member of the Taliban.

Ganna Mae, the old woman, was in her stateroom listening to static on her radio while having a heated conversation on the boat's satellite phone. Yasnaya and Lisa were on the top sundeck catching rays and knocking back Yellowbirds and Bahama Mammas quicker than Tidwell could mix the sweet concoctions from the fly bridge bar one deck below.

Phillip Moole and Tim Ridell, on the rear sundeck, were engaged in a pissing contest to see who could best handle the manliest version of bourbon. Moole, after hearing Tim's order for bourbon and water, dropped his request for bourbon and coke and decided on bourbon with a splash of branch. Ridell, circled in front of Moole and polished off his drink in one gulp, sneered, then ordered bourbon on the rocks, straight up. Moole, turned his back to Ridell, gulped his drink, gagged, made a prize winning lemon-sucking festival face, and then went with bourbon straight up, no ice, for his next routine.

Tidwell, sensing the rising level of testosterone on the lower sundeck, and a good shot at halving his bartending gig, filled two shot glasses with bourbon then dropped both drinks into iced mugs of Kalik beer. Both men eyed the boilermakers; Ridell leered at Moole and slammed the shot down. Moole, in the same cowardly way he had done during the entire contest, turned his back on Ridell and polished off the drink as he suppressed another gagging reflex. Five minutes later, both drunks were body surfing the aft railing and spewing like sperm whales.

As Tidwell had figured, the inebriates passed out a short time later. Part of his duties as a mate was to make sure no harm befell the passengers. One look at the four entwined shark belly white legs and he knew he'd have to get them back inside the main salon. But nothing in his orders said he couldn't have a little fun with them once they were safe.

Clark had seen odd-couple pairings on boats, old men with young girls, old women with young men, women with women, men with men—hell, once on the Med he had seen a man and sheep pairing—goddamn crazy Europeans! But the couple he saw splayed on the main salon sleeper damn-near rivaled the bestiality scene.

Moole was coupled in Ridell's corsage decorated arms. Ridell had his face snuggled against Moole's neck and hibiscus adorned ear. "Sons of bitches, looks like two hippie weenie washers passed out at Woodstock." Clark shouted to Tidwell on the bridge, "You have anything to do with that?"

"Got no idea what you're talking about."

Clark settled back into the captain's chair on the bridge. "Funny how they've been at each other the whole time then—poof! They're in each other arms, all lovey-dovey." Remembering the man and sheep on the Med cruise, Clark mumbled aloud, "Yep, one thing's for sure...salt air sure as hell seasons kinky."

A blip on the surface radar screen pinged in Clark's peripheral vision. Like an ape checking for ticks on an only a cub, Clark bent low and peered into the green-tinted screen. "Damn thing gotta be doing over 90 knots. But what's his hurry? Ain't nothing out there but open ocean."

Tidwell grabbed the binoculars and zeroed in on the southwest quadrant of the horizon. The silhouette of the 42' Fountain against the darkening magenta sky was familiar, but the actual image of the pock-marred vessel was much different from the sleek craft he had boarded only weeks earlier. "Something screwy here—give her a look, Captain." Clark fine tuned the Lexica 8X power binoculars until the fake blemishes stood out clearly on the Fountain's skin. "Yeah, if she had that much damage she'd be limping to port not racing for the open sea."

"Come on, Clark. You know what I mean."

Clark Guilford gave the speeding image a good look from stem to stern. Even with the fake splotches, different color, and new registration number, there was little doubt about it. This was the boat that Wyatt Kincaid was last seen aboard. But admitting it could get Clark and his passengers into a bad situation. "I'll give you this much, it looks a lot like her. But this boat's different—check out the rod holders and look at the coolers. She's rigged for fishing."

"Rigged for fishing, my ass! Those are Penn 9's in the rod holders. Where are they going to bottom fish out here? We're in blue water. For Christ sakes, it's all for show. You know it."

"I know this." Clark pressed the eyecups hard against his face. "The fellow on your boat wasn't Bahamian—and unless I'm crazy as all get out—that ain't the case here."

Tidwell grabbed the binoculars and studied the boat's crew. Even from this distance it was easy to see their faces weren't white, but neither did the faces have the rich dark chocolate color of Bahamian fishermen. Then it dawned on him, "War paint, they wearing war paint, Clark! When was the last time you saw fishermen with camo-paint? Who do you think they're hiding from—the fish?"

Clark moved closer to Tidwell on the outside chance some of the passenger might over-hear him. "If you're so sure about the boat, why don't you call down the thunder? Hell son, if you can get a jet over Chub for show, this should be a piece of cake."

Clark was right. Calling down the thunder was no problem and the force sent in would be overwhelming. All of the perps would be dead, including Wyatt Kincaid, if a rendezvous with Wyatt was the Fountains destination. "Clark do you remember the Bahamian cop who was killed in Nassau the other day?"

"Who doesn't? Damn shame, too. Killing a good man like that."

Tidwell paused before continuing. Cops killed in the line of duty deserved any honorarium or accolades the public cared to bestow upon them. But before dead cops were turned into national heroes, international in the case of Rene Jacobs, the facts should be sifted first. Pressure to hold the actual findings from the Jacob's crime scene was already coming from the Bahamian government to the Miami office. Facts didn't match the story being touted by local officials. Nothing unusual about that, even small nations and local governments had learned the value of spinning information. Someone once said that truth has no versions, there is only truth. That someone never had met the spin-miesters hired by governments, politicians, and even news services around the world. Ironically the capitol of truth spinning, Washington D.C., was demanding a full and truthful report on the Jacobs killing. National Defense was at stake, but putting the Jacobs' hero image back in the bottle was going to be hard. Once the press, the same press who had helped perpetuate the Jacobs' myth, found out the truth, some version of gate--Bahamasgate, Nassaugate, Jacobsgate, take your pick, would dominate the headlines and lead stories. Some good cops would be sacrificed to save some fat cat politician and it would take years for the dirty cop image to die down. No matter, the facts would come out. If the FBI and the CIA had learned one thing it was that— crap smells a lot better when aired out. So, even if what he had to tell Clark was classified, it would only be a matter of time before the truth was leaked by an opposition party politician, generally identified as a high-placed administration official.

"Clark, I've been watching TV too. Maybe what we heard about Jacobs wasn't exactly the truth."

"What do you mean?"

"Look, Clark, I went to the crime scene in Nassau...what we're being told and what actually went on there are different."

"So, you're saying the Bahamian government is lying?"

"I'm saying I don't understand what's going on. Not the crime part. That I've got down. It's the diplomacy inflections I don't understand."

Clark grabbed a handful of peanuts and shook them like a shooter at the craps table.

"When I don't understand something I just ask a question. You tried that?"

"Yeah," Tidwell watched as seagulls snapped up the nuts Clark tossed into the air. "I was told the explanation was above my pay grade and beyond my need to know."

Clark reached into the bags for more nuts. "You know, I served, too. Some uppity-up told me that…well, that'd be that for me."

"Even if it meant someone innocent may suffer, or worse, die?" Tidwell looked at the circling flock of gulls overhead and waited for Clark to respond. He didn't. "You ever buck the system?"

Clark threw more nuts to the gulls. "I bucked it once, got all hung up on doing the right thing. Ruined a promising career. Should have kept my mouth shut." Clark's hand flicked skyward and plucked a gull from the air. Tidwell jumped back as the flapping mass of feathers and talons zipped by his face. "What the hell?"

"Goddamn polluters!" Clark held the gull down and undid the loop of a plastic six pack holder from the bird's neck and claw. "Been watching him all day—little fellow was having a tough time." As quickly as the bird had appeared he was gone. "There you go, Bud. Stay safe."

An easy feeling came over James Tidwell. Trusting people came hard for undercover operatives. Sure the guys you worked with, that was innate. But part of his job was to develop allies when on a mission. Until this moment, as close as Clark had become, his trust in Clark had been tentative at best. Something as simple as saving a squawking gull had turned the tide. After all, animal lovers, other than the Birdman of Alcatraz, had a pretty good record in the criminal justice system, and for the moment that was good enough. Miami wasn't listening, or they were buried deep in the developing political fog and time was running out. Either make a move now or watch a bad deal go down, and without help he had no move to make. "Clark, let's follow that Fountain I've got a hunch…"

"Partner, unless you want to officially commandeer this vessel, I'm not about to endanger my passengers." Clark jabbed his finger on the glass covered compass. "This heading doesn't change until you act in your official capacity, and that's final."

Tidwell looked at Clark's set jaw, blazing eyes, and don't screw with me expression. No way in hell voluntary cooperation was coming tonight. Without a word, he slipped from the bridge and headed for the bow pulpit, a place he often retreated to when the vessel was underway. The orange glow of twilight in the western sky silhouetted the Fountain as it raced away at a 90 degree angle to the Hatteras. Nothing he could do. If getting an explanation for the screwed up report on the Rene Jacob's killing was above his pay grade, then commandeering this boat sure as hell was.

Ganna Mae Ferguson had spent no time on the bridge; as a matter of fact, Clark didn't remember her even passing through the bridge since she had been onboard. All of that had changed. No longer did she look or act like a mere passenger. Confidence glowed around her like a halo of bitchery, "Captain, bring her around to this heading, maintain this speed and input these coordinates in the autopilot." Clark glanced at the paper and placed his pen under the new bearing, "Ma'am that heading takes us to the high seas. We run that course for long and we may not have enough fuel to return."

Why the hell did men always think they could undermine her? Hadn't she buried a boatload of them figuratively and literally just to prove they couldn't? "Returning isn't a concern I have, nor should you. I own this damn boat and I'm ordering you take up this heading. If you have a problem with that," Ganna pointed to Tidwell in the pulpit, "get his sweet little ass up here and put your captain's hat on him 'cause, one way or another, we *will* make this waypoint."

The big Hatteras leaned into the waves and over rode the hard working stabilizers. Tidwell beamed a smile up at Clark and headed back to the bridge. "Thanks…" Tidwell's voice trailed off as he watched Ganna Mae stuff a Beretta into her calf holster. "Is there something I should know, Clark?"

The brother's Yantikov did not notice the bone rising on the bow as the Hatteras Motor Yacht changed course and reached full speed. Further away on the darkening eastern horizon a stealthy H-733 hard ribbed Zodiac armed with twin 50 caliber machine guns initiated a quartering flanking maneuver, moved into firing range and zeroed in on the Hatteras.

Chapter 35

The damage from Konstantin's punches and weakness from the diarrhea that had indeed been induced by the brackish water his parched tongue had lapped at earlier, pushed Wyatt back into an inviting unconsciousness. For days he teetered between the worlds of light and dark. At times he heard voices fading in and out like cell phone conversations on 1-bar signals. The speakers and a few key words were all that he could remember. Kozlov's rants fell like fire and brimstone, *devastation, capitalist imperialist, America be damned.* Svetlana's words were like refreshing sips from an effervescent mountain stream, *rest, stay with me,* even *love.*

Chills and fever racked his body while dreams and horrible nightmares churned his mind until, finally, total exhaustion plunged him into fits of restless sleep. The vicious cycle continued for days. At times he clutched the bedding to stop his fall into the black abyss of nothingness at the bottom of his dreams. In his darkest moments he kicked the covers and his security blanket away and freebased to oblivion. Lunacy and lucidity were toe-to-toe, apathy was in a high state of arousal, and Wyatt Kincaid didn't give a damn who won.

Bony hands massaged the coldness of the grave into his extremities, inward the icy tide surged ,drowning vital organs one by one. "Order of passage" his father's doctor had called it. The first time he heard the phrase he was standing at the foot of his father's death bed, watching the last breath leave the frail body that once had been vigorous and strong.

Seeing the loneliness and pain spread over his mother and replace sixty years of love that had stood the test of time had been hard. To his knowledge, she never smiled again and, a few weeks later she died. The hardest part had been living with the forgiveness that never came, from either of them.

Once, father and son had been close. Other boys wanted to be like heroes in comic books or on television. The only hero he worshiped had just died without absolution. Svetlana had lied about that. "The Code" had endured and, if there was a reward after death, then Wyatt Kincaid Sr. knew his son made the right call and that was all that mattered. *"To keep good deeds good, keep them to yourself."* I did it Daddy, I kept them good. Wild with fever, Wyatt repeated the phrase until he was sure the words echoed down every crevice and up every hilltop in heaven, *Keep'em good, keep'em good, keep'em good.*

After days of darkness, the swelling around his eyes abated and he began to see the green-hued flash of the Caribbean twilight sparkling around the cabin. Dream or not, this was pleasant and the pain, dull and throbbing, was numbing, almost euphoric.

IV tubes dangled around him like a life-giving spider web. The hiss of the ventilator as it cycled through the inspiration-exhalation circuit explained his forced breaths. As soon as consciousness was detected the sedative dose was increased on the IV meter.

As the contusions and inflammation around his spine subsided his movement and dexterity increased. Each day, when he could sense no one in the cabin, he pushed the increments of his new found mobility until the limitations were defeated. He used Canadian Army isometric exercises to strengthen and tone his muscle.

During the times he could sense or hear movement of others in the room he exercised his mental capacities by solving mathematical and word problems. At night he avoided the programmed sedative by plugging the IV into his mattress. The resulting clarity helped him formulate a plan. No doubt Kozlov would tear him down as soon as he awakened, but he would circumvent Kozlov's plan by playing 'possum. With any luck he would learn if the conversations between Kozlov, Svetlana and Phillip Moole were real or imagined, and more importantly, he would know friend from foe.

The warm sponge baths spiked with baking soda and scented with rosemary awakened his senses. Free from the horrible odor of the bilge he relished the just-washed scent clinging to his body and bedding. Each time he moved he could he feel the sheen and richness of the sheets covering him; 400-500 thread count, at least. Fine Irish linen shams and a pure silk duvet cover, reminiscent of resplendent European hotels he had stayed in, completed the luxury of his new berth. Figuring out his new surrounding didn't take much imagination. Though he had seen the Captain's Quarters only briefly while swabbing the decks, this was definitely Kozlov's quarters.

Plush quarters, sophisticated medical equipment, prescription sedatives…there was no doubt he was under medical care but by who, how, and why the hell would anyone bother?

It was on this day, that Svetlana came into the cabin humming a Russian lullaby. As she ran warm water into the basin, he admired the easy swing of her hips as she moved to the cadence of the ditty. Ah, the days of rest and force fed broths laced with vitamins and minerals had worked wonders.

Gentle strokes from her warm sponge soothed the aches and pains stored in his muscles. As she had done with each bath since Wyatt had been moved to Kozlov's quarters, Svetlana reinforced her patient with a steady stream of positive instruction. "Rest, save your strength, fight for your health." The words and sponge worked their magic in unison.

Even the broken ribs and torn ligaments from the beating responded to the treatment. From the darkness and safety of his feigned coma, Wyatt floated back to the woman who had saved his life. Light strokes nudged his genitals and stirred his libido like a double-shot of *Cialis*. Svetlana stroked him with the sponge just long enough to acertain the full measure of Wyatt Kincaid. "Hmm, I think someone has been faking it."

"Oh maybe a little bit, but then again," Wyatt let out a raspy chuckle, "kinda hard to hide that much trickery."

The voice of the man she had given up for dead excited her. Having the fortitude to laugh after all the pain he had suffered was amazing. That he had chosen to engage in sexual banter after being so close to death was proof that Wyatt Kincaid was still Wyatt Kincaid. Her instincts of flight and fight folded in her gut like batter being stirred by a whisk and finally settled in smooth resolve at the bottom of her heart. She vowed to never again side against this man again and she would stand by him even if it meant death for both.

"Umm, yes!" Svetlana teased, "Not even a *napyerstuk* could hide so much trickery."
For the first time in weeks the mischievous glint returned to Wyatt's eyes, "Russian for bucket, right?"

"You are asking me for the definition of *napyerstuk ?*"

Like a kid playing fort in the bed Wyatt fluffed the sheet into the air and let it settled upon his makeshift tent pole. "Well it's gotta mean something big enough to hide this ole…support, right?"

Svetlana laughed, "Your first guess was closer, think cylindrical."

"A barrel!" Wyatt beamed.

"Smaller."

"Keg?"

"Smaller."

"Ah, come on. I give up. Tell me…. Hey, I got it. We can name my ole boy *napyerstuk*.

"I beg your pardon."

"My boy." Wyatt nodded toward the tent pole. "It's an American custom…well, maybe it's Southern? But it's a custom. Women always give *it* a pet name…"

"And what did your last wife call *it?*"

"I can't tell you that, it's too personal. Besides that'd be like cheating. We have to decide on a name with no outside influence. If you don't have any objections I like *napyerstuk* sounds kinda manly and manly suits old Wyatt Kincaid mighty fine."

"*Napyerstuk* it is then. I certainly wouldn't want break with tradition."

"All right, then." Wyatt laced his fingers and cradled his hands behind his head, "So what's it mean?"

Svetlana made a mocking bow towards his lap like a servant to her master. "Oh great thimble may you bring much joy to our lives--"

"Great, wait... what was that? I didn't quite catch the name."

"Thimble."

"Ah baby, that won't work."

A sound so seldom heard on this ship of misery and oppression suddenly cascaded over the steel deck and splashed out upon the blue waters of the Caribbean. Not even Kozlov could silence such laughter.

There is the first kiss of youth, the prelude kiss before virginity's farewell, and the kiss of love that seals the wedding vows. Each immediately recognized as milestones along life's path. The kiss Svetlana and Wyatt shared was a milestone passed only by those who have touched Death's cloak.

If eyes could engage in foreplay, both pairs, which had avoided contact for months, were now in the midst of intense activity. Their bodies came together in perfect rhythm. The fullness and vitality of the love making pleased and surprised both. Powerful thrusts countered gentle caresses and neither time nor space was a barrier to the lust they gave in to. Slowly, soft intelligible murmurs and groans turned to intelligible conversations.

"Well! Some one was definitely faking..."

"As long as it wasn't you." Wyatt beamed, "I don't have a problem with that."

Once, a hundred years ago, it had been impossible for him to hold a woman after love making. Now, their hour long embrace seemed like only seconds. "Are you strong enough to go outside?" Svetlana asked. "I think the fresh air will do you good."

"Svetlana, I need to play possum for a few more days."

"Possum?"

"You know faking being almost dead. I need more time before I take another shot at that som bitch."

The sound of Kozlov's footsteps echoing off the steel walls announced his impending arrival. "Ah, good, the patient is up," Kozlov eyed the mussed sheets then stared at Svetlana. "and well, I presume?"

"No, captain, he has just now awakened. He is still weak."

Kozlov broke open a smelling salt capsule and shoved it under Wyatt's nose which caused a fit of coughing. Before Svetlana could move, Kozlov shoved her palm in front of Wyatt's mouth. "In her hand, Mr. Kincaid. Spit in her hand."

Dark splotches of coagulum floating in red tinted spittle stood out against the paleness of her palm. "Good, the internal injuries are clotting; you have done well, Svetlana. Our guest will live."

Kozlov, opened the sea chest at the foot of his berth and began to gather items from his desk, including the newspaper article from the Wilmington paper. "I hope you find your new quarters satisfactory, Mr. Kincaid?"

Wyatt screwed his face into a sarcastic snarl; before he could speak Svetlana twisted the ball of sheet still draped over Wyatt's groin. Though he was stronger and refreshed he was in no position to take anymore of Kozlov's punishment. One more beating and there would be no recovery next time. The uncomfortable constriction around his middle caused Wyatt to look at Svetlana.

Only a nanosecond passed as their eyes locked. The message sent by Svetlana was clear and strong. No more machismo, play it straight, or he could endanger her life as well as his own.

"Probably should have gotten around to this a little sooner," Wyatt said as he brushed a thin film of scarlet drool from his chin. "I know we haven't seen eye-to-eye…and I know I haven't been the most appreciative guest, ah." From the corner of his eye Wyatt could see the relief wash over Svetlana's face, as humiliating as it was to kowtow to Kozlov it was worth every crumb of humble pie to give a little security to one that had given so much to him. "I know you moved me to your quarters and I know without your generosity, I'd be dead by now. There'll be no more mutinous behavior on my part Captain I'm done. From here on out, your plan is my plan."

For the very first time since, Wyatt Kincaid, bigger than life, had stepped aboard the ship Svetlana was actually proud of the man she was certain she loved. Americans were famous for adapting the world to custom fit their needs. Wyatt, from day one, had resisted the obvious. Kozlov, was in command even if by some fluke Wyatt could have succeeded in one of his harebrained schemes, he could never have taken command of the ship. Not that that had stopped the big galoot from trying and for that she admired him, badly named penis and all.

"So, you have seen the error of your ways, as they say, Mr. Kincaid," Kozlov said as he inched closer to Svetlana and gently massaged her shoulder. "I do not believe you old friend." Kozlov slid his hand down Svetlana's blouse while tightening his grip on the ever present Tovlov revolver. In one quick motion he tore the buttons from the blouse exposing the full bosom of Svetlana Yankovich.

Rage, blood red, darker and more powerful than surging seas stirred by a Cat 5 hurricane pummeled Wyatt's gut. But, rather than the mad charge Kozlov expected, Wyatt eyed him with total calm. "Not many things have gone my way on this ship, and I know I deserved a lot of the punishment that I received." Wyatt pointed at Svetlana. "She didn't deserve that, and frankly, I expected better from you."

Yuri Kozlov had given many commands and overseen many deeds during his years at sea. None disgusted him more than the one he had just preformed. Svetlana stood before him tall and erect with her bared chest and made no attempt to hide his misdeed. Sailors, Kozlov believed, had always represented the moral fiber of the countries they served. Even the Nazis' perverted beliefs had failed to afflict the German Navy as it had the Fatherland's army during World War II. Shame bowed his head and shoulders. Never again would he embarrass his nautical brethren, no matter how bad he wanted a reason to beat the Capitalist Pig, Wyatt Kincaid.

"Please, cover yourself, Svetlana." Kozlov grunted as he spun on his heels and headed for the bridge, looking neither right nor left.

Chapter 36

Ganna Mae, satisfied the boat was on course, left the bridge and returned to her stateroom. As she did every time she made a call or had a private conversation, Ganna Mae tuned the radio to a static band to interfere with any bugs or listening devices. Some people, like Yasnaya, thought her paranoid, but those people weren't familiar with Pre Perestroika Russia. In those times she hadn't seen a need for secrecy either; after all she was a darling of the Soviet elite and untouchable. But an encounter with Yegor Kulakov, a KGB section chief, who made a very public play for her affections, changed that status and her frivolous view of life forever.

Kulakov was a disgusting pig and she laughed at his audacity; that little show of disdain on her part had deadly consequences. Thousands were imprisoned and hundreds sent to their deaths because of clandestine reports assembled by her unsavory jilted suitor. When Kulakov played a subversive recording between her and one Adonis look-alike actor she understood her new role. Kulakov was no longer the ugly frog. Overnight he became a dashing prince to her enamored princess, her most believable performance yet. Oh, yes. She screwed him like her life depended on it. It did.

To her everlasting shame, Ganna perjured herself at a state trial and gave damning testimony against her young and doomed Adonis. If the wolves had not gotten to them, his bones remained in an unmarked grave deep in a Ukrainian forest.

James Tidwell slammed his headset down. The old woman was at it again with the damn static. The only way he could hear her phone conversations would be if the Agency was recording them, a request he had made dozens of time to no avail. Disgusted, he left his makeshift spy nook in the engine room and headed back to the bridge.

Moole and Ridell's snoring serenaded Tidwell as he eased about the cabin dimming lights and closing blinds, doing his best to put the shiny white Hatteras into stealth mode. Careful not to wake the love birds, Tidwell slipped a hard plastic case from beneath the salon divan and shuffled his prize back to the bridge. "Som bitch," Clark whispered as he eyed the two Uzis and M-79 grenade launcher. "I didn't realize the Bossman had that kind of armory aboard."

"He didn't," Tidwell said. "Believe it or not, this is government issue."

"How the hell did I not know about this?"

Tidwell gave Clark a grin, "Come on, Captain. When's the last time you've done housekeeping?"

"You got me there," Clark grunted. "Where's Miss Ferguson?" Clark eyed the passageway to make sure they were alone. "Are you good with us headed toward open waters?"

"If it means we hook up with Fountain I'm very good with it." Tidwell said, and stashed the weapons in the narrow pilothouse closet. "You know where they are if you need them."

"I hope that's not the case," Clark grunted.

Tidwell grabbed the binoculars. "Wish we had night vision goggles...I'm going topside. Got this funny feeling we aren't alone."

In the dim salon Phillip Moole snatched the corsage off Tim Ridell's arm as he squirmed from his embrace. His clothing was soaked and reeked of alcohol. Though he had swallowed a fair amount of the contest drinks he had managed to spill more on himself. Quiet as a kid checking the milk and cookies left for Santa, Moole made his way into the galley and grabbed a clean chef's smock hanging in the pantry. Fools actually thought he was stupid enough to get into a drinking contest with a lowlife like Ridell... a Harvard Man participating in such stupidity, really!

Moole unsnapped his briefcase and removed the unsigned proxy assignment papers. Drunks, most drunks anyway were lovable, and Tim Ridell was no different. Moole had witnessed his affability many times...the man just could not hold his liquor or his emotions intact, a malady from which many undereducated people suffered. "Ridell, wake up," Moole whispered. "The captain needs you to sign an Entry Declaration Form before we get to port."

Tim Ridell sat up, looked at Moole, fell back against the divan and slurred his response, "Leab me balone, you blasturd."

Perfect, Moole thought, this idiot has finally reverted to his native tongue.

"Tim, wake up! This will just take a moment..."

"I need coffee," Tim mumbled. "And food."

"Sign these papers first..."

"Hell, no! I'm the boss and I'm not signing anything until I get coffee and food, got it?"

"We don't have a chef and the captain and mate are busy." Moole said.

"There is a new sheriff in town Mooley, and he ain't signin' nothin' until there is coffee."

"All right, all right... I'll fix you coffee and eggs. Just sign the damn papers!"

"And bacon. The boss wants bacon."

"Very well. Coffee, bacon, eggs and how about some toast? Now will you sign the papers?"

"Eggs *and* bacon? You'd do that for me old Mooley Wooley? I was wrong about you old buddy old buddy Phil o' mine...you're OK."

Moole cringed as Tim Ridell continued to paw at him. Soon that would never again be a problem. But, for just a little longer, he had to play along. "And you are my little buddy, too" Moole crooned. "Just sign right here."

Tim sat up and tried to focus on the papers. Red Flags should be flying all over the place, since from the very outset of Moole's *position* offer he had been careful to never sign a document without thoroughly reading it. For that matter he made no moves without discussing it with Yas. This was different. All he wanted Moole to do was shut up and cook him some food. He held the paper close to an indirect lighting fixture and scanned them. Bold official looking script across the top of one page affirmed Moole's request: ENTRY DECLARATION:

Harmless, anything to shut Moole up...besides, he had his own insurance against Moole. When Lisa and Yas had recounted the story of Grover and Iris Ferguson as told by Ganna Mae figuring out the mystery of the chiffonier stored in the Crown Kincaid basement had become a passion. In his spare time he had made a point of examining the furniture more closely. His first inspection had revealed the obvious handwritten crop reports and accounting notes Grover Ferguson had scrawled on the bottoms and sides of the drawers. From those he surmised Ganna Mae's reason for putting the furniture was motivated by sentiment. But, after getting to know Ganna Mae, he realized there were no sentimental bones in her body.

It was only after rereading what he had first taken to be scripture that he figured out the real reason Ganna Mae had stored the chest of drawers. *Our blessit neighbor gave us Demon for ourn poor crops this year...praise God..* Another read: *Dynymite and caps...blessit is the Lord and mr. kincaid.*

To Ganna Mae the furniture was a record of Wyatt Kincaid Sr.s' plot to kill the Fergusons and make it look like an accident. At some point and time Wyatt, no doubt, would be forced to face the evidence, hence the reason for its safekeeping.

The lawyer in Tim Ridell told him there was another story. It couldn't be that cut and dried. Determined to solve the mystery or leave it alone forever, Ridell turned the furniture upside down and reexamined it one last time. On the bottom of each drawer was what looked to be faded crayon scrawl in a child's hand, and he had almost ignored it. Almost. Though the writing was illegible for the most part, it was repeated on the bottom of every drawer, over and over. Finally after several days of searching for hours in various types of lighting, the word revealed itself. That word and his new high-paying position provided the impetuous and the resources for his detailed investigation. An investigation that had proven the word was written in blood, not crayon, and, with the help of a chemical called Luminol® the homophone that would destroy Phillip Moole was safely recorded on a video.

Tim rested his head on the back of the divan and the alcohol in his stomach made a break from his gut. He barely made it to the kitchen sink before he hurled. "Nice!" Moole shouted as he turned his head in disgust and stepped out onto the outside cabin passageway.

To steady himself Ridell braced against the counter and in the process splayed the pages Moole had given him. The declaration form was neatly folded in half covering the top half of the proxy form. Even drunk Moole chicanery wouldn't have gone unnoticed but why not have a little fun? Tim slid the papers back into a neat stack, rinsed his mouth with water and spit it back into the sink. "You know they prepare food in that sink...disgusting!" Moole yelled from the passageway.

"Okay I get it! I'm going below and shower. I'll sign the paperwork there."

"No need for that. Just sign here and I'll take them up to the captain and you can go straight to bed," Moole pleaded.

"Nah, I'll be right back. You just wait right here and I'll bring'em back...and don't forget my coffee and eggs, Mooley-Muley...oh, funny story about your name and a mule name Demon when I get back," Tim said as he rounded the first steps of the spiral staircase leading to the main staterooms.

Rather that the hot soothing shower he wanted Tim Ridell turned the water full cold and hoped the refreshing stream would clear his head. Moole was at it again, but this time the Harvard prick was drawing dead. Exposing the truth would be almost as damning to him as to Moole, but, again, why not have a little fun before his cushy job vanished? After all, it wasn't like he would be taking any real perks with him when he left this gig.

Moole had done a half-way decent job of folding the papers and making them appear as a complete page. And, he had to admire the way Moole had bated him into a drinking game; no ordinary drunk could have spotted Moole's deception.

Using Moole's folding technique, Tim creased the proxy agreement, but rather than leave the folded signature part on the paper, he cut along the crease with one of the double sided razors Yasnaya used to shave her legs. Once that task was completed, he made a paste from Ganna Mae's denture power and glued the signature section of the declaration agreement to the proxy paper. Under close examination, the papers were obviously mismatched, but under the dim lighting in the salon, this could work. If Moole was stupid enough to try to use the doctored proxy in court to gain control of the company, wouldn't that be a moment in the annals of Wilmington Legal lore? "Excuse me, Your Honor. Permission to examine the evidence?" With subtle pressure he would pull the document apart and show each half to the judge and jury...ahh, wouldn't that be a moment? It would never get that far, but just seeing the surprise on Moole's face when he realized he'd been sucker punched by a drunken Campbell University lawyer would suffice.

As he stepped into the salon Moole was on him. "What's this about a mule?"

The intensity in Moole's face was unbelievable. During all the time Tim Ridell had known Moole he never had seen him so visibly shaken. "Oh, that was nothing. Just a little drunk talk. Forget."

"What do you know Ridell, or what do you *think* you know?"

Maybe it was the way Moole was fidgeting, or maybe it was having the power to toy with Moole as he had toyed with him that day in the restaurant with the job offer. What ever the reason Tim Ridell did what a good lawyer never does; tipped his hand."

"I know enough to send you to prison for the rest of your life...unless we get a particularly mean jury. Then you may get the death penalty."

"Are you accusing me of murder?" Ridell gave Moole a long cool stare. "No Phillip, that's the DA's job. But he can't charge you until I turn the evidence over to him...and that's going to happen as soon as we roll back into Wilmington."

"What evidence...there is no evidence. I've never killed anybody." Moole studied Ridell's face to expose the bluff; there was no bluff. The cool steady stare from Ridell told Moole all he needed to know. After all these years someone had finally put all the pieces together. He was a dead man walking unless he could stop Ridell now. "Even if you did know something a lot can happen between here and Wilmington."

"You know, Moole, if that's more than a threat and something happens to me, three people will get copies of a video divulging everything I know, along with the location of physical evidence that will prove your crime."

Moole tossed the plate of bacon and eggs on the dinette in the galley. "Listen, I'm sure you've misinterpreted what you think you have discovered, but that's irrelevant. You need me to keep this job, and without this job, that sexy little number upstairs goes away. Come on, you don't really want to go back to the 'gherkin days' do you?"

Tim smiled. "You must have gotten a kick out of that Moole. But guess what? Yas is no Sally and I'm not one of your lackeys. We get back to Wilmington and you're going down."

"We'll see. Enjoy your meal. I'm going to bed."

Tim Ridell downed the food like a man who hadn't eaten in weeks, generally the feeling a drunk has after he pukes dry. Sated, cozy, confident in his new position of power and still loaded with alcohol, he dropped off into a deep sleep, snoring loudly.

Cued by the deep and reverberant sound of his accuser's snores, Moole rose from his stateroom and made his way back to the salon where he sat beside the sleeping Tim Ridell. The papers were partially under the dirty plate. With one hand Moole tugged the declaration form from under the plate. A quick shuffle of the paperwork revealed the signed documents and Moole breathed a sigh of relief. Now to carry out the plan.

He checked the entire deck to make sure he and Ridell were alone. Satisfied the area was secure Moole made his way into the galley and eased the utensil drawer open. As he searched with his hand, Moole kept his eyes on the sleeping Tim Ridell. Suddenly, he jerked back as he sliced his finger on the serrated blade of a filet knife.

A quick wrap around the finger with paper towels stopped the bleeding and Moole once again sat down next to Tim Ridell. With the skill of a surgeon, he traced his fingers across the top of the third rib pressed the blade against the bottom of the fourth rib and buried the knife to the hilt. Tim Ridell clinched his fists, glared up at Moole, exhaled one long last breath, and ignominiously became the only CEO of the Crown Kincaid Development Company to never cast one vote at a stockholders meeting.

Moole searched the salon over for traces of blood; other than the initial spurts from the beating heart, little soiled the area. Like an artist with blank canvas, the killer daubed and smudged the evidence of his crime with a handful of damp paper towels. Satisfied the diluted red stain and prominent maroon thread of the divan resembled a manufacture's flaw; he wrapped the body in a sheet and pulled it to the aft sundeck. At the conclusion of the unceremonious burial at sea, Moole poured himself a cognac and toasted the corpse headed for Davey Jones' Locker. "As I said son, a lot can happen between here and Wilmington." Moole wasn't worried about the three people who would receive Ridell's packages. Ridell was a loner. He had no friends. Two of the three people who would likely receive a video, if a video even existed, were on this boat. The other likely recipient was the only professional Ridell had trusted since he became president of the Crown; L. Robert Lee, president of Farmers and Maritime Bank and a long time family friend. No threat there. Once again Moole lifted his glass and faced the blackness of the open ocean and toasted the objectives of his new Plan B. "One down, two to go."

Chapter 37

Taylor Averette, watched as the Hatteras changed course. As soon as the heading change matched the Fountain's course, he locked and loaded the 50 calibers and aborted his flanking maneuver. Concealed by darkness, he jammed the throttles full ahead and tucked the Zodiac into the gap between the yacht and speed boat. Soon his days of under-paid and under-appreciated public service would be over. Let the agency be enamored with Tidwell. Hell let them celebrate his exploits posthumously. Who really cared? His secrets died with Tidwell and he'd be rich and long-gone by the time anyone noticed. All of this made possible by Old Lady Luck. *Old* as in Ganna Mae old.

At first her plan had seemed like a mistake. The vast array of characters and resources provided by the Odessa had drawn the attention of not only Interpol, but almost every country's security agencies. And that, it turned out, had been the genius of the *Last Kincaid* plan. Although America had learned the value of inter-agency communications, the same could not be said for the rest of the world. The gaps created by the lack of communication between international agencies and the vast sums of money created by criminal enterprises, had been too large to ignore. Idiot criminals were making billions of dollars and world governments were slow to react, but once they had, their pursuits had become myopic. Only the most dangerous criminals were targeted and the Kincaid Plan players had all slipped under the radar, except for Wyatt, Kozlov and Fyodor Yantikovs.

Moole's double crossings had perfected a plan that would likely escape international, as well as federal, scrutiny. All that was needed to grab the billions lying around in the *Last Kincaid Plan* was a few scapegoats…and they were currently being fattened for sacrifice.

Averette pulled the Zodiac out of the mini convoy and switched on his night vision goggles. As the Hatteras passed by on his starboard side, he spied Tidwell on the fly bridge scanning the waters in front of the Hatteras with standard binoculars. "Good luck magnifying the dark…dumbass," Averette murmured. Movement on the swim platform of the yacht piqued his interest. He quickly pressed the 10x zoom feature on his goggles and got an eyeful of Moole wrestling something, or someone, off the platform. "What the hell?"   Just as Averette expressed his thought, Moole rolled the object into the ocean.

Averette, cloaked in pitch-blackness, eased into the wake of the steaming Hatteras and waited until the flotsam was abeam the Zodiac. "Well, well, what do we have here?" Averette pulled the throttles to idle and gaffed the shrouded body. Air pockets in the sheet could have kept the body floating long enough to be seen by a passing boat tomorrow. True sharks probably would find the carcass long before then, but no need for Moole to be careless. In a flash, Averette gutted the corpse, punctured the lungs, and weighted the remains down with Zodiac's lead anchor. When the weight of the body pulled the anchor line taunt, Averette released Tim Ridell to the sea.

One more peek to make sure Tidwell was still on the bow and Averette eased the Zodiac close to the Hatteras and secured the inflatable to a rear cleat on the yacht. Phillip Moole celebrating with a postmortem drink, never saw the maneuver. In one swift moment, Averette pounced on Moole and choked him down to a sitting position. Moole flailed his arms and tried to grab the mass of muscle behind him. Fear welled up in his throat but the death grip prevented him from crying out. Just before Moole blacked out, Averette clamped his hand over Moole's mouth and backed away from the yellow pool spreading across the deck. "I can't believe you peed yourself, damn!"

Moole rolled over onto his hands and knees, "I've done more than that. Damn you!." Moole growled, as he gasped frantically for air. "What do you mean choking me like that?"

"That's the way we handle anyone who puts the mission in jeopardy."

"Jeopardy? I've gotten the proxy signed and killed Ridell." Moole cleared his throat and stood up. "Perhaps you should choke yourself if you want to punish the weakest link?"

Averette, ignored the smart remark, but appreciated the accomplishment. Frankly, it was much more that he expected from Moole, no doubt about that. "I'd throw you a celebration, but I don't think we have much time left--"

"What's gone wrong? I thought you said you had everything under control? "

"I do as far as the agency and Tidwell are concerned...you didn't see the jet earlier?"

Moole looked around as if to spot the plane. "What would a jet have to do with anything?"

"Thought maybe you could tell me? Did the captain or Tidwell mention anything about seeing a plane?"

"No, not that I'm aware of...and why is an airplane a problem?"

"Maybe it's nothing. It would have been hard to spot from here, but the plane made a low pass. I'm almost certain it was Kincaid's plane."

"Nothing unusual about that. The crew and pilot are friends. He may have been just doing a friendly flyby. They do that all the time unless you warn them not to, and I always do--"

"I know that. I know that, but these guys are legendary for their flybys. It's like a contest to see how damn close they can get. This time it was different. It was like they wanted to see but not be seen."

Moole looked behind him. "Umm, while we're on the subject...what if Tidwell sees you?"

"He won't. I'm leaving. Just wanted to warn you about the plane and our time constraint...don't screw this up."

"Don't worry about me. I'll handle my end."

Averette hopped back into the Zodiac. "One more thing. I cleaned up your Ridell mess. Next time you put a body in the ocean, weigh it down or at least gut it and puncture the lungs. That'll bring the sharks and keep it from floating."

"Hadn't thought of that," Moole said. "But my agenda has been rather full, in case you haven't noticed." Before Moole finished speaking Averette disappeared into the night.

Finally the satellite communication line blinked ready. "About time," Moole whispered as he dialed the Wilmington number and cursed when he heard the recording. "This is Big Jim, leave your message and I'll get back to you when I feel like it."

"Pick up, pick up, damn it! Jim...it's Phillip. Pick up! This is important." Moole thought about leaving a message, and then decided to forgo what could be incriminating evidence.

Big Jim yanked up the hand set. "Yeah, what do want? Thought you were done talking to me after the declaring Wyatt dead thing?"

Moole was still pissed about that. Sheer luck had kept the old woman from finding out. Even if she had, there was no way to connect him to the stupid deeds of Jim and Sally Boykin-Bryce.

"That's not important now. You have to convene the board. I have the proxy papers signed. Wyatt's vote is in the bag, now it's up to you to get the board to follow through."

"Even with the board's vote you're still going to need the old lady's, or her hot-ass daughter's vote...it's a financial resolution. Simple majority won't do it. All these proxies and no-show stockholders could be a problem, too."

Phillip Moole jammed the knife he used to kill Tim Ridell into a cutting board on the counter in the galley. A damn MBA from Harvard and he had to be lectured about corporate law from a freaking neophyte. Things would just go so much smoother if he had killed Jim and Sally when he had the chance in Paradise Island, and it wouldn't have to have been by his hand. The Yantikov's would have been more than willing...adding a little chaos at a posh resort like Atlantis would have replaced some of the furor over the Bahamian cop killing. Without the greed of Sally and Jim, things at the Crown wouldn't fall into place. Good call not killing them in Atlantis. He could always do that after the money was safe.

"That's right, and I do know that, Jim. The old lady will sign and I will email the papers…"

"Emails, might not work. They may want a hard copy, and they'll want stockholders in person--"

"*They* who? You idiot! L. Robert Lee will accept the paperwork and the instructions. Why the hell would he question paperwork that will make him a multi-millionaire?"

Big Jim bristled. No one called him an idiot, not even Moole. Little egotistical son-of-a-bitch, maybe he'd forgotten who his room mate was at Harvard.

"L. Robert Lee is not the only board member with brains…and that idiot remark is free, Phillip but if you ever talk down to me again I'll kick your ass over your shoulders. You got it?"

Boykins was just like the Kincaids…always using their mass to intimidate. What the hell else would they use? Certainly not their mental capacities, hell they had none. In case Big Jim had forgotten the only reason he had a Harvard degree hanging on his office wall was work done for him by one, Phillip Moole.

"Jim, what the hell is wrong with us? Best friends about to pull off the deal of the century and we're at each other like two rednecks? I'm sorry, you're right." Moole twisted the knife boring out an oval gash in the cutting board. "I'm just a little on edge with the Ridell thing and all."

"Yeah, all we need to do is endorse the check and we're, ah…What if Ridell balls up and decides to…"

"Tim Ridell is no longer a problem."

Big Jim was never sure when talking to Moole exactly how to interpret his statements. Like now, if he didn't know better he'd think Ridell was dead. But not even Moole was that cold. The thought to ask crossed his mind, then a cold shiver shook his spine…nah, better to be in the dark than an obstacle for Phillip Moole.

Chapter 38

"Captain, traffic, twenty kilometers," Vitya Baranov said as he shielded the radar screen depicting the fringe area of the ship's radar. Kozlov glanced at the screen to verify the helmsman's assessment of intersecting traffic. Good. Right on time. "Steady as she goes. Stop all engines when she is within two kilometers, Mister Baranov."

Kozlov surveyed his crew. Vitya, Konstantin Nikolayev, six mercenaries and himself, fit for duty. Kirill Petrov, Nicholas Gurov, walking wounded...Damn Wyatt Kincaid. The Indonesian maintenance crew? Totally useless if things went bad.

"Konstantin, arm the crew, stockpile ammunition on the bridge, and ready the Acom Ladder."

Wyatt pressed his hand to Svetlana's mouth, steering her behind a fire hose reel and turned her head toward the buzz of activity emanating from the crew quarters hatch. Metallic clangs rang out as Konstantin quick-clamped two M-60 machine guns to the deck railing and slapped belts of ammo into each.

"What does it mean?"

"Trouble, unless I miss my guess." Wyatt grunted. "Is this the way this little shindig was supposed to play out?"

Guilt for having to answer a question about information she should have shared with Wyatt prompted a quick response from Svetlana. Rather than speaking, she spit the words from her mouth as if expediency could regain his trust.

"No, the rendezvous was planned. This must be something else..."

Wyatt weighed her words. In spite of everything that had transpired, he wanted...*needed* to be able to depend on Svetlana. Without an ally there was no way to save their lives. He turned his back and gave Svetlana a chance to yell out to crew. If that's how it played out he didn't plan to resist Kozlov again. Without a team mate the game was over. Instead of the betrayal he half expected, Svetlana slid her hand around his and squeezed.

Wyatt nodded, "In that case, this is a double cross..." before he could add to his words, two grappling hooks, like those favored by Somali Pirates, snagged the deck railing. "Make that a double-double cross."

"How do you know?"

"Gang plank's ready to be lowered; I figure that's for the invited guest. Those grappling hooks mean some uninvited guests aren't planning on using the stairs. The machine guns obviously indicate the invited guests aren't trusted." Wyatt snatched the reel cover from the casing and covered himself and Svetlana. "This is going to get bad. Until we sort this out, we stay here. After we figure out what's going on we stow away under one of the cargo hatches and come out only after the King of the Mountain has been decided, got it?"

Once the hooks were secured to the railings, Boris piloted the Fountain along the hull of the old freighter as Fyodor attached the C-4 explosives near the Baltic Queen's waterline. The number of charges was overkill, but nothing could be left to chance and especially no chance could be left to Boris, idiot. "Remember," Fyodor grimaced as pain shot up his mangled arm when he tested the grappling line. "Blow the charges as soon as I signal, and do not leave the area until everyone is dead. No survivors understand?"

Boris winched as he saw the pain his younger brother felt. Always he had cared for Fyodor more than Fyodor had cared for him. That *weakness* as Fyodor described it came from Liliya Yantikov, a saint even if the church would never canonize her. "I spit on the church," Boris muttered under his breath. His *weakness* was nothing more than a dutiful son obeying the admonishments of his mother. *Boris, always watch over your brother. He does not see dangers as you do. Be safe my ongel* [angel]. *Ongel.* Fyodor never had been angel and yet his mother loved Fyodor more. Not that a saint like Liliya Yantikov could show partiality to one of her children, but the tenderness in her heart was always reserved for Fyodor.

"Pay attention!" Fyodor shouted. "Do you want to sink your own boat, idiot?" Boris reversed the Fountain and revved the engine just before it slammed into the steel hull towering over them. "I see it. Just testing your nerve," and added his own, "idiot" for good measure. As much as he was maligned by Fyodor and as much as he was tempted sometimes, he could never kill his younger brother…the C-4 explosives they were attaching to the hull of the *Baltic Queen* may as well be boxes of cornflakes. Boris looked upward toward movement he sensed more than saw. "Fyodor," Boris whispered. "I think the cat has let the shit out of the bag." Fyodor Yantikov followed his brother's stare up the hull and down the barrel of the M-60 machine gun being pointed at them by Konstantin Nikolayev.

"What is this, Fyodor?" Konstantin asked as he whipped loops down the grappling line like a cowboy roping strays.

Ganna Mae, coiffed and partially polished, went topside to check on Yas and Lisa. Both had given up on the sweet libations and were stuffing themselves with canapés from the service bar. Like two tipsy college students on Spring Break, they burst into laughter when they caught a glimpse of the old woman's toes separated by toilet tissue. Another chorus of laughter ensued and ended abruptly as soon as they felt Ganna Mae's icy stare.

"Yasnaya Polyana. Shower and dress…it's show time!"

Unaccustomed the real Ganna Mae Lisa gather a towel around her torso to shield herself from the stranger standing before her. "Yas and I have some business to take care of. You stay on the boat with the crew." Ganna Mae instructed.

Yas squeezed passed the bar and disappeared down the stairwell. Finally, after all these years, *"Last Kincaid"* was about to end and the end couldn't come soon enough. Life without vengeance, what would that be like? She pondered a life without Ganna Mae influencing her every move, approving or disapproving her every relationship. Personal time, leisure time, no more pissing Ganna Mae off for any reason…or no reason. How wonderful life was about to become! Tim? She had to find him, tell him that he had passed the test. Let him know that his life of poverty and misery was over. Even without the Crown, Ganna Mae had agreed to a settlement that would allow them to live comfortably if they never worked another day. However, all these things she had to tell him could wait; right now, all she wanted to do was complete *Last Kincaid.*

Thinking of the lies and deceit associated with the plan made her feel dirty. Yas scrubbed the sea sponge hard against her skin until all the imagined crud swirled down the drain at her feet. With one hand gripping the shower head, she managed to maintain her balance in the rolling seas. Suds splashed into her eyes and she braced against the stall to catch clear water in her cupped hands. The stateroom door opened and quickly clicked closed, Tim no doubt. "Hey baby…ooh, my eyes, hand me a towel." Yas' hand swept the air in slow circles until she felt the towel. "Want to join me while I'm all hot and steamy, big boy?"

From the foggy mist a cold steel blade nipped across her throat and a voice she hated made a request, "No. I want you to make me steamy." The sound of a zipper silenced the cascading water. "On your knees," Moole said, as he pushed her in front of his groin and forced her to kneel.

As bad as the moment was, it was not a situation Yasnaya had not faced before. Drunken patrons during private dance sessions had tried the same move and there was a tried and true method of regaining control, she remembered as she balled a fist. Before she could swing, the knife blade slid between her lips and scraped across her teeth. "If you scream or try to escape, I promise I will kill you." OK, she was plowing new ground here. Private dance partners were rarely armed and never committed to murder. Time to go cerebral on this freak, "Tim will be here in a minute. Get out and I'll pretend this didn't happen. He's a trained boxer, you know."

Phillip Moole thought of the corpse he floated off the aft ski platform less than an hour ago…definitely eaten by sharks now after Averette's butchery.

"Oh, I hope you are not clinging to the idea that your White Knight is going to rise from the dead and save you," Moole said as he pulled Yas' head back and pushed the blade between her teeth to pry open her mouth. Yas twisted her head to avoid the blade and paid the price…*Dead?* Warm blood filled her mouth as she formulated her words. "Moole, if you've hurt Tim not even my mother will be able to save your ass. Damn the *Last Kincaid* plan! I'll kill you, I promise."

"Don't threaten me," Moole pressed the blade into the corners of Yas' lips until blood ran down both sides of her neck, "and for the record, *Last Kincaid* is already damned. Now get busy, bitch!"

"Looks like the surprise party's over," Wyatt said as he watched Konstantin tow the Fountain toward the newly lowered gangplank. The welcoming party for the man Wyatt knew as John Smith had been about as inhospitable as the one he had been subjected to months earlier, maybe worse. Rather than the quick knockout punch Konstantin had used to deck him, the man the crew called Fyodor was being pounded with body shots. Even though he had no love for the guy who had helped imprison him, it was hard to watch a man suffer like this.

"So, you came back to steal the electrical components for Renee Jacobs a man we both know is dead!" Kozlov shouted as he joined Konstantin in the pummeling of the barely conscious Fyodor Yantikov. "No", Kozlov said. "Stop. Bring his companion, the one he barely knows."

Boris fidgeted like a rabbit facing the stew pot. Bullies were always the biggest babies, and unlike Wyatt, Svetlana had no human compassion for the pain about to be inflicted upon her one-time nemesis.

"You know him?" Wyatt asked.

For a moment Svetlana was in the cold of Siberia and draped over her shoulders was a fine Russian sable. The richness of the garment blocked out the starkness of the prison. Just as she allowed herself a moment to savor her escape from reality, two beastly hands crushed her breasts until milk seeped from her nipples. "Oh, yes." Svetlana unconsciously covered her bosom and turned from Boris, "That one I could not forget...in a thousand years I could not forget that bastard." Svetlana delighted in the fear smeared across Boris' face, "And, he is the coward I always knew he was."

Chapter 39

Yasnaya watched Moole in the vanity mirror she was bent over. Two final jabbing thrusts, an infantile whimper and her ordeal was over, or so she thought. Incredibly, the idiot leaned against her bound hands and kissed the nape of her neck. "I do hope it was as good for you as it was me?"

How the hell could this have happened? Of all the men who had ever pawed, bribed, hit-on and even punched her, none had made her feel this helpless. She forced herself to look at the sickly sight in the mirror: Rounded shoulders, concave chest, paper-white paunch, and shriveled arms with matching gnarly hands...Ah, yes. The knife.

Moole placed the tip of the blade between her shoulders, for a second she imagined what the pain would feel like as steel split her heart. "Oh, it won't be as painful as you think." Moole whispered in her ear. "I have an M.B.A. but as a hobby, I studied anatomy. Killing can be relatively painless once you learn how to stop the heart. When oxygen doesn't reach the brain the senses dull. As a matter of fact, I dare say your White Knight felt little more than a prick..."

"Stop it, you liar. You would not kill Tim. You need him..."
Moole pushed the blade into Yas' back until it burned like a branding iron. "No, I never needed Tim Ridell," Moole grinned as pain etched across his victim's face, "I needed his signature and he was stupid enough to oblige me. Little did he know when he signed that proxy he signed his death warrant."

Yas scoured Moole's face like a navigator looking for a route home. When their eyes met in the mirror, she saw joy dancing off the blackness of his soul. Tim Ridell was dead and, for the first time in her life, she was terrified.

"YAS," Ganna Mae banged on the door. "Let's go or I'll drag your ass out of there...and if that drunk-ass Tim is in there, tell him to come, too. I want to show him what kind of man Wyatt Kincaid isn't...Are y'all decent?"

Moole put his finger across his lips demanding silence and then made a slashing motion across his throat portraying the penalty for disobedience.

"Ask her to come in. Tell her you are having trouble with a zipper," Moole whispered. "Then tell her how you enjoyed the treat behind the zipper." Again the sickening sneer filled Moole's face and again terror shot through her gut. Ganna Mae would not take this. Her soul was blackened too and she would not back down. Moole would kill her just as he had killed Tim Ridell.

Both, Moole and Yas watched as the door handle turned, horror-flick slow. Yas filled her lungs in order to project her scream all the way to the pilothouse and loud enough to reverberate against the conflictions of heaven and hell. She would likely die for her efforts, but Moole would not be able to mount anymore sneak attacks. The crew would be on to him. Tears mixed with the thin streams of blood running down her neck. After all the years of wondering, Yas realized that she did love Ganna Mae, enough to die for her.

Clark pointed to lights on the steamer dead ahead, "Looks like we made the intercept. I don't know from where the old woman is getting guidance, but this is pretty impressive."

"Not that impressive," Tidwell said. "A simple variation of a basic Slope Intercept Formula. The key is to keep everyone on the same page, heading and speed." Almost as a footnote he added, "What *is* impressive is that this is being coordinated by satellite. Suggests some form of government involvement...or a very powerful organization."

Clark pushed his cap back on his head. From the moment he had been given the heading and coordinates, he assumed the Coast Guard was monitoring his every movement. Tidwell's statement wasn't making him feel as warm and fuzzy as he had earlier. "A *friendly* government or organization we know about, right?"

"Not exactly."

Clark crammed the binoculars to his face and scanned the ship's silhouette for an origin marking, flag state, anything to indicate a sovereign entity that recognized Maritime law...nothing. "Damn son. Do we have back up or not?"

"Not exactly."

"Well, to hell with that. We're out of here. Damn that old woman. She can just fire my ass." Knickknacks, flower vases and partially filled drinks spilled across the deck and, chaise lounges from the sundeck tumbled into the ocean. Seldom were heading changes this severe on luxury crafts and Clark Guilford didn't mind. It was time to put some distance between his ship and potential danger. Danger, damn it to Hell!

As the Crown Jewel bit deep into the swells, almost keeling over, Yasnaya flew across the vanity and smashed headfirst into the shower stall. Her last image before unconsciousness was the knife flying from Moole's hand and heading straight for her gut.

Ganna Mae was thrust against the cabin door slamming it shut. She fought against the G-forces and pulled herself along the hand railing leading to the pilothouse. "That bastard Captain!" Ganna Mae screamed, "Yasnaya, get your ass dressed and meet me upstairs."

Gradually, the ship began to level and walking with both hands against the wall wasn't necessary. Ganna Mae took advantage of the conditions and sprinted toward the wheelhouse.

"Stay on the heading," Ganna Mae yelled from the sundeck. Her words were lost in the slipstream, and before she could holler again, a line of dual 50 caliber rounds peppered across Clark's retreat route.

"What the hell... are they shooting at us?" Clark asked Tidwell.

"Back it down, Clark," James Tidwell said as he slid the throttles into neutral. From the first time Jim Williams\James Tidwell stepped onboard, he always addressed Clark as "Captain". Though the name change was hardly a mutinous act, the transfer of power was effective and immediate. Clark looked at Tidwell for instructions, half expecting his mate to order him to retrieve the weapons stowed under the main salon's divan.

No such order came, and for a second, rage welled up inside the old sea captain. This bastard Tidwell was part of the problem. He wanted to lock eyes with the traitor before he let Tidwell know exactly what he thought of him. Instead, he followed Tidwell's gaze along the deck of the rusting steamer. Four M 60 machine guns clamped on the railing were pointed at the Crown Jewel. "They must be pretty good shots. They damn near hit us," Clark whisper to Tidwell. Rather than answer, Tidwell scanned the steamer's silhouette, searching in vain for the weapons that had fired on the yacht. "Clark, there's another vessel out here and it's not packing those little pea shooters. See if you can pick it up on the radar."

"HELLO, yoo hoo!" Ganna Mae shouted to crew on the Baltic Queen.

"Shoot this mutinous bastard!" Clark and Tidwell turned to face their irate passenger. "You're both fired! You don't think I know what you did?"

"Ma'am"...

"Don't *ma'am* me you old bastard. I gave you an order and you disobeyed...that's grounds for firing!"

"Ma'am, I was trying to save us," Clark said.

Ganna Mae ignored Clark and made her way beside Tidwell. "Young man, I'm willing to give you a second chance...Yasnaya, get your ass up here, now!" Ganna Mae turned back to Tidwell, "Whatever it is that has to be done to get us on that ship is what I'm ordering you to do." Ganna Mae pressed the pilothouse intercom and shouted again for Yasnaya. The woman she saw coming up the stairs was barely recognizable. Yasnaya's face was not as marred as Lisa's was before surgery, but it was very close. Her collision with the vanity had fractured bones and caused dark contusions across her face. Ganna

Mae put her hands to her mouth then rushed to comfort Yasnaya. "Stay back Mother, he has a knife!"

Moole shoved Yasnaya toward the helm and stepped into full view. "And a gun if anyone is interested," Moole said as he twirled his Beretta around his finger. "Oh, and before anyone gets any ideas...those weapons you stowed in the salon? Well, they are about as useless as Tim Ridell." The laughter filling the pilothouse was unmistakably evil. Even the crew aboard the Baltic Queen was put on edge by the menacing cackle.

Tidwell strained to recall the last time he had seen Ridell. Mate or government agent made little difference. The safety of these people was his responsibility. He had to contact Miami while he still had the chance. The Sea Tel phone was in easy reach and, unfortunately, in plain view.

"Moole, you can forget our deal," Ganna Mae said as she stroked Yasnaya's hair. "And as soon as the destruction of the *Last Kincaid* is complete, I will kill you."

"Oh, I didn't beat her up if that's what you think. You can thank your captain for her injuries." Moole saw Tidwell easing toward the phone, "Go ahead make your call, Jim...or is James... Williams or Tidwell?"

Tidwell looked from Clark to Moole. "Don't worry. Your friend didn't betray you. But I've known about you since day one, *Jim*."

Of all the people who popped up on his radar as a potential threat, Moole had not been one of them. Too pedigreed. Now, his mistake was endangering them all and it was time to correct that. "It's Tidwell, Special Agent James Tidwell. Now put the gun down or--"

"Or what?" Moole motioned to the phone. "Let's put the illusion that you control this situation with the full backing of the United States government to rest. Make your call Tidwell."

Tidwell looked at the blinking light indicating satellite coverage. If Moole didn't shoot him within minutes, the full backing of the United States government would be headed to this location. Tidwell dialed a private emergency number, entered a coded text and put the phone back on its base.

As soon as the hand held made contact with the base the phone rang.

"Verification that the cavalry is on the way?" Moole sneered.

There would be no need for a call back. The message was routed directly to a quick response team.

"Answer it Special Agent Tidwell, I'm sure it's for you."

Tidwell let the phone ring and tried to make sense of the situation. No one in his right mind would let him make the call to bring down the thunder. No intercept on earth was capable of disrupting a call to that number...

"Answer it, Tidwell, damn it!"

Chapter 40

Taylor Averette flipped the commo/intercept switch to monitor and surveyed his weapons inventory list…eight Stinger missiles (absconded from Bahamian Police evidence room) and five Hae Sung-1 anti-ship missiles; all classified as defensive weapons…talk about irony. But how they were used was not his problem. Like any businessman he was only concerned with the inventory's value and demand. As long as splinter sects of radical religious and political ideologues kept popping up, global demand would certainly drive up prices…and the best part, his quality of life.

Averette's thoughts of riches vanished as the capture light on the intercept panel blinked with urgency. Almost simultaneously he hit affirm, redirect, and source buttons, sending James Tidwell call straight back to the Crown Jewel.

Provoked by the ringing phone Moole pointed his Beretta at Tidwell and made his demand, "Put it on speaker and answer it this time, or I will." Tired of Moole's theatrics, Tidwell pressed the speaker button and addressed the call, "This is the motor yacht, Crown Jewel. Agent James Tidwell speaking. Who's there?"

Rather than the silence Tidwell expected, or the sound of a voice others in the pilothouse likely expected, a high-pitched digital tone sequence filled the air. A meaningless annoyance to all aboard except James Tidwell whose perfect pitch hearing detected the same rapid response request he sent earlier. There was no doubt that the encrypted digital channel, installed on the Crown Jewel by the agency months earlier, had been compromised. More likely, a virus programmed to lie dormant until needed had been awakened.

"You there, Jim?" After a moment of silence the voice spoke again, but this time in a voice Tidwell recognized as the Miami Station duty officer he had filed most of his reports with during his time on the Crown Jewel. "More comfortable with this dialect, Jim?" The voice drawled in a South Carolina Low-Country accent. "The voices, the people you've been reporting to…they're all the same, Jim. That's right, just me, Taylor Averette, agent voted most likely to never succeed because not one of you agency shits were smart enough to figure out the real genius among you…assholes!"

Tidwell's gaze shifted from face to face. No doubt Moole was the inside connection, but who else was on his team? Ganna Mae was armed, but it was a safe bet that she and the other two women were against Moole. That left Clark, who Moole had declared innocent, but was he?

As Tidwell's heart beat slowed, his Methodical Assessment training kicked in: Moole said the weapons stored in the pilothouse closet were useless, but were they? And even if they were, he didn't need a weapon to take down Moole. A well placed kick would dislodge the gun, but Moole still had the knife and potential victims at arm's length. Then, there was Taylor Averette; whereabouts unknown, but certainly in close proximity. To intercept encrypted messages from the yacht's communications system required shadowing. No doubt about it, Averette was close and probably watching the events unfolding in the pilothouse right now. All things considered, it was best to sit back and wait for clarity.

Moole pulled Yasnaya into the corner of the pilothouse and placed the Beretta to Clark's head. "Dock this boat and no funny business. I'm getting real tired of your crap."

Clark Guilford switched on the Crown Jewel's flood lights and wheeled the bow toward the rusting freighter. As the lights illuminated the ship a reminiscent sight greeted him; rather than the side-slung boarding ramp he expected to see, the Baltic Queen was outfitted with a floating dock and grappling netting. The exact same setup he had seen once before when he was boarded by Pirates off the Somalia coast and delivered to the Mother ship. The only difference now and that day off the African coast was that he still had choices.

Taylor Averette aimed the deuce 50 calibers at the Crown Jewel's engine room intake vents as he monitored the yacht's docking progress. If the yacht made a break for it the adventure wouldn't last long. With the vessel schematic Moole had provided he could destroy the engines and avoid hitting the fuel tanks, theoretically.

The roll of the sea caused the superstructure of the freighter to block out the lights illuminating the docking platform. Clark took the temporary darkening of the platform to be a sign from above. It was time to roll as fast and as far from this place as he could get. There was no way in hell he was delivering his passengers to such an ominous place without at least attempting to save them.

With his right hand Clark shoved Moole toward the open pilothouse door while simultaneously revving the throttles to full ahead. With surprising agility that suggested martial arts training, Moole utilized the force from Clark's shove to spin kick the sea captain in the groin. To avoid the onrushing deck, Clark tucked and rolled and kept his head from smashing into the wheel stanchion. Moole quickly asserted his aggressive stance and pounced, knee first, into Clark's chest. From his genuflect posture Moole spoke, "If anyone makes any sudden movements, you die."

Before Moole could inflict more pain on Clark, James Tidwell held up both hands to indicate surrender. "Let me get her in there," Tidwell said as he straddled the injured captain and grabbed the wheel.

Under Moole's direction and the watchful eyes of the machine gunners and Yuri Kozlov, the boarding party assembled on the swim platform of the Crown Jewel. Like the living dead, Yasnaya shuffled toward the platform, pushing her wet hair from her face. Lisa noticed Yasnaya's partially opened blouse and reached over to button it for her. Yas barely noticed the favor and intensified her scan of the boarding party, hoping against hope that Tim Ridell would appear. But after noting Moole in the pilothouse there was no longer any doubt; Tim Ridell was dead. Soundlessly, she mouthed the words she could not bring herself to say: "Tim's dead."

Lisa Cox, horrified by Yasnaya's statement, put her hand over her mouth. "Yas don't say that!"

"It's true, Lisa." Yasnaya raked her hair away from her face. "Just before Moole made me...I can't talk about it now." Yas bowed her head and whispered "Moole told me Tim was dead. He did it. He killed Tim. I know it."

"No, he wouldn't. He's a *lawyer*. Are you OK?...*mwah,mwah,mwah.*"

To Yas, Lisa's words suddenly sounded like those of the adults on the old Peanuts cartoon. Of course she wasn't OK, nor would she ever be again unless she somehow managed to reclaim at least some of her dignity and pride. Her choices were either to forget what happened or pretend it had never happened. Neither choice was appealing, but how could she admit that she let Moole...no, not *let*. He had a knife. He *still* had it and the gun. He could take her again, or take Lisa, or even Ganna Mae, and there was nothing they could do about it. Moole was in charge. He proved that in the pilothouse. Everyone on board was at Moole's mercy...and the irony was that Moole had no mercy. He was a heartless bastard who had killed once and was ready willing and able to do it again...and again.

"Yas." Lisa shook her friend hard. "Tell me what happened!"

"He forced me to do things to him...then he raped me. And he'll do the same to you. We're not safe Lisa. Moole's a psychopath--"

"No! I won't let that happen to me again. I won't let it happen to you. We have to call someone."

"Who!" Yas shrieked. "We're on our own out here in case you haven't noticed."

"He's only one man--"

"Damn it, Lisa. Moole killed Tim...and he'll kill us!"

Yasnaya looked at Moole herding everyone toward the gangplank. "And God only knows what's in store for us once we board that ship."

"No," Lisa said. "Look at Ganna Mae. She's in charge...just look at her."

Sure enough, somehow Ganna Mae looked completely in charge, even though Moole kept jamming his pistol into her back. Not one hint of worry furrowed her brow. Instead, a small flirtatious smile spread across Ganna Mae's face and she extended her hand to the seaman leaning from the boarding platform of the Baltic Queen. "Thank you, Captain Kozlov," Ganna Mae whispered as she made the transition from one vessel to the next. Yuri Kozlov, touched the brim of his cap with forefinger and thumb, but otherwise made no response to Ganna Mae's comment.

James Tidwell's welcome aboard the Baltic Queen was not as uneventful. As Tidwell reached for the railing surrounding the platform Kozlov slammed his gun into the base of Tidwell's neck. Partially paralyzed from the blow, Tidwell could only watch as Kozlov steel-toe zeroed in on his exposed flank. The explosion of pain spread through Tidwell's body like fissures racing across thin ice. As Tidwell gasped for air, Kozlov explained his actions. "Mister Williams. I usually wait until a guest breaches protocol before I explain the rules, but in your case I have to make an exception."

Lisa grabbed Yasnaya and the two women clung to one another. "Why doesn't she stop this?" Lisa Cox asked. "And why is she smiling?"

Yas put her fingers to her lips. "I'm afraid you're about to meet the real Ganna Mae Ferguson...stay close to me, Lisa."

Kozlov dug his boot back into Tidwell's ribcage, "Do you know why I have to make an exception for you, Mister James Albert Tidwell?"

Tidwell tried to spot Ganna Mae. If he could get the pistol from her calf holster he had a chance. "The jig is up Captain. I'd re-think this if I were you. There is a team on the way."

Kozlov motioned for two crew members to hold William's feet and hands.

"Stretch him out, comrades. I will show you how to break a man in minutes." Kozlov looked at Moole. "This is what I should have done to Wyatt Kincaid the first day he came aboard and he would not have damaged my crew." Kozlov stepped over Tidwell and rammed his boot into the uninjured half of his ribcage. "I'm not worried about your team, Mr. Tidwell. But you should be very worried about me."

"Leave him alone, Kozlov. He's one of mine," Wyatt said as he tore from Svetlana's grip. "I know why the others are here and I'm willing to meet their demands if you let my crew go."

Svetlana pushed against Wyatt's chest as he leaned toward Kozlov. "Stop it," She whispered. "You are in no shape to bargain."

Wyatt pressed his mouth close to her ear. "See the blonde with the old woman, Ganna Mae?"

Svetlana's focus turned to the blonde in the boarding party line. Yasnaya, as if guided by divine intervention, gazed up at Wyatt and Svetlana.

Svetlana looked back and forth from Wyatt to Yasnaya and mumbled, "My God, you look like--"

"Brother and sister," Wyatt finished Svetlana's thought.

Chapter 41

Kozlov stopped his assault on Tidwell with the same abruptness he had begun the beating. "Very well, Mr. Kincaid, your crew can stay with your boat. But I can assure you if you cause any trouble at all, I will kill them and you, understand?"

Wyatt hung his head. "I'm done fighting, Kozlov." And then turned to Svetlana, "You don't have to pretend anymore. I get it."

"Pretend? I don't understand."

"Do you think I'm stupid? Your daughter, Yasnaya Polyana, is on Moole's team and how hard is it to figure out whose side you'll choose?" Wyatt clinched his teeth. "Moole found her and that's how he was able to take control of my company." Wyatt slammed a fist into his palm. "I'd rather have my balls nailed to a board than see Moole get The Crown. Now I know why my father set up that LUBOVA account He never wanted me to have the company. Well, that's just fine by me. It's all yours. Go with Moole and your friends, Svetlana…and you can all go to hell!"

"Wyatt…you can't mean--"

"Go, damn it!"

As the group from the yacht made their way to mess deck, Ganna Mae pulled Yasnaya close to her side and whispered, "Don't worry about Moole. He thinks he has the upper hand; I can assure that is about to change." Ganna took in the bruising across Yasnaya's face, "And I promise you that son-of-a-bitch will pay for what he did…"

"I don't need your promise. I'll take care of Phillip Moole. He won't get away with what he did to me!" Yas glanced up… "Mother, the man on the ship. Who is he--"

"Yasnaya, this day is the day of reckoning. The *Last Kincaid* hasn't only been about vengeance for me. Today is the day you reap your rewards as well. That man you see on the deck stole your birthright, and he has hunted you down for years just so he could end any threat you pose to his ownership of his company. He is your half-brother, Wyatt Kincaid. The woman standing next to him is… your birth mother--"

"No talking, syka!" said Gurov.

Ganna Mae swung at Gurov but the agile seaman ducked the blow.

"Don't ever call me bitch again." Ganna Mae snapped. "I'm your captain, numb nuts!"

"Nyet! A woman brings only ill winds at sea. I will not serve under her, Captain."

"Gurov." A menacing scowl etched across Kozlov's face. "Do not provoke me with your insolence or you will pay a price you cannot afford."

Finally, the respect she deserved, Ganna Mae thought as she smiled and faced Kozlov.

"While you are in a disciplining mood," Ganna Mae cooed, "there is something I want to share with you about Moole. He has compromised the *Last Kincaid plan* by killing a key player, and he has damaged another," she said as she nodded toward Yasnaya, who was already seated in the mess deck. "Take that pistol Moole is carrying and whip him with it. Kill him when I no longer need him."

Svetlana rushed Kozlov. "Captain, the young woman...may I have a moment with her in private?" Svetlana acknowledged Ganna Mae. "Your friend won't mind, Captain. My request is but a promise she made to me years ago in--"

"Svetlana, back to your station." Kozlov roared. "I care nothing about promises of yesterday. Go!"

"No, captain. She is my daughter, please."

"Svetlana," Kozlov shook his head. "Were you not such a good cook, I would throw you overboard for disobeying my order. Don't test my benevolence, and understand this. Your insanity and this fantasy family reunion of yours is of no concern to me." Kozlov placed his boot on Svetlana's backside and shoved her across the room. "Back to your station!" As Svetlana stumbled out of his reach Kozlov pointed the pistol at Ganna Mae. "And you madam, never give orders on this ship!"

"What? I'm not one of your deckhands you Ukrainian peasant," Ganna Mae snarled. "And may I remind you, if I hadn't pulled you from the gutter, you would be just another drunken sailor on a state pension. I *made* you Yuri Kozlov!"

"How does one ever forget? For years all you've done is remind me! But the debt is paid. Wyatt Kincaid is yours--"

"Wyatt is only the beginning of the plan."

"Damn you, and damn the plan...I've had a better offer, as you business people say."

Ganna Mae glanced around the room hoping to spot Moole. No luck. "Be careful how you choose your partners, Yuri. Moole is--"

Moole filled the gap between Ganna Mae and Kozlov. "Is *what*, Ms. Ferguson?" Moole put the barrel of his pistol between Ganna Mae's eyes then twirled the barrel back into his palm and handed the gun, butt first to Kozlov. "I believed you wanted Captain Kozlov to have this...and now he does," Moole sneered. "But there will be no pistol whipping, Ms. Ferguson."

"Moole, as soon as the Odessa find out that you don't--"

"*Odessa?* Do you really think *that's* who I'm dealing with...a bunch of low-class thugs?" Moole walked in front of Kozlov and motioned for him to move away so he could address Ganna Mae alone. Moole circled Ganna Mae and stopped just as he exited her field of vision, a tactic used by police when they interviewed suspects to unnerve them. "See, Ms. Ferguson, that is the fundamental and philosophical class difference between you and me. I deal with the elitists of the world; my breed. You, on the other hand, deal with the scum of the world...your breed. "

Ganna Mae turned and pointed at Moole, "You have no idea how bad my scum of the earth breed is going to f---."

"Silence!" Kozlov screamed. "We have held up our end of the bargain, Mr. Moole. The ship is yours. Now let's get down to the business at hand."

"As you wish, Captain. But first we have to complete Ms. Ferguson's plan in order to obtain the resources and allies needed to accomplish our goals."

"What the hell is going on, Moole? What are you up to?"

Moole wasn't about to answer it was time for some bank psychology, the kind L. Robert Lee of the Farmer's and Maritime Bank had practiced on Tim Ridell.

The crew of the Baltic Queen circled the new arrivals like a pack of wolves intimidating each other with leering scowls. None was more intimidated than Yasnaya, as she suffered lewd stares, flicking tongues and air kisses aimed her direction. Instinctively, she moved toward the largest and most powerful of the prisoners, Wyatt Kincaid.

Moole, Kozlov, and the ship's officers separated from the group and assembled in the galley around a stainless steel metal table. Gurov slammed the steel hatch separating the two compartments and spun the hatch shut.

Ganna Mae, Yasnaya, Wyatt and Svetlana stared at the larger of the two compartments before them. White-hot light from bare halogen bulbs intensified the stark contrast between dinghy white primer and curling flakes of gray paint clinging to the steel walls and ceiling of the mess deck. Only centerfold posters of half naked women holding tools softened the glare of the floodlights beaming overhead.

To the left of the mess deck was the smaller officer's mess. A surprisingly tasteful soft, eggshell blue paint adorned six evenly spaced pilasters which supported an oak beam that ran the width of the room. Tapestries hung from brass rings separated the crew from the officer's mess. In front of the drapes were seven gunmetal gray tables bolted to the floor with stainless steel hex head bolts. Metal chairs used at mealtimes were stacked against the poster-covered walls and secured to eyelets in the floor with thick woven cotton straps.

In the center of the room was a square-shaped void, created by the removal of four tables. At what would have been the center of each missing table sat a metal folding chair. The "guests" were seated facing each other. Wyatt in front of Ganna Mae and Svetlana in front of Yasnaya. At the head and foot of the arranged seating were Boris and Fyodor Yantikov, hog-tied and bleeding from the beatings each had received earlier. Gurov, armed with an Uzi, stood in the center of the group. "Do not speak and do not move. My orders are to shoot to kill, do you understand, Mr. Kincaid?"

"I hear you Gurov...how're are those ribs I busted up?"

"Wyatt, shut up," Svetlana whispered.

Gurov squeezed the Uzi's safety latch to fire. "Silence!"

To avoid eye contact with Wyatt Kincaid, Ganna Mae gave the room another going over. As she scanned the harsh surroundings, it suddenly dawned on her how absolutely dismal life must be on a tramp steamer. The vessel was designed to carry freight, and at every juncture commercial-function overruled aesthetics.

The tapestry and gaudy posters were the only life in the austere bleakness of the mess deck. Exposed steam pipes, wrapped with asbestos sheeting and painted electrical conduit, webbed the room in engineered chaos. The exterior surfaces of the portholes were awash in rust and salt spray; the interior surfaces were smudged with the greasy fog flowing from the ship's galley. As a result of the filth, the port holes looked like yellow stained glass.

God, how Wyatt Kincaid must have suffered in this place...no creature comforts, no cadre of peons to satisfy his every spoiled-whim...Good. Hell, better than good, excellent!

But Wyatt's misery hardly brought her comfort, not as long as Moole was running the show. Ganna Mae looked at Gurov and wondered if he would obey his shoot to kill orders. Nothing to wonder about. Russian soldiers under Lenin had committed horrors beyond imagination upon their own people. Yeah, Gurov would follow orders. She would bide her time and get Kozlov away from Moole then plead her case.

Just as she finished her thought, Boris begged for water and first aid to stop his bleeding. His requests were met with a jarring kick to the gut from Gurov's boot.

"Oh yeah," Ganna Mae whispered. "*Good* idea."

The ship's officers and crew exited the galley and entered the officer's mess in a single file, forming a circle around the perimeter of the room.

Yuri Kozlov moved to the center of the square avoiding eye contact with the occupants. "All of you have questions about why you are here. Your concerns are of no importance to me and your fates are sealed." Kozlov made a sweeping motion with his arm in the direction of the galley, "But, Comrade Moole thinks it important that your predicament be explained."

"Thank you for your generosity, Captain Kozlov." Phillip Moole, dressed in officer's whites and unarmed, stepped across the threshold of the galley hatch and entered the mess. "Captain, once you hear the story, I think that perhaps even you will appreciate my request." As soon as Konstantin stationed himself behind Wyatt Kincaid, Moole moved between Wyatt and Ganna Mae. The hatred oozing from Ferguson to Kincaid was invigorating. Only a genius could set such a perfect stage. "Tell me, Ms. Ferguson. Who do you hate most at this moment? Me, or the Kincaids?"

Ganna Mae squirmed in her chair and half stood, but a quick glance at Gurov and she decided to remain seated. "You can throw Yuri Kozlov in the bunch. I hate *all* of you…and all *men*, for that matter!"

"Why do you hate me, Ms. Ganna Mae?" Wyatt growled. "Hell, all I ever did was over-pay you for that old piece of land that got in the way of my development."

Moole could not have asked for better response. His plan was to coax the old woman into divulging her ridiculous "Last Kincaid" plan to Wyatt. But leave it up to dumbass Wyatt Kincaid to say the wrong thing at exactly the right time.

"You lummox!" Ganna Mae stood and faced Wyatt. To hell with Gurov. "You have no idea who I am and what I know about you and your sorry-ass family, DO YOU?"

"Ma'am, we never--"

"Oh, shut up! Enough of that syrupy southern charm…I know how your father killed my parents and destroyed my family!"

"Are you referring to the mule theory?"

"Theory?" Ganna Mae spit the word at Wyatt. "*Theory* didn't kill my parents. That was done by a Kincaid-trained mule named Demon."

"Ma'am…that's a rural legend. My Daddy never did your family harm."

"Harm? Hell no! He didn't harm them, he killed them! And I know how he did it. He trained that damn mule to sit when a shot gun fired. Then he gave my parents a plunger and dynamite and waited until the mule was in the right spot…damn you to hell! And you *will* pay for the sins of your father, trust me!"

"Bravo, Ms. Ferguson! Bravo!" Moole said as he clapped and made a slight bow to Ganna Mae. "You have repeated the story exactly as my father created it years ago."

"What are you talking about? I was there." Ganna Mae said. "And that's exactly how it happened."

Moole laughed. "You were there after the fact, Ms. Ferguson." Moole circled Ganna Mae again, but this time she was having none of it. Ganna Mae faced Moole each time he tried to flank her.

"You can't imagine the irony I felt when you 'recruited me' to help with your vengeance against Wyatt Kincaid."

"I recruited you because the Kincaids tried to frame you for killing that girl who bled to death after Kincaid's blotched abortion. You said yourself that Kincaid tried to blame you for impregnating--"

Wyatt leaped from this chair and was promptly knocked to the floor by Konstantin.

"Damn you, Moole! You know I never had sex with--"

"With that *whore*," Moole sneered. "No, you never did Wyatt…but everyone *else* in the county--"

"Liar!" Wyatt stood and glared at Konstantin. "You're a liar, Moole. Jenny told me exactly what happened. You told her you loved her…that you would take care of her and her family. They were--"

"*White trash,* Kincaid. That's all they were. You could never separate the cream from the milk, Wyatt. Just like that stupid father of yours." Moole turned and faced Ganna Mae. "Actually, Miss Ferguson, my father, Judge Moole, and I destroyed the Kincaid family long ago. We forced Wyatt to admit that he impregnated the girl and used his father's money to buy the abortion. You see, he had this crush on that slut, and as youth is apt to do, he displayed those feelings in every nuance of his being."

Moole sneered at Wyatt the same way he had done in the judge's chambers when they had met with the Kincaids all those years ago. "I was a young trial attorney then and was very good at reading witnesses. I turned up the heat and promised that I would have a conga line of men swear that they had sex with…the girl…and I do believe her name was Jenny. Not that she did. Actually, I believed she was quite faithful to me and she did seem to be in love with me. But, why not? Rich, handsome, and the best education money could buy. Oh, I was quite the catch, and this gold digger wasn't about to let that slip from her grasp, so she spread her legs and let me sow my seed in hope that she would conceive and have blood ties to my wealth. Oh, she knew what she was doing."

"You are a liar Moole!" Wyatt said. "You even told her you wanted to marry her, and don't deny it."

"Deny? No, what you said does sound familiar. I suspect I told her exactly that...like I've told a whole whorehouse of money-grubbing-harlots. And they all did the same things Jenny did. It's amazing they could imagine someone of my background marrying down to their level...astonishing really, don't you think Miss Ferguson? I'm sure high class clientele baited you with similar promises and I'm sure you couldn't wait to trap them so you could have divorce attorneys rob them later. How else could you have amassed such a fortune?"

Ganna Mae blew off the question and stared at Moole. "What happened that day?!" Ganna Mae yelled. "They were my parents...I have a right to know."

"I can't blame you for not wanting to talk about you past. Screwing your way to the top and amassing a fortune along the way. Whore--"

"Damn the past, and damn you, Moole. I want to know what really happened that day."

"You may not want to know." Moole crossed his arms and rocked back and forth. "You see, Ms. Ferguson, I'm afraid you've spent your whole life devising a plan to end the Kincaid Dynasty based on a lie." Moole looked at Wyatt. "She calls it *The Last Kincaid Plan*. And make no mistake, it's a solid plan and it will, or rather *has*, finished off the *Last Kincaid*. Surprised, Wyatt?"

Wyatt thought of the cold nights he and his father loaded blankets, quilts, and bundles of freshly washed clothes his mother purchased from the Good Will store. He remembered how content his dad looked as he settled in behind the steering wheel of an old pickup used to haul hands on the farms. All around Wilmington they drove, attending to families, black and white, who needed a hand to get back on their feet. Wyatt's father had explained it this way: *Give a man a hand and he'll pull himself up; give him a handout and you'll condition him to fail.* In keeping with his father's philosophy, this charity work was done late at night when no one could see who was doing the giving or the getting.

"Yeah." Wyatt looked at Ganna Mae. "You may have reasons to hate me, but not my Daddy. Let me tell you something about that family that you hate so much--"

"No." Moole repositioned himself so Ganna Mae and Wyatt could see him clearly. "Let me tell the story...it's only fitting since I was there," Moole said. "Wyatt wasn't even born when your parents died, or if he was, he was still soiling his diapers."

Moole turned to make sure the crew and Kozlov were listening. "Let me share a little background about myself." Moole smiled at Ganna Mae. "Had I been your counsel when you were searching for a kindred spirit to ruin the Kincaids, I would have advised you to check me out thoroughly, by the way."

"Don't treat me as an idiot, Moole. I knew exactly who you were—the Kincaids made you and your old man look like idiots for years."

"Shut up!" Moole snarled. "The Kincaids had one talent, and that was making money. They gave a lot of the money away. But unfortunately for them, they didn't know how to leverage their benevolence."

"Yeah, we gave anonymously, like the Bible requires…but you and ole Judge Moole, now there was a pair! They would take credit for everyone's good deeds. Hell, half the county still thinks you two are responsible for most of the charitable works of my dad."

"As I said, Wyatt, you Kincaids were never smart enough to leverage your benevolence. No telling how many political favors we reaped from the Crown's efforts. Thanks to you stoic self-righteous Kincaids" Moole rested his chin on his thumb and forefinger. "But that's old news. Tell me this. I've often wondered…why *abortion*? Why didn't the girl just raise a little bastard Moole instead?"

"Because Jenny hated your guts, Moole. In her mind abortion was the only option she had to cleanse her soul."

"And you couldn't wait to help--"

"She was going to get rid it…no matter the method or the cost. Her words."

"Yeah, but using Kincaid money? That must have really ticked your old man off."

Wyatt sagged down in his seat. "He couldn't understand. There were no options back then—the guy said he was a doctor." Svetlana moved her hand over Wyatt's and gave it a squeeze. Wyatt snatched his hand away and glared at Svetlana.

"Oh," Moole smiled. "So you finally figured out your caretaker is part of the plan. Huh, Wyatt?"

"That's not true," Svetlana rushed her words. "Maybe at first--"

"Liar!" Moole yelled. "See why you should never trust a woman, Wyatt?"

"Go to hell, Moole."

"Silence!" Gurov shouted as he made his way to Wyatt. Moole held up his hands to stay Gurov. "Thank you, seaman, but I have it now…Let's see. Where was I? Oh, yes. Abortion." Moole paced as he formulated his thoughts. "Abortion is a wonderful tool for improving populace purity—lowlifes can't keep their pants on and so we clean up their mess for a few bucks rather than support another moron for life. Why is it so hard to understand?" Moole asked.

"I can see both sides. Good and bad in each." Wyatt said. "Jenny died for no reason, but then, we don't have another Moole like you on the face of the earth. I just wish I had told my dad the truth. It was never the same for us after the abortion."

"Too bad," Moole snickered. "At any rate, we thank him for his generosity. I'm just thankful my father had the smarts to leverage Kincaid altruism into all those votes against the evil rich."

Wyatt nodded, "Yeah, just let a reporter get within hollering distance and Judge Moole would brag all day about *his* good deeds. It made me mad, but Dad said it didn't matter who got the credit as long as the wrong was made right."

"Too bad your old man didn't subscribe to the idea that free-will is not always best for the governed. I know you don't believe that either, Wyatt. But there is an elite who knows best. Trust me, the 'all men are created equal' part of the constitution was rhetoric, not policy. The Founding Fathers were not stupid enough to believe that." Moole glanced at Kozlov and the crew, and smiled when he saw them nodding in agreement with his statements. And why wouldn't they? They had been brought up under the exact system his father had advocated for years.

"But enough of politics. Let's get back to the story at hand." Moole paced up and down the narrow space between the four prisoners. The crispness of his steps ringing across the steel deck. "Anyway, just imagine how elated I was when Miss Ferguson came to me with a plan to not only destroy the *Last Kincaid*, but to give me control of my family's most hated nemesis...The Crown Kincaid Company...just think how absolutely rich that made me feel, Wyatt?"

Ganna Mae stood and addressed Moole. "We get it Moole. You are brilliant and the rest of us are stupid. Now tell me what happened to my parents."

Moole glared at Ganna Mae. "You know, Ms. Ferguson, I could just tell you what is in store for you, but then you won't know the depth of my distain for you and those like you." Moole leaned down eye to eye with Ganna Mae. "Have a seat, Ms. Ferguson, while I expose the ridiculous legend of the mule trained to be an assassin...Gee, Haw!" Moole strolled back and forth working himself into frenzy. When it seemed as if he would explode, he took several deep breaths and began his story in the calmer voice of a closing attorney. "That day started early for me. I was a boy of eleven, and I had gotten sick and tired of my father always complaining about the exploits of ignoramuses and never doing anything to stop them. So, early that morning around 4:00 A.M., I heard old man Kincaid rumble by in his farm truck. I knew his first stop, so I jumped on my bike and cut across the pasture to beat him to the Ferguson house.

As usual, he left a basket of side meat, flour, salt and potatoes. I waited until Kincaid left and then dashed on the porch and pissed all over the--"

Ganna Mae flew from her seat like a hawk after a field mouse, talons poised. Moole ducked behind Wyatt. "Get her under control!" Moole yelled. "The next time she tries something like that, shoot her."

"Damn you, Moole! If I had a gun, I would kill you right now!"

"Sit down." Moole eased from behind Wyatt's chair and faced Ganna Mae.

"Since the truth bothers you, why don't I stop? We do have other business." Ganna Mae stared at Moole. A bullet to the head was too kind. "No...I have to hear this." Ganna Mae looked at Wyatt. "So I can make things right."

Moole purposely walked by Ganna Mae, close enough for her to grab him if she dared. "Very well then. Let's see. Oh, yes. After I relieved myself." Moole eyed Ganna Mae to make sure she wasn't about to pounce. "I hid in the bushes and watched as old man Ferguson retrieved the food. Urine dripped from the bottom of the basket and the old man dabbed his fingers in my piss and sniffed it. He knew what it was, but rather than throw it away like any normal person would do, he rinsed the meat off under the old hand pump they had on the back porch. Then he separated the soiled salt and flour from the dry. I thought he would at least throw the spoiled flour and salt away, but instead he put it on the drain board to dry. I'd never witnessed such filthy behavior in my life. That's when I knew something had to be done." Moole, with his hands clasped behind his back, walked in a circle around the prisoners as he continued.

"Earlier that week, I put my plan into action, I delivered a box of dynamite and blasting caps to that old stump they battled every year. I then buried half of the dynamite deep around the stump to make sure the explosion would be massive. Any competent farmer could have cleared that stump away in no time, but the Fergusons damn near killed that magnificent mule Kincaid sold them trying to remove that stump.

My plan was working to perfection. The Fergusons thought the blasting material was a gift from Kincaid, so there was no suspicion. The only snag was that half-wit brother of yours."

"Caleb was no half-wit! He could read and write when he was five." Ganna Mae saw the disgust on Moole's face. "Go on. I just wanted to make sure you knew the truth."

"Duly noted," Moole sneered. "At any rate...I couldn't get close to him without that damn mule charging me like a vicious watch dog. That's when I discovered a Tootsie Roll Pop in my pocket. I tossed the sucker toward the stump and the boy chased after it. Even with the mule cutting across his path to stop him, the boy keep heading for the stump and the TNT. When old man Ferguson realized what I was doing, he and his wife sprinted across the field, running toward certain death, hand in…quite glorious really. But time was up for them…Ka-BOOM!" Moole trickled his fingers like falling rain.

"You miserable bastard!" Ganna Mae screamed." How can you take pleasure in killing two innocent people?"

"Oh, killing your parent wasn't a pleasure Ms. Ferguson. That was my duty. The pleasure came when those idiot rednecks, who believed my father's story about the mule sitting on the plunger after Kincaid fired his shotgun, formed a firing squad to execute the assassin mule. They couldn't know that the reason for the mule's hoof tracks around the plunger was because the damn mule kept charging me trying to get me away from the box. But once I threw the lollipop, Demon took off after the halfwit to keep him away from the charges they had set.

My father and the sheriff were so serious when they pointed out those hoof prints around the plunger and kept insisting it had to be that the mule purposely sat on the handle. Of course, my footprints were there too, and I was even placed at the scene by a field hand, but my father convinced them that I tried to pull the mule away from the plunger box and that the mule was just pure evil... and with a name like Demon he didn't have to do much more convincing. Then, as they say, ole' Demon's fate was sealed.

And the irony? Your idiot family could never pronounce my name correctly because all they could speak was *Cuuun-treee..*" Moole rolled the word out in his best redneck dialect. "So, when the half-wit kept saying: 'Mule did it, mule did it, mule did it'…that convinced them without a doubt that the mule, indeed did it." Moole snickered, *"Gee Haw!"*

"Months later, suspicions started turning toward me, because some of the brighter sharecroppers figured out that it was much more likely that I, a person who was known to hate the lowlifes, was much more motivated to push that plunger than that mule. Though my father didn't approve of what I did, he wasn't about to sacrifice me to bunch of rednecks, so he and the sherriff starting speculating out loud on the campaign trail, in country stores and churches, about whether Kincaid might have actually trained the mule to sit when he heard a gun fire. It turns out that mules are highly intelligent and can easily be taught to do something like that. Rumors somehow started that Kincaid was seen quail hunting in the adjacent field. Truth is, Kincaid was nowhere near that place. Others had seen him miles away in another part of the county. Eventually, people forgot about the explosion, but my father and the sheriff always gave credence to the idea that Kincaid trained that mule and fired the gun.

"Mule did it. Mule did it'. Ignorant slug! Had his IQ been above room temperature and his diction somewhat normal, I suppose he could have pronounced *Moole* properly…Perhaps I would have been found out. But, luckily ah…what's the half-wit's name…Caleb?"

Ganna Mae, with no regard for Gurov or his Uzi, charged Moole. Before Wyatt could reach Gurov, the Uzi's stock smashed into Ganna Mae's head and she hit the deck. Yasnaya and Svetlana covered her with their bodies to protect her from the blows that were about to come.

Chapter 42

Taylor Averette maneuvered his Zodiac behind the bow of the Baltic Queen and out of sight of the Crown Jewel. As he floated down the length of the freighter, he noticed the blocks of C-4 explosives attached to the hull. Nothing in his meetings with Kozlov gave him any indication the sea captain would rig his own ship with explosives. That being the case, then this had to be the work of the Fountain docked to the mother ship. As methodically as Boris and Fyodor had planted the explosives, Taylor Averette removed them and separated the remote detonators from C-4 blocks.

As he mechanically switched off each device, the earlier low-flying maneuver of the jet nagged at him again. Had it been a military jet, no problem. Those guys flew on the deck all the time…but private jets, never. The jet he had observed looked an awful lot like Kincaid's plane, but maybe not. Even if it was and the pilots decided to alert authorities, by the time alarms were raised and interceptors scrambled, only flotsam and an oil slick would mark this spot.

Averette smacked his face with both palms. The jolt helped clear his jitters. Time to get his head in the real game. Little was left to do now but wait. The jamming had fried the communication frequency on the Crown Jewel and, with night vision goggles, he confirmed the three souls aboard the yacht were under the intense scrutiny of the Baltic Queen security detail.

Averette's past assignments made him a perfect choice to be a liaison between Moole and the Odessa, a group he had infiltrated during a human trafficking case three year earlier. Though his undercover work nearly dismantled the crime ring, he was never suspected as the mole. That suspicion fell on a young Chechen who was eventually fed feet-first into a commercial sausage grinder and later served to his family at a wedding reception.

Thought to be incapable of resurrection, the Odessa dropped off Interpol's radar, but that turned out to be a big mistake. The mob laid low, but used their inactivity to become smarter and more subtle in their standard operating procedures. Once, profits from lucrative dope deals and kidnappings were used to finance flashy life styles and obscene displays of nouveau riche. The new and better managed Odessa plowed profits from illegal deals back into the organization and used the proceeds to hire knowledgeable, if immoral, financiers. In return the financiers, figured out ways to penetrate the international medical records field flush with government monies. Money scammed from medical record billing flowed into their coffers. Just when the Odessa thought profits couldn't get any higher, a sinister genius from the medical records branch hit upon the most profitable and diabolical plan ever devised.

The Odessa had always been major players in human trafficking. But new management, like corporate raiders before them, determined it was easier and more profitable to deal with the parts rather than the whole.

Scores of kidnapped victims pressed into domestic service and prostitution were suddenly in play for the very lucrative black market human organ trade. In the old days when escapees from Odessa prostitution and slave rings were captured after futile attempts to flee, they were beaten back into submission. Now offenders were quietly transported to makeshift hospital ships, like the Bratva Mercy, stationed on the high seas to avoid the pesky international laws forbidding the taking and selling of human organs.

Corneas, skin, kidneys, livers, lungs and hearts once in short demand started turning up on black markets in multiples. Kidneys alone were fetching over a hundred grand and hearts were bringing five times as much. Harvest-to-order requests were being filled for millions and the demand increased daily.

And, just like that, flight prone assets became cash cows rather than problems. The new business model was so successful the Odessa began to phase out riskier drug operations and concentrate on the organ harvesting.

Through gossip and well placed rumors, prostitutes learned quickly the concept of loyalty equals long shelf-life, and since none of them wanted to end up on a parts list, escape attempts dwindled to a trickle.

Tonight, those not fortunate enough to be crucial to the *Last Kincaid* plan, would be traded to the Odessa transplant division. A very profitable way to get rid of potential eyewitnesses. Tidwell, Lisa Cox, Svetlana, Clark Guilford and most of the Malaysia crew on board the Baltic Queen fell into that category. Yasnaya was vital to the *Last Kincaid* plan, but she could still be used as compensation for the ship's crew. Salary bonuses were rare on freighters, unlike the crab and fishing vessel so popular on reality TV that shared the value of the catch. Freighter crews were paid scale, and as a result morale was nonexistent. A little time alone with Yasnaya would go a long way toward restoring morale and loyalty of the crew, no doubt about that.

Already climbing over 4000 feet per minute, Trent Rayle pushed the throttles against the housing assembly. "You think anyone saw us?"

"If they did, it was a quick peek," Mason Lexford responded. Trent nodded agreement. "Still, I should have cut the nav lights and delayed my climb."

"Don't sweat it. By the time anyone figures out what's going on, we'll have a team on site."

"I know. It's just that I don't want to get those guys hurt. Hell, they're my friends." Just before he lowered the Challenger's nose, Rayle scanned the array of choices on the Collins Pro Line stack until he found the new waypoint option.

"You sure that will store lat and long?" Mason Lexford asked. "The team will need coordinates, not waypoints."

"They'll have both. Good job with the triangulation by the way."

"Thanks, but your friend the boat captain made it easy for me. Is he ex-military?"

"Maybe, I don't really know," Trent said. "But Clark's a sharp guy."

"I hope so. This could get real ugly real quick. He won't get any second chances."

Trent eased back on the throttles to begin his descent. "What if the agency doesn't buy your assessment?"

Lexford looked out the starboard cockpit window and remembered back to the last time that happened. "Innocent people will die."

After the clearance to land, only the white noise of the GE 34 engines could be heard in the Challenger cabin. Both men were silently praying for the same results for different reasons.

"This is about as secure as it's going to get. I'll make my call from here," Mason said as the line boy crossed his batons, a signal for the jet to stop.

Trent Rayle slid his seat aft and softly exhaled. That was the good thing about Mason; he didn't put things off, except for making time for family. That bad habit turned out to be the reason Cheryl divorced him. The divorce had been hard on Mason and Cheryl. Their split was a perfect example of two good people growing apart. It had been hard to honor Cheryl's request to see her ex-husband before she died, but now Trent was glad that had transpired. What other Special Ops person would he have called to help the Bossman and Clark? Cheryl, even in death, seemed to be watching over him.

Mason Lexford's voice was calm but urgent. "I don't have proof that it's a hijacking, but the captain asked for assistance. "

"Why didn't he send out a Mayday?"

"I don't know. It could be a hostage situation."

"Pirates?"

"No, it's more complicated than that."

"What's the name of the vessel?"

"She's a Hatteras called the Crown Jewel, North Carolina registry. You may have the owner under surveillance. Wyatt Kincaid? "

"Hold on."

While Mason waited for his information to be verified, he gave Trent the cut-power sign and waited for the engines to spool down.

"We are aware of the situation."

"So you have agents onboard?"

"You know I can't give out that information, Mason. But we have the situation covered."

"Come on. I taught you this business and I still have a Top Secret Clearance. What gives?"

"Look, enjoy your retirement, Mason. I appreciate the heads up, but seriously, we have this covered."

"Ok, let me ask you this. Are you aware there is another ship on a rendezvous course with the freighter, Baltic Queen?"

"Now, how do you know that?"

"We verified it by sight and Slope Intercept Formula. Four boats heading for the same destination in the middle of the ocean and the waypoint isn't on any shipping lane."

"Sounds like coincidence to me, Mason."

"Yeah? Well try this on for size. The ship is the Bratva Mercy."

"You're kidding?"

"Nope."

"I'll get back with you on this."

Mason Lexford ended his call and made a beeline for Trent Rayle. "Your friends have a problem."

"What's wrong?"

"The agency indicated to me that they have agents onboard, but if that's the case they would have known about the Bratva Mercy."

"What the hell is the Bratva Mercy?" Trent asked.

"The Bratva Mercy is an Odessa hospital ship we calculated will rendezvous with the Baltic Queen and your friend's yacht."

"Why is that trouble?"

"Bratva is Russian for Brotherhood. The irony is there is no mercy in The Brotherhood. You have heard of the Odessa?"

"Only on in the news. It's something like the mafia, right?"

"Mafia, mayhem, and terror," Mason said. "Take your pick."

"But the team can handle it, right?"

"They aren't sending the cavalry, Trent. They'll try to contact the agents. If that fails, they may try to get a visual on them within 12 hours. The only thing that will launch a team sooner is a request from the agents."

"I don't get it. Why are you so sure they are in trouble? I mean, the agents must feel like they have the situation under control, right?"

"Trent, I was with Delta Force for 14 years. If I knew a Brotherhood ship was en route to my location, I would have sent out the alarm. They may have an agent on board, but I don't think he has any idea what's headed his way."

"You said it was a hospital ship. What--"

"Take my word for it. There's nothing hospitable about that ship."

"There's nothing we can do?"

"Nothing timely enough to help those folks."

Chapter 43

Fyodor Yantikov looked at Svetlana. She had hardly taken her eyes off Boris. Even as she aided the bleeding old woman on the deck, her cold stare rarely left his face. He followed Svetlana's gaze and observed the damage done to his brother's features by Konstantin. Why hadn't he studied the freighter longer before they decided to rig the explosives? Four or five charges were more than adequate to sink the vessel. He should have set that amount and demanded Boris leave. No sense wasting time analyzing such a stupid plan. It was time to come up with a new one and quick. Boris couldn't hold out much longer without medical attention. First business at hand was to save his brother. As Svetlana pulled Ganna away from Moole and toward him, he made his move. "Comrade, can you help my brother, too?" Fyodor whispered. "He will die if the bleeding--"

"Then he will surely die, *Comrade.*"

He could not let his mother down again. She had to have at least one son to look out for her. "Please, madam. I know who you are and I know something of the history you and my brother share--"

"We share nothing!"

"What my brother did was wrong, but he did try to provide you with warm clothes. He is awkward, clumsy, and he has no social graces, I will admit that. But he is my brother and he is my mother's pet. I can't let him die. Please help us...for a mother's sake, I beg you."

Before Svetlana could answer, Ganna Mae propped up on her elbow and waved all of them away. "Give me some room so I can breathe!" Ganna Mae sat upright. As she did, Fyodor Yantikov realized his last chance to save his brother. He leaned down and whispered, "Help my brother or I will tell Yasnaya Polyana about the prevention part of the *Last Kincaid* plan."

"Who the hell are you?"

"That doesn't matter, but what does is that I've had your plan for months--"

"You're not that commie bastard," Ganna Mae whispered. "I would recognize him."

"He's the one beaten to a pulp." Fyodor jerked his head toward Boris. "Help me get him medical attention or I will tell everything I know. In light of what we've just heard, do you really want the real last Kincaid to know what you've done to her?"

"No!" Ganna Mae struggled to sit up. "Moole is twisting the truth. It was never my intent to hurt Yas. You'll get your help and money too. Just keep your damn mouth shut until I can speak with my daughter."

"Very well," Fyodor said. "But if my brother doesn't get help soon, I will tell my version of the *Last Kincaid* plan."

"Yuri Kozlov." Ganna Mae strained to see Kozlov. "You'll pay for this. I promise you that." Kozlov parted Ganna Mae's hair, revealing her gaping wound. "Take her to my quarters. Now!"

Kozlov looked at Fyodor and Boris. For them to have value they would have to be alive. "Take these two with you, and see that they all get treatment. Svetlana, go with them."

"Nyet," Svetlana pointed at Boris. "I will not be alone with this one. If I am, I will surely kill him."

Kozlov seemed to leap the width of the room to get to Svetlana. "Do as I say Svetlana, or so help me, you will need medical attention yourself, I swear!"

As Kozlov threatened Svetlana, Ganna Mae pulled Fyodor close. "I can handle her and I'll see that your brother gets excellent medical attention. Just keep *quiet* until I can explain."

"I believe you mentioned money? How much money were we talking exactly?"

Ganna Mae glanced at Yasnaya to make sure she had heard nothing. But who was she kidding? There was no such thing as paying off a blackmailer. There would be no final payment. Fyodor, like the Odessa, would never take his bloodsucking fangs out of her till. It had to end now. She had to tell the truth and hope Yasnaya would understand. Ganna Mae pretended to faint and Yasnaya rushed to catch her. On her way to the floor, Ganna Mae crushed Yasnaya's ear to her mouth. "Stay with Moole and Wyatt if you can. I want to know everything they say."

"Mother," Yasnaya whispered. "Haven't you heard enough? My God, the Kincaids were your saviors, not--"

"I know that now, damn it!" Ganna Mae hissed, "But corporate takeover is an issue I need to discuss with Kincaid. Moole needs you or me for the take over. We have to stand together or we have no chance of survival. If Ridell signed that proxy, Wyatt Kincaid is as good as dead. Try to save him if you can." Ganna Mae kissed Yas on her cheek and whispered, "And be careful--"

"Old woman, shut up!" Gurov yelled.

"Yuri, please, a moment with my daughter?" Ganna Mae pleaded.

"Leave the girl Gurov, but take Kincaid to the brig. Konstantin and I will join you shortly."

Svetlana wrapped her arms around Kozlov's ankles. "No, please Captain. He can't take another beating." Kozlov jerked his foot away and kicked Svetlana in the ribs. Wyatt belted Gurov in the face and pinned Kozlov's arms to his side before he could fire his pistol. "Yasnaya, get his gun."

Yasnaya tore from Ganna Mae's embrace and wrested the gun from Kozlov.

"Nobody move or I will shoot." Yasnaya yelled.

"Oh, how nice. Sister saving big brother. But I'm afraid it's all for naught," Moole said as he put his Beretta at the base of Ganna Mae's skull. "Drop the gun, or I shoot."

Yasnaya tightened her grip and aimed at Moole. "You won't shoot her Moole. You need her to complete your takeover of The Crown."

"Well, Wyatt," Moole said. "She does have Kincaid blood in her."

"Guess so. Too bad for you, Moole."

"I do hope you didn't mistake that as a compliment? I meant she is as rash and ignorant as you." Moole leered at Yasnaya. "I don't usually dispense free legal advice, but I suppose that little favor you did for me on the boat constitutes payment. Let me explain to you why I'm going to shoot this woman and it won't affect my taking over The Crown. You see lover, you have remainder interest in Ms. Ferguson's shares of Crown stock. That is to say, when she dies, and she surely will die when I pull the trigger, her shares pass to you. And you will beg to sign any paper I put in front of you. I promise you that," Moole sneered. "Say good bye mothers. Yes, I said *mothers*. I've decided to kill them both, just to prove my point."

"No." Yasnaya threw the gun down. "Don't hurt them. I'll do anything you want."

"Anything?" Moole laughed. "Oh, you should really choose your words more carefully around an attorney, lover."

"Konstantin, get him," Kozlov said, as he scooped up his weapon and pointed it at Wyatt. "You just sealed your fate…and that of your crew."

"Let them go, Kozlov."

"Oh, no, Mr. Kincaid," Kozlov sneered. "You made a deal and you knew the price."

"Moole, you've won. You have my company and you've squandered my fortune. Show a little mercy, will ya?"

"How funny. Macho Wyatt Kincaid begging for his life--"

"I'm not that stupid, Moole. I know Kozlov will never let me leave this ship alive. I'm asking mercy for my crew…and the women. My God, man. You know Clark and Jim. They don't deserve to die for my mistake. Not even you could be rotten enough to kill innocent people for no gain."

"Enough!" Kozlov shouted. "There will be no mercy. Konstantin, take Kincaid to the brig. Gurov, take the others to sick bay, then join us."

"Wait, I want to watch…but first I need to get all the paperwork in order." Moole said. "Can you postpone it a little, Kozlov?"

Kozlov nodded.

"What about the pretty one, captain?" Gurov asked.

"Oh, yes!" Moole screamed. "Why didn't I think of this earlier? Take the girl to the brig with Wyatt. I have a little surprise for him...and her."

Kozlov nodded. "Secure them in the brig, Konstantin, then report back to me."

Onboard the Crown Jewel, James Tidwell finally regained consciousness. Beside him on the opposite divan was Clark. "They rough you up too?"

"Naw," Clark lifted the icepack from his face. "That scrawny little Moole did all this. It's nothing compared to what you got." Clark sat up. "What the hell did you do to deserve that beating?"

"That's enough." Lisa Cox said as she gently pushed Clark back down. "You boys can compare boo-boo's later."

Tidwell felt the ace bandage around his chest and a chilled compress behind his neck. "I don't know how you got them to stop, but thanks. I thought I was a goner." Lisa smiled. "You can thank the man on the other ship. He made a deal with them and they stopped hurting you."

"What man?"

"Big guy, graying hair? He said he'd go along with some deal if they agreed to free his crew."

"Bossman," Tidwell and Clark said in unison.

"Still think he's a bad guy?" Clark asked Tidwell.

"No, and I haven't for sometime." Tidwell thought back to his conversation with Averette. "Problem is my concerns never got back to the agency. He's a marked man, Clark."

"I know I'm new to all this," Lisa Cox said. "But I'm part of it now. What's going on?"

"Do you hear that?" Tidwell asked

"What?"

"The beeping noise...someone's phone is dying. Quick! Help me find it!"

After a mad scramble, Lisa Cox held up Ganna Mae's bag. "It's in here."

James Tidwell checked the battery life on the satellite phone. "Barely enough power left to make one call...maybe."

"Yeah, but how about your friend out there? He's cooked our communications. Wouldn't take much for him to burn that little thing up."

"That's true, but he probably isn't anticipating anymore jamming. Besides, Ganna Mae was using this phone and he wasn't jamming her signal. I do know that."

"Hell, call down the thunder, Jim. What have we got to lose?"

"I can't chance that. Averette knows all my contact numbers. He probably has them programmed for automatic capture. We have to call someone we can trust and someone sharp enough to understand what's going on in a few words. This battery is almost gone."

"Call Trent. I could have sworn I saw the plane earlier, but I didn't want to say anything." Tidwell snapped his fingers rapidly. "Clark, dial Trent's number and here's what I want you to say..."

Chapter 44

Yasnaya's first whiff of feculent scented air in the ship's hole made her gag. She held her breath and tried to make sense of Ganna Mae's uncharacteristically loving behavior, but the stench made her vomit. As she wretched, Wyatt pulled two bundles wrapped around a long steel bolt from under the corner basin. "My secret stash. I never know when I might get stuck in here. Svetlana makes sure we have a couple of these just in case." Wyatt handed her a paper towel stuffed with rosemary leaves. "You can have this one." Yas grabbed the homemade concoction, pressed it to her face, and extended her free hand to Wyatt. "Pleased to finally meet you. On behalf of my mother, thanks for helping her family."

Wyatt acknowledged her graciousness with a slow smile. "And I want to thank you for backing me up there...we almost pulled it off."

"I didn't have time to think. It just felt like the right thing to do."

"It was." Wyatt hid the bolt in his shirt. "My father is owed your appreciation." Wyatt smile turned into a full out grin. "Hey, come to think of it, he was your father too, and Ganna Mae is *not* your mother."

"I know. She told me. I mean, we do favor. But it's so weird to think we are brother and sister," Yas said. "And the woman, Svetlana, is my mother?"

"Yeah, that's true." Wyatt stood and walked to the hatch. "If we could get out of here, I could prove it to you. Truth is, I've been searching for you a long time. But, for now, why don't you just take my word for it." Wyatt rattled the chain hanging from the hook in the ceiling. "We got more pressing matters."

"This all seems so surreal. Why is the captain so set on killing you?"

"Long story...but it probably has more to do with Moole than Kozlov. Kozlov's a psychopath. He just wants an excuse to kill."

"So is Moole. He killed my boyfriend, Tim Ridell. That's why I was so quick to give up earlier. I know he's capable of killing...and more."

"Ridell from legal? Why the hell would Moole kill him?"

"They made him president." All the horror of the past hours flooded Yas, and the realization that Tim was really dead hit her. Overwhelmed, she closed her eyes and slowly slid down the wall.

Wyatt squatted beside Yasnaya. "I'm sorry for your loss. He was a good kid. I didn't know him that well. I do know he didn't deserve the treatment he got from Sally and Jim...and he sure as hell didn't deserve to die." Yas pulled herself together and stood. "I think Moole knew from the moment he made Tim president that he was going to kill him."

"Moole...man, that guy has never found a moral boundary he won't cross."

Yas nodded agreement. "You may be interested to know that Tim took the job seriously. He cared about the company and its people." She smiled. "I never understood why he was so concerned about your safety, but then he told me about all the employees who told him stories about how you helped them. Those stories inspired him to also find ways to help others."

"I'm glad he helped folks, but those stories were not supposed to be told. Poor guy, I should have done more for him." Wyatt shook his head. "I did make Moole give him a bonus once so he could get a decent car...jeez, that smoke-blowing car."

"Strange you would bring that car up. It's one of my favorite memories of him."

"Ridell, uh Tim, had to know Moole hated him. It's not like Moole tried to hide it. Why did he agree to take the job?"

"Tim wasn't stupid. He read over the paperwork numerous times before he decided to accept the position." Yas looked down. "We had a big fight when he demanded to know what Gan and I knew about your disappearance."

"I'm sure Moole made certain the offer passed the legal sniff test. And no doubt that chicken-shit board of mine rubber stamped the resolution that included authorization to vote my shares. The fact that they kept me alive this long means Tim understood that signing that proxy meant the end for both of us. Moole must have tortured him."

"But even with your vote, Moole still needs me or Ganna Mae, right?" Wyatt paced the room like an expectant parent. "Hadn't thought about it that way, but it would be odd for a company to transfer ownership by proxies only. Not even that idiot board of mine would approve something that fishy."

"There is something you should know. Moole has my proxy. Tim and I found it going through some corporate minutes."

"I'd like to hear that whole story sometime. Blows the hell out of my security measures. If Moole has your proxy, why is he dealing with you? Why wouldn't he just vote your shares?"

"Maybe he forged the paperwork?"

"That would open some doors," Wyatt mused

"Even if the paperwork is legal, can we stop him?"

"The meeting will have to take place in Wilmington, that's in our corporate bylaws...that means Moole has a big problem. How does he control you and Ganna Mae now that you know the truth? Having majority stockholders there to vote their shares certainly would make things go smoother, but you two are the only ones left who fill that bill."

Yasnaya, revitalized with the brainstorming, began to match Wyatt step for step. "Gan is a very shrewd person. I'm sure she has a contingency plan on the chance Moole double crossed her. She never shoots straight from the hip. She's been planning the *Last Kincaid* since I can remember. Moole has to know that about her, too."

Wyatt stopped and faced Yas. "You don't think her contingency was Kozlov, do you?" Yasnaya smiled so big it struck Wyatt as odd. "You don't know Ganna Mae Ferguson at all, do you?"

"Not really, but what's that got to do with anything?"

"Gan would never trust her life to a man. Whatever her backup plan is, I promise you, it doesn't involve Kozlov."

Wyatt let out a long heavy breath. "Damn, that's a load off! Well, if she's got a magic bullet, it's about time to lock and load." Wyatt pointed to the hatch. "Uh, oh. Company."

Yasnaya and Wyatt watched as the hatch spun open. Konstantin, Gurov, and Kozlov entered, followed by Moole. "Well, Wyatt I do hope you two had time to get acquainted?"

"Yeah, we had a nice little chat. I was telling her how easy it would be to snuff out a little weasel like you, Moole." Wyatt pointed at the Russian threesome. "*If* you didn't have the Brothers Karamazov with you."

"Oh, that is so *Kincaidian*, if there is such a word. But, you don't bother me, Wyatt. Once I take over the Crown, your bullying days are over."

"Just curious, Phil. How did you get Ridell to sign the proxy? Torture?"

"Oh, nothing that Draconian, Wyatt. I simply bribed him."

"That's a lie." Yas shouted. "Tim couldn't be bought."

"We can all be bought. Ridell was no different. Look how fast he jumped into your grave, Wyatt. He couldn't wait to do a deal."

"That's bullcrap, Moole," Wyatt said. "Ridell figured out this *Last Kincaid* plan. Unfortunately for him, and for me, he didn't figure on your total lack of humanity."

"That's your problem, Wyatt. You think you know everything. The *Last Kincaid* plan was never about killing *you*." Moole looked at Yasnaya. "The plan was to stop the Kincaid bloodline… that ends with *you*. Tubal ligation ring a bell?"

Yasnaya turned to Moole. "How do you know about that? My medical records are private."

"Not really. I wanted to make sure the Kincaids would be finished once and for all before I signed on. The old woman told me about your operation, but that's no longer permanent birth control in today's medical world."

"It wasn't for birth control. I had ovarian cancer--"

"Read those medical records lately? You never had an imminent cancer risk, Ms. Polyana."

"You're lying, Moole."

"*The Last Kincaid?* Think about it. How could she be sure you were the *last* Kincaid? It's my favorite part of her plan, and the main reason I signed on. Diabolical people fascinate me."

"Say what you want. But I know she would never hurt me. She loves me."

"Really, why do you think she never bestowed the Ferguson name on you?" Moole again sounded like a lawyer doing his closing statement. "Oh, yes. I checked more than your medical records. I know every thing there is to know about you, Yasnaya Polyana." Moole let out a wicked chuckle. "Something Wyatt could never accomplish, even with all his millions. Don't let your hatred of me hide the facts. Without heirs, it was never in doubt that Ganna Mae would receive your shares through survival rights. If you don't believe me, look at the certificates she had you sign."

Yasnaya thought back to all the forms Ganna Mae had ever shoved in front of her, and true enough, she *had* signed most without reading them.

"Even with Wyatt's votes," Moole continued, "she would have needed your shares to finish off the Crown and the Kincaids."

"Shares I would have gladly given her, so she would have had no need to kill me."

Moole toyed with his Beretta. "That's true now, but then her problem has always been that, in spite of your Russian name, you *are* a Kincaid. And Ganna Mae Ferguson had no plans to live in a world with Kincaids."

Yasnaya moved closer to Wyatt as she remembered the day Ganna Mae had explained why she needed the operation. Was it all a lie? Was Ganna Mae that evil?

Moole continued, "That's right. Think about it, see the truth for what it is, Ms. Kincaid."

"Give it up Moole. You can't conquer and divide," Wyatt said.

"Can't conquer? Ask her about her earlier submission on the boat?"

"Submission! Don't you mean *rape*?!" Yas screamed.

Wyatt's rage boiled as he went eyeball to eyeball with Moole. "You raped her?"

"Grab him, Konstantin," Kozlov yelled.

The big Russian wrestled Wyatt into the corner, away from Moole.

"Hold on! That's not true," Moole panted.

"Not true?!" Yasnaya bellowed.

"You got what you deserved, whore! Wearing those little skimpy outfits…" Moole closed his eyes and thought of the many times he had salivated over every move the gorgeous blonde made on board the yacht. Oh, she knew what she was doing all right. "That's not important now, however."

"Not *important?*"

"Not as important as your *lives,* is it?" Moole looked from Yasnaya to Wyatt. "Oh, just shut up and listen to my proposition and you both may live."

"Why should I believe you?" Yasnaya asked

"Yeah, Moole. We all know you can tell a lie."

"Shut up, Wyatt. Even if you don't care about your own life, remember the safety of your crew is also at stake."

"Go to hell, Moole. Nobody is getting a pass out of here. Do what you have to do."

"No! What must we do?" Yas asked.

"You have to vote Ganna Mae's shares after they revert to you, and vigorously support me at the stockholders meeting. No monkey business." Moole said.

"And if I do that, no harm comes to anyone, including Wyatt and the crew?" Yasnaya's expression changed as something else occurred to her. "When you say 'revert', you mean after she signs a proxy, correct?"

Blood vessels around Moole's temples pulsated wildly. "I'm sure you and Wyatt have figured out that I have a dilemma. The board is not going along with an ownership transfer by proxy only. I have to have shareholders present. Wyatt's not expected to be there, Jim and Sally will vote their shares in person, no problem. Still, I need majority stockholders there to assure the board. But if I allow you and Ganna Mae to make the meeting, she will have a plan to stop me. You see, what I need is a death certificate for you or Ganna Mae to explain why another proxy is nothing unusual. Now, who will it be? You or Ganna Mae?"

"That's sick! Only God should decide who lives and who dies."

"That may be true on most days, but today think of me as God. Now, who's it going to be?"

"You'll have to kill both of us and take your chances with the board. I can't choose and I know she won't either."

Moole started a slow walk around the room. "You are wrong about that. I made Ganna Mae the same offer and she agreed to vote your shares. But I don't trust her. That's why I'm making you this offer."

Yasnaya pointed at Moole. "Liar! She wouldn't let me die."

"I wrote down the address of her half-wit brother's hospital and promised her that he would die if she did not play ball."

Yasnaya felt the truth burning in her gut, Ganna Mae would agree to that. Nothing was more important to her than avenging the Ferguson family, even the life of her adopted daughter. "You bastard!"

Moole sneered, "Did it just hit you that blood is thicker than water, Miss *Kincaid*? OK, I've wasted enough time." Moole turned to Kozlov. "They're all yours, Captain. Do with them as you will."

Yasnaya thought of what Moole had said about the tubal ligation. Could Ganna Mae's reason for the operation be as sinister as Moole suggested? "Wait. I need more time, please?"

"What's to think over? These are you choices. Agree to work with me so I can take over the Crown and only one person dies, Ganna Mae. Don't work with me and Wyatt, your real mother, and two innocent crew members die. The half-wit dies either way. Oh, and I shutter to think what will happen to you once Kozlov turns his crew loose." Moole's face was so close Yas could feel and smell his breath. "I need your decision. Right now."

Yasnaya clasped her hands together and bowed her head.

Wyatt stared down Moole. "You can let both women live and still get control of the company. They've suffered enough, Moole. Just take your spoils and go."

"And then wouldn't life be grand?" Moole again turned to Kozlov. "Again, they're all yours. I need to get out of here."

Yas ran the numbers through her head. Five lives for one. "No, wait. I'll do it," she countered.

Careful to keep his back to Yas and Wyatt so they couldn't see the big smile spreading across his face, Moole answered, "Smart girl. Why don't you and Wyatt wait here while I go deal with Ms. Ferguson? I'm sure you don't want to be present when it happens, do you?"

Yas buried her head into Wyatt's chest. "God forgive me."

"Moole, you taken everything I own. I've got nothing left to bribe you with. I'm begging you, don't do this."

"Oh, you have something left Wyatt."

"What?"

"Two big fat bank accounts at the Farmers and Maritime--"

"How did...Hell! That damn L. Robert Lee!"

Moole smiled. "We think we have a way to gain access, but it would be a lot cleaner if we have the passwords."

Wyatt looked at Yas and back at Moole. "My Daddy left that money for her and she's going to get it."

"I don't have a problem with her having money, Wyatt. I just want to make sure you don't have any. You see, your life was never in danger. I want you to live forever, but penniless. I'll tell you what I will do, Wyatt. If you give me your account password," Moole proposed, "I'll spare the old woman, but she has to remain a prisoner aboard the ship with you…get a feel for what she put an innocent man through. A little *retribution*, eh, Wyatt? But, if either of you tries to stop me from getting control of the Crown," Moole gestured at Yas. "she dies."

"How do I know you'll do what you say?

"You don't, Wyatt. However, if you don't give me the password, I'll bring the old woman down here and shoot her in front of both of you, right now. I--"

"OK, OK, I'll do it."

Moole grabbed Yas. "Have your friend on the Crown Jewel to pack you a bag, and then bring the old woman and Svetlana down here so Kozlov can keep and eye on them."

Yasnaya nodded and headed off for the main deck.

Moole motioned for Kozlov to step outside the brig. "I want to kill him," Kozlov ranted. "I made a promise in front of my men. He has to die. I'm tired of babysitting him!"

"That hasn't changed, Captain. Kill him as soon as Yasnaya and I depart the ship. As a matter of fact, kill them all."

"And when do I get the power units for my weapons?" Kozlov asked

"Right away. I'll make the arrangements in just a minute."

Kozlov smiled as he watched Moole climb the stairs. Soon the world would no longer be ruled by capitalists. A new world order was coming. Kozlov looked at his watch. In less than one hour actually.

Moole caught his breath as he topped the main deck and punched numbers on his phone. "Averette, get here quick."

Chapter 45

Taylor Averette floated the Zodiac up to the makeshift dock and gave a furtive wave to the crew manning the machine guns. One crewman returned his wave. The other three kept him in their sights. He passed the sentries and headed straight for Moole who was standing near the stern. "When do I get my money and cargo?"

"The money as soon as I get back from Wilmington, but the cargo may be a little harder to work out."

"We promised the Odessa they would have organ donors and weapons with firing mechanisms. If that doesn't happen, there is no place on earth that I, or you for that matter, can hide."

"Kozlov is under the impression that he is going to get the weapons. Without them he won't release the hostages."

"Why does he think this?"

"It was the only way I could turn him against the old woman, and it isn't like Kozlov doesn't know the weapons are onboard. Besides, with half the government armories in the Mid-East being ransacked as we speak, getting more weapons won't be a problem."

"You're right, Moole. Weapons are cheap and plentiful but firing mechanisms aren't. Think of all the weapons the Mujahedin had to shitcan when the power units went dead and we wouldn't replace them. Our friends need these weapons now. They have some target practicing to do on some low and slow flying airliners…and remember they have paid for them with services already rendered." Averette looked at his watch. "Don't expect me to protect you from the Odessa. It's not too late for me to kill Tidwell and switch back to the other side, you know."

Moole paled as he thought of the brutalities the Odessa could inflict upon him. He should have let the old woman deal with them, but without the double-cross, his plan would have failed. Ah, if a double-cross worked once, surely it would work again? "Then there is only one thing to do. You have to kill Kozlov and his crew. We really don't need him anymore, and I have no interest in hiding from the Odessa the rest of my life."

"I'm one person, Moole. What will *you* be doing while I'm killing Kozlov and his crew, plus trying to keep an eye on the prisoners?"

"I have to leave to take over the Crown. The meeting has been called and we certainly don't want to miss our payday, do we? I will take care of the prisoners. Wyatt is likely dead by now. The girl, Yasnaya, will do as I say and I will get the women prisoners onboard the Crown Jewel. We can tie them up, kill Tidwell and Clark, transfer the weapons, and blow up this rusting bucket--"

"What about the maintenance crew? Organ providers are valuable."

"Our friends will have prisoners and weapons. Not as many as they want, but things don't always go as planned. Surely they will concede that point?"

"They aren't interested in excuses. We need more organs."

"Give them Fyodor and Boris?"

"Still, not enough," Averette said. "Unless I make a deal with Fyodor to help me get the maintenance crew off this ship before we blow it."

"Yes, then give them the two brothers," Moole whispered. "That should satisfy them."

"Where is Kozlov?"

"He and two of his henchmen are in the brig finishing off Kincaid. I'll transfer my things back to the yacht and take care of Tidwell and Clark—damn! I can't kill Clark. Someone has to pilot the boat."

"You can't hold heading and speed?" Averette snapped. "Never mind. I'll call the Bratva Mercy and get them to send a launch. I need backup. I don't trust Fyodor and I have no confidence in you."

"Go to hell, Averette! I'll do my part!"

"Well, see that you do!" Averette started out for the brig, then stopped, turned, and walked back to Moole. "One more thing. So far everyone you've partnered with you've double-crossed. I wouldn't advise trying that again."

Back on the mess deck, Phillip Moole unlocked his briefcase and gave the proxy agreement a cursory scan. The half-folded page with Tim Ridell's signature fluttered to the desktop. "What the hell? Ridell, you conniving bastard!"

Moole raced through the hatch and attempted to rail-surf down the stairs as he had seen Kozlov and sailors do. Instead of a graceful slide, he crashed headlong into the steel deck. The men manning the machine guns turned and laughed. "Shut up!" Moole yelled as he scrambled toward the next stairwell. "See who laughs last, jerks!"

From the deck above, Yasnaya heard Moole and leaned over the railing just in time to see him running back toward the brig. She put her fingers to her lips and then motioned for Ganna Mae and Svetlana to stay put. Before either woman could protest, she eased from the sick bay and followed behind Moole. Half way down the stairs, she heard footsteps behind her. "What are you doing?"

"Going with you," Ganna Mae whispered. "Besides, you said Moole told you to bring us to the brig. On top of that, I don't want you alone with Moole."

Yasnaya stopped and faced Gan. "Moole said you had my tubes tied to stop the Kincaid bloodline, not because you were concerned about my ovarian cancer risk. Is that true?"

"No, that's not true." Ganna Mae opened her eyes so Yasnaya could see her truth. "I was worried if you found my day planner and read the *Last Kincaid* plan that you would think this. It's *not* true. Moole is lying!"

"Just coincidence, then? Come on, admit it. You never loved me. I wasn't even good enough to share your name?"

"Yasnaya, please. When we get away from all this, read the cancer risk literature. It's still in your medical records! The doctors discovered a mutation of your BRCA1 gene. Your risk of contracting ovarian cancer was over 70%. I couldn't--"

"It would require genetic research to uncover that..." Yasnaya twisted Ganna Mae's collar around her fist. "You had the research done to make sure I was a Kincaid...and then you had my tubes tied. I should take a cue from Kozlov and beat the crap out of you. Right here and right now!"

"No, Yas. Without genetic research, I wouldn't be able to know what your risks for certain diseases were, like birth parents from the get go. It's not like I knew, *her*," Ganna Mae pointed to Svetlana.

Svetlana pushed the two women apart. "I can't believe you would do such a thing to her without having her best interests at heart."

"I didn't. The doctor said the only way to be 100% sure she wouldn't get ovarian cancer was to remove her ovaries. I wouldn't let them. Tubal ligation brought her chances down to 50% or less. I opted for that procedure and was told as medical advances were made, she might have an excellent chance to have it reversed if she ever decided to have children. Read her medical records, please!"

"I hope for your sake that is true." Svetlana glared at Ganna Mae. "Lubova." Svetlana stroked Yasnaya's hair. "That is your real name. As a mother, it pains me to know how lonely and unloved you felt at times. It breaks my heart that you may never bear me grandchildren." Svetlana turned back to Ganna Mae. "But if not for this woman, we both would have died long ago."

"In Russia, you mean?"

"Yes, it is a long story. For now all you need to know is that the day you left is the day I stopped living." Svetlana pointed at Ganna Mae. "She said to me back then, 'I can't tell you when, but one day, I promise you will have your daughter back.' Those words kept me from ending my own life."

"Is that why you never gave me the Ferguson name?" Yasnaya directed the question to Ganna Mae without looking at her directly.

"Yes, and I tried not to love you. That turned out to be impossible, Yas." Ganna Mae wiped the tears now flowing down her cheeks, real tears.

Yasnaya placed her hand on Ganna Mae's back and felt the pain the old woman was feeling. "I believe you...and even though you never have been much of a mother, you were all I had, so I loved you...as much as I could anyway."

Svetlana savored the tentative laugh the three women shared and prayed there would be many more moments like this. But without Wyatt, those moments may never come. "We have to save Wyatt. Kozlov will kill him this time."

Ganna Mae patted her ankle holster. "Way ahead of you, and after we save Kincaid, it's payback time for what Phillip Moole did to our daughter."

Kozlov stepped back inside the brig and coolly scanned Wyatt. "Konstantin, put him on the hook." The head of the bolt he had honed for months braced against his palm, Wyatt waited. Just as Konstantin reached to handcuff him, Wyatt drove the bolt up the giant's nostril. Blood and bits of gray matter spewed across the room and onto floor. Kozlov jumped back, but Gurov was not as lucky. Wyatt grabbed the sinewy sailor and slammed the bolt through his ear, sending another spray of crimson into the air. Kozlov scrambled toward the hatch but Wyatt pinned him on the floor and ripped the pistol from his holster.

As he tightened his arms around Kozlov, he could hear the sailor's ribs cracking. Blood on his hands from the earlier slaughter made it hard to maintain pressure. For a moment, the thought of the lives he had just taken overwhelmed him. Being locked up like an animal had turned him into one. He discovered that, rather than remorse, he felt empowered and justified. He looked at the hook dangling from the ceiling and then at the bodies of Konstantin and Gurov. *Better them than me.*

Kozlov took advantage of his momentarily lapse and slithered from Wyatt's grasp. "HELP ME!" he screamed desperately.

"Your tyranny is over, Kozlov," Wyatt said as he rammed Kozlov into the steel wall. "From now on we'll be operating by *my* rules."

Wyatt hit Kozlov so hard he flew across the room and crashed head first into the steel desk bolted to the floor. "Rule Number One: Never mess with Wyatt Kincaid!"

Wyatt went over and grabbed Kozlov by the collar with one hand and cocked his haymaker. "Rule Number Two." Wyatt sent Kozlov flying back across the room. "See rule Number One!"

Kozlov slid down the wall and crumbled into a bloody heap in front of the hatch. Wyatt leveled Kozlov's pistol at the slowly opening hatch.

"Step inside and drop that gun," Wyatt said to Taylor Averette. "Who are you anyway?"

Averette surveyed the carnage strewn about the room and slowly let his weapon drop to the floor. "I'm one of the good guys, Mr. Kincaid. You're safe now."

"Who are you?"

"I'm a United States Navy Seal."

Wyatt relaxed his grip on the pistol but still kept it pointed at Averette. "Not that I don't trust you, but since you aren't wearing a uniform, I'd like to see some ID."

Averette held both hands in the air. "I'll be glad to show you my ID but I'll have to reach inside my vest. I don't want you to shoot me."

"Not a problem, just use one hand and keep the other where I can see it."

Averette felt the metal disk around his neck and snapped the chain from his neck. "Dog tags work for you?"

"Yep, toss them over here and put your hands against the wall."

Averette did as instructed and Wyatt scooped up the dog tags and held them to the light. "What the hell took you guys so long?"

Averette smiled. "We've been looking for you a long time. Mind if I get my weapon?"

"No, of course not," Wyatt said. Averette picked up his weapon. "You know Mr. Kincaid, we thought you might be involved in the operation run by Captain Kozlov." Averette swept the room with his eyes. "That's obviously not the case, but just to be on the safe side, maybe you'd better hand me that weapon. We don't want some trigger happy sailor shooting you before we can get you to safety."

"No we don't," Wyatt said, and handed Averette the gun, butt first.

"On your knees Mr. Kincaid", Averette said as he pointed his pistol at Wyatt.

"What the hell?" Wyatt asked before doing as instructed. "Oh, I get it. You need to search me for weapons?"

Averette straddled Wyatt's feet from behind and pressed Kozlov's pistol to Wyatt's head. "No, Mr. Kincaid. I'm going to kill you."

"I thought you were one of the good guys?"

"I was, but I gave that up." Averette screwed a silencer onto the barrel of his Ruger. "You see, Mr. Kincaid, I want the kind of wealth you have and on military pay that ain't happening."

"Can't we work a deal? I'm part of the 1% who doesn't mind sharing."

"Nice try, Mr. Kincaid, but I don't think you can match the offer already on the table."

Moole gave the rail surfing one last try and landed upright on the deck this time. He wheezed with each breath as the stale air below decks burned his lungs.

"Koz...lov stop!" Moole panted as he ran. "We need Kincaid!"

As Averette tightened his finger on the trigger, Wyatt lurched against him with all his might. Averette's round ricocheted off the ceiling, pinged around the room for what seemed like minutes, finally cracking a rib bone and searing its way into Wyatt's lung. Wyatt snorted like a bull impaled by the matador's final estoque. With his last surge of adrenaline he charged headlong at his assassin. Averette sidestepped and aimed at Wyatt's head. "No!" Moole shouted as he rushed Averette, knocking him to the floor. "Without Kincaid we have nothing...Ridell tricked me."

Chapter 46

Tidwell rolled off the Divan and headed for the pilothouse closet to check his weapons. "Damn, these are useless." Tidwell looked at Clark. "Don't you have a weapon aboard? Anything?"

"You're in no shape to go anywhere. Help me sit him down, ma'am." Lisa ran over to Tidwell. "He's right. I'm no doctor but I'm sure you have some broken ribs."

"Clark, Wyatt is probably up there right now paying the price for sticking up for us. We have to do something."

"Our responsibility is to passengers first, and we have a passenger in case you haven't noticed."

"Yeah, and we let three others get away from us. Hey, where is Ridell?"

"Yas said Moole killed him." Lisa said.

"*What?* How? Why?...When?" Clark pushed his cap back on his head. "Damn, with all the excitement, I forgot to do a headcount."

"Moole raped Yas, too...just before he took over the boat."

"Damn It!" Tidwell growled. "It's my fault Clark. I should have made sure we were under surveillance before we took off after the Fountain."

"I'm going to look for him." Clark said.

"I did that while you two were knocked out." Lisa said. "Tim is not on this boat."

"That damn Moole!" Tidwell looked up at the Baltic Queen. "I've been watching those guys on the machine guns. They aren't patrolling the ship's perimeter. They're only manning their positions."

"So?"

"If I had a hand line and a grapple I could go to the bow, snag the railing, and pull myself aboard."

"Why take the chance?" Clark asked. "I got through to Trent. I'm sure they figured out your code and are on the way."

"Look Clark, I think we both know that ultimately I'm responsible for everyone on this boat. I lost Wyatt, Ridell is dead and we have only one passenger left and she's not safe. The person responsible for kidnapping Wyatt and killing Ridell is right up there." Tidwell nodded at the Baltic Queen again. "I going to get Moole. And maybe I can help Wyatt. You stay here and watch out for Lisa."

"I don't need to be watched over. As a matter of fact," Lisa said as she unbuttoned her blouse, "I'm pretty sure I can distract those guys while you get aboard,"

"Hell, I'm going with you, Jim."

While Lisa flirted with the sailors, Tidwell fashioned a grappling hook from a hand line and small lead anchor from the lifeboat. On the second try, the line wrapped around the deck railing of the Baltic Queen. Tidwell scampered up the line with Clark's buck knife clamped between his teeth.

Once topside, Tidwell cut the line and tossed the rope back down to a perplexed Clark. "Look after Lisa. I've got this", Tidwell mouthed.

The first order of business was to get inside the ship without being seen. That was proving difficult since the only inward passages were beyond the machine gunners. Getting by them would be an impossible task, or at least it seemed that way until Lisa Cox walked out on the aft deck of the Crown Jewel looking quite luscious. Even an old port hag would have appealed to these sailors who had been at sea for months, but the beauty before them was like a Venus flytrap. Tidwell used the same hose reel Wyatt had used to conceal himself and Svetlana. At first the crew was cautious and continued to glance around to see if Kozlov was lurking nearby. But finally, Lisa's performance became all consuming and they were lost in imagined possibility.

Tidwell bagged and gagged the first and second gunners before Clark realized what was going on. As soon he understood Tidwell's plan, Clark pretended to be caught up in the moment and danced around Lisa with his back to the crew. "Hey, see if you can get one to come down and take my place dancing with you." Lisa looked up and saw Tidwell in a sailor uniform, manning one of the three guns. She nodded to Clark, then shoved him out of the way and started gyrating and motioning for the youngest wide-eyed sailor to join her. Like many sailors before him who had succumbed to a siren's song, the sailor jumped ship and rushed headlong into Clark's fist. Tidwell slammed the last gunner over the head and waited for Clark and Lisa.

"Did you notice the Zodiac docked down there?" Tidwell asked Clark. "Yeah, you know the owner?"

"I'm pretty sure I do, and he's our first target. We have to find him."

"He met with Moole." Lisa said. "Moole went upstairs and your friend from the Zodiac went downstairs."

"Clark, grab one of the 60's and a belt of ammo."

"Yas--Ganna!" Lisa squealed. The trio of women rushed down the stairs and circled around Lisa.

Ganna Mae broke from the crowd and approached Tidwell and Clark. "I've been a fool. I need your help to find Wyatt Kincaid."

"First lay out the scenery for me," Tidwell said as he pointed to the bound and gagged sailors on the deck. "These guys won't be a problem, but I need to know how many more armed sailors are aboard."

"You've got the bulk of them here. The others are barely able-bodied seamen. They didn't try to stop us when we left the sick bay. Kozlov and two sailors are the remainder of the Russian crew. The others are Malaysian for-hire hands, or that's what one told me, anyway."

"Hired maintenance crew? That's sounds about right," Tidwell said. "Everyone is trying to cut costs. Cruise ships do it all the time."

"The ones in sick bay were banged up by Wyatt according to the Filipino medical officer. They are probably capable of combat, but not spoiling for a fight."

"How about Averette?"

"Who?"

"The guy on the Zodiac." Tidwell pointed to the docked boat.

"First I've heard of him." Ganna Mae touched her bandaged head. "But, I've been preoccupied."

"We need weapons. Haven't seen an armory have you?"

Ganna Mae pulled her Beretta from her calf holster. "Just this one and I'm not giving it up."

"I can help you with that," Svetlana said. "There are more in the room next to the galley. Come. I will show you."

"Are you part of the crew?"

"I was, but no longer."

"Do you still have free rein of the ship?"

"Yes, I'm still cook."

"No need to set off an alarm. Can you get me a pistol and some ammo?"

"Yes, no trouble."

"Thanks." Tidwell said. "Ma'am I need for you and the ladies to get back aboard the Crown Jewel so Clark can get y'all to safety."

"You can forget that." Ganna Mae chambered a round. "I got us in this mess, and I'm going to get us out of this mess."

"Ma'am, I'm a federal agent. I'm ordering all of you back to the yacht. There is a team on the way. You are in extreme danger--"

"And that's exactly where I plan to stay," Ganna Mae said. "I was doing espionage behind the iron curtain before you were born. Trust me, I can handle a weapon and myself."

"Ma'am, back in the day, maybe--"

"Don't patronize me, boy. I said I'm staying and that's it! I'm not leaving this ship until Wyatt Kincaid is with me."

"Fine! Clark, get the other ladies on board and get out of here."

"We're not leaving either," Yas said. "I can handle a gun."

"And so can I," Lisa Cox added.

"Great." Tidwell looked at Svetlana. "Guns for me and the ladies, if you don't mind?"

"I'm staying, too, Jim. Better get me one, I reckon."

While they waited for Svetlana to bring back the guns, Yas laid out the floor plan and location of the brig. "Moole was on his way to the brig and we were tailing him when we bumped in to you guys," Yas said. "You must have just missed him."

"We have to find Averette, he's--"

"Ours." Six Navy Seals in full armor and war paint swung from the deck above on rappel ropes. "This ship is secure from the top deck to here. We've got it, Tidwell. Get these people on board the yacht and get out of here."

"I told him and I'm telling you," Ganna Mae said. "I'm not leaving this boat without--"

"Ma'am, that order I just gave wasn't an invitation to discuss how this operation is going down. You'll get on the yacht now or I'll have one of my men tie you up and gag you. Either way, you're going to leave."

Ganna Mae looked past the group of Seals and saw another dozen descending to decks below like spiders on webs. "Well, looks like you have it under control. Will you call and let us know when Wyatt is safe?"

The Seal handed a backpack to Tidwell. "I'll do you one better than that. You've be able to see the operation in real time on this monitor. But, hurry. We need you off this ship before we can conclude our mission."

Chapter 47

While the remaining members of the Naval Special Warfare Development Group (DEVGRU), or simply Seal Team Six, viewed footage of the ongoing operation from the live satellite feed being shone on the intercept ship's numerous plasma TV's.

Tidwell tied the monitor, given to him by the Seal, into one of the Plasma screens on the Crown Jewel for better viewing. They held their breath as the Seal team amassed outside the brig door. The warning was simple. "Averette, give it up. Come out with your hands up. We own this ship. The Bratva Mercy launch bumped into our contingency team. There were no survivors. You don't have backup."

"Tidwell with you?"

"Nope."

"Tell him no hard feeling, will you?"

"He can hear you."

The group huddled around the TV on the Crown Jewel recoiled in unison as the only shot fired on the Baltic Queen echoed throughout the salon. Seconds later, the Seals opened the hatch. Taylor Averette was slumped against the wall with most of his head blown off. Moole was jumping around waving his hands in the air, screaming, "I give up! I surrender!" so loud and long that one of the Seals knocked him down to shut him up.

Wyatt Kincaid had fought the valiant fight. With the amount of blood pooling around his body, the corpsman was certain he did not survive his wounds. As he felt for a pulse, Wyatt grabbed his arm. "There are others on board. Save them!"

"Calm down, Mr. Kincaid. They're fine."

The steady beat of the medivac's rotors cutting through the heavy sea air did, indeed, calm Wyatt Kincaid. For the first time in months he closed his eyes, knowing with absolute certainty that the next day would be better.

Crisp clean sheets crackled as Wyatt rolled over on his back. Scents and sounds he hadn't heard or smelled in months soothed the rising panic in his gut. It wasn't until he felt a familiar hand sponging the sweat from his face that he spoke. "Svetlana, is that you?"

"Yes, Wyatt."

"I want to open my eyes, but I'm afraid if I do we'll be back on the Baltic Queen. Please tell me this isn't a dream."

"Open your eyes, Wyatt. You're in Wilmington."

From the balcony of the Cape Fear Memorial Hospital sunroom, the view of the Crown Kincaid building was nothing short of spectacular. "That's the second most beautiful sight I've seen in my life."

After months of hearing nothing but gushing praise for the edifice, Svetlana was shocked. "Pray tell, what's the first?"

Wyatt pulled Svetlana to him and looked steadily at the tall brunette, refusing to blink, afraid she would disappear if he did. "You are...and when I get you home I'm going to--"

"Wyatt." Svetlana pressed her hand over Wyatt's mouth. "We aren't alone!"

Wyatt rolled over and surveyed the room. A sheepish grin covered his face as he nodded to Ganna Mae, Lisa Cox, Yasnaya, and an unknown Wilmington cop. "Sorry, folks. I was just having a little fun."

"You deserve it Wyatt, and so much more," Ganna Mae said. "I, on the other hand, deserve to be shot. I can't begin to tell you--"

"Hold on, Ms. Ganna Mae. I don't mean that to sound condescending. It's the way I way raised."

"I understand."

"What you did was wrong." Wyatt sat up. "And I swore I'd kill the person who imprisoned me, but that's changed." Wyatt pulled Svetlana to his side. "Ganna Mae, I can't let you apologize for giving me the happiness I could never buy." Wyatt locked eyes with Yas. "I don't know you that well, yet. But even though I was raised as an only child, somehow I knew I wasn't. That's part of the reason I spent so much money, searching for Yasnaya Polyana, my family." Wyatt laughed, "Hell, I may sue to get back some of that money. After all, you're living proof I was ripped off."

"You may rethink that once you realize what a pain family can be. Or, hopefully, you'll learn, as I did, that family will never be perfect...far from perfect most times." Yasnaya shot Ganna Mae a quick glance and Ganna Mae hung her head. "I want you to know that no matter how my relationship with Wyatt and Svetlana plays out, you will always be my mother and you will always be part of my life," Yasnaya said.

"Oh, Yas... I love you. Thank you."

"Lubova, mother. My name is Lubova."

"Ahem...I hate to intrude, Mr. Kincaid, Ms. Ferguson...I'm Deputy Pamela Diffee, with the New Hanover County Sheriff's Department. I've been asked to review this video that was forwarded to our department by Mr. Tim Ridell. He asked that most of the people gathered here be present at the viewing. Are you up to doing that today?"

"I'm up to conquering the world today, ma'am."

Diffee smiled. "After your ordeal, I understand why. Glad to have you back, Mr. Kincaid." Diffee plugged an IPod into the AUX feed of the TV. "I've seen this before, so I'll narrate what's going on. If you have questions, I will pause the video and answer them before we continue. Is that agreeable to everyone?"

A chorus of OKs and nods circled the room. The video began with Tim Ridell standing alone in a room with an antique piece of furniture. "This is a chiffonier, or 'chest-of-drawers' if you hale from Mount Olive, North Carolina. But it is more that than. I was instructed to retrieve this from a house on a tract of land that was owned by the Ferguson Family. After falling in love with a member of that family and learning some of their secrets...I mention this because if you're watching, Yasnaya, then I'm dead, and wanted you know that I love you."

Yasnaya swallowed hard and nodded for Diffee to un-pause the video.

"Years ago a murder took place on this farm. Rumor has it that Wyatt Kincaid Sr. trained a mule to kill Grover and Iris Ferguson. Since the only eyewitness to this crime was a just-turned-five-year-old boy named Caleb, the police had little to go on but the rumor. Caleb was so traumatized by the murders that from that day until this, all he has ever been able to say is 'Mule did it. Mule did it. Mule did it.'

Though evidence suggested otherwise, the rumor substantiated by local officials and Caleb's testimony sealed the mule's fate. Demon was executed by firing squad the day of the murder and Caleb Ferguson was forced to watch."

"Oh, my God!" Ganna Mae exclaimed. "I made him watch. What was I thinking?"

Diffee paused the video. "Do you want me to stop?"

Ganna Mae shook her head and the video continued. "But, after extensive research, I have another version of the Ferguson murders and the evidence is irrefutable. Phillip Moole, a boy of eleven at the time, was seen and admitted to being at the scene of the murders. As a matter of fact, newspaper articles at the time showed him to be a member of the firing squad. In these same articles, Moole is portrayed as a hero who tried to pull the mule away from the plunger to save the Fergusons. I submit to you today that wasn't the case. I tracked down family members of eyewitnesses who swore on their death beds that Phillip Moole was the perpetrator, not a hero. There is even an eyewitness who swore in an affidavit that Moole was at the plunger when the blast occurred, not the mule. But Moole's father was a judge and good friends with the sheriff at the time, so the affidavit disappeared and the rumor of the assassin mule became the accepted version of the Ferguson murders."

Tim pulled the drawers out and stacked them alongside the furniture. The camera panned in tight enough to see writing in the bottom and sides of the drawers. "At first this appears to be a simple ledger by Grover Ferguson covering his income and crop productions. I questioned Yas about why we had to store it in the Crown Kincaid building. As I suspected, it was an artifact Ganna Mae planned to use to make Wyatt Kincaid understand her family, and why she brought about his downfall. For a while, I accepted that, but the lawyer in me kept bringing me back to the chiffonier. One day I turned the drawers over and I could see a faint outline that looked like words." Ridell turned the drawers upside down and the camera panned in tight again. "You are seeing what I saw and there is really no way to make out the words. But I hired a police lab to develop what I consider to be evidence. The lab sprayed the drawers with a chemical called Luminol. Under a black light this chemical illuminates bodily fluids like blood. I will turn the black lights on now."

On the bottom of the four drawers written in child's scrawl were these words: *Moole did it. Moole did it. Moole did it.*

Diffee turned off the video. "Any questions?"

"We already know Moole did it. He confessed." Ganna Mae said. Wyatt, Svetlana and Yas nodded agreement. "So you say, but Moole said that it's a story all of you concocted to frame him."

"But it's four against one."

"Four who have a reason to frame Moole," Diffee said.

"But, Lisa, Tidwell, and Clark, "Yasnaya's voice trailed off "…weren't on the ship when Moole confessed. He made sure they were on the yacht."

"He killed Tim Ridell." Wyatt added.

"Moole said Ridell was drunk and went on the swim platform to relieve himself and must have fallen overboard."

"Forensic turned up Ridell's blood in the salon, but Moole said Ridell cut himself slicing a lime for a drink. There is not enough evidence to charge him with a crime."

"How about working with Kozlov…he's a terrorist for God's sake!" Ganna Mae shouted.

"Should we charge you too? You developed the relationship with Kozlov. You funded his ship and crew," Diffee said.

"But not for terror purposes. I was trying to destroy Wyatt and the Crown Kincaid Company."

"That's what Moole is saying. Except his version is that you were funding the terrorists and once he realized you weren't after Kincaid, he reported everything to agent Taylor Averette. He has phone records to prove his assertions." Diffee explained.

"Will I be charged?"

"That's up to federal authorities. But then there are the kidnapping charges--"

"I voluntarily got on that ship, officer. It was a surprise vacation Ganna Mae gave me. There was no kidnapping." Wyatt said.

"Moole raped me." Yas said. "You have to charge him for that."

"We can and we will, but Moole said he paid you for sex...and I'm not being judgmental, but he says you did lap dances for him, too."

"I did not."

"Your word against his." Diffee said.

"So Moole walks?" Yas asked.

"Not completely. Mr. Ridell gave us enough evidence to charge him with murder and the D.A. is prepared to do that. Problem is, we'll have to try him as a juvenile."

"How long will he get?" Ganna Mae asked,

"Moole is lawyered-up, claiming insanity as a defense, and he may get it. Judge Moole sent him to a mental hospital after the Ferguson murders. I think he was laying the groundwork for an insanity plea way back then." Diffee explained.

"So he won't go to prison?"

"Maybe a few years in a mental hospital, but it's not likely he'll get hard time."

"Justice delayed is justice denied. Rings a little hollow, don't you think officer?"

"Sorry, but it's the way the system works."

"Or doesn't." Ganna Mae added.

Chapter 48

Phillip Moole surveyed the room; white walls, white ceiling, and gray tile floor. Just like every other room in the private hospital, with the exception of the grand entrance... a domed atrium affair replete with lavish furnishings and original oil paintings. A masterful ploy by some genius hospital administrator to justify the ridiculous costs bled from the families of the patients milling about the spartan room.

Thank goodness his stay would be short. First he would have to convince them he was insane, and as soon as practical, convince them that he was *sane* and absolutely no danger at all to society. Idiots! How could they possibly believe that he was going to prison on trumped up murder charges? Still, he would be locked up in here for a few years at least. Someone would have to pay for that and, if his hunch was correct, that someone was here.

Moole settled into the most comfortable chair in the day room and waited for his victim to arrive. Within seconds a giant of a man ambled across the room and stopped at the juice canister. With one arm, he held the 30 gallon cylinder over his head and guzzled from the open tap. Attendants rushed across the room and bargained with him to put the canister back on the table. While one coaxed him with fresh brownies, two other grabbed the almost two-hundred-pound vessel and let it slam back down on the table.

Moole walked over to the attendant. "Wonder if I might have a word with you?" The attendant looked agitated. "Man, don't you see I got my hands full?"

Moole squeezed a twenty dollar bill into the man's palm. "They look a little empty to me, but I'm sure we can fill 'em up if you are, as they say, willing to work with me?"

"Whatcha want?"

"Information."

"Yeah, I can probably help you with that. But one of them bills ain't gonna buy much."

"Oh, there's plenty more, but I'll need your services as well, not just information."

"That can be arranged. Whaddaya need to know?"

"The patient there," Moole pointed at the giant. "What's his name?"

"Caleb."

"And his last name?"

"I might could look it up. But ya know man, that bill you give me is getting real thin."

Moole took out a hundred and wadded it in his palm. "I'm sorry, I'm Phillip Moole and I don't believe I caught *your* name?" Moole stuck his hand out for a shake. "My name's Norbert and I'll get back with you on the big guy's name."

"No, no, don't bother, Norbert," Moole smiled. "Tell me is there anything unusual about Caleb?"

"Hell, yeah! Old Caleb is strong as an 800 pound gorilla…he does anything he wants."

"No, I mean…well, anything different about his vocabulary?"

"Man, Caleb ain't got no vocabulary…all he ever says is: 'Mule did it. Mule did it; Mule did it."

Moole turned and looked at the security camera. No doubt some psychiatrist was observing his every move. "Nobert, this is going to seem crazy to you, or at least I *hope* it does. Now, you have to keep our conversations to yourself. If you'll excuse me, I have to go prove I'm temporarily insane."

"Huh?"

With arms flailing, Moole rushed the giant and struck him across the face and shoulders. Caleb shed the attendants like a dog drying off after a swim and grabbed Moole with a crushing vise-like grip.

The raw power in the arms wrapped around his chest sent fear so deep and paralyzing across Moole's solar plexus he could barely squeak out a whimper. His last memory before passing out was the residual shock of the 50,000 volt taser used to fell Caleb.

Norbert humming softly as he replaced the plastic cups in the room stirred Moole back to consciousness. "Where am I?" Moole asked.

"Oh, you still in the hospital…but you lucky your ass ain't in the morgue."

Moole strained to see the mirror and could barely make out his face which was covered in dark bruises. "What the hell happened to me?"

"You got you a big ol' dose of Caleb Ferguson. Got that name for you boss."

Unable to sit up Moole, let his head fall back into the soft foam pillow and savored the coolness of fresh linens. He had never felt pain like this. To his recollection, this was the first time in his entire life that he had felt pain caused by a physical altercation. He was certain it would be his last. There had to be a saner way to prove insanity. "Norbert, are there cameras in this room?"

"Yeah, but I know a place that don't have 'em."

Moole propped his arms behind his head and stared at the ceiling. "Come back tomorrow and take me to that place. I have more of those bills for you."

"You got it."

It took all of that day and most of the next before Phillip Moole was finally able to leave his room. Norbert pulled the wheel chair up close to his bed. "You ready to take a little ride, boss?"

"Yeah, let's go…and Norbert, henceforth refer to me as *Ironhand*. I don't care for the 'boss' moniker."

"Never heard of Boss Moniker," Norbert said. "OK, so you want me to call you Ironhead?"

"Ironhand, if you don't mine."

Norbert stopped the chair in a small nook that held a broken water cooler and janitorial supplies. "Are you sure no one can see us?" Moole asked.

"Naw, we good, Ironhand."

Moole palmed five one hundred dollar bills his attorneys had delivered that morning into the attendant's hand. "I need to know where Caleb is--"

"Man, your ass is crazy! Caleb liked to killed you--"

"Norbert…I'm not crazy, but I'm rich as hell." Moole scanned the area to make sure no one could see them. "I need your help to make me appear crazy, and I need to have access to Caleb Ferguson. You help me accomplish those two things and you will have a lot more money when I'm 'cured'. Do we understand each other?"

Nobert looked around the area, and, satisfied it wasn't a set-up, nodded his head. "Yeah, I understand real good." Nobert held up a hundred. "How many more Benjamins are we talkin'?"

"About ninety-five more. Sound fair?"

"Hell, yeah. You got a deal, Ironhand!"

Moole nodded and held his finger to his lips, "You can't tell anyone."

"You couldn't beat it outta me, Ironhand."

"Good. Glad we understand each other. Look, I need to see Caleb but I don't want him to see me." Nobert pushed Moole further into the nook and whispered, "He's in solitary. He can see you, but he can't get to you…that might be important."

"Perfect. I see this is going to be a very beneficial relationship for both of us. You make sure I'm protected and I'll double that offer I just made."

Solitary was a holding cell in a cinderblock building that also housed the hospital's assortment of four-wheelers and golf carts. The building was an eyesore left over from a farming operation before the main campus was constructed. Architects had planned around a natural stand of trees to conceal the storage building for aesthetic reasons. What the building was about to be used for had nothing in common with aesthetics or morality, as far as that was concerned.

Dawn broke gray and dreary, but Phillip Moole's mood was anything but. He took one look at the fruit and dry toast breakfast beside his bed, tipped it onto the floor, then hustled out to find Norbert. As soon as he stepped into the hallway, he could hear the booming voice of his new accomplice. "I done told you dummies not to trash this place. Who the hell you think gonna clean it up?" The unmistakable sound of trashcan being kicked across the room followed Norbert's short tirade. "Naw, you asses is wrong…old Norbert ain't cleaning up none of this mess. Y'all are. Now get to it!"

Moole stood at the threshold of the day room and motioned for Norbert. Before joining his new employer, Norbert fired off another warning. "I got some important business to take care of…this damn place better be ship-shape when I get back. I ain't playing neither!"

"When can I see Caleb?" Moole muttered without moving his lips.

"Well, Ironhand, to tell you the truth, it's going to be a lot easier for you to see him when he gets out of solitary. See, the hospital, they don't like for new patients to be out on the grounds…you know… until they see that they ain't gonna run off."

Moole calmed his anger at Norbert's ignorance. Why the hell would he run off… so they could stick him in prison? "You don't have to worry about that. Trust me I want to be here."

"Yeah, I get that, but the hospital--"

"Damn the hospital. I'm paying you to make sure--"

"Hold on Ironhand, Ol' Norbert already thought of that…I'm going tell them you got this real talent for grounds keepin' and I'm taking you in as my apprentice yard maintenance man. See the hospital likes it when a patient finds something that calms them. Sounds good don't it?"

"Real good. Now, let's go see that big ape."

Only a few yards of the foot path to the maintenance shed was visible from the hospital. Getting there unnoticed would not be a problem. That fact quickened Moole's pace and Norbert had to half-jog to keep up. "Damn boss, it ain't like he's goin' no where. An elephant couldn't break outta that place." Moole's ignored the comment and plowed down the path at full speed. The building was more substantial than he expected and; the first thing he noticed were the heavy iron bars across two small windows and one full-length door.

He leaned against the building to catch his breath and turned just in time to see Caleb's arm grabbing for him. "Oh, so you want to hurt me because I slapped you, don't you?" Before continuing his conversation the careful lawyer came out in Moole. "Norbert, why don't you find something to do while I have a private conversation with my old friend?"

"Unless you just want to hear about a damn mule...you just soon forget that little talk, Ironhand."

"Thank you kindly, Norbert, but I believe I speak this gentleman's language. Now leave us."

Moole found a small green, gum branch on the ground and whipped it across the bars, stinging Caleb's arm in the process. The big oaf moved to the rear of cell to get away from the switch. Moole stood close to the door looking Caleb straight in the eyes. Caleb slowly repeated his ever present phrase, "Mule did it. Mule did it. Mule did it."

"That's right, my old friend. But who could have guessed that a half-wit like you could write at five years old? You see, that's why I'm here, because you wrote my name in blood using your parent's blood. That's why you have to die. But listen to this. I'm going to kill you while I'm insane, and that way I get off with *three* murders...well *four* if you count Ridell."

Moole took a lollipop he had purchased earlier from a vending machine and held it up to Caleb. "You remember me don't you big fella? Oh, you weren't very big then, but you remember this."

Caleb paced the cell like a big cat and memories from long ago rushed into his head. "Mule did it. Mule did it. Mule did it."

"No. Come on. Say it like you wrote it...Moole—Moole---Moole."

"Mole—Mole."

"Come on you dumbass redneck." Wild-eyed and crazy Moole continued. "Say Moo like a cow. MOO, MOOLE-MOOLE!"

"MOOLE!"

"Yes, that's it, Caleb. Say it again; Moole did it. Moole did it. Moole did it."

"Moole did it. MOOLE did it. MOOLE DID IT!

"Ha ha.... Yes! Moole did indeed do it. You dumbass!"

Moole hurled the lollipop as hard as he could at Caleb. When Caleb ducked, Moole yelled: "Ka-Boom!"

As he had done so long ago, Caleb sat on the ground and repeated his phrase over and over. But this time something was different. The big man rose, walked to door and grabbed the bars, never taking his eyes off of Moole. Eye to eye, the two traveled back to that day in the newly plowed earth, when Iris Ferguson had danced her little jig and Grover and Caleb had laughed.

Moole beamed satisfaction as tears ran down the giant's cheeks. "So, you do remember me?"

Caleb battered the door so hard the building began to shake like it would fall down. Norbert raced over to them. "Damn, what's wrong with him...I ain't never seen him like this--back away...he crazy!"

"Not crazy, my friend…angry, very, very angry."

Norbert pushed in front of Moole, "That may be, but you need to get back…Calm down Caleb! What's the matter with you? Brownies…you want some brownies?"

Moole eased back around Norbert and to the front of the cell. "Leave him alone. Let him feel his anger…KABOOM, ha ha ha ha KABOOM!"

Caleb rammed against the bars with full force. The building shook and the mortar around the cinderblocks cracked. "Damn Ironhand! Don't say that no more! He's coming outta that thing!"

Moole turned back toward the hospital. "Come on Norbert. Let's leave my friend so he can calm down…Caleb, I'll see you tomorrow."

None of the law enforcement officers nor any of the hospital staff could explain how the explosion happened. Some speculated that teenagers stole dynamite from the rock quarry across the road from the hospital and stashed it in the maintenance building for safe keeping. Others surmised that an old artillery round from nearby Fort Bragg had been unearthed by the hapless victim, and that's what had blown him to kingdom come. Another, less popular, version was that somehow after all the years of watching charges being set off in the quarry, Caleb Ferguson, in spite of his infirmities, had found a way to play with fire.

What there was no disagreement on was the macabre spectacle before them. There, in the loamy soil in front of the gigantic hole caused by the explosion, sat Caleb Ferguson saying the only words that, until the day he died years from then, he would ever say again, "Moole did it. Moole did it. Moole did it." Cradled in his arms were the entwined hands of Phillip Moole.

Despite eyewitness accounts, investigators decided not to pursue leads that reported sightings of two attractive women walking with Caleb and Moole minutes before the explosion. Besides, the women identified as one very pregnant Lubova Kincaid and a Lisa Cox Tidwell, had airtight alibis…both were on a yacht cruising the Caribbean with Ganna Mae Ferguson, and Mr. & Mrs. Wyatt Kincaid.

The End

Coming December 2012 the Jigsaw sequel:

Venomous Reckoning

By: Ted Miller Brogden